GRACE ... WITHIN AND WITHOUT

GRACE ... WITHIN AND WITHOUT

A Novel

By

Shirley Riley Seltzer

"Where Fairy Tales Don't Always Come True"

iUniverse, Inc.
New York   Bloomington

Grace ... Within and Without
A Novel

iUniverse books may be ordered through booksellers or by contacting:

iUniverse
1663 Liberty Drive
Bloomington, IN 47403
www.iuniverse.com
1-800-Authors (1-800-288-4677)

ISBN: 978-1-4502-0763-8 (sc)
ISBN: 978-1-4502-0765-2 (dj)
ISBN: 978-1-4502-0764-5 (ebk)

Library of Congress Control Number: 2010901722

Printed in the United States of America

iUniverse rev. date: 5/10/2010

This novel is lovingly dedicated
To the memory of my beloved
Aunt Celeste
and to my mother, EvaRae, who has been my rock when I needed
strength, and my soft place to fall when I needed comfort.
To my husband Edward, without whose help and
encouragement this novel would never have been written.

Special Acknowledgment to my granddaughter
Elizabeth Poteat whose diligence in proofreading this
novel has been a blessing beyond measure.

And after you have suffered a little while, the God of all grace, Who has called you to His eternal glory in Christ Jesus, will Himself complete and make you what you ought to be, establish and ground you securely, and strengthen, and settle you.

1 Peter 5:10
    The Amplified New Testament
    by The Lockman Foundation

Prologue

Like a seed blowing in the wind such are our lives on the landscape of life. We are on a journey toward an epicenter that is yet unknown to us. Only God knows where we will be planted. Once planted we either thrive and grow, or wither and die, sometimes leaving no trace that we ever existed.

Sometimes our seed gets trampled on and the inner core is damaged . . . left to struggle even harder to survive. We may journey through storms of great magnitude, or go through periods of drought. If we survive the struggle, we can grow even stronger than we ever were before, but if we are too injured we may just give up.

It is what is within our inner core that determines whether we survive that which comes from outside our inner being.

CHAPTER I

▼

MY SEED IS PLANTED

It was a beautiful day in sunny South Florida as I sat on my grandmother's front stoop. The year was 1949 and I was three years old. I wasn't thinking about what game to play next, or what new toy I wanted. I was thinking about God. That day and those thoughts are my first memories of deep and significant cognition. Although that was many years ago, I still spend a lot of time thinking about God, and I find myself in awe of the magnificence of his many creations. The broad spectrum in which he performs his many miracles are so vast and so varied. Allow me to introduce myself. My name is Grace . . . Grace Murphree.

I was born thirsty for knowledge. The wheels of my mind were always spinning in full throttle. My imagination had no boundaries, and it was a broad and open field that my mind traveled across. I was always searching for knowledge and adventure. Let me share with you a look into what life was like for a first generation baby boomer such as I.

I grew up in a little town on the southeast coast of Florida called Ocean Shores. It was a sleepy little town back then, and life was relaxed and leisurely. My neighborhood was on an unpaved gravel dirt road with about seven houses on my block. I knew everyone in my neighborhood and they knew me, as I was a precocious little girl.

My grandmother, Sarah Murphree, along with my Aunt Esther and Uncle Marty, lived right next door to us. With just a short walk across our yard I could be at their door. I was in and out of there every day, and they were all a big influence on me during my formative years.

For the most part it was all good stuff, especially when it came to my grandmother.

Grandmother Sarah had a chicken pen in her back yard, and there were many times that I would have to sprint across the yard in order to get away from her rooster who would escape from the confines of his pen quite often. My mother would use the calico sacks that the chicken feed came in to sew dresses for me and my sisters.

I don't have a single bad memory of my grandmother. To me, then and now, she has always embodied all that is good, honest and pure in this world. She had the kindest eyes and the sweetest face. Whenever I looked in her eyes all I could see was sweetness and love reflecting back at me. She was a fine woman of southern heritage, having been born in southeast Alabama in 1884. Her hair was silvery gray in color and it hung down to her waist. She always wore it braided, and she would pin the braids up in a circular fashion around her head.

When I was very small I was always amazed by her false teeth. I thought it was so neat the way she could take them out of her mouth whenever she wanted to. I just couldn't wait for the day to come when I would be able to have my own set that I could take out whenever I pleased.

I'm a tender and sensitive person by nature, too much so maybe. Some people may see that as a weakness. I see it as a blessing. I would hate to be cold-hearted or mean spirited, but I can be tough when the occasion calls for me to be. Grandmother Sarah taught me about love and kindness, not only for other people, but for all of creation. I'm so glad for that because it makes me feel connected and at peace with the universe.

Grandmother Sarah had a lot of fruit trees in her yard. There were two giant avocado trees, several orange and grapefruit trees, and one guava tree. She was an avid gardener. She always said that even at the tender age of three, I would get out there in the yard with her and help her pull up weeds. She said I always knew just how you had to grasp the weeds from the bottom before pulling them out because if you didn't get the root out, the weed would break off and grow back. In my mind's eye I can still see her out in her garden with one of those calico bonnets on. The ones I've seen in pictures like the early American settlers wore.

Aunt Esther and Uncle Marty's influence on me was more in the realm of teaching me proper etiquette and appreciation of a more cultural nature. They taught me the importance and value of having the proper social graces in life. Whether it is right or wrong, I think that people are judged by their knowledge of proper decorum. Ignorance, or lack of these qualities, can and does have a vital impact on how we are perceived by others.

Just a little way down from Grandmother Sarah's house was where Mr. And Mrs. Hertz lived. They were very old and always made me laugh because they talked funny. They were from Brooklyn, New York, and I had never heard anyone talk with that kind of an accent before.

The last house on our side of the road was where my friend Bobby Adams lived. He and I had great fun together playing cowboys and Indians, or sometimes just walking up and down the road using the big elephant ear leaves that grew in his front yard as our umbrellas. The only time I remember the two of us getting into trouble was the time my mother caught us playing doctor in my bedroom where Bobby was pretending to give me a shot on the behind. Neither one of us really understood why Momma was so upset, but we both quickly learned that playing doctor was not to be played anymore.

Across the road and a little way up from Bobby's house was where Harry Flanders lived. Harry was a couple years older than me. Harry and my older sister Dinah were born in the same hospital just one day apart. My mother and Harry's mom had shared the same hospital room. I remember Momma saying that she had felt sorry for Harry's mom Alice. The reason being that whenever the doctor would come during the course of making his rounds, he would always comment on what a pretty baby Dinah was, but he never mentioned what a handsome baby Harry was. That aside, Momma and Mrs. Flanders were good friends, and my sisters and I played a lot at Harry's house. There was a big Mulberry tree in his back yard that was good for climbing, and the mulberries were really good for snacking on fresh from the tree.

A little further up the road from Harry was where Molly Boyle and her family lived. Molly was four years older than me, and she was a real live wire and always into mischief. She just about drove her mother Mildred crazy trying to keep up with her. Molly spent a lot of time at our house. When it would come time for her to go home, my mother would tell her that she needed to leave. Later we would hear her mother frantically calling for her to come home, and that's when we would find Molly hiding around our house somewhere.

Next door to Molly was where Maude and Jedadiah Morton lived. They were old and very eccentric. On just about any given day you could see old Mrs. Morton out in her yard surrounded by all of her cats. She had about fifty of them and they would all be swarming around her legs and meowing to beat the band. At night you could hear them fighting and caterwauling till the early morning hours. Mrs. Morton also had a couple of squirrels that she kept in a cage. I remember Momma always warning my sisters and me not to touch them because they were wild and would bite us. We were also warned, that not only would they bite us, but that they would likely give us a disease called rabies, and that would require us to get a lot of shots in our stomachs. Momma didn't need to tell me twice. I hated shots.

What I remember most about Mrs. Morton is the way she looked and dressed. She reminded me of a scarecrow because she always wore men's pants and shirts with an old straw hat on her head. She smoked cigars that she would let dangle from her mouth even when she talked.

Although Mrs. Morton outdid her husband when it came to being a real character, Mr. Morton was no slouch himself. He looked like Jeff from the comic strip characters "Mutt and Jeff." His favorite style of clothing was an old pair of stained and faded blue jean overalls that he wore along with a cap that advertised his favorite brand of chewing tobacco. He always kept a wad of it in his mouth, along with a spit cup for spitting into as was needed. His teeth, what were left of them, were stained the same rich brown color as his chewing tobacco. I never saw him clean shaven. He always had several days of scruffy beard growth, and his skin had the look of well-worn leather with very deep lines and wrinkles. I guess he had spent too much time in the hot Florida sun. His eyes looked like large round brown beads and they seemed to follow you without him even having to move his head. He hardly ever spoke, but he grunted a lot.

I'm glad that I was born in the 1940's because I think that life was much more relaxed and carefree back then. There were no cell phones, fax machines, beepers or computers to keep us all running around like some frenetic machine on a treadmill that never stops. The rat race never has been my cup of tea.

My early childhood was happy for the most part. As I have told you, I had plenty of playmates on my street. Back then kids had to use their imaginations and make their own fun because most people didn't have a T.V. until the early 1950's. We got ours when I was four.

It may sound like it would have been boring with no T.V. and all, but actually we had great fun that made a lot of great memories. Those memories still bring a smile to my face, and an inward chuckle at remembering our creativity. Looking back in retrospect on that time always brings a flood of memories to mind. Those memories never fail to bring a strange mixture of both happiness for what was, and sadness over the loss of it.

I was a tomboy that loved to climb trees and play cowboy, and other times all girl, playing with my dolls with my best friend Nancy. I played out my fantasy games in vivid detail, and with heartfelt earnest. I can remember tears streaming down my face when I would conjure up an incident that would supposedly have my doll crying.

Aside from climbing trees, playing cowboy, and playing with my dolls, we kids had a few make believe games that were our favorites. One was playing "witch" and the other one was called "getaway." Witch was my favorite.

We always played "witch" in my grandmother's back yard under the big avocado tree that grew just outside her back porch. Who would be the witch was determined by one person reciting "eeny, meeny, miney, moe, catch a tiger by the toe. If he hollers let him go. Eeny, meeny, miney, moe. My mother said to choose the very best one and that is y.o.u."

Everyone would be sitting in a circle and each one would put both fists out toward the middle. With each word of the rhyme one person's fist would be touched by the person doing the reciting. The person whose fist was touched last by the letter u of y.o.u., would be the witch. Once who would be the witch was determined the witch would then have to start gathering the ingredients to make her "witch's brew."

My grandmother had a huge aloe plant that grew at the side of her house and that's what we used to make the witch's brew. The plant was about two feet high and about four feet in circumference. An aloe plant is a green plant with thick sharp pointed leaves and bitter juice that is often used in making medicine. My grandmother always put it on our scrapes and burns, and my father used to mix the juice with water and drink it to treat his ulcer, so we knew that it was safe to ingest.

In our game of "witch" the juice from the aloe plant would be mixed in a little bowl with water. The bowl would then be placed on a small stack of twigs that was supposedly the fire the witch used for cooking her brew. The other people playing the game would hide like you do when playing hide and seek. The witch would then have to find them and bring them back to her campfire where she would then cackle like a witch and say, "Now my little pretties, I have fixed a special brew that you must drink as your punishment for trying to run away and hiding from witchy." She would then cackle again and take a spoon and make each one take a spoonful of her brew in their mouth. I don't know if you have ever tasted aloe, but it has a very bitter taste that lingers in your mouth long after you have had to drink the "witch's brew" that is concocted from it. Ooh, better not let that witch getcha my little pretties. Cackle! Cackle!

When we played "getaway" we used Uncle Marty's old red Jeep as our getaway car. We would conjure up some unsavory characters in our minds and pretend that they were trying to capture and kill us. We created our own imaginary dialogue and events as we sat in the "getaway" car. We did a lot of yelling and screaming during the course of trying to get away, and the situations were limited only by the boundaries of our imaginations.

Let me tell you about the rest of my family. My father, Walter, is a very handsome man with a kind and gentle nature. He served in the Navy during World War II, but luckily he came home with no visible scars. I never heard him talk about the war. I guess some memories evoke too much pain and are too horrifying to speak of. Daddy served on an LST, (Landing Ship Tanks) and was seasick most of the time.

I've always been proud of the fact that the men in my family served their country in times of war, as well as in times of peace. My great-great-great-grandfather fought for our country's freedom in the American Revolution. Having taken part in the unsuccessful rebellion in Ireland against the English government, he and two brothers were forced to flee in disguise from their native country. They fled for their lives from Ireland and settled in Louisburg, Franklin County, North Carolina in 1754.

My mother, Evangeline, is a very beautiful woman of southern heritage. This may sound insignificant, but she instilled in me, among numerous other things, the importance of good grooming and personal hygiene. Among the ones I deem to be of the greatest importance are to keep your teeth brushed, wash your hands often, keep your hair clean and brushed, and wear clean and pressed clothing. Although that may sound overly simplistic, if you are like me, those qualities are among the first things that I notice in a person, and you know how important first impressions are.

When I was little, I was sick a great deal of the time with asthma. There were many sleepless nights that the rocking chair served as my mother's bed as she would rock me and try to soothe me all night long. I would be gasping for every breath. During those long exhausting nights she never wavered from her loving care and devotion to me. She was always the loving face I gazed into, with the loving arms that held me tenderly.

I have two sisters. We look pretty much alike, having blonde hair, blue eyes, and a smidgen of freckles splashed across our noses. We were pretty children, but I always thought that I was ugly because we got teased so much about the freckles, and I was skinny from being sick most of the time with asthma.

My sisters and I are similar as far as physical appearance, but our personalities are different. Dinah is very sociable, whereas I am more into make-believe. I have a very active imagination. Colleen's personality kind of falls in the middle of Dinah and me. The one thing that we do have in common is that we are all likable.

Dinah is two years older than I am. She is my idol. I want to be just like her because she is charming and funny. In later years she will become my confidante and adviser, teaching me how to dress insofar as what goes together and what is stylish. She will also teach me how to be witty and charming.

My younger sister's name is Colleen. She is a couple of years younger than me, and to me she is the cutest little girl on the face of this earth. I spoil her like crazy because I love her so much. I'm going to have to cut that out though because she is becoming a little bratty and getting into trouble for doing things I have allowed her to do, unbeknownst to our parents.

So this is where I have been planted. I wonder . . . will I thrive and grow . . . or wither and die?

CHAPTER 2

▼

A LITTLE FURTHER ALONG

My early childhood years were what I consider to be typical of the day. Our household was that of a stay at home mom and a working dad. Daddy was the district manager for a life and health insurance company. Although Momma didn't have a regular job, she stayed busy around home and she did volunteer work. She served as a room mother at my sister Dinah's school, and she taught preschool Sunday School at our church, The First Presbyterian Church of Ocean Shores.

I always loved it when Momma had to go to Dinah's school to help out with parties and such on special holidays, because I would get to go too. Colleen had to stay home with Grandmother Sarah because she was too young and squirmy to control in the classroom. Although Dinah's classmates were only a couple of years older than I was, they always fussed over me and I loved being the center of their attention. I could hardly wait for the day to come when I would start going to school.

When that day finally did roll around it was the most exciting day in my life thus far. I can still see my classmates sitting at our little desks. Our little faces were so fresh and eager. We were so anxious to learn, so full of vim and vigor, and so innocent.

The initial excitement over going to school didn't last very long for me. After the first week or so it no longer held the allure that it had in the beginning. Sometimes I loved it, but more often than not I would find myself looking out the window daydreaming, and thinking that I would much rather be at home playing than sitting there learning about the adventures of Dick and Jane.

The daydreaming was something I couldn't help. I did it without even being conscious that I was doing so until I would be awakened from my reverie when my teacher, Miss Meadows, would say, "Grace, you better start paying attention, or you're going to be in trouble."

Another hindrance with school was my preoccupation with trying to do everything exactly right. I've always fretted over doing everything perfectly, and when I wasn't able to I would look for an escape, hence the daydreaming would come into play.

My interest in the opposite sex started early. I developed my first crush on a little boy named Bobby during the first week of school. I remember making a visual survey of which boys I thought were the cutest, and I would steal a sideways glance at them whenever possible.

I never really thought of school as being that important to my future. I didn't plan on having a career. It was more or less expected that girl children would just get married, keep house, and raise children. Most women didn't have careers or even work back then. That was okay with me because all I really wanted to do was to grow up and have a family.

I had a very clear picture in my mind of what my family would be like. Of course my children would be beautiful, and my husband would be very handsome and dashing. He would come home from work, pick me up, kiss me, and whirl me around in his arms. Meanwhile, our children would be looking up at their father with adoring eyes, waiting for their turn at being kissed and whirled. Our dog would be prancing around wagging her tail, and waiting for a scratch behind the ears and a pat on the head from my handsome dashing husband.

All of this would be followed by our going to the dining room where I would already have the table set, and a piping hot delicious meal awaiting us. But there I go daydreaming again. Let me get back to the classroom where Miss Meadows is calling, "Grace, Grace, you're not paying attention."

By the time my first year of school was over, I was more than ready for summer vacation. Aunt Esther and Uncle Marty had bought a farm in North Carolina and that's where Dinah and I would be spending the summer. The farm consisted of 800 acres, with horses, riding trails, and mountains and streams. It was a perfect haven for a little adventurer like me.

I remember that first trip to the farm very well. Daddy had just bought a brand-new dark green Mercury, which I christened with vomit after getting carsick. As if that wasn't bad enough, on the final leg of the journey we had to travel over a rut-filled, gravel dirt road for four miles in order to get to the farm. It just about killed Daddy to have to drive his brand new shiny car over that dusty, rocky, rut-filled road. The day was topped off with me getting stung by a wasp while trying to pick an apple off a tree.

It was love at first sight for me the first time I saw the mountains. I couldn't wait to start climbing them. I remember asking Daddy, "How do you climb up them?", because from a distance it looked like the only way to climb up them was to climb from branch to branch, tree by tree. The foliage was so dense that from a distance you couldn't see any ground beneath it.

Daddy laughed and said, "No you walk up them. You'll see."

From day one being at the farm was one big adventure. Dinah and I pretty much had free range of the place and every day we cooked up new mischief and fun. It's a wonder we lived through some of our shenanigans.

One day we decided to pretend like we were bullfighters. We went in the house and got a red shirt to wave in front of Uncle Marty's biggest bull, whose name was Mike. Then we went down to the pasture and started waving it like mad at him. We thought it would be fun to get him to chase us. Lucky for us he just stared at us like we were out of our minds.

When we innocently mentioned what we had done that evening at the dinner table, Uncle Marty thought that it was anything but funny. I remember that there was a moment of stunned silence and then Uncle Marty's fist came crashing down on the table. Everything on that table jumped and rattled. Uncle Marty had a booming voice, and when he got done lecturing and reprimanding us, we knew that the next time we would keep our games to ourselves. We still thought that we were invincible.

One day when Aunt Esther was having her bridge club over for the afternoon, Dinah and I were instructed to stay outside and play. That was perfectly fine with us. The only problem was that at one point we started laughing so hard that I wet my pants and had to sneak in the house and get dry clothes. Afterward we buried my wet clothes in the woods so that no one would know about it. Years later Dinah and I wondered if anyone had ever found them, and if so, what they may have speculated had happened to the little girl to whom they had belonged.

The farm wasn't actually a working farm. It was more like Uncle Marty's piece of heaven on earth where he roamed the property on his tractor. Oh, he did have vegetable crops, some Hereford cattle, chickens, hogs, a billy goat and a nanny goat. He even had a peacock, but he had farmhands that took care of all the work. He had bought the farm strictly for his own pleasure. Uncle Marty had enough money to be able to afford such extravagances and self-indulgence.

Midway through the summer Uncle Marty bought Dinah and me each a horse. Colleen was still too little and didn't spend the summer at the farm yet. My horse was a filly. Her coat was taupe colored. She had a white star on her forehead and a fringe of white fur around each hoof with a long shiny black mane and tail. She was a beauty. I named her Prance because she moved with such a lively pace.

Dinah's horse was a beautiful gelding, charcoal gray roan. He liked to trot around the pasture bucking periodically and annoying the other horses. Dinah named him Ruff.

I was the first person to ever ride Prance, but nobody ever told me that. The first time I got up on her I was in for the ride of my life. She bucked and jumped like there was no tomorrow . . . remember, I was only six years old. The thing is, every time she bucked me off, Uncle Marty was right there insisting that I get right back on her. "And don't let that horse know that you're afraid of her," he would bark at me. Trust me, when Uncle Marty issued a command to you, you did it. Even though his bark was bigger than his bite he didn't stand for any nonsense, and his authority was never questioned. That being said, I would hold back the tears, and with my heart pounding and my legs shaking, I would get right back up on her.

Another great thing about being at the farm was that there was a large family with six children that lived about a mile's walk through the woods from us. The fact that we had to walk through the woods to get there was a plus for me. I loved the woods. The family's last name was Elder. They were just as adventurous as Dinah and me, and together we never lacked for imaginative activities to keep us happily occupied.

Our first summer at the farm was to be the first of many. By the time the end of the summer rolled around and it was time to go back to Florida, we were already eagerly anticipating our return next summer.

Chapter 3

▼

Life Gets More Complicated

Life seemed to roll along pretty smoothly at a somewhat idyllic even keel for the next several years. However, that peaceful and serene existence was not to last. Trouble was brewing. When I was nine years old, my parents decided to get a divorce. All hell broke loose. I had no clue as to the storm that had been brewing inside my home. It seemed to have come out of nowhere without any warning. Up until then I didn't even know what a divorce was, but once the cat was out of the bag events took place rapidly.

One day I came home from school and my mother was gone.

I started calling, "Momma, Momma!", but there was no answer.

When I went in her room and found all of her things gone, it was as if she had vanished into thin air. My heart started pounding so hard I thought it was going to jump out of my body. All that remained of her presence was the faint scent of her perfume that lingered in the air.

Suddenly I felt the presence of someone behind me, and I desperately hoped that it was Momma, but when I turned around it was Daddy standing in the doorway. The expression on his face was somber and that made me feel frightened. When he opened his mouth to speak, I felt a deep sense of dread as to what he would say, but no words came out . . . only tears. I had never seen a man cry before, and it was quite a jolt to see my father in tears.

"Daddy, where's Momma?"

I could hear my voice rising as I asked the question. I knew I was on the brink of hysteria, but there was no stopping it. I could feel myself careening down a slippery slope into a very dark and empty abyss. Still, no answer came from Daddy.

"Daddy, I asked you where Momma is. What has happened? Where is she? Tell me what is going on?" I screamed. Still, no answer came from his lips.

He turned to leave and went into the living room and sat down. Instinctively I followed him. By now I was teetering on the verge of panic. I felt my anger toward Daddy quickly rising. Why didn't he answer me? I frantically searched inside and outside the house for Dinah and Colleen, but they were nowhere to be found. That was when I stopped teetering and plunged into a full-blown panic attack. It was just me and my sobbing father.

I took a few moments to try and gather my courage and calm my nerves before going back to the living room. Thoughts whizzed through my mind as I tried to figure out what to do. Was I going to have to slap my father in order to get an answer? My first inclination was to run, but my feet seemed to be frozen to the floor. Where were Dinah and Colleen? Did they know what had happened? Then I heard Daddy calling, "Grace, please come back in here." I snapped out of my reverie and went back to the living room.

"Come and sit with me Grace." he said as he patted a spot for me to come and sit in his lap.

I hesitated for a moment, but quickly decided that this was probably the only way I was going to get any answers. Reluctantly I crossed the room, knowing I wasn't going to like what I feared he was going to say. Tears were still streaming down his face.

He said, "Your mother has left Grace. She doesn't love me anymore."

There were so many unanswered questions I wanted to ask, but I couldn't right then. All I could do was run outside and find a place to hide so I could cry. I don't know how long I stayed hidden in the bushes. I cried until there were no tears left. Then, with great trepidation I went back in the house to face whatever fate lay before me. I felt sure that I would never be happy again . . . not ever.

Dinah, Colleen, and I were never given any explanation as to why our parent's marriage had ended. We were expected to simply accept it with no questions asked, but it sure did hurt.

After Momma left Grandmother Sarah tended to my sisters and I. She would come over every morning and see that we got off to school okay, and in the afternoon when we came home she would be there waiting for us. She fixed us dinner and stayed until Daddy got home from work. Once Daddy was home she would walk across the yard to her own house.

I was very angry during this period. I resented just about everyone except my sisters. We stuck together like three peas in a pod. I blamed my mother's leaving solely on my father, but it wasn't just him that I took my anger out on. I lashed out at my grandmother too, even though she didn't deserve it.

Grandmother Sarah had broken her hip the year before and the doctor had operated and put a metal pin in her hip. She had to walk with a cane after that, and even though she didn't complain, I know that it was probably painful for her to get around, but I didn't care if she was suffering. I was hurting too.

Sometimes Grandmother Sarah might ask me to do something for her like, "Grace could you please bring me my glasses?"

I would reply with a haughty answer, saying, "Go get them yourself." I've never quite been able to forgive myself for being so ugly to someone who was so loving and kind to me, and whom I loved with all my heart.

During this time my father was trying very hard to assure my sisters and I that we were loved beyond measure. He was also trying to make us feel safe and secure, but I felt so angry toward him that I returned his love with hostility. When he would come into our room to tuck us into bed at night, I would cover my face with the sheet and tell him not to touch me. Looking back I know that this must have hurt him a great deal, but at the time I didn't care because I thought it was his fault that Momma had left.

Dinah and I decided that we would devise a plan to uncover the mysteries surrounding the divorce. We were going to be like private detectives and get to the truth of the matter. We decided that we would write a letter to a judge and ask him if he would assign some private detectives to the case to find out exactly what had happened that caused Momma to leave.

We believed that if he would do this for us then justice would prevail and Momma would come back home. Then life would resume as it had been. Of course our plan was never carried out. We were just frustrated and hurt little girls that were desperate for answers.

Those first few months after Momma left were difficult for my family. Dinah, Colleen and I felt like our lives were ruined forever. We learned very quickly that life is much more complicated than the innocent play of childhood, and that we do have to grow up, sometimes much sooner than we should have to, or want to.

One good thing to come out of the divorce was that Dinah, Colleen and I became much closer. We didn't seem to have as many sibling quarrels as we had in the past. We sought assurance from each other and felt that everything would be all right as long as we were together.

A routine was quickly developed to accommodate the new circumstances our lives had taken on. Momma would come and pick us up every Sunday and we would always do something fun. A typical visit would be to go to the movies, an amusement park, shopping, or to the beach, and afterward out to dinner. The only bad part about the day would be when we had to say goodbye. That was always tough and usually ended in tears being shed.

Colleen and I seemed to have a harder time adjusting to the divorce than Dinah did. I believe that it was just as hard for her as it was for us, but being the oldest she was trying to put on a brave front for our benefit.

Colleen became very clingy toward me. She was always hanging on me and following me around. It was annoying at times, but I always acquiesced to her demands. At night she would cry uncontrollably if I didn't let her climb in bed with me and cuddle. She was afraid of any shadows that appeared on the wall from the reflected images of the bushes and trees outside our bedroom window. No amount of cajoling could calm her fears.

She was afraid of the sandman. She didn't want him coming and putting sand in her eyes at night. I tried to tell her that he wasn't real, but she could not be convinced. When she lost her first tooth she was terrified of the tooth fairy coming, but she wanted the money that the tooth fairy was supposed to put under her pillow. She was still my little "munchkin," but she was no longer my real live baby doll to play with. She had become my real live protégée and I had become her protector.

I was still suffering with severe asthma attacks, and since Momma wasn't around to sit up with me, Daddy would sleep in Dinah's bed, and

Colleen and Dinah would sleep in Daddy's room. I know that he really tried to help and give me comfort, but he snored so loud that even if I had been able to sleep, I couldn't. His snoring was so loud that I would have to keep waking him up to tell him.

"Daddy, I can't sleep with you snoring so loud."

He would always apologize, but before I knew it he would go back to sleep and start snoring again.

Another problem was that the medicine I took for my asthma attacks had bad side effects. It caused me to have nightmares and hallucinations. I remember one such episode very vividly. In it I was lying in bed, when all of a sudden all of my books and dolls on the bookshelf facing my bed, started being hurled violently at me by some unseen and unknown force. It was terrifying.

The nightmares and hallucinations weren't the only side effects from the medicine. It made my heart pound and my hands shake because it increased my heart rate. Sometimes it would make me so jittery that my hands would start to shake uncontrollably. At other times, out of the blue, it would cause me to suddenly start crying for no apparent reason.

Whereas before our parents were divorced it had seemed that nothing ever did, or ever would change, but as life began to unfold we learned that life brings perpetual change, and that along with it more often than not, comes stress.

Just as we were starting to feel a degree of acceptance and stability in our lives everything got turned upside down. Once again my sisters and I felt that we had been betrayed. The reason was that our parents had both started dating. That was hard for us to accept. I think the main reason it was so difficult for us was that we all three harbored the secret wish that our parents would be reunited. The other reason was because we were afraid that they might fall in love, and start to love their new-found love more than they did us.

It all started one Sunday morning when Momma came to pick us up for visitation day. She wasn't alone. In the car with her sat a very handsome man with jet black hair. As we approached the front door to go to the car we all three stopped dead in our tracks.

We all said in unison, "Who is that?"

Dinah was the first to regain her speech after the initial shock wore off a bit. "I don't know. Do you know who it is Grace?"

"No, I don't have a clue. Have you ever seen him before Colleen?"

"Nope."

After confirming that none of us had ever seen him before, we just kind of looked at each other as if saying, okay what do we do now? The stunned silence was finally broken when Dinah said, "Okay, let's go find out who he is."

With that said we took our first tentative steps out the door and down the sidewalk to the car. As we were walking to the car, we could see that Momma, and what's his name, were laughing and talking. We didn't like that. It looked like they liked each other too much, and were having way too much fun. Right away that made us not like him, even though we had never met or spoken to him before.

Once the three of us were in the car, Momma introduced us. She said, "Samuel, I would like for you to meet my daughters." She then motioned toward each of us individually, saying, "This is my oldest daughter Dinah. This is Grace, and this is Colleen. Girls, I would like you to meet my friend Samuel."

We didn't smile and say, "Hello, it's nice to meet you," instead we replied with a very unenthusiastic, "Hello." We sure weren't going to be friendly with this what's-his-name. Forget about it— no way, no how.

Samuel was to be the first of many boyfriends Momma would have, and we never liked a single one of them.

It wasn't long after we had met Samuel before Daddy introduced us to his new girlfriend. Her name was Susanna. She was very pretty and likable. She had an unassuming and down-to-earth demeanor about her. She was one of those people that you meet and can't help but like. Even though we tried not to, Dinah, Colleen and I took a liking to her right away.

Susanna was fair complected. Her build was tall and lanky, and she had a very casual appearance about her. She was athletic and very much an out-doors-man. She wore her long blonde hair pulled back in either a ponytail or hanging loosely about her face. She didn't wear much makeup, but she didn't need to. She was a natural beauty. She had a gung-ho personality with a kind and generous spirit.

She seemed to fit into our family circle very naturally and easily, and unlike the feeling we had gotten about Samuel, Susanna tried to mend the fences and bring us closer to Daddy. She encouraged us to do more things together as a family. For instance, instead of just her and Daddy going to the beach, she would suggest that we all go. Many times when they were going out, say to dinner or a movie, she would say, "Let's take the kids." Daddy wouldn't want to most of the time.

By this time Dinah was twelve and thought to be old enough to babysit for me and Colleen. Consequently, we were now left on our own a good deal of the time, and that wasn't good. We started getting into mischief.

Dinah and I being the oldest were the most mischievous and daring. Colleen was only eight so we didn't include her in most of our shenanigans. One such afternoon we found an open pack of Daddy's cigarettes and decided to smoke them. Back then the dangers associated with smoking were not known, and so the notion that it was unhealthy for us wasn't an issue. Most of the movie stars we had collected pictures of smoked, and we thought it looked very glamorous. The hacking coughs that ensued after our first few tentative puffs, however, were anything but glamorous. We were not deterred by it though because the reckless danger that we perceived our antics to be was very exciting.

Another time when we were left alone, Dinah and I decided to shave our legs. Afterward I was scared to death that Daddy would notice and we would be in a heap of trouble. That premonition did come true and I received a stern lecture. Dinah wasn't in trouble for shaving her legs because Daddy said that she was old enough to do so. However, she was scolded for enticing me to do it.

About this time I started going through adolescence and started growing pubic hair. I felt very ashamed and embarrassed by it. Whenever I would sleep over at a girlfriend's house, or they would sleep at mine, I made sure that they didn't see me get undressed and ready for bed. I thought I was a freak because none of them had it yet. The arrival of pubic hair brought along with it, an awareness of my sexuality. I began to notice that this was a very sensitive and titillating part of my body.

My grades at school began to suffer. I wasn't failing, but I was just making average grades. Somehow I just couldn't buckle down academically. I liked to socialize too much. Since I had always done well in school up to this point, I think there were two contributing factors that affected the change in my grades. One reason was that I was going through adolescence, and the other reason was that I really didn't see the importance of academic achievement in my life. What did I need it for? All I planned on doing after I grew up was to fall in love, get married, and raise a family. I had no interest in having a career.

I only had one more year to go in elementary school and I was very happy about that. It just sounded, from what Dinah told me, that middle school was a lot more exciting because you didn't have to be around little kids anymore, and you got to change classes. That appealed to me because I wouldn't be stuck in the same old classroom all day, and there would be different people in each class. The best part about it though was that I would be in the same school as Dinah.

CHAPTER 4

▼

COMING OF AGE

I felt like the coming year would be a new and better chapter in my life. I would finally be entering middle school. For the first time since first grade I felt really excited about school. This is where I would complete the seventh, eighth and ninth grades.

I was very proud of my sister Dinah. Now that we were in the same school, I felt like I had extra clout just by being her sister. Dinah had it all. She was very pretty. People always said that she looked like Doris Day. She was extra smart and hardly ever had to study because she could read or hear something once and completely grasp and understand its' content and meaning.

Dinah was very popular in school. Every year she would get voted "Most Popular," or "Best Personality," sometimes winning several superlatives. I felt in awe of her, and I didn't think that I could ever be as wonderful as she was.

Lately, Dinah seemed more like a grownup than a kid. I loved to eavesdrop on her and her friends when she had them over. I could hear them talking and giggling over the latest gossip in school. They would talk about who liked whom, and who were the cutest boys, etc.

I heard her tell one of her friends that next year when she started high school, she was going to ask Daddy if she could start dating. Dating sounded exciting to me, but it also sounded scary in a way. I mean, like what were you to do if your date wanted to do "*it?*"

This time in my life aroused a new kind of excitement and adventure in me. On the one hand I looked forward to exploring new and uncharted territory, but on the other hand it brought about melodrama and inner turmoil within . . . due to the confusion of adolescence.

Although I felt happy about going to the same school as Dinah, I felt as though I had to prove myself worthy of being her sister. What if I couldn't measure up to the challenge? What if I wasn't pretty enough, or smart enough, or funny or charming enough? I was sorely lacking in self-confidence, and I was feeling very alone and bogged down by my insecurities. As I looked around, no one else seemed to have those problems.

The biggest hurdle I felt that I initially had to cross was getting through gym class. We were required to change into our gym suits at the beginning of the period, and get completely undressed and take a shower at the end of the period. I was very modest and self-conscious about my body. Although my breasts were beginning to sprout little nubs, they were by no means as big as some of the other girls. That made me feel very inferior and inadequate because I thought that I wasn't a real woman if I didn't have big breasts.

Another, and even more troubling source of concern, was the way the boys behaved toward us developing girls. They were always snickering between themselves and making rude remarks about girls' bodies, especially our breasts.

There was one boy in particular that I tried to avoid at all cost. He taunted me without mercy, causing me pain and torment the likes of which I had never known. His name was Tommy English. He would always seek me out when classes were changing, and the corridors were crowded with students. His favorite chant was, "Grace is a pirate's dream . . . a sunken chest." I just wanted to crawl under a rock and die when he said that.

It was during this time that I started to consider buying some of the breast cream I had seen advertised in the movie star magazines. The cream was supposed to make your breasts grow. I was afraid to order it though, because I was afraid that someone would find out about it. I would have been mortified if that were to happen, so I decided that it was too risky to take the chance. Instead I decided to start doing some of the breast exercises I had heard were suppose to make your breasts big. I started doing them like crazy. As I did them, I had my own little chant that I would recite. This is the way it went, "I must, I must, I must increase my bust!" After several weeks of fervent dedication in doing the exercises, I could see no change and decided that it was an exercise in futility, thus I abandoned the routine.

By this time I had a new concern. I had started menstruating. I had been eagerly awaiting for that passage into womanhood, but once the pain and cramps started, I quickly changed my mind. It was for the birds! Growing up wasn't turning out to be as great as I had thought it was cracked up to be. It no longer held the glamour that I had envisioned it would.

I was learning that what may seem like a personal calamity one day, may not even give us pause to consider the next, and that adversity can often make us stronger. My attitude was beginning to change in more ways than one. I don't know why, but I was beginning to feel a protective and caring regard for myself, and an intolerance for people such as my tormentor, Tommy English.

I had definitely had enough of him. I decided that it was high time to turn the tables and start to torment him. I was beginning to realize that the bullies of this world are the weak ones. They can't stand their own self-worth and so they prey on others in order to draw attention to themselves. They have the mistaken idea that this behavior builds them up in stature with their peers. Wrong! Duh!

In addition to the various changes I have already mentioned, I began to feel a new and empowering sense of my own self-worth. I decided that if I tried to flee from the Tommy Englishes of this world, they would only continue to seek me out and bring me down. I decided that the only way I could rid myself from problems of this nature was to face them squarely, look them straight in the eye, and not be the first to blink. It was with this steadfast determination that I decided to face off with Tommy.

The next time he decided to ridicule me, Lord help him! The first time the opportunity presented itself, instead of fleeing from him as fast as I could, I intended to calmly turn around to face him and block his path. That would completely catch him off guard. The more I thought about it, the more I began to relish the idea. The opportunity presented itself the very next day as I was changing classes and the corridors were full of students.

When I first saw him my heart started pounding, and for just a second I had the urge to bolt. I took a deep breath, and decided it was now or never. Just as he was about to start with the pirates' joke, I turned around and looked him squarely in the eyes. I almost laughed when I saw the look of alarm cross his face. This was going to be even better than I had imagined, and I could hardly wait to get the words out.

"Are you talking to me you little weasel?"

He froze on the spot, and just stood there with his mouth agape. He was dumbstruck and so flabbergasted that I expected a puddle to form around his feet at any second. His eyes started darting around as if looking for an escape route, but there wasn't anywhere to go because the halls were full of students changing classes.

By this time everyone had stopped dead in their tracks to see what was going to happen next. It was almost quiet enough to hear a pin drop. Tommy was speechless, but much to his chagrin, I was anything but. I was determined to make him look like a fool in front of everybody.

I said to him, "Who do you think you are you little weasel? God's gift to women? I don't see any girls around here drooling over you. Girls, do any of you think that this little weasel is God's gift to women?"

For a few heart-stopping moments there was dead silence, and then everybody started to laugh at Tommy as he slunk away in humiliation. After that Tommy English went out of his way to steer clear of me.

Wow, that was empowering, not only in the eyes of my peers, but in my own eyes as well. It had given me infinite courage, and a self-respect that had been sorely lacking.

Not too long after the "Tommy incident," I developed my first serious crush on a really cute boy named Carl Fellamy. He gave me his ring to wear and we started going steady. I put the ring on a chain and wore it around my neck. Our romance consisted of nightly telephone conversations and Saturday afternoon movie matinees. My biggest fear was that he would try to kiss me or hold my hand during the movie, but to my great relief he never did.

CHAPTER 5

▼

EXPECT THE UNEXPECTED

I haven't said too much about Susanna, but what little I did say, I think pretty well painted the picture of her as a person. She was lovely, inside and out. She and Daddy had been dating for about two years now, and she had become a very significant person in our lives. She was at our house just as much as she was at her own apartment. We girls loved her, and more or less took it for granted that she and Daddy would eventually get married. At least that's what we hoped would happen.

That said, you can imagine what a shock it was when Daddy came home from work one afternoon and told us that he and Susanna had broken up.

"Why Daddy?" We all asked in amazement.

I was getting the feeling of déjà vu. It brought back memories of when Momma left. Suddenly I was starting to feel sick to my stomach. "Daddy, you're just kidding, right? You can't be serious, Daddy?"

Then Dinah jumped in. "Did the two of you have a fight? Just call her and work it out. If it was your fault just tell her that you're sorry."

"No, there is more to it than that. We both decided that it is for the best, but I don't want to talk about it right now." he said.

Colleen said, "But, I thought you loved each other. I know you do. It just can't end this way. We all love her. You can't do this. It's just wrong Daddy. Fix it."

"I'm sorry girls. It can't be fixed. It's too late for that." he said with a grim look on his face. He then turned and left the room, leaving us in utter dismay, with tears running down our cheeks.

Daddy would never talk about Susanna after that, and no further details were ever revealed, but my gut feeling told me that there was a lot more to the story than just a simple argument. I didn't know exactly how I was going to do it, but I planned to find out. I just didn't know I would be finding out so soon, and in such a shocking way.

It all became crystal clear very soon. A couple of weeks after Daddy had announced the breakup, the true reason was revealed. It was a Saturday night and Daddy had come to pickup Colleen and me at the skating rink. There was nothing unusual about that, except he wasn't alone. There was a woman in the car with him.

When we got in the car, Daddy said, "Girls, I'd like you to meet Ellen. Ellen these are two of my daughters, Grace and Colleen."

Colleen and I both said "Hi," but neither one of us was being friendly toward her. We were both fuming about the fact that she was there at all. When we looked over at each other, we could see the contempt we were both feeling on each others' face.

In the weeks that followed our first encounter with Ellen, we would be seeing a lot of her, but nothing could have prepared us for the shock we experienced the first time we saw her in broad daylight. It was very obvious that she was pregnant . . . very pregnant. Furthermore, much to our horror, we were told that Daddy was the baby's father, and that he and Ellen would be getting married in two weeks. The reason for the breakup between Daddy and Susanna was suddenly staring us right in the face. Daddy had been a very bad boy!

I was feeling a great deal of anger and disgust toward Daddy, and so were Dinah and Colleen. We wondered if and when the betrayals would quit coming. At this point, Daddy had once again lost the respect of his three daughters. None of us liked Ellen.

I had begun to feel a chilling coldness toward Daddy and Ellen course through my body, the likes of which I had never known before. I had a chilling premonition that there was going to be hard times ahead for me and my sisters.

As the plans for the wedding were being finalized, I could see a deep sense of dread overcome Daddy. It was very clear by his demeanor that his heart was growing heavier with every day that passed, and the impending marriage loomed closer. I often found him sitting in the dark, brooding and smoking one cigarette after another. He was downing cans of beer like they were water.

My cold heart couldn't help but feel sympathy for him when I would see him that way, but the warm feeling would only last for a few fleeting moments before my heart turned cold once again, and I would start to feel that he deserved all the misery he was feeling because of his betrayal to Susanna.

I missed Susanna a lot and I called her a couple of times a week. She never talked about Daddy during our conversations. I'm sure it was hard not to show a hint of the heartbreak and disappointment that I know she must have felt, but being the kindhearted person that she was, she only wanted to know all about how Dinah, Colleen and I were doing. She always wanted to know what we had been doing, and if we were okay, etc.

I told her whatever I was feeling in my heart. I told her about my sense of the impending doom I felt concerning Daddy and Ellen's upcoming marriage. I had the feeling that Ellen was going to make life a living hell for me and my sisters. She would always try and make me laugh, and tell me not to jump to conclusions about Ellen. "She is probably a lot nicer than you think. Give her a chance before jumping to any preconceived conclusions."she would say, but I knew better. I could feel it deep down in my soul.

Whenever we were around Ellen, superficially she seemed pleasant enough, but her smiles and conversation appeared insincere to me . . . like they were stilted and forced. I could physically feel the tension in the air when she was around. It seemed to suck the breath right out of me . . . making it hard to breathe. Inwardly I would feel like I was going to start gasping for air, and I would have an almost uncontrollable urge to run out of the room before I suffocated. Laughter and fun no longer lived at our house.

There was nothing that I liked about Ellen. Nothing! She was devious and phony as far as I was concerned . . . with no redeeming qualities to be found. There was never any single word or gesture that I could pinpoint to base my feelings on, but I knew that the feeling of dislike was mutual between us. It showed itself when our eyes would meet indiscriminately. A knowing that was felt by both of us. It never failed to send shivers down my spine.

As the day of the wedding loomed closer, I tried very hard to sort out my feelings about Ellen. I became withdrawn and aloof. I felt that if I stayed clear of everyone, no one could touch me, and therefore no one could hurt me, but it was a lonely and sad place in my inner sanctum. I cried a lot. It was a painful place to be.

Meanwhile, in the midst of all this hullabaloo, Aunt Esther was trying in every way that she could to prevent the marriage from taking place. She and Daddy were trying to convince Ellen to give the baby up for adoption, because apparently, Daddy wasn't even sure that it was his baby. Forget about it. There was no way that Ellen was going to consider the adoption option. In fact, the very mention of it enraged her even more.

Although Ellen was short in stature, she was a voice to be reckoned with, and she was definitely on the warpath now. Aunt Esther usually got her way, whether by hook or by crook, but neither her will nor Uncle Marty's money were buying Daddy out of this fiasco !

As for Momma, she was having the time of her life living it up and partying. She was far too busy having fun to get involved in this soap opera. I wish she had helped us to get through this somehow. We needed her to be around to help us get through all of the emotional distress the situation was creating, but what we really wished was that she would come to our rescue by physically removing us from it and take us to live with her. I didn't hold out much hope for either of those scenarios taking place. We were on our own with this.

I don't think any of the adults even had a clue as to how Dinah, Colleen and I were being affected by all that was going on. They were all too caught up in their own agendas to notice. Perhaps they thought that if they didn't acknowledge the problem, there was no problem. In retrospect, I came to the conclusion that maybe the reason that Momma had left so abruptly when she and Daddy split up was because she didn't know what to say . . . so she said nothing. In other words, it seemed that my family's way to handle a problem, was simply not to handle it. Ignore it, and hopefully it will just go away.

Momma had experienced her own share of run-ins with Aunt Esther, and knew that she was no match against her and the power that her money could buy. I'm speaking of the high-powered attorneys that Aunt Esther was able to hire, and did hire for Daddy when he and Momma got divorced. That's how he was able to attain custody of Dinah, Colleen and me.

Momma and Daddy had gotten married when Momma was just sixteen, and she really hadn't had much of a chance to experience much of life before having the responsibility of a family to care for. Now that she had the chance to sow some wild oats, that is exactly what she was doing. It was party time, big time !

Getting back to the Ellen problem. The reason that I didn't like her is because she didn't like me or my sisters. I knew this strictly by intuition and the gift of discernment. It wasn't because of anything that we had said or done. It was simply that we existed. The truth was that she wanted Daddy all to herself, and we stood in her way.

She had tried to have Daddy all to herself from the start. She was always fawning over him in order to detract his attention away from us. In essence, she was doing her best to build a wall between Daddy and us. A wall that had no door, and was too big to climb over. She wanted to make it clear to Dinah, Colleen and me that she came first in his life . . . not us.

I think that Daddy had an inkling about what Ellen was up to, because he seemed to go out of his way to compensate for Ellen's callous behavior toward us by doing activities that excluded her. That tactic didn't work out though because we soon found out that Ellen would always find a way to intrude upon our time together. Her behavior took a toll on all of us. At times Daddy looked like he was suffocating from her overbearing manner. His face would get the look of a caged animal desperately wanting freedom.

I think the reason that Ellen clung to Daddy so tightly, and tried to shut Dinah, Colleen and me out as much as possible, was that she must have known that she was on shaky ground. She probably thought that if she loosened her tight grasp on him, or allowed him to ever focus on anything or anyone other than her, she would more than likely lose him.

I could never figure out how Daddy had gotten involved with Ellen. She certainly didn't have a sparkling personality, and she wasn't that good looking. She was short, with a stocky muscular build that would probably have made her look overweight even if she hadn't been pregnant.

Her facial features were severely defined, with a nose that was on the long side, but it made her look distinguished and did not detract from her appearance. Her eyes were hazel, and very penetrating. Her hair was her best feature. It was a deep auburn and fell softly around her face.

Her eyes always seemed to be following my every move, looking right through me to my very core, yet not seeing me for my true self. Whenever she looked at me, I got the feeling that she was trying to put a hex on me. It was intimidating, which is probably the effect she was trying to achieve. Nevertheless, it worked, even though I did my best not to let it show.

At any rate, by the time the day of the wedding rolled around, I had achieved better insight into the situation. It didn't matter though because it didn't change anything. In fact, if anything, it had made things worse because I had lost all hope for any improvement.

The wedding took place at The First Presbyterian Church of Ocean Shores. The only people in attendance were Dinah, Colleen, me, Aunt Esther, Uncle Marty, and Grandmother Sarah. It was a solemn occasion for everyone except Ellen, whose face was flushed with excitement.

After the ceremony, Colleen, Dinah and I went home with Aunt Esther and Uncle Marty. We stayed with them for a few days while Daddy and Ellen were away on their honeymoon. They went to the Bahamas. By this time, I was wishing that they would never come back.

CHAPTER 6

▼

MOVING ALONG

I didn't get my wish. They came back, and the problems started as soon as they walked in the door. The initial problem was that the house wasn't really big enough to accommodate all of us comfortably. Our house was a small wood frame house with two bedrooms, one bathroom, living room, kitchen, and Florida room. The Florida room was the biggest room in the house. Dinah, Colleen and I shared one bedroom.

Due to the cramped space we all kept bumping into each other. Nobody had any place they could go to get away and have some privacy. Given the way that we three girls and Ellen felt about each other, the cramped space made an already tense situation even more awkward and harder to cope with. With the arrival of the baby expected in about four weeks, it was clear that something would be done to remedy the situation as quickly as possible.

As things stood now, there was no room for the baby's crib except either in the living room or the Florida room. The baby was due in mid-February, and even though the weather is generally warm in South Florida during the winter, we do get some cold spells. Since the only heat we had in the house was a small gas heater in the living room, putting the crib in the Florida room was not an option due to the possibility of cold weather. However, there was a little wiggle room with this problem because the baby could sleep in a bassinet in Daddy and Ellen's room for a month or two. Nevertheless, it was clear that we would be needing more space as soon as possible.

It was decided that an addition of two bedrooms and a bathroom would be added on at the back of the house, just off of the Florida room. Dinah, Colleen and I liked that idea because it meant that we would have the bedrooms in the front of the house, and therefore have that part of the house to ourselves at night.

Another immediate problem was that Ellen was a terrible cook. It seemed to Dinah, Colleen and me that she deliberately cooked things that she knew we didn't like, and then she would insist that we eat it . . . all of it. If we didn't clean our plates we were made to sit at the table until we did. Since Daddy usually worked late into the evening, we were at her mercy.

After dinner we were made to clear the table, do the dishes, and mop the floors in the kitchen and Florida room. We had to do the Florida room because that is where the dining room table was. We complied with her demands because her demeanor toward us was threatening. The way that she would glare at us as we did our chores was frightening to me because I didn't know what she might do if we didn't obey her rules, which were very rigid.

You are probably saying to yourself that you don't think any of that sounds too unfair, and under normal circumstances I would agree, but Ellen was never satisfied with the results of our cleaning. She always found something wrong; such as a crumb that had been missed, a spot of grease that had been overlooked, or condiments not put away correctly, etc.

It was imperative that each bottle, jar, and can be wiped perfectly clean and put away in perfect order according to size. The taller items went in the back, with their labels perfectly centered and facing forward. They also had to be grouped into the proper categories. We were never excused or permitted to leave the kitchen until Ellen had inspected everything and given her final approval, which she took her own sweet time in doing. If she found something wrong, we were detained. She seemed to delight in finding a reason to detain us because a gleeful expression would cross her face as she gave us further orders. When we voiced our complaints to Daddy, Ellen would twist things around and make it appear as if we were just lazy and unwilling to help her. She would say something to Daddy, such as, "Don't you agree that the girls are old enough to share in some of the household responsibilities? They are exaggerating the situation because they are trying to get out of doing anything; I'm the one who is being given a hard time, not them." She would keep up that type of argument until she had Daddy believing her, and agreeing with her. Then, as soon as Daddy turned his back, she would flash a gleeful look of triumph at us as if to say, you will neither defy nor defeat me . . . ever.

Our feelings toward Ellen aside, Dinah, Colleen and me were excited about having a baby in the house . . . especially me. I was the one who had always been so naturally drawn to the motherly instinct. There was another reason that I was eagerly awaiting the baby's arrival. I felt that the attention the baby would require might take away some of the tension and stress that we were all feeling due to our new living arrangements.

I was still trying to hold on to the hope that we would all be able to live with each other in an amicable manner one day. I guess that I'm a born optimist because I always cling to the hope for better things to come.

I had found that if I put a smile on my face and looked like I was willingly cooperating with Ellen, that things went a lot better. I was trying to convey to her that I was willing to do so because I wanted our relationship to be a happy and mutually respectful one. It seemed to help, because it seemed to relieve her feelings of competitiveness that she had toward Dinah, Colleen, and me. I wanted her to realize that we didn't have to be foes, but could possibly be friends. I needed harmony in my life.

To my amazement and delight, I could see that Ellen was responding to my overtures of cooperation in a very positive way. At that point, my hope for a congenial environment and relationship among all of us was re-born. At any rate it seemed to be working. Ellen actually started to be a nicer person to be around, and we all started trying to work together . . . instead of against each other.

I've always believed that the attitudes of those we are surrounded by are contagious. A negative attitude breeds negativity, and a positive attitude breeds hope, happiness, and contentment. I wonder why there are so many people that feel life is a competition that they always need to be the lone winner of? Why not be a team player? That way there are more winners.

One afternoon Ellen, Dinah, Colleen and me all sat down at the table and started looking at catalogs together. We were planning how to decorate the baby's room. We enjoyed each others' company, and even laughed some that afternoon.

Once the plans for the new addition on the house were decided on, the work seemed to go quickly. It looked as if the addition might even be completed before the baby even got big enough to need his or her own room. Even so, the baby's arrival fell a little short of that.

Ellen went into labor shortly after I got home from school one day. Nora René Murphree was born on February 14, 1958. She was a beautiful and healthy baby, weighing in at eight pounds four ounces. She was twenty inches long, with red hair the color of a carrot stick. I loved her the minute I laid eyes on her.

CHAPTER 7

▼

LIFE GOES TOPSY TURVY

Ellen and the baby stayed in the hospital for three days. During that time Dinah, Colleen and I tried our best to make sure that the house would be in good order when they came home. We dusted, vacuumed, mopped, cleaned the bathroom, did laundry, and had Daddy take us to the grocery store so that Ellen wouldn't have to worry about a thing when she and Nora came home. We hoped that Ellen would be pleased with all of our effort, and for once she was. We felt relieved and happy, and we had a renewed sense of hope that we all may just be able to get along after all.

The baby was good, and slept most of the time during the day in between feedings. Night time, however, was a whole different story. At night she would have the whole house awake with her crying and fretting. Consequently, we were all seriously sleep deprived, and along with the construction on the new addition going on, it wasn't long before tension was running out of control among us once again.

Due to the sleep deprivation, it was hard for Dinah, Colleen and I to get up in the mornings to get ready for school. Daddy's eyes were always red from lack of sleep, and Ellen was suffering with postpartum depression. Whew ! What a mess we all were ! It is amazing how one small baby can turn a whole household topsy turvy in no time flat.

Things got so tense, that after a week or so went by, Aunt Esther and Uncle Marty came to our rescue by offering to hire a combination nanny/housekeeper for a couple of weeks as a gift to Ellen. They also suggested that Dinah, Colleen and I come and stay at their house until the new addition on ours was completed.

Daddy was pushing the construction crew to hurry and finish the work, and they were doing their best to get it done as quickly as possible. All that remained to be done was the finishing touches, such as painting, and finishing up the installation of the wood flooring.

Ellen and Daddy went shopping for the furnishings that were needed. That seemed to give Ellen a lift, and her postpartum depression seemed to be subsiding. I don't know if that was because of the natural progression of things, or if it was because of the extra help from the nanny/housekeeper that had taken a lot of pressure off her shoulders. That, and seeing some light at the end of the tunnel from all of the construction, seemed to give her some relief as well. Whatever it was, it was a welcome relief, and a good sign that things were improving.

Dinah, Colleen and I stayed with Aunt Esther and Uncle Marty for about two weeks. At that time the new addition on the house was completed and ready to be moved into. All we were waiting for were the drapes, etc. to be hung, and for the new furniture to be delivered. That would be forthcoming within the next few days.

It was decided that since Dinah was the oldest she would have her own room, and Colleen and I would share the larger bedroom. Colleen and I were a tad bit envious of Dinah getting her own room, but we knew it was only fair to do it that way.

Daddy said that he would paint our rooms whatever colors we wanted, and get us new curtains and bedspreads of our choosing. That worked out well for Dinah because she had no one but herself to please, but for Colleen and me it was a little tougher to agree on what colors and patterns we wanted. Daddy's solution to our standoff was simple; either come up with a mutual agreement that we could both be happy with, or live with it just the way it was. That ultimatum gave us the necessary incentive we needed in order to reach a compromise. It worked ! We reached a decision. The painting was completed a couple of days later, and the new furniture was delivered. A few days later we hung the new curtains, bought new bedspreads, and finally got moved into our new quarters.

Dinah, Colleen and I loved having the front of the house, more or less, all to ourselves at night. There were several reasons why we liked it so much. As long as we didn't turn up the volume on the radio too high, we could listen to music until the wee hours, unbeknownst to Daddy or Ellen. We could sit and talk in whispered tones to each other, or lay in bed and read a good book late into the night without being detected.

Dinah did a great job decorating her room. She chose a four poster double bed with a canopy and a high double dresser that had four drawers on each side. The dresser had a mirror that you could tilt to various positions. The furniture had a rich cherry finish to it, and the paint she chose for the walls was a dusty rose color. The area rug was sea foam green with small roses along the border and a large rose in the middle. The sheer swag curtains were the same sea foam green as the area rug. For privacy purposes white window blinds were installed. On the walls Dinah had a picture of her two favorite singers, Elvis Presley and Frankie Avalon, along with a pennant that said, "Ocean Shores High School."

I was satisfied with the choices Colleen and I had made for our room too. We chose a pale lavender color for the walls, and a white French Provincial bedroom set with two twin beds. I had the double dresser for my clothes and Colleen had the chest of drawers for hers. Our curtains were white with lavender polka dots that were the same color as the walls. Our area rug was a pale pink with a white fringe around the border. For privacy we had chosen white window shades.

We were all very tired, but happy by the time we finished getting our new rooms set up. Although the move from one room to another was only a few short steps down the hall, it had involved moving all of our clothes and personal possessions, and had taken a good deal of work to get everything organized.

By this time the baby was sleeping better at night, and we had all developed some sort of routine as far as what was expected from each of us toward contributing to the running of the household. We were all still working out the kinks and trying to adjust to each other, but things were getting better. Ellen even seemed to be working harder at trying to get along with Dinah, Colleen and me. The road was still rocky, but getting smoother.

One Saturday morning shortly after completing the move, I was going through my box of photographs, and came upon some photos of Susanna that I had taken one day when we had all gone to the beach.

Looking through the photos and strolling down memory lane made me miss her. I decided that I would call her the first opportunity I got when Ellen would be out of the house. I knew that if Ellen ever came across the photos, or knew that I was calling her, she would be furious.

I didn't have to wait very long. Shortly after lunch Daddy and Ellen said they were going grocery shopping. Daddy said that Dinah, Colleen, and I didn't have to go if we didn't want to. We were not to go anywhere. If we needed anything, we should tell Aunt Esther or Uncle Marty because they would be at home.

As soon as I saw them pull out of the driveway I made a beeline for the phone and dialed Susanna's number. Much to my astonishment a recording came on announcing that the number I had dialed had been disconnected and was no longer in service. I sure hadn't expected to hear that.

I decided that as soon as Daddy and Ellen came home I was going to ask them if I could ride my bike downtown. I told them that I wanted to go to Woolworth's Five and Ten to buy an album for my photographs. My plan was to hurry up and get the photo album, and then ride my bike to Susanna's apartment, which was only a few blocks from downtown Ocean Shores.

As soon as Daddy and Ellen pulled in the driveway, I ran out and asked them. The baby was crying and Daddy said that if I would feed Nora her bottle while they put the groceries away, I could go. That was okay by me. I loved holding Nora. She was so sweet looking, and she stared at me so intently as she sucked on her bottle. As soon as the groceries were put away and Ellen had taken over the care of Nora, I took off for town as fast as I could. Ocean Shores was just a small town back then with hardly any traffic, consequently there wasn't any cause for concern about a young girl riding her bike to town.

I went directly to Woolworth's and got the photo album. I put it in the basket on my bike, and headed for Susanna's. I was feeling a rush of excitement over the prospect of getting to see her, and also because I felt like I was on a daring secret adventure.

As soon as I pulled up in front of her apartment building, I saw her landlord, Mr. Ornby. He was outside doing some yard work. He recognized me right away and looked surprised to see me. I supposed that he knew about the breakup between Daddy and Susanna.

"Well, well, look who's here," he said. "How are you doing? What has brought you over to this part of town?"

I said, "I came over to see Susanna." Once again his face took on a look of surprise, followed by a look of concern.

He said, "Susanna has moved back to Georgia in order to be closer to her family. She moved about two weeks ago."

I suppose his look of concern was in response to the stricken look I must have had on my face. I felt devastated, not only by her leaving, but also because she had never called to tell me that she was leaving, or to say goodbye. I turned away and ran quickly back to my bike. I could feel the tears welling up in my eyes. I had to find a private place where I could go and cry my heart out.

CHAPTER 8

▼

SUCK IT UP . . . AND STAY TOUGH

The remainder of my first year in Junior High School seemed to slip by at a slow crawl. With all of the changes that I had recently gone through, both mentally and physically, at home and at school, the stress of it all seemed to finally be taking its' toll. I was feeling kind of dazed by it all . . . shell shocked.

I was always on edge, never knowing when *that* Ellen might reappear. Her acid tongue had reared its ugly head sporadically from time to time, mostly just to Dinah, Colleen and me, but there had been times when we had friends over that she had lashed out at them. It was embarrassing and awkward, not only for us, but for them as well. Consequently, we soon cutback on having our friends over.

All of these incidents changed me. I became withdrawn, keeping my feelings locked up inside because I couldn't trust their revelation to anyone. I was afraid that if I shared my feelings with anyone, they would see how conflicted my emotions were, and use them as a weapon against me . . . thus capitalizing on my vulnerability.

I was feeling very insecure and fragile as a result of my inner turmoil. Many people misinterpreted my withdrawn demeanor as being aloof or stuck-up, but it was simply that I felt if I kept myself isolated from others, and never let anyone penetrate the invisible barriers that I had surrounded myself with . . . then no one could hurt me. I just felt that I couldn't take any more hurt without completely cracking up. I was finding out that the road of life is infinitely a very complex highway system.

Although things were better at home than they had been during the first days of Daddy and Ellen's marriage, we were all still trying to adjust to the changes that our lives had undergone. With all of the commotion from the construction of the new addition on the house, and the arrival of Nora in our lives, I think that we had all been left in a bit of a stupor. I couldn't wait for summer vacation to begin.

Ellen was being much nicer to Dinah, Colleen and me than she had been when we had first met her, but I still felt like I was walking on eggshells when I was around her. I couldn't help but remember the mean looks and angry outbursts that were so common in the beginning of our relationship.

Another reason that I was anxious for summer vacation to start, was that Colleen, Dinah and I were going to spend a month with Momma before going to the farm for the rest of the summer. Our agenda was to spend a week in Key West and then drive to the farm. I'd never been to Key West before so I was really excited, but what I was looking forward to the most was getting to spend a whole month with Momma. I still missed her daily presence in our lives a lot.

I missed all of the little things that she had always done for me; the special touches she had given my life that had shown me how special I was to her. The things I had taken for granted were the things I missed the most. Things like the lemon meringue pies that she knew I loved and would often make for me to have as a treat when I came home from school hungry and wanting a snack, or the way she would fix my lunch for school. She would always make sure that there wasn't a speck of fat on my ham sandwiches because she knew I hated the fat.

Most of all I missed the comfort of knowing that I could always run to her for any reason that I might feel a need to, even if it was something that she might get mad about. I knew that I could still go to her, and that she still loved me unconditionally, but the comfort that love provided for me was no longer close at hand.

CHAPTER 9

▼

DRIVING DOWN THAT HIGHWAY

Summer vacation finally arrived. I left school that day with great expectations that I had envisioned in my head over and over again. I was anticipating a wonderful summer full of fun and laughter. I knew that I would soon be free from the stress that I experienced daily at home and at school. I was giddy with happiness.

At school I was stressed out just by trying to live up to the reputation of being Dinah's sister. She was a tough act to follow . . . her being so popular and all. I always felt like I could never measure up to her greatness, and that made me feel depressed and inadequate.

At home I felt the same way in a different sense. Dinah somehow seemed to be able to fly under Ellen's radar. She was somehow able to go undetected as a target for Ellen's scorn, as was Colleen. I seemed to be the target that she was always able to hone in on, and she never missed hitting the bulls' eye squarely in the middle. That added to my feelings of isolation. I felt myself slipping into a deeper sense of rejection. I wondered why I seemed to be singled out more often than Dinah or Colleen. What the determining factor in this particular equation was, I could never figure out. I don't know if my assessment of the situation was accurate, or something that I merely perceived because my own self-worth was so diminished.

There was another reason that I felt so helpless and abandoned in the situation. That was because my father never seemed to protect me from Ellen. I felt very vulnerable and alone. I think my father was afraid to tangle with Ellen, and that made me lose respect for him. Part of being a parent is to protect your child from those sort of things.

I was afraid of Ellen, and it is tough to live in a state of fear . . . especially when you are thirteen going on fourteen years old. Adolescence is a tough stage to have to navigate through under such pressure. The situation was made worse because I have always been a very sensitive person. I take everything literally. I can't help it, and I don't know how to do otherwise.

On my way home from school, I tried to put all negative thoughts out of my mind. In order to do so, I started singing happy songs inside my head, and visualizing myself doing all the fun things I had planned. By the time the school bus came to a halt at my stop, I had almost managed to put all negative thoughts behind me. After disembarking from the bus I went skipping merrily down the street.

I was thinking that I wasn't going to let anyone rain on my parade. As soon as I got home, I went straight to me and Colleen's room. She got out of school earlier than I did, so she was already there waiting for me. A few minutes later Dinah came strolling in and the three of us started talking a mile a minute about all the fun we were planning on having over the summer.

Then we started packing and trying to decide which clothes to take.

"I'm taking my old and my new bathing suits." I said. "That way I'll always have one that is dry to put on. I can't stand having to put on a wet bathing suit. It just feels so icky. Do you think my new bathing suit makes me look too skinny Colleen?"

"Grace, you aren't too skinny. Okay? So my answer is no, it doesn't make you look too skinny. How many pairs of shorts do you think we should take?"

Dinah hollered from her room, "You should take a dress and a pair of jeans in case we go out to dinner or something. We're not going to be in the pool twenty-four seven you guys."

"We need to remember to pack our toothbrushes and that sort of stuff too." I hollered back.

"Yes, and *please* don't forget your deodorant!" Colleen said jokingly. "It gets really hot down there, if you get my drift."

After about an hour and a half of bantering back and forth, we finally finished packing. We weren't packing the extra things that we would need to take to the farm, because after our month with Momma was up we would be coming back home for a couple of days, and would pack that stuff then. We went to bed fairly early that night because Momma was supposed to pick us up around eight o'clock the following morning.

The next morning when Momma picked us up all three of us started bombarding her with a million questions.

"How long will it take to get there?" Colleen asked.

"What's the name of the place where we'll be staying? What's it like?" Dinah wanted to know.

"What are we going to do first?" I asked.

Finally, Momma had heard enough, and put an end to our incessant questions.

She said, "If you all don't hush, it won't take long for us to get there because I'll turn right around and take you right back home. Furthermore, I have no idea what the place we will be staying at looks like because I haven't made reservations anywhere. I figure we will decide once we get there and find a place we feel will be to our liking. Last, but not least, I don't have a clue as to what we will do first, but putting on our bathing suits and jumping in the pool sounds good to me. We'll figure it all out as we go along, okay?"

We all answered in unison, "Okay."

That bit about turning around and taking us back home had really gotten our attention. After that we just started singing, playing travel games, and laughing.

Momma's current boyfriend, George, wouldn't be joining us because he had to work. That suited us just fine because we didn't like him. He was too possessive of Momma, and we wanted her all to ourselves.

Once we got settled in our hotel, we rushed to put on our bathing suits and made a beeline for the pool. From that moment on, it was a nonstop, fun-filled month of fun in the sun. We hardly gave Momma a chance to catch her breath. We swam every day, and for the first few days we got as red as lobsters from over exposure to the sun. None of us could stand for anything to touch our skin because it was so tender from the sunburn.

Momma went to the drugstore and got several different kinds of ointments to soothe the burning. We slathered it all over each other, but

Momma made us stay out of the sun for a few days until our sunburn got better.

The sunburn didn't stop us from having fun though. For the next few days we simply found other things to do. The first day of our respite from the sun we went to the movies to see Elvis Presley in "Jailhouse Rock" and let me tell you, that movie theater was really rockin and a boppin! Every young female in the theater was in a frenzy over Elvis. They were swooning and screaming, and placing their hands on the sides of their cheeks like they were just beside themselves. They were spiraling out of control from the sight of that sexy, handsome face, and those swiveling hips. I think Momma was very relieved when the movie was over and she could get away from all those star struck girls.

Afterward we went back to our room with the kitchenette and Momma fixed us some dinner. The next day we decided to go sightseeing. The first thing we did was go for a ride on the Conch Train. It was a lot of fun because it was an open-air sightseeing tram that gave you an overall view of the island and its history. Afterward you could return at your leisure to special points of interest.

The next day we decided to go and visit the Audubon House. That's where the naturalist John James Audubon stayed while working in the Keys. After we left the Audubon House, we decided to go check out the Hemmingway House. That's where the famous author, Ernest Hemmingway lived when in Key West. By the time we finished touring the Hemmingway House we were all getting tired and hungry. We decided to call it a day and go back to the hotel.

Momma said, "After the sun goes down, we can all go swimming."

The next day we went to Grassy Key, where Flipper, the porpoise movie star was trained. The Sea School there had porpoise shows and we got to see one while we were there. On the way back to the hotel we spotted a Key Deer. It was so little and so absolutely adorable. It reminded me of Bambi.

Finally, on our last two days in the Keys, we were sunburn free and able to spend more time in the hotel pool. Momma smeared Noxema all over us so thick that we looked like ghosts. We were embarrassed about going to the pool that way, but when we complained Momma said, "Okay. If you are too embarrassed, take off your bathing suits and we'll find something else to do."

We all three begged and pleaded with her not to make us go looking that way, but she wasn't willing to budge an inch. Dinah was really mad because there was a cute lifeguard at the pool that she had a crush on, and she was mortified that he would see her looking so ridiculous. She knew better than to argue any further about it though, because once Momma told us to do something, there was no changing her mind. In the end, I guess Momma knew best, because when we left the Keys we were sunburn free, and we all had a deep golden tan.

From the Keys we went to Momma's house in North Miami where she and George lived. We weren't too sure about how we were going to like being around George for the next three weeks, but we ended up having a great time with Momma. George wasn't around too much anyway because he had to work. We were glad that he wasn't around because, even though he was nice enough to us, we still didn't like him

The next three weeks went by very fast, and before we knew it, our month with Momma was over. Nevertheless, we weren't too sad because we still had the remainder of the summer at the farm to look forward to.

Before going to the farm, we made a pit-stop at home to pack a few more things that we needed to take . . . mostly jeans for horseback riding, a few long sleeve shirts, sweaters, and a lightweight jacket because it sometimes gets chilly up in the mountains. After a couple of days we were good to go again. Dinah, Colleen and I started singing, "She'll be comin' round the mountain when she comes."

We always had a blast at the farm. We had made a lot of friends there in the last seven years that we had been going. This year my cousin Claire, who lived in New Jersey would be spending the summer at the farm as well. She had been coming to the farm for the past several years. She is one year younger than I am, and we've always felt very close. I was really excited about getting to spend the summer with her.

I love the country life. Even as I was growing older, I found that I still loved many of the things that had endeared me to that lifestyle since day one. I loved to roam through the woods, and I loved horseback riding with my sisters, Claire, and our friends.

This summer Uncle Marty had let Dinah start driving his old jeep. What a ball we had with that. We went tearing through the woods and down every dirt road on the place . . . wind blowing through our hair and laughing like crazy.

There was never any stress at the farm until one rare evening when Uncle Marty and Aunt Esther went over to some friends' house to play bridge. They left strict instructions that Dinah was not to drive the jeep while they were gone. Of course we told them that we would never even consider doing something like that. We reassured them that we would be fine, and that we would just stay in the house and lock all of the doors. They left feeling assured that we would be just fine.

Ha! What stinkers we were! As soon as they pulled out of the driveway we all went running up the hill to jump in the jeep and go for a joy ride. What the heck, we thought. No one would ever know. Ha! We decided to drive over and pick up our friends, the Elders. Wheee! Hee! They all jumped in and off we went.

We were all squealing and laughing our heads off. Dinah was giving us the joy ride of our lives. She was going very fast and whipping around the curves so fast that we were all hanging on for dear life.

There were no side panels or roof on the jeep, just the two front seats and two built-in metal benches that were attached to the floor on each side in the back. We were really having to hold on tight to whatever we could grab onto. Nobody was concerned about speed or safety whatsoever. After all, we thought we were invincible. Weren't we? We're just having some pure wholesome fun, right? And it was pure fun, Lord knows . . . until we decided we better put the jeep away before Uncle Marty and Aunt Esther came home.

In our rush to get the jeep put away, we came down a steep hill in the mile long driveway way too fast. Dinah was unable to make the sharp curve in the road at the bottom of the hill. As she tried to make the turn, she overcompensated her steering. In the next, what seemed like a split second, our joy ride had turned into our worst nightmare. We ended up in a gully that had originally, many years ago, been the dirt road going up to the house. When Uncle Marty bought the farm, he put a white gravel driveway in. The gully hadn't been used as a road for years. Consequently, it was overgrown with thick weeds and dense brush.

Added to our dismay, was that someone had thought it would be a really good place to dump some old rusty barbed wire, and that is what got tangled up and caught on the bottom of the jeep. You never would have believed how quickly we all stopped laughing. It was as if someone had pulled the plug out of a wall socket and stopped the sound of our laughter. For the first couple of seconds we all just sat there dumbfounded and in shock. We quickly regained our composure because we really had to hurry now. Uncle Marty and Aunt Esther would be home any second.

Everybody started to go a little haywire until Dinah said, "Calm down everybody. This isn't a problem. All I have to do is re-start the jeep and drive it out of the gully."

Everybody relaxed and felt reassured by her words. She jumped back in the jeep with a big grin on her face and feeling very confident. Sure enough, the jeep started right back up. We all let out a big sigh of relief and jumped back in the jeep. Our smiles were back on our faces, and we were ready to roll, but the jeep wouldn't move and it was making a noise that wiped the smiles right off of our faces. We jumped back out to investigate further, and that is when we discovered that we were tangled up in barbed wire. Alarm bells started going off in our heads, and Dinah and I started having a full-blown panic attack.

Suddenly my cousin Claire took off running down the road as fast as she could toward the house. When I called out to her, "Claire, where are you going?"

She yelled back, "I'm not going to get in trouble for this. It wasn't my idea to take the jeep for a joy ride."

She always had been kind of skittish. I started running down the road after her yelling, "Claire come back. We need your help! ," but she just kept running away, and I just kept running after her. By the time I caught up with her, she was already in the house.

I went in and started searching every room in the house for her, but she was nowhere to be seen or heard. I started calling, "Claire, Claire!" I was becoming alarmed when I couldn't find her. Finally I saw her feet sticking out from the bottom of Aunt Esther's bed.

"Claire, why are you hiding under the bed? "

All she would say was, "No! No! I'm not coming out. Go away."

Finally I just gave up, and started running back to see what was transpiring with the jeep situation. When I got back to the scene, everyone had crawled under the jeep to try and untangle the barbed wire. Everyone was working feverishly at it, and sheer panic had just about taken over. However, they were making some progress.

Dinah yelled, "Grace, run up to Uncle Marty's workshop and get some wire cutters. Hurry!"

I took off lickety-split. I was getting worn out from all this running, first from chasing Claire, and now having to run about a mile straight up a hill to Uncle Marty's workshop. By the time I got the wire cutters and was running past the house, Claire was standing on the front porch. She had decided that it was too scary to stay in the big house under the bed all alone. She fell in beside me to go back to the scene of the crime, so to speak.

By the time we got back down there it was starting to get dark. That just added to the pressure we were under, and by this time we were all getting wigged out. After about thirty minutes, we finally got the last piece of barbed wire untangled from the bottom of the jeep.

We all started jumping for joy, and smiling and laughing again . . . until we heard a car coming down Sweet Creek Road. Could that be Aunt Esther and Uncle Marty? Dinah, Colleen, Claire and I made a mad scramble to get back in the jeep, and hopefully get away in time before Uncle Marty could catch us. The Elder's said they would just run home from there. The car didn't turn out to belong to Aunt Esther and Uncle Marty. This had turned into a real live form of the game "getaway" that we use to play. What an exciting evening we had.

By the time Aunt Esther and Uncle Marty got home, the four of us were all sitting at the table playing canasta.

"Were there any problems?" they asked.

We all looked at them very nonchalantly and said, "No. No. No problems. We've just been playing canasta all evening."

As soon as they left the room, we all just looked at each other with a look that said, boy, that sure was a close call.

We were on our best behavior for several days following the jeep scare. In fact, it had scared us so badly that we all vowed never to do anything like that again. We really meant it at the time, and several uneventful days went by before we decided to break our vows of goodness. Then it was onward to more rollicking and hilarious adventure.

We decided that we wanted to start smoking cigarettes again. We decided to sneak into Uncle Marty's office and steal some of his Lucky

Strikes. We did that for a few days until he started making the remark that he just didn't understand why his cigarettes were disappearing so fast. He would look right at us with his eyes kind of squinted when he said it. We knew we'd been had. After that we decided we had better find another way to get cigarettes.

We remembered that he had told us once, that when he was a young boy, he and his friends had made cigarettes out of corn silk that had turned brown. He had said that all they had to do was go to the store and buy cigarette rolling papers. Well, we could do that.

The next time we went to town we went to the drugstore and bought some cigarette rolling papers. We couldn't wait to get back to the farm and get us some brown corn silk. The corn silk caper didn't work out too well though. The problem was in the rolling of it. Every time we would lick the glue and roll the cigarette up, we got the paper too wet causing the paper to tear. Oh well, we tried. We would just have to find some other form of mischief to get into.

We weren't deterred for long. We decided that we would get us a few plugs of Uncle Marty's chewing tobacco and see how we liked that. The bad thing about that was that we didn't know that you were supposed to spit the tobacco juice out, and we swallowed it. The four of us got so sick that we thought for sure we were going to die. The only thing we could do was to suffer in silence because we certainly couldn't tell Aunt Esther or Uncle Marty why we felt so sick.

Before we knew it, another summer was drawing to a close, and it was time for us to leave and go back home. Time for Claire to go back to New Jersey, and time for Dinah, Colleen and me to go back to Ocean Shores and get ready to go back to school. Yes, it was time for us to go back to our *real life*, the one with you know who in it. The one with all the stress in it.

CHAPTER 10

▼

SCHOOL DAYS

Well, here we were, back at home sweet home again. As usual the summer had flown by way too fast. It was going to be tough getting back into the old grind of getting up early for school every day. We had come back a week before school was to start so we could go shopping for new school clothes, and get all our school supplies bought. Going shopping was the bright spot in this scenario. I love, love, love, shopping.

This year Dinah would start going to High School. I had mixed feelings about that. On the one hand, I liked us being in the same school. I was so proud to have her for a sister, but on the other hand, it might be a relief not to have to walk in her shadow.

I decided that I wanted to try out for cheerleading this year. Dinah had been a cheerleader for the past three years, and she said she would help me practice and learn the cheers. Every afternoon we went out in the yard to practice. Learning the routines and the words to the cheers was a snap, but no matter how hard I tried, I could not do the different jumps. My body just could not do them. It just wasn't going to happen, even with Dinah's help. I don't care if I had tried for a thousand years, I still wouldn't have been able to do it. Rather than make a fool of myself, I abandoned the idea.

It was probably just as well that I didn't make the cheerleading squad because the classes I was taking were much harder than they had been in previous years. Algebra class was the bane of my existence. I have no idea how I ever managed to pass that class.

Dinah hardly ever had to study in order to make good grades. When she did study, she would turn the volume on the radio up really high, and it never interfered with her ability to study at all. It was a different story for me though. I had to really concentrate, and it had to be really quiet with no distractions. I really wasn't into academics. I had found that it was much more fun to socialize, and there really wasn't enough time to do both.

Somehow, over the course of the summer, a lot of the stress that had so engulfed me at school and at home, had for the most part miraculously disappeared. I no longer felt so bogged down with problems. I wondered what had changed me, but I couldn't put my finger on it. I felt so much lighter in spirit, and I had more self-confidence. Even when I didn't feel all that confident, I found that I could just pretend like I did and nobody knew the difference. I was quite the actress when the occasion called for me to be.

I was much happier that way, but sometimes I wondered if I was being true to myself. I didn't want to come across as being someone that I wasn't. I can't stand phonies and hypocrites, and I certainly didn't want to be one. It wasn't long until it got to the point that I had acted and pretended so much, that I found myself asking the question, who is the *real* me?

That matter, who is the real me, is one that I continued to give a great deal of thought to when I was in an introspective mood, or when I was thinking reflectively. I came to the conclusion that I was not being a phony or a hypocrite because I was being myself. The necessity for having to sometimes act, or pretend, is one that is just part of the human element.

Even though I still felt a little anxious around Ellen sometimes, I wasn't afraid of her as much as I had been. She was still hard to please and very critical, but I think having had a child of her own had softened her and brought out her motherly instincts. She seemed to be much happier within herself, and I think that trickled down to the rest of us.

Nora had learned to sit up by herself, and was starting to crawl and make all kinds of baby talk. She was quite the little chatterbox. Too bad we had no idea of what she was talking about. It probably would have been very funny.

Dinah was loving High School and had made the cheerleading squad again. Daddy had let her start dating, and there was no shortage of boys calling her.

Colleen turned twelve and had started getting her period. The first time she got it she freaked out and cried hysterically. She was really mad about having to put up with the cramps every month, and got severe PMS. Dinah and I steered clear of her as much as we could during those times because she could get really grouchy. Once she slipped and showed that bitchy side to Ellen. I held my breath because I was afraid Ellen was going to get really mad, but she didn't. She knew why Colleen was so moody, and I guess she understood how PMS can affect a person, having suffered with it herself every month.

So far this school year was going very well for me. Every Friday night my best friend Nancy and I would go to the dances that were held for teenagers at the Recreation Center and hang out with our friends.

Saturdays were movie matinee day. That's where Nancy got her first kiss by a boy she had a crush on, whose name was Donald. She said, "Grace, I got goose bumps all over when he kissed me." She was lovesick for about a month until she developed a new love interest.

I had developed a crush on several boys, but I wasn't ready to be kissed yet. I was afraid I wouldn't know how to do it right, and that would have been extremely embarrassing. I couldn't take a chance on that happening!

The holidays were approaching. Thanksgiving was a week away, and Ellen's parents, whom we had never met before, were coming from Michigan to spend Thanksgiving with us. Ellen had everyone in the house scurrying around. She wanted everything to be perfect, and that was understandable. Her parents would be staying in Dinah's room, and Dinah would be sleeping in me and Colleen's room. Dinah wasn't too happy about giving up her room.

Dinah, Colleen, and I spent a lot of time talking about what we thought Ellen's parents would be like. The general consensus was that we didn't think we would like them, based on what we had to go on . . . you know, seeing as how Ellen was and all. The night before they were scheduled to arrive the following morning, Dinah waited until Daddy and Ellen had gone to bed and came into our room. We started conjuring up some hilarious ideas about how we thought they would look and act. We were laughing so hard that we just about wet our pants.

I don't know about you, but when I make a prediction about somewhere I've never been before might be like, or how I think someone I've never met before might look or act, I'm almost always wrong. This time was no exception. Dinah, Colleen and I were very pleasantly surprised to find out that Ellen's parents were very nice people.

They were both very congenial, especially her dad, Benjamin Forester. He was always joking around. Ellen's mother, Adele, was more mild mannered than her husband, but she was very kindhearted. Dinah, Colleen, and I were all wishing that Ellen had taken after her parents more. We wondered why she had turned out so different from them. Why hadn't she inherited the good humored and kindhearted genes?

They asked us to call them Mr. Ben and Miss Adele. They stayed for a week. Dinah, Colleen and I were actually sorry to see them go because Ellen had been being extra nice to us ever since they had arrived. We surmised that she wanted them to think she was such a good stepmother. She sure had them fooled.

I know that I'm making Ellen out to be a really miserable person. She was a lot of the time, but in all fairness to her, I'm sure it wasn't easy for her to come into a ready-made family with three very lively girls.

Before we knew it, Christmas was approaching. Dinah, Colleen, and I were going to spend Christmas day with Momma and George. We were very excited about it because we were going to be having Christmas dinner with Momma's sister, Aunt Christine and her family. They lived in Luna Beach, which is about twenty miles north of Ocean Shores.

Aunt Christine and her husband, Uncle Alvin, have two children. Thomas, who was nine, and Penny who was twelve, the same age as Colleen. We always had fun at their house because there was always a lot of merriment. The day went way too fast, and before I knew it, New Years Day had also come and gone.

On February fourteenth we celebrated Nora's first birthday. She had a blast tearing the wrapping paper off of her presents. She surprised us all when she got up and took her first few tentative steps. We all clapped and said, "Oh what a big girl you are." Then she started clapping too. She didn't know why we were having a party, but she knew she was the center of attention for sure. She ended up getting birthday cake all over her face, in her hair, and even in her ears. She was a delightful little baby girl, and I just loved her to pieces. We all did.

After the holidays came and went, the rest of the school year seemed to just fly by, and before we knew it summer vacation had arrived. Once again, we would be spending the first month of our vacation with Momma. Her boyfriend George was no longer in the picture. As far as we knew, he hadn't been replaced yet.

Our month with Momma was a lot of fun. First we went to Silver Springs where we went for a ride on a glass-bottom boat. All of the passengers were given little pieces of bread to feed the fish. One fish jumped up and touched Momma's hand. It startled her so, that she jumped out of her seat and let out a yelp. Everybody got a laugh out of that.

Another feature at Silver Springs was the show put on by underwater mermaids. They really looked like the pictures you have seen of mermaids, and they put on a wonderful underwater ballet. It made me wish that I was a mermaid. They were so pretty, and such free and unencumbered spirits.

Next on our agenda was for us to visit Cypress Gardens the next day. It was a beautiful place. The gardens were full of the most fabulous flowers and trees. There were pathways in the gardens and women dressed in antebellum, true southern belle attire, walked through the gardens fanning themselves with beautifully designed fans.

After enjoying the beautiful gardens, we saw a water-skiing show that was truly amazing. It was one of those things that you experience, and just go, "wow." The tricks and maneuvers that the water skiers did were truly amazing. Some of them had people standing on their shoulders, others did flips, and some danced while on skies. We were wowed by their performance.

We left the following day, not because Momma had to get back to work, but because it was expensive staying at hotels and eating out every day. Momma was working for a company that provided temporary office workers to companies that were short-handed and understaffed. That particular job worked out well for the month we were spending with her, because she was able to either accept or reject taking the job. During our time with her, she only took the jobs if she really needed the money.

Because of the flexibility her job afforded her, we were able to spend a lot of time together. We went to the beach a lot, which was great, because we got to see our friends, and spend time with Momma as well. We stayed busy, whether it was going to the movies, playing cards or board games at home, or whatever. The bottom line was that we really enjoyed being together, and we had fun no matter what we were doing. Before we knew it, it was time to leave Momma, and go to the farm for the rest of the summer.

We had our share of mishaps that summer. First of all, Dinah got bucked off of her horse, Ruff. As she fell, her foot got caught in one of the stirrups and she was getting dragged on the gravel driveway. It was horrifying to watch, and to hear her screaming in pain. I tried to catch up with Ruff and grab the reins to stop him, but he was running too fast for me to catch. Fortunately Uncle Marty was close by and heard Dinah screaming. He was able to grab the reins and stop the horse.

Dinah was really banged up. Her legs and arms weren't too bad because she had on blue jeans and a long sleeved shirt, but her back was rubbed raw. She was laid up for about a week until her back was healed well enough for her to resume her regular activities.

The next mishap took place down in the basement one day when I was helping Aunt Esther with the laundry. She had an old-fashioned wringer washing machine. One tub was for washing, and the other was for rinsing. Once the clothes had washed long enough, they were put through a wringer where they fell into the tub with the rinse water. I was putting a handkerchief through the wringer, when suddenly one of my fingers got caught in the wringer. Before I knew it, the wringer was pulling my arm through it. Thank goodness Aunt Esther was there. Just before my elbow was fixing to get put through the wringer, Aunt Esther pulled the reverse lever, and my arm started to roll back toward me. It hurt, and it was debated as to whether I should be taken to the doctor or not. In the end, we were convinced that my arm wasn't broken and after a few days went by, it wasn't sore anymore.

Not one of us kids were spared from having some form of bad luck that summer. Claire and Colleen made out the best. They only got stung by some wasps while picking blackberries.

Another summer had come to an end. It was time to go back home and get ready for the coming school year. It would be my last year in Junior High, and Colleens' first. I liked the idea of having my little sister at the same school with me again.

Chapter 11

▼

Time Marches On

Yes, time does march on. There is no stopping it. When I was growing up I didn't mind it. In fact I had always looked forward to it with great anticipation. I couldn't wait to get out on my own. I wanted to experience life on my own terms, as I saw fit. I would find out one day that being an adult, and on my own, wasn't all that I had thought it was cracked up to be.

Dinah would soon experience the trueness of that reality. One afternoon shortly after the new school year had begun, October the fifteenth to be exact, I came home from school as usual. Dinah hadn't come home yet, but I didn't think anything was wrong because three times a week she stayed after school for cheerleading practice. However, as time passed and there was still no sign of her, I began to wonder where she was. She was always home by five-thirty, and it was going on seven o'clock.

I'll never forget what happened next. I was sitting in my room doing homework, when all of a sudden the phone rang. It made me jump because I was beginning to feel uneasy about Dinah not being home yet. I grabbed the phone right away. It was Dinah calling, but she wasn't calling to say that she would be late for dinner, she was calling to inform us that she was in Norfolk, Virginia, and that she had eloped with my cousin Claire's stepmother's brother. He had come to the farm last summer to visit with Claire's dad and stepmother while they were on vacation at the farm. His name was Vincent Borrelli and he was twenty-six years old.

She said, "Grace, I'm in Norfolk, Virginia and Vincent and I just got married. A buddy of his from the Navy lives here, and he and his wife were our witnesses."

I was struck dumb when she told me that. I said, "What did you just say? What do you mean you're married? Why did you do this? When are you coming back home?"

"I'm not coming back home, Grace. Vincent and I are going to live in New York City."

I just couldn't believe that Dinah, who had just turned sixteen, had run away and married a twenty-six-year-old man that she barely knew. Evidently he and Dinah had become much closer friends than any of us had even an inkling of. To say that I was stunned would be an understatement.

That did it for me, I was in too much shock to continue speaking. Daddy wasn't home from work yet, so I handed the phone to Ellen. She warily took the phone from me, sensing that there was something wrong by the look on my face.

As soon as Ellen hung up the phone, she called Daddy at his office and told him what had happened. He was home in a flash. The rest of the night is mostly a blur to me, partly because I was truly in a state of shock, and partly because Colleen and I weren't privy to any of the discussion that transpired after Daddy came home.

The first thing Daddy did when he got home was to go over to Aunt Esther and Uncle Marty's house to discuss it with them, and to get some advice.

I called Momma and told her what was happening. She called Aunt Esther and told her that she was coming over. "I want to be a part of the discussion, and I want to have my say about what should be done about the situation."

Ellen wasn't too happy about the fact that Daddy had gone straight to Aunt Esther and Uncle Marty for advice. She didn't like being excluded as if she was an outsider, and she was especially livid when she found out that Momma was coming over to be a part of it. Too darn bad she was mad is what I say. After all, Momma was Dinah's mother.

It was decided that early the next morning Momma and Daddy would fly up to New York where Vincent and his family lived. The plan, as I understood it, was that Momma and Daddy would get the marriage annulled and bring Dinah back home.

Colleen and I felt an immediate sense of relief because we were confident that what was planned would be carried through to fruition. We had no reason to think otherwise. Unfortunately, even the best of plans fall through sometimes, and what you expect to happen just doesn't happen. As it turned out, Dinah and Vincent were not in New York. Evidently they were still in Norfolk, but no one knew for sure. If Vincent's family did know, they weren't saying so. Momma and Daddy flew back that very evening without Dinah.

The whole family, with the exclusion of Ellen, was tremendously upset by this totally unexpected chain of events. Colleen and I were devastated. Dinah had been our rock. As long as there had been the three of us, we had felt a sense of security from the insecurities of our dysfunctional family life.

With each day that went by Colleen and I began to lose hope that Dinah was ever going to come back home. On the fourth day of her absence she finally called again. I rushed to grab the phone, as I had been doing every time it rang, always with the hope that it would be her.

"Hello."

"Hi Grace, it's me Dinah." I was happy, but only for a brief moment.

I said, "Dinah! When are you coming home?"

"I'm not coming home Grace. Vincent and I are back in New York, and that is where I want to be. I'm sorry, but I'm not coming back."

My heart sunk. She had no intention of ever coming back, or continuing her education. She was dropping out of school.

I never did find out why Dinah had decided, seemingly out of the blue, to get married, especially to someone that she barely knew, and that was so much older than her. Colleen and I came to the conclusion that she just wanted to get out of the house, and that was her way of escaping. We both felt like she had abandoned us, but we didn't harbor any bad feelings toward her. We understood her reasoning.

The only positive thing to come out of Dinah getting married, was that Colleen and I got to have our own rooms. Since I had seniority over Colleen, I got to choose which room I wanted. I chose Dinah's. Colleen didn't care, so she wasn't mad at me.

At first it seemed so strange not having Dinah around. Colleen and I really missed her. Momma told us that during our month with her next summer she would take us to New York, and the three of us would go and visit Dinah. That made Colleen and I very happy. We were so excited, not only about getting to see Dinah, but also about getting to go to New York City. We had never been there before, and everything we had ever heard about it sounded so glamorous and exciting.

The plan was that we would leave for New York about two weeks before our vacation time with Momma was up, and we would go by car. When it came time to leave New York, Momma would pick up my cousin Claire in New Jersey, and then drive us to the farm where we would stay for the rest of the summer. The knowledge that we would see Dinah that summer really uplifted our spirits. In the meantime, Daddy let us call her every Sunday.

Every time we talked to Dinah she sounded like she was happy. The subject of why she had decided to run off and get married never came up. Eventually it was just accepted, and Colleen and I gradually adjusted to her absence. What else could we do?

The fact that we now just had each other to lean on made us closer than we had ever been before. There was no subject that couldn't be broached between us, and that closeness was worth its' weight in gold. We made a vow that we would always be there for each other no matter what, and we just kept trudging along.

One thing about going through adversity is that it does make you stronger. At least that's what I believe. At any rate it was true for Colleen and I, not that we necessarily wanted to have to become stronger at our age. We would have liked to have had a carefree childhood, but it just wasn't in the cards for us. We had been dealt a tricky hand. We weren't bitter about it, but maybe we hadn't acquired the resentment that bitterness harbors yet.

We did our best not to make any waves at home. For one thing we tried to please Ellen. We made that effort for our own well being. We hadn't sat down and said, lets try to please Ellen more. I think it was an unspoken resolution that we felt would make our lives better, and we knew that intuitively.

Looking back in time, I think that was pretty mature of us, but it once again brought into play my inner conflict of not wanting to ever be a hypocrite. The only way I was able to resolve that conflict, was that in this case, I felt like it was for the greater good.

The Thanksgiving and Christmas holidays were approaching, and Ellen was on a crusade to try and convince Daddy into going to Michigan for the Thanksgiving holidays. Since Daddy only had four days off, it wasn't feasibly possible to consider driving, and it was too expensive for all of us to fly. Since Colleen and I didn't really want to go anyway, and Ellen was giving Daddy a fit over it, Colleen and I came up with a plan that we thought would make it look like we were making a sacrifice, while being thoughtful and considerate at the same time.

We told Daddy and Ellen that since it was so important to Ellen to spend Thanksgiving with her family, and since Nora was so young they wouldn't have to buy a ticket for her, that we would stay behind and spend Thanksgiving with Momma. Much to our delight the plan worked, and we even gained some brownie points with Ellen to boot.

On Thanksgiving Day Momma, Colleen and I decided to call Dinah to wish her a happy Thanksgiving, and to see how she was doing.

She answered the telephone sounding kind of pitiful. She said, "We're having Thanksgiving dinner at Vincent's parents' house."

She was freaking out. She said, "They butchered their own turkey, and they eat every single part of it except for the feathers."

Then she started to cry. "I can't eat turkey eyes, feet, or God knows what else. I can't just pick and choose the food that doesn't have undesirable body parts in it because even the vegetables are seasoned with broth made from the turkey's feet, eyes, and who knows what else." Even though she was speaking in a hushed tone, we could tell that she was on the verge of hysteria.

You know how sometimes someone can be in a stressful situation like Dinah was, and it is all you can do to keep from busting out laughing, well that is how Momma, Colleen and I were feeling. Whichever one of us was on the phone with her, we would repeat what she was saying. That way we all knew what was being said. I'm telling you, it was all we could do to keep from busting out laughing. We had to clamp our hands over our mouths to stifle the laughter. In the end we just couldn't keep our laughter contained. Once Dinah knew that we were laughing at her she really got mad, but by the end of the conversation she was laughing too.

The serious side of the situation was that she was scared to death that she might somehow offend her new in-laws, and that wasn't the least bit funny because it was rumored that her father-in-law was connected to the mafia. Yikes!

When it came time to say goodbye, I said, "Be sure to let us know how the turkey feet and eyes tasted."

Colleen chimed in with, "Yea, let us know if you were able to make it through the meal without gagging."

Momma tried to be more helpful. She asked, "Do they have a dog that you might be able to sneak some food under the table to?"

"No, they don't have a dog." Dinah replied, somewhat pitifully.

We ended up suggesting that she pretend to chew and swallow the food, and then under the pretense of wiping her mouth off, discreetly spit it out into her napkin.

When we spoke to her a week or so later, she said, "Somehow I managed to make it through the meal without gagging, or having a contract put out on me." Hearing that we were once again able to get a good laugh out of it.

Christmas came and went. It seemed weird for Dinah not to be having Christmas dinner with us. Aunt Esther fixed a delicious meal for everyone at her house. Ellen made a few pies, but Aunt Esther took care of everything else.

The remainder of the school year was for the most part uneventful. Nora had her second birthday. She was talking a little and really starting to develop her own little personality. So far it looked as if she had inherited Ellen's father, Mr. Ben's good humor, and Miss Adele's gentle and sweet nature, but her looks were all Murphree. Her hair was still reddish, but it was more of a strawberry blonde than the carrot top red color that it had been when she was first born.

It wasn't long after her birthday that the terrible twos kicked in and made her quite a little stinker. I loved her to pieces, but I didn't like it when Ellen let her go in my room and get into my things while I was at school. She broke my record player, and went in Colleens's room and broke her radio. The most aggravating thing about it was that Ellen just let her go and do it without any sort of reprimand. Colleen and I were furious.

We spoke to Daddy about it, but all he said was, "Just make sure you close your bedroom doors when you leave for school."

"We already do that, but it doesn't make any difference because she has already learned how to open doors."

"I'll talk to Ellen about it," he said.

I don't think he ever said a word about it to Ellen. For some reason he seemed to be intimidated by her, and that just burned us up. We really needed him to stand up for us, and he just wouldn't do it. Because of that we had no alternative, but to take whatever Ellen dished out to us, and we resented it. The one thing that we did have going for us was that we stuck together no matter what. I don't know what we would have done without each other.

CHAPTER 12

▼

LIFE GOES ON

Before we knew it we had completed another school year. Hip, hip, hooray! We would be seeing Dinah soon.

Momma was still working for the temporary employment service, and was currently nearing the completion of a work detail she had been assigned to. She had about another week's worth of work to do, and then she would be free for us to leave on our trip to New York. Colleen and I were so excited. We could barely contain ourselves.

Eight days later we were on our way. I had gotten my drivers license learners permit when I turned fourteen. Consequently, I was able to help Momma with some of the driving. There weren't too many freeways or interstate highways at the time, so there were lots of stretches of highway where traffic wasn't congested. Momma felt comfortable letting me drive under those conditions.

Maybe I should say that for the most part she felt comfortable. There were times when I thought her foot was going to go through the floorboard when she thought I was going too fast. Sometimes she would brace herself when she thought that I was following the car in front of us too closely. The thing that scared her the most was when I went screeching around curves too fast.

"Grace, are you trying to get us killed? You don't pass cars unless the yellow line is on the right of the center line, and you most certainly do not pass when you are approaching a hill or going around a curve! Get back in your own lane! Don't you see that car approaching us in the other lane? Are you crazy, or what?"

Colleen and I thought it was hilarious to see her carrying on like she was, that is until she shouted, "Pull over and stop this car immediately." She was boiling mad.

We stopped laughing immediately. There was fury in them there eyes. Colleen was sitting in the back seat where I could see her face in the rear view mirror. She looked like she was about to bust a gut to keep from laughing. That is until Momma turned around and gave her the evil eye. We knew we were in for a stern lecture, and we sure weren't laughing anymore.

As soon as I could, I pulled over into a restaurant parking lot, and stopped the car. Momma was so mad.

She said, "Grace Murphree, get out of the driver's seat right now young lady."

Then, she turned around and said to Colleen, "You better get that smirk off of your face right this minute young lady."

I got out and went around to the passenger side and got in. Momma scooted over to the drivers' side. She then proceeded to inform us of the danger I had put, not only the three of us in, but also of the potential danger that I had exposed other drivers and their families too as well.

We ended up sitting in the parking lot for about half an hour while Momma very carefully went over all of the things I had done wrong, point by point. She then explained what the possible consequences of my actions could have been. By the time she had finished and we were back on the highway, I was so worried about all the potential automobile accident scenarios she had brought up that I really didn't know whether or not I ever wanted to drive again. That concern didn't last too long though, because about an hour later I had come to the conclusion that nothing like that would happen to me because I was invincible. Things like that only happened to other people. Yea, right.

Mommas' lecture had done some good though. In my mind I knew that she was right, now that I thought about it. It made me realize that driving a car is a big responsibility, and not to be taken lightly. Lives are on the line. A few hours later she asked me if I wanted to drive awhile. I didn't hesitate to say yes, and we both knew that I would drive in a responsible manner. We could see the knowing in each others eyes.

The first day of our trip we drove four hundred and ten miles. We stopped for the night at a motel in Valdosta, Georgia. We stayed up late watching television and talking about everything under the sun. We did a lot of laughing. It always felt so wonderful to spend time with Momma.

The next morning we were up bright and early. By the time we had eaten breakfast, filled the car up with gas, and gotten back on the road again, it was about eight-thirty. We still had a long way to go and by mid-afternoon we were all getting antsy. You would have thought that Colleen and I were still little kids the way we started pestering Momma.

I asked Momma, "How much further is it? How much longer do you think it will be until we get there?"

Then Colleen started. "What town are we in? I'm hungry Momma, and I have to go to the bathroom really bad."

It didn't take Momma long to put an end to that nonsense. She decided that we would drive as far as Washington, D.C., get a motel room and stop for the night.

She said, "How would you like it if we stop for the night in Washington, D.C.? It isn't too far from Washington to New York, so if we get up early, we can do some sightseeing before we get back on the road. I think it's only about five hours from there to New York. I just want to make sure that we get to New York before it gets dark. I most definitely do not want to be driving in New York City in the dark."

Colleen and I both enthusiastically said, "Yes Momma, that sounds great." That put an end to our pestering.

There were so many places we wanted to see in Washington, and so little time to do it in. It was hard to decide what to see first. After a brief discussion, we decided to go to The National Gallery of Art. Once we got in there, we knew that we weren't going to be able to get much more sightseeing done because the place was so enormous, and there was so much to see. All three of us loved art, and we didn't want to rush through. We wanted to take our time and enjoy the experience thoroughly.

We ended up staying there for two hours. That didn't leave us much time to do much more sightseeing if we wanted to get to New York before dark. We were able to get a glimpse from the car of The Washington Monument, The Jefferson Memorial, and The Lincoln Memorial.

We all wished that we had more time to spend there, but we were happy that we had been able to be there at all. It was wonderful to see some of the sights that we had only read about, or seen pictures of. We all remarked about how proud it made us feel to be an American, and decided we would come back when we had more time to take it all in.

Momma had been very nervous about driving in New York City, but nothing could have prepared us for just how nerve-wracking it was actually going to be. We did make it into the city before dark, but not before the afternoon rush hour. Momma was pretty much freaking out. None of us had ever seen anything like it.

Huge skyscrapers were everywhere and buildings were as far as the eye could see in every direction. Thousands of people were running hither and yon at breakneck speed, whether on foot or by automobile. Cars were cutting in front of us, and people were honking their horns at us like crazy. People in cars were yelling at other people in cars about each others' driving, and some were giving each other the finger.

Momma didn't know which way to go or where to turn. She looked like she was going to have a nervous breakdown. All three of us kept gasping and wincing, thinking we were fixing to get killed.

Momma, in a panic, said, "Lock all the doors." She was afraid that some unsavory character was going to jump in the car and get us. We kept looking for somewhere to pull over and gather our wits, but there wasn't anywhere. All we could do was to just keep on driving until we found some place to stop and find a pay phone so that we could call Dinah and Vincent to get directions to their apartment.

We finally came upon a diner on Houston Street, and pulled into the parking lot to make the call. Dinah must have been sitting right by the phone waiting for our call because she picked it up before the first ring was over.

Vincent was already home from work, and since he had lived in New York all of his life, he knew his way around the city very well. He must have picked up on how nervous Momma was by the sound of her voice.

He graciously said, "Just tell me exactly where you are and Dinah and I will come and rescue you."

That was a huge relief for the three of us. Although we were enjoying the excitement of being in this huge and bustling metropolis, we were also a little bit leery of it, and very wary about trying to find Dinah and Vincent's address on our own.

Dinah and Vincent lived in Greenwich Village, and after giving him our location, he said, "You are only about ten minutes away from us."

Momma said, "We'll be waiting for you inside the diner. Thanks for coming to our rescue Vincent."

"No problem, we'll see you in about twenty minutes."

The first thing we did when we got inside was to go in the restroom to wash our hands and to do a little primping. After all, we wanted to look pretty for Dinah. We had no sooner sat down and taken the first sip of our drinks when we saw Dinah and Vincent pull in the parking lot. You couldn't miss his car because it was a red 1958 Corvette.

As soon as we saw them pull in all three of us jumped up and went running out. We just couldn't wait to get our arms around Dinah and give her hugs. The waitress came running out after us because she thought we were trying to skip out without paying our bill. We all got a laugh out of that, including the waitress.

Dinah looked great. She looked different, but in a good way. She no longer looked like a sixteen-year-old high school girl. She looked more sophisticated . . . more glamorous.

I had mixed feelings about Vincent. I wasn't sure what my reaction to him was going to be. I was wondering if we were going to feel a little awkward and uncomfortable around him. I knew that my feelings toward him were conflicted. On the one hand, I wanted to like him because he was Dinah's husband, but on the other hand, I resented him for taking Dinah away from us. As it turned out, my feelings weren't one way or the other, but rather somewhere in between.

After we got through with all of the hugging, we went back inside the diner to finish our drinks and pay our bill. Since it was dinnertime, we decided that we would just go ahead and eat dinner there instead of going back to Dinah's and cooking. Besides, we weren't too sure about Dinah's culinary abilities, and we were hungry.

One of the first things I noticed about Dinah was the way she talked. In the short time she had been living in New York, she had picked up that New York accent. It seemed funny to hear her talk that way.

It was still daylight outside when we finished eating dinner, so Dinah asked us if we wanted to go for a short walk. She thought we would find Greenwich Village a very interesting and unique place. She was right. It was nothing like anything we had ever seen or experienced before. We walked down to a place called Washington Square where there were all kinds of colorful characters lolling around.

There were all kinds of artists on the sidewalk. Some were painting, some were singing and playing music, others were reciting poetry. Most of them were dressed like beatniks and seemed to be living a Bohemian lifestyle. Colleen and I couldn't help but gawk. There was so much going on everywhere we looked. We thought this was the most interesting place that we had ever been.

Once it started getting dark, Vincent suggested that we go back to the cars and follow him to their apartment while there was still some daylight. Dinah, Colleen and I really wanted to stay, but Momma said that she would feel more comfortable not driving in the dark.

She reminded us that we would be there for a week, and that we would have plenty of time in the coming days to get our fill of Greenwich Village. That said, we acquiesced to leave.

It took about fifteen minutes to get to Dinah's from the restaurant. They lived in a brownstone on MacDougal Street. Colleen and I were really loving this place. Dinah had the apartment decorated in a style that seemed to reflect the Greenwich Village lifestyle perfectly. She had acquired several very nice paintings done by local Village artists. They depicted the Bohemian lifestyle that was the heart and soul of Greenwich Village. The style was very eclectic and formed a very tasteful and charming atmosphere.

Vincent was a journalist for The Village Voice and Dinah had gotten a job at a boutique on Bleecker Street. They seemed to be happy. Dinah had arranged to take a few days off from work, so the next morning she was to be our tour guide.

We had never ridden on a subway before, so that in itself was very exciting to us. Colleen almost got shut out because she didn't realize that the doors closed so fast. The first place we visited was the Empire State Building. By the time we got there our necks were already getting sore from looking up, down, and all around trying to take everything in.

We took the elevator up to the top floor and went out to the observation deck. It was a clear day and we were able to see the whole city below. I couldn't stand real close to the wall at the edge of the observation deck because it made me feel dizzy when I looked down. It made me feel like I was going to topple over and go plunging to the ground, which was one hundred and two floors below.

Colleen thought it was funny that it made me feel dizzy, so every time I ventured to the edge to sneak a peek, she would get behind me and give me a little shake. That made the feeling of falling even worse. She was cracking up laughing, but it wasn't the least bit funny to me, and that made her laugh even more.

After we left the Empire State Building we walked over to the Automat at Times Square and got us some lunch. Next we were going to Battery Park to take the Statue of Liberty Ferry over to see the Statue of Liberty. By the time we had walked up the three hundred and fifty-four steps to the head of the statue we were pretty tired, but it was worth it because the view was spectacular.

During the remaining days of our visit we went all over the city. We went to the Central Park Zoo, the Metropolitan Museum of Art, and of course to Macy's and Saks Fifth Avenue. At night we would usually go to a sidewalk café in the Village and people watch. It was so much fun just watching all of the unusual people.

Our visit with Dinah just flew by, and before we knew it, it was time to leave. We wished that Dinah could come with us to the farm just like always, but things were different now. She was no longer a carefree teenager in high school. She was a married woman with a job to go to every day. Momma, Colleen and I all felt the full implications of that sad, but true fact, even though not a word was said about it. We knew it because we could see into each others' hearts as we hugged and kissed goodbye. Our tears fell like rain as we got in the car and waved goodbye.

Vincent had given Momma written instructions on which route to take when leaving the city, and that made it a lot less stressful for her. It was about an hour drive to pickup my cousin Claire in New Brunswick, New Jersey. It cheered us up to see her, which helped to alleviate our sadness over having to leave Dinah behind.

We drove as far as Richmond, Virginia and stopped for the night. The motel had a swimming pool, so the first thing we did after checking in was to put on our swimsuits and jump in the pool. Everyone got big laughs over my attempts at diving.

One wisecracking boy about my age said, "You're the first person I've ever seen dive in head first, whose feet hit the water at the same time as the hands."

I was kind of embarrassed at first, but it was said in fun so I ended up laughing just as hard as everyone else did. I never did learn how to dive. It was always scary to me, so I would just hold my nose and jump in feet first.

It was about a seven-hour drive from Richmond to the farm in Franklin, North Carolina. There was still some daylight hours left when we got there, so Colleen, Claire, and I decided that we wanted to go ride the horses for a while. No one wanted to take the time to put the saddles on, so we decided to just put their bridles on and ride them bareback. Claire and Colleen were going to ride double on Ruff and I was going to ride Prance.

No one had ridden them since last summer so they were kind of hard to catch, but we finally caught them and put their bridles on. I helped Colleen and Claire get on Ruff first, and then I got on Prance. I had no trouble getting Prance to go, but Claire and Colleen couldn't get Ruff to budge. Uncle Marty was watching nearby, and came over and gave Ruff a hard slap on the behind. That got Ruff moving. He trotted for a minute or two and then decided to start bucking.

From that moment on it was only a few seconds until both Colleen and Claire were on the ground. At first they both seemed to be okay, and then all of a sudden Claire passed out. Evidently she had gotten the wind knocked out of her. She quickly snapped out of it, and was okay after a minute or two.

After that incident, Uncle Marty said, "I think we should call it a day. You can ride again tomorrow when Willard and Floyd are around to catch and saddle the horses." Willard and Floyd were two of Uncle Marty's hired hands.

Supper must have been ready anyway because we could hear Aunt Esther calling us in that high pitched singsong voice she used. "Gray-ace, Coll-lee-een, Cla-air!"

We had a lot of fun at the farm that summer, but it would never be the same again without Dinah.

CHAPTER 13

▼

THE HIGH SCHOOL YEARS BEGIN

Before Dinah got married I had really been looking forward to High School. I had thought about how neat it was going to be for us to be going to the same school again. Daddy was going to let me start dating that year, just as he had let Dinah. I had anticipated us going on double dates together. I thought I would feel a lot more comfortable with Dinah along until I got the hang of it. You know what I mean? Like how to keep the conversation going, and what to do if the boy wanted to kiss me . . . stuff like that. As it turned out, it all worked out. I learned on my own.

A few days after we got back from the farm, Nancy and another friend, Carolyn, asked me if I wanted to go to the beach with them. They said they were going to meet the two boys they had started dating over the summer. Their names were Chad and Bruce, and they had a third friend whose name was Trevor. The three boys were best friends. Nancy and Carolyn were real excited about me going because Trevor was going to be there.

They said, "He is really cute, and he doesn't have a girlfriend. We think that you and Trevor will really hit it off. He's a senior in high school." So, off we went to the beach.

At first I felt kind of shy when they introduced me to Trevor. I still didn't have too much confidence in myself as a developing young woman. I felt especially shy because I was in a bathing suit. I was still very self-conscious about my body image, particularly the breast part. Even though I was above average in breast size, I think the taunting

I had received from Tommy English had left a lasting impact on my psyche.

But, getting back to the day at the beach and meeting Trevor. Nancy and Carolyn were right about him being good looking. He was tall, about six feet, with a good physique, brown hair, and big brown eyes. I liked him right from the start because he was kind of shy himself, and he was very polite.

We had fun that day, and Trevor asked me if I would like to go to the movie the following night. Nancy and Carolyn were going with Chad and Bruce. We were all going together in Chad's parents' station wagon.

"I'll have to check with my father first, but you can call me tonight if you want to. I should know if I can go by then."

"Sounds good.," he said. I gave him my phone number, and thus my first date was launched.

I was kind of nervous about asking Daddy, but since we were going to be going with two other couples, he didn't suffer too much angst over it. The fact that he had known both Nancy and Carolyn since they were little girls made it even more acceptable.

Daddy seemed to take a liking to Trevor right away. Trevor made a good impression because he was so well mannered and respectful toward Daddy.

When he came in to pick me up and I introduced him to Daddy, he shook Daddy's hand, and said, "It's very nice to meet you Mr. Murphree. Thank you for allowing me to take your daughter to the movies. What time does she need to be back home sir?"

I think he scored extra brownie points because he was dressed very neatly. His clothes were perfectly pressed, and he was very well groomed. Those things are very important to parents.

After we got in the car the six of us had a discussion about which movie we should see. We ended up unanimously deciding to go see the movie "Gidget" starring Sandra Dee and Troy Donahue. After the movie we went to a drive-in restaurant that was popular with the high school kids and had a burger, fries, and a soda. By the time we left there it was time for the boys to take us girls home.

Since my house was the closest to where we were I got dropped off first. I was so nervous about the possibility that Trevor might try to kiss me good night as he walked me to the door. After I got to the second step, I turned around to thank him for the evening and to tell him that I had a really nice time, and before I knew what was happening he kissed me. It was a sweet and tender kiss, but I can honestly say that I did see the proverbial fireworks go off in my head. When the kiss ended I felt dizzy and a little wobbly for a minute. From that moment on, I never felt afraid of being kissed again. Trevor had cured me of that malady.

Trevor and I dated for the rest of the school year. We always triple dated with Carolyn and Bruce and Nancy and Chad. All three guys would be graduating from high school in June. Although none of them had really said what they planned on doing after they graduated, we were shocked when about a week before graduation they announced that they had all joined the Air Force, and would be leaving for basic training a week after graduation.

Carolyn, Nancy, and I decided that we wanted to give them a going away party. I asked Aunt Esther and Uncle Marty if we could have the party at their house, and they said we could. I wanted to have it at their house because they had a really big Florida room with plenty of room for dancing, plus, we wouldn't have to worry about being quiet in order to keep from waking Nora, or disturbing Ellen and invoking her wrath

Carolyn, Nancy, and I were going in together on the planning, sending out the invitations, buying the food, and splitting the cost of everything three ways. We made out the guest list together, making sure that all of their best friends, as well as ours, were included. We tried to work it out so that there would be an equal amount of boys and girls there, but it ended up with one extra boy. Oh well. We told everyone that it was a surprise party, so mum was the word.

Since the six of us had already made plans to go out that night, all we had to do was to figure out a way to get the boys over to Aunt Esther and Uncle Marty's house. That was pretty easy to do. We decided that we would come up with a reason for me to be picked up last instead of first, which was the usual routine.

What we came up with was to say that I had to babysit for Nora until seven o'clock. We told them that Colleen couldn't do it because she was going to a slumber party that evening. Since all of the party peoples' cars would be parked next door at Aunt Esther and Uncle Marty's, we hoped that the boys wouldn't get suspicious about it. There probably wouldn't be that many cars anyway, because a lot of people either came together, or were dropped off by their parents.

We had decided beforehand that when they came to pick me up, and Trevor went up to my front door to get me, he would find a note saying that I was next door at Aunt Esther and Uncle Marty's house. At that point Carolyn and Nancy would say that they would run over and get me. Once they were inside, I would go out to the front door stoop and motion for the boys to come over on the pretext that Aunt Esther and Uncle Marty wanted to see them and wish them well before they left for basic training.

It worked like a charm. All of the guests were hiding in the next room, and once the boys were inside everyone came out blowing horns and yelling, "SURPRISE!" They were absolutely caught off guard, and for a moment they just stood there with their mouths agape, looking totally dumbfounded. The looks on their faces were hysterical, and Uncle Marty had been able to catch it all on his camera. Everyone had a ball that night.

Nancy and Carolyn spent the night at my house that night. We cried on each others' shoulders off and on for most of the night about the boys leaving. They stayed until the next morning to help me clean up over at Aunt Esther's. I had promised her we would.

After they left, Aunt Esther told me that she wanted to talk to me for a minute. I said, "okay," and we sat down on the couch. I had no idea as to what she wanted to talk to me about, so you can imagine my astonishment when she said, "I saw you and Trevor kissing last night."

I took a big gulp, and I'm sure that my eyes must have gotten real big because I was totally alarmed and embarrassed at the same time. Oh my, I was in big trouble now. I tried to brace myself for whatever was coming next, but what I actually wished I could do, was to make a mad dash and bolt out the door.

"You are at the age now when kissing can stir up feelings that can lead to inappropriate touching, and from there to sexual intimacy, which is totally unacceptable for a girl your age." She went on to stress the importance of, and the need for absolute adherence to, the notion that a girl must remain a virgin until she got married.

She said, "The girls who do not adhere to this rule are considered nothing but tramps. God considers sex before marriage to be fornication, and that is a really big sin. A husband can tell if his wife is a virgin on their wedding night, and if she isn't he may hold it against her for the rest of their lives. In other words, the marriage is troubled from the very beginning."

She then stopped talking and just stared at me as if she was trying to determine what impact her lecture had made on me. It had made a big impact. I felt like I couldn't breathe. My mind and eyes were frantically darting around for an escape route. I could feel my eyes blinking really fast, as they always do when I am real nervous. I didn't know what to say, so I just said, "okay" and got up and left.

I was shaking like a leaf when I got outside, and I was wondering if she was going to say anything about it to Daddy. I held my breath for a day or two and nothing happened, so I figured that she hadn't mentioned it to him. What I did know for sure was that my fear of being kissed was back.

CHAPTER 14

▼

SWEET SIXTEEN

The first few days after Bruce, Trevor and Chad left, Carolyn Nancy and I moped around like little lost puppies. Colleen teased me a lot about being "lovesick", as she put it.

Me, I started reading my Bible. It brought me comfort. I asked God to help me be strong in adhering to the rules that Aunt Esther had laid out for me during our talk. I got the impression that Colleen thought it was somehow kind of weird that I had started reading my Bible because she would grimace at me as she walked by. I shouldn't have cared what she thought, but for some reason it made me feel like I should be embarrassed about it. That made me feel sad, and at the same time it made me feel annoyed at her for making me feel that way. I don't like people that make fun of others.

The talk with Aunt Esther had embedded deep in my brain, that above all else, I must absolutely be a virgin on my wedding night no matter what, but I still didn't feel that kissing Trevor was wrong, and I felt reassured that God didn't hold it against me either.

Our plans for the summer were a little different this year. Momma was going to drive Colleen and I to the farm where we were going to meet up with Dinah and Vincent who were going to pick up my cousin Claire in New Jersey on their way down. With the exception of Vincent, we would all be at the farm for a month. Momma and Dinah had each been able to take a month off from work so that we all could be together during that time. Vincent had only been able to get a week off, but at the end of the month he was going to take another week off to come pick up Dinah, Colleen, Claire and me.

Our trip to the farm was not all that great. Almost right off the bat, (about a hundred miles into our trip) for some reason the car horn started blasting, and there was nothing we could do to make it stop. We went roaring down the highway with the horn blasting away like a siren. It was so embarrassing. People looked at us first with surprise, then with confusion on their faces, like why are those people blowing their horn like newlyweds? We stopped at the first town we came to and found a garage and a mechanic to check it out. Fortunately it was a problem that was easily fixed, and we were on our way again in about an hour.

We drove until about three o'clock in the afternoon and got a motel room in White Springs, Florida, which is right on the Suwannee River. When we checked in the owner of the motel told us about a great place to swim that was nearby. The spring was the most crystal clear, sparkling water that I have ever seen, and we had a great time swimming. The beautiful clear cool water and the swimming revitalized us, and we felt very refreshed. We swam for about an hour and went back to the motel to change clothes and find someplace to eat.

As we were driving around looking for a restaurant we passed the Stephen Foster Museum. It was still open so we decided to go in. Stephen Foster was one of America's best-loved songwriters. He composed many well known songs back in the 1800's that are still remembered by many to this day. Among his most famous are, "Old Folks At Home," (also known as "Swanee River,") "Oh! Susanna," "Camptown Races," and "Beautiful Dreamer." I remember his songs very well because when I was growing up I heard them a lot, and "Beautiful Dreamer," is the only song I learned to play fairly well on the piano.

I hated piano lessons and I hardly ever practiced. Consequently, Aunt Esther and Uncle Marty discontinued my piano lessons after only one summer. I wish now that I had taken them more seriously because I would really like to know how to play the piano.

The next morning we were up and on our way by eight o'clock. I drove for about the first 150 miles, then Momma took over. I was feeling kind of tired so I crawled into the back seat to take a nap. It was very hot so we had opened all of the windows, but we were all miserable because of the heat and humidity, although we were making good time.

When we were just the other side of Macon, Georgia, I started feeling really sick. I was feeling very nauseous and asked Momma to pull over because I felt like I was going to throw up. She pulled over on the shoulder of the road just in the nick of time. After I threw up I felt much better, but I still didn't feel very well. Momma said, "You're probably car sick." It was horrible! We kept having to pull over to the side of the road so I could throw up, and that was making us lose a lot of time. We were still able to make it to the farm by dusk. We were thankful that it stayed light so late this time of year so we could get there before dark.

As soon as I got out of the car I started to feel a lot better, but my legs were feeling a little shaky, and I had the sensation that I was still riding in the car. Luckily it didn't last too long and by the time we had eaten dinner I was back to feeling normal.

Dinah, Vincent and Claire had arrived the day before us. We had so much to catch up on that we ended up staying up half of the night just catching up with each other. Although my family was still feeling some ill will towards Vincent for eloping with Dinah, as we were getting to know him better, that ill will was slowly diminishing. We were getting to the point that we were actually starting to like him. He was funny, but he wasn't the type that I would ever have imagined Dinah marrying.

I had always pictured her marrying someone that was real good-looking, and Vincent certainly filled that qualification, but his personality was not what I would call sophisticated. He worked as a journalist at the Village Voice newspaper, and he fit in very well with the Bohemian lifestyle that was so prevalent in Greenwich Village. Actually that is why I started to like him.

I have often sought out that free-spirit type of person to be friends with because I find it so interesting and invigorating to be in their company. It makes knowing them an adventure, and it is a lot more fun than being with your ordinary run of the mill type person. I need that excitement and interest in my life, because for the most part, I am easily bored. My mind needs that edge of stimulation and variety. It makes for a sort of paradox in my personality, because in a lot of ways I am very traditional and conservative in my beliefs.

After Vincent left to go back to New York, Dinah returned to being like her old self. Instead of acting like a grown-up lady, she became the lighthearted Dinah that she had been before she got married. Once again we were zooming all over the farm in Uncle Marty's old red jeep, our hair flying in the wind and squealing with delight. The bumpier and faster the ride was, the better we liked it.

As always we did a lot of horseback riding. My horse, Prance, was being very obstinate that summer. Subsequently, I had a lot of mishaps. One time Prance took off running through the woods with me. It was scary. I ducked as best I could, but I still got pretty well banged up by all the branches hitting me in the face, and even though I was wearing jeans, my legs were getting scraped up from rubbing up against all the trees. I think what spooked her was a small sapling that had grown up in the middle of the bridle path and rubbed against her stomach.

Another time, as we were approaching the barn she started running into the stall with me. That was a close call because it was so unexpected. Good thing I have good reflexes and ducked before getting my head knocked off.

Dinah had a close call too. One day as we were heading back to the barn after an afternoon ride, Ruff knew that we were in the home stretch and suddenly took off galloping towards the barn. Dinah was able to stop him from running, but then he started bucking and threw her off. Just like before, her foot got stuck in one of the stirrups, and he started to run again and was dragging her along the gravel road. Fortunately, one of Uncle Marty's hired hands happened to be nearby and saw what was happening. He was able to grab hold of the bridle reins and stop him before Dinah was severely injured. Nevertheless, she was pretty well shaken, and scraped up.

Claire and Colleen managed to avoid getting hurt by any of the horses that year, but they did suffer from other hardships. They both acquired severe cases of poison ivy. Colleen had the worst case of it. Practically every inch of her body was covered with it, and she itched miserably for about a week before it cleared up. Claire only got it on her right arm. I suppose the reason she had a less severe case of it was because she was wearing jeans, whereas Colleen had been wearing shorts.

Another time they got bitten by a whole bunch of wasps while picking blackberries, and once while they were out in the woods they picked up a head full of ticks in their hair. That night when they went to wash their hair and started feeling all of the ticks that had burrowed into their scalps, screams were heard all through the house. They were totally freaked out.

At the end of the month Vincent came to pick us up. Momma would be driving back to Florida, and Colleen and I would spend a month with Dinah and Vincent in New York. On the way, we would drop Claire off in New Jersey.

Colleen and I were ecstatic about being in New York again. I just loved hanging out in Greenwich Village with all of the artists. I could never get my fill of it. Dinah would have killed me if she had known how much time I spent out there. She thought it was way to dangerous for me to be out there alone . . . but she was at work all day, and I knew that I could trust Colleen not to snitch on me.

Sometimes Colleen would come out with me, but she really preferred to stay inside and read or watch television. She had turned into a real bookworm. The Nancy Drew series was currently her favorite reading source. I didn't care because I really liked being out there by myself. I enjoyed being able to do exactly as I wanted to. I loved the feeling of unencumbered freedom that having only myself to please brought with it.

It wasn't long before I started becoming friendly with some of the "regulars", and they started inviting me to parties. I would have loved to have gone, but I knew that Dinah would never stand for it. Looking back in retrospect, that was more than likely a wise decision. I was so young and naive that there is no telling what kind of trouble I could have gotten into.

At the time I really didn't realize what a sheltered life I had been living. On the one hand I had been exposed to a lot of hardships, due to the fact that, for the most part, I was being raised in a dysfunctional family environment. However, the other side of the coin was that having come from a small town, I had no street smarts. Not only that, basically it was just a much more innocent time. We weren't really exposed to the ugly side of life. Maybe if I had been born in a big city I would have been, but in nineteen sixty-one, southern Florida hadn't yet experienced the colossal growth that would come later.

We didn't have gangs or slums yet. I had never even heard the word marijuana, let alone known anyone who used it. The only reference I had of people taking drugs of any kind was from the movie, "The Man With The Golden Arm."

I still believed that most of humanity was good for the most part. If someone was nice and friendly to me, I believed that they were sincere. It wouldn't have occurred to me that they might be trying to con me. Unless it was obvious that there was clearly something mean or deceptive in a person's demeanor, I saw no reason for mistrust. I'm still convinced that most of the people I met in Greenwich Village that summer were very nice people. Some were just different. I am also convinced that had not Dinah been as vigilant and protective of Colleen and I as she was, something very bad could have happened to us.

My new-found freedom was very short-lived anyway. One night when we decided to go to a sidewalk café for dinner, I ran into one of the young artist that I had become friendly with. Since he wasn't able to support himself fully on his artwork sales, he worked at night as a waiter in the café where we were having dinner, and he was our waiter. Naturally he started talking to me. Uh oh, this was not good.

When he came to take our order, he said, "Hi Grace, guess what? I sold the painting of you today. I got a good price for it too."

Upon hearing that, Dinah and Vincent just sat there for a moment with a look of pure shock on their faces. Their mouths were agape and their eyes got really big, just for a few seconds until they could regain their composure. Then as they looked at me their eyes got real narrow and squinty. That's when I knew that I was in big trouble.

Forcing myself to appear calm, and wanting to draw their attention in another direction other than squinting at me, I quickly introduced him. I said, as nonchalantly as I could muster up the nerve to do, "Hey Ryan, I didn't know that you worked here." Believe me, if I had known, we wouldn't be sitting here right now.

"Ryan, I'd like you to meet my sister Dinah, and my brother-in-law Vincent, and this is my sister Colleen."

Stretching out his hand to shake theirs, he said, "Hi, it's very nice to meet you. I've already met Colleen. How are you Colleen? I haven't seen you around lately."

Uh oh, this seemed to be getting worse by the minute. Now Dinah and Vincent were not only glaring at me, but they were glaring at Colleen too. I could see Colleen looking at me out of the corner of my eye. I knew that she was expecting me to come up with something to say that would make this conversation go away, but I was at a loss as to what to do about it. I knew that she was mad at me for putting her in the middle of this uncomfortable situation, but what could I do? I hadn't held a gun in her back to make her come out with me.

"Are you all ready to place your order, or do you need a few more minutes?" he asked.

I saw my chance for a reprieve, so I quickly said, "I'm ready." Colleen saw her chance for an escape too, and quickly replied, "I'm ready too." With that said, Ryan began taking our order. As soon as he left the table, the inquisition started.

Dinah was the first to start. "What in the heck is going on here Grace?"she demanded to know. "What have you and Colleen been up to? I want the truth Grace, and I want an explanation right now."

Dinah continued to bombard me with questions until our food came. After Ryan left the table I started eating right away. I knew that as long as I kept my mouth full, it would be improper etiquette for me to talk with food in my mouth.

"We will continue this conversation when we get back home."Dinah said in a stern tone.

Even though I had been very hungry when we had arrived at the café, I had suddenly lost my appetite. I knew that more than likely I was in for a very stern lecture. I recalled the lecture that Aunt Esther had given me, and felt that this would probably be on the same level. I didn't expect that it would be about kissing and what that could lead to, but more about the dangers of hanging out on the street with Bohemian type people.

Sure enough, as soon as we got home, Dinah directed everyone to sit down on the couch, and the inquisition started.

Before she could say anything, I said, "First of all Dinah, you are blowing this all out of proportion. I met Ryan one day when I went out for a walk. I like to go and watch the artists working, and I see no problem in doing that. The reason that I know Ryan is because I like his work and I think he is a very talented artist, so I stopped and watched him while he was painting one day, and we struck up a conversation."

I stopped talking only long enough to take a deep breath, and I went on to say, "Colleen doesn't usually go with me on these walks.

She just happened to go with me one time, and that's why Ryan said he knew her."

I hoped that explanation would be sufficient enough to keep Colleen from getting into trouble for being a party to my escapades.

Colleen asked, with a sudden glint of hope in her eyes, "Since I have nothing to do with this, can I please be excused?"

The glimmer of hope in her eyes quickly vanished when Dinah said, "No, you may not be excused. I want you to stay and hear this because I want you both to be aware of the dangers that lurk out there on the streets, especially for two young and naive girls such as yourselves."

Colleen and I shot each other a glance, as if to say, that's ridiculous. We know how to take care of ourselves.

That was a mistake, because Dinah caught the look and knew exactly what we were thinking. She was narrowing her eyes at us again. So far Vincent was keeping his mouth shut.

Dinah then began her discourse on all the things that could happen to us. "Both of you are very trusting girls, and I don't think that you realize how many people are out there just waiting to lure you into thinking that they just want to be friendly. There are also people out there, such as your friend Ryan, who probably are genuinely nice. The problem is that you might not be able to distinguish between the two."

"There are stories in the paper everyday about girls getting raped and murdered. There are also drug addicts and people trying to sell drugs. There are pimps trying to enlist girls into prostitution. These people might just grab you, and we will never see you again. I'm not trying to stop you from having fun, I'm simply trying to make you aware, and to keep you safe."

The next morning when Colleen and I got up, we found a note from Dinah on the kitchen table. It said that under no circumstances were we to go and hang out on the street with the artists. If we did, she said that she would tell Daddy what we were doing while she and Vincent were at work. She went on to say that if we both wanted to go out together and get some lunch or go shopping, that was okay, but if Colleen didn't want to go, I wasn't to pressure her into doing so.

After the discovery of my activities were uncovered, it wasn't that much fun being in New York. Every once in a while, I was able to convince Colleen to take the chance and accompany me. She was starting to like it too, but she was too afraid of getting caught to do it very often.

We didn't have too much longer to stay anyway. The following week we flew back to Florida to get ready to begin the new school year.

I had several letters from Trevor waiting for me when I got back home. He was close to finishing his basic training, but he hadn't been told where he would be stationed after that. He said that basic training had been really hard, and that the rules and regulations that they had to follow were very strict. He went on to say that he had gotten the vocation he had wanted, and that was photography. He was very happy about that. He said that he missed me. I miss you too, I thought to myself.

I was glad to see Daddy and Nora. Nora was talking pretty good now, and some of the things she said were really cute and funny. So far, Ellen was being very nice to us, but there was no telling how long that would last.

Mama came and picked up Colleen and I the Sunday after we got home. She told us that she and Samuel had broken up again, but she didn't seem to be upset about it.

"Why did you break up?" Colleen asked.

"We just weren't getting along very well, and we decided it was time to go our separate ways." We could tell that she didn't want to discuss it any further so we just let it go.

Actually, I was glad to be back home and see my friends. Nancy, Carolyn and I went school clothes shopping and caught each other up on what we had done that summer.

I hadn't had a chance to tell them about the talk that Aunt Esther and I had about Trevor and me getting caught kissing. They about died on the spot when I told them. They stopped dead in their tracks with their mouths agape and their eyes as big as saucers. "You're kidding." they both said in unison.

"If she saw you, she must have seen us too."Nancy said, all aghast with the very thought of such a thing.

"I've never felt so embarrassed in my life." Carolyn said, as her hand flew up to cover her mouth from the very shock of such a thing.

"I'll never be able to face your Aunt Esther again." Nancy said.

"Me either." Carolyn chimed in.

Then they started to worry about whether Aunt Esther might say something to their parents about it.

"If she was going to say anything, she would already have done so." I told them, trying to dispel their mounting concern. That relieved them somewhat, but they still had worried looks on their faces.

CHAPTER 15

▼

GOODBYE CHILDHOOD, HELLO CRUEL WORLD

When Trevor left to go in the Air Force, I had initially intended to be faithful to him, and not date anyone else. After all, he had given me my first taste of love, and I had thought that it was the real thing. I didn't realize at the time that I was far too young and inexperienced to even know what true love was, let alone be faithful to it.

What I did realize very quickly was that fidelity to someone that is no longer around, especially at the tender age of sixteen, wasn't going to work for me. It simply was no fun. Plus, there were so many cute boys around. Every week I compiled a list of boys that I liked. The list usually included about fifteen or twenty boys that I found attractive for one reason or another. My list was always a work in progress, and I don't think that there were ever fewer than ten boys in the running. My rating system was simple. Number one being, well, number one, and whoever the bottom number was the last in the running.

There were exceptions to that rule however. There were a few times that I went "steady" with someone for a month or two, but for the most part, I was pretty fickle. Plus, I liked the challenge of pursue and conquer. It was a game with me to see how many boys on my list I could get to like me.

Don't think that I had forgotten about my talk with Aunt Esther though. If anything, it was more on my mind than ever. I just liked to flirt. Aunt Esther's advice had merit, and I had every intention to abide by it. I also appreciated the fact that she had cared enough about me to sit down with me and approach a subject that many parents, or caring aunts are too embarrassed to broach.

She knew what she was talking about. I know that because my hormones were raging, but because of our talk, my belief about the importance of being a virgin until marriage was engraved in my mind with indelible ink.

At that time in my life, I followed my family's tutelage without question or exception when pertaining to such matters. It wouldn't have occurred to me to do otherwise. At that stage in my life I didn't know that I had any choice or say in such matters. I was very innocent and naive, and I know that my family had my best interest at heart. I have since adhered to the values that I was raised by for the most part, but I still could be considered to be naive and gullible in some ways.

I suppose my behavior was not that different than most girls my age. I smoked cigarettes on the sly, and sometimes Nancy, Carolyn and I would snitch a drink of liquor from our parents' liquor cabinets. We were far from being angels, but we were very aware of the importance of having a good reputation. We never smoked or drank alcohol in public for that reason, and we certainly never intended to become sexually active until we got married.

There was always gossip going around about a few girls that, according to rumor, went *all the way,* but I didn't hang out with that crowd. They had a bad reputation, and my upbringing mandated that I would not be in that category. It wasn't easy trying to stick to the good girl rules, especially when it came to keeping the boys at bay while on a date.

The problem was that I had fallen in love. The relationship had started at the beginning of my senior year. That's when Tom Walker came into my life. He pursued me hard, not that he really had to try that much. I was pretty much smitten with him from the start. He made no bones about going after what he wanted, and he wasn't the least bit shy about it. In fact he was very confident, and a little cocky. I liked that.

I like people who come across as being comfortable in their own skin, with no false pretense. Who needs it? Be yourself, and don't feel the need to portray yourself in any other way. What I'm saying is like yourself. If you don't, than change what you don't like, or learn to live with it.

I felt very comfortable and happy being with Tom. We really had a lot of fun together. He was very straightforward and easy to be with, his sexual drive notwithstanding. That is where we were running into trouble. The longer we were together, the harder it became not to go to the next level of intimacy in our relationship. That became an issue that we had a hard time handling.

So far it had just been a lot of kissing and touching, but we were reaching the point where that was no longer enough for either one of us. By the end of my senior year all that kissing and rubbing and touching had gotten out of control, and the inevitable happened. I lost my virginity.

It happened one night at his house when there was no one else at home. Afterward I felt a little uneasy about what had just happened, but not ashamed. I loved Tom, and he said that he loved me. What we hadn't counted on, or even considered during our abandoned state of desire, was that I could become pregnant. I know that sounds unbelievably stupid, but I didn't think that I was actually woman enough to get pregnant.

We only had two sexual encounters, but shortly before graduation I started to feel like I was getting sick. It started with a sore throat that quickly got worse until it was very painful to swallow. I started having chills and felt so sick that I actually thought I might die. I went to the doctor, and he thought that I had mononucleosis, but as it turned out, I had strep throat. He prescribed some antibiotics and my sore throat got better, but the feelings of nausea did not go away. They only got worse.

By the time that my period was two weeks late, I decided to tell Tom that I thought I might be pregnant. At first he seemed to take the news very well. In fact, he even seemed to be kind of happy about it. He hugged me and said, "It's okay. We'll get married. Don't worry, it will be alright."

Unfortunately Tom's positive response to the news was short lived. By the time graduation exercises had come and gone, he was having nothing to do with me. He stopped coming over, and there were no more phone calls . . . nothing. If I called his house and he answered the phone, he would just hang up on me. I was scared to death, extremely hurt, and feeling totally alone.

We weren't going to the farm that summer because Uncle Marty was very sick. Instead, Colleen and I were going to New York to spend the summer with Dinah. Needless to say, I wasn't having carefree days hanging out on the street with my artists friends that summer. I had no inclination or enthusiasm to do anything. I was very depressed. The only thing that I could think about was me and my baby, and what was going to happen to us. What were we going to do? I loved my child that was secretly hiding in my womb. The whole summer went by, and still I had shared my secret with no one except Tom. I was afraid to. I had no idea what I was going to do, or how my child and I were going to make it through this.

After Colleen and I got back to Florida, I asked Momma if I could come and live with her. She said okay. Shortly after moving in with her I made an appointment with a doctor to find out for sure if I was pregnant. I knew deep down that I was, but I still held out a little hope that maybe there was some other reason that I wasn't getting my period. I made the appointment under a fictitious name. I told the doctor that I lived in New Jersey and was visiting my sister who lived in Florida. I picked the doctor out of the Yellow Pages, and I made sure that I picked one that wasn't in Ocean Shores. I didn't want to take a chance on running into anyone that I knew.

Sure enough the doctor said that I was about three months pregnant, and gave me a due date of February the fifth. I was beside myself in a state of panic. My worst fear had turned into a living nightmare. As I got in the car to leave the doctor's office, I was shaking like a leaf. I started driving and stopped at the first phone booth that I came to.

With trembling hands I deposited my dime in the phone and dialed Tom's number. He picked up the phone on the third ring. I hadn't spoken to him in a couple of months. I was praying that he would not hang up on me, and that maybe, just maybe, he would have had a change of heart after thinking things over during the summer, but my hopes were quickly shattered. If anything, he was colder than ever toward me.

I hung up the phone and got back in the car. I couldn't hold back the tears any longer. I started sobbing uncontrollably. I don't know how long I sat there crying. I was mired in hopelessness. What my next move would be, I had absolutely no idea.

Somehow, through all my tears, I made it back to Momma's house. She was still at work. I was supposed to pick her up at five-thirty. It was now two-thirty. I was glad that I had some time to collect myself before going to get her.

I went into the bathroom because I felt like I was going to throw up. I was wishing that I would because I thought it would make me feel better, but all I could do was to hang my head over the toilet as I started convulsing with dry heaves. That lasted a few minutes and then I splashed some cold water on my face. What I saw in the mirror looking back at me was a face I no longer recognized. It was the face of a stranger. A person I no longer knew. It was the face of hopelessness.

I took a deep breath and tried to summon up whatever strength I had left. I knew that I must make myself presentable by the time I had to pick Momma up from work. I kept splashing cold water on my face, hoping that it would help make the blotches from my tears go away. My eyes were all red and my face looked puffy.

I sure didn't want Momma to know that I had been crying because I didn't know what I would say by way of explanation. I went to the refrigerator and got some ice to make an ice pack with. I wrapped the ice up in a washcloth and went to lay down with it held to my face. I knew that ice was supposed to help swelling go down, and I was fervently hoping it would do the trick this time.

I laid there until about four-thirty and decided I had better go look in the mirror and see if I recognized the face looking back at me this time. The ice had helped, but my face was still kind of splotchy looking. I tried to cover it up with some liquid makeup, and by the time it was time to go pick up Momma, I felt that she wouldn't be able to tell that I had been crying. Just to make sure I grabbed my sunglasses and put them on as I headed out the door.

As Momma approached the car I said a prayer. I asked God to please not let her know that anything was wrong, and to please help me not to break down and start crying. If that were to happen, I had no clue as to how I would explain my actions. It started to get quite difficult though when she started asking questions like, "Have you had a good day? What have you been up to? Did you look for a job?"

"I haven't done much of anything because I haven't felt good all day. I got my period and I've had terrible cramps, so I've pretty much just laid around the house all day."

"Do you want to stop at the drugstore and get some Midol?" she asked.

"I've already taken some, but they didn't help that much." I replied.

When we got back home Momma headed straight for the shower. "I've got a dinner date with someone I met at the beach last week." she said. "After dinner we're going to the movies.

She gave me a few dollars and said, "Why don't you call Nancy and see if she wants to go out and get something to eat with you, and if she wants to spend the night, that's okay too."

"I'll probably give her a call." I said, but I knew that I had no intention of doing any such thing. I had come up with a plan to take care of my situation.

I knew exactly what I was going to do. As soon as Momma left I went and got some paper and a pen. I had decided that I would kill myself, but first I wanted to write a suicide note to Tom. The gist of the letter was to tell him that, regardless of everything that has happened between us, I still love you. I told him how hurt I was by his indifference toward me. I expressed how scared I was, and how utterly alone and abandoned I felt. I went on to say that I couldn't come up with any other way out, except to kill myself.

I sealed up the letter and laid it on top of my dresser. I planned on mailing it to him in the morning, but first I would go to the drugstore and buy some sleeping pills. I figured that I would need to go to several drugstores in order to get enough without raising suspicion. I planned on getting four bottles with two hundred pills in each. That ought to do the trick, but I never got there.

Chapter 16

▼

My Broken Heart

I awoke with a start. Momma was bending over me, shaking me, calling my name and telling me to wake up. At first I thought I was dreaming, then I saw the open letter in her hand. Oh, no!

"Grace! What is this about?" she asked, shaking the open letter in her hand. "Why are you saying that you're going to kill yourself? Grace, get up! Now!"

She half led, half drug me to the kitchen, and sat me down at the kitchen table. I was so scared. I don't think I have ever felt as afraid as I did at that moment. Momma sat down in the chair across from me and laid the letter down on the table between us. Then she looked directly at me. Her face was very intense and pale, like she had seen a ghost. She looked as frightened as I felt.

I could tell that she was at a loss as to why I would be writing a letter to Tom, saying that I was going to kill myself. For a few seconds neither one of us said a word. There was dead silence. We just looked at each other, then it was like a light bulb went on in her brain. That was when I knew that she had figured it all out. One more fleeting moment of dead silence went by. She was staring at me with a look of disbelief. Suddenly her hand flew up to her face and covered her mouth, as she tried to stifle the inescapable gasp, brought on by the dawn of recognition that was invading her psyche. After what seemed like an eternity, she finally spoke and the silence was broken.

"Suicide is not an option Grace. Are you and Tom going to get married?"

I could feel the tears welling up in my eyes. I didn't trust myself to speak. How could I tell her the awful truth? I felt so ashamed and humiliated. I covered my face with my hands, and broke down in inconsolable sobs. I stayed like that, crying my heart out for a few minutes. As soon as I felt able to speak, I raised my head and decided to try and explain the devastating situation to her.

In between sobs, this is what I said to her. "He doesn't want to marry me. He won't even discuss it any further. At first he seemed to be okay about it. He said that we would get married. The last time we really had a heart to heart talk was about a week before graduation. I tried to call him about a week after we got back from Dinah's, but he hung up on me. I think what happened is that he told his friend Mike about it, and I think Mike talked him out of getting married. I think Mike told him that he didn't *have* to get married and be tied down with a wife and a baby. He convinced Tom into abandoning me. I can't believe that he is treating me like this. I'm so hurt Momma."

She said, "If he won't marry you, you'll have to get an abortion Grace, and soon. How far along are you?"

"I'm three months, but I don't want to get an abortion. I want to keep my baby."

"That's not an option." she said quite adamantly. "How do you think that you can take care of a baby?"

I didn't know what to say. I had assumed that she would help me, or Daddy would, but it was beginning to become apparent that I shouldn't count on that happening.

Momma got up from the table and went to the phone. It was almost midnight, and I wondered who she would be calling at this late hour. I had no sooner finished thinking that, when she turned around and said, "I'm going to call Dinah."

They only spoke for a few minutes. I could hear Momma's voice, but I couldn't make out what she was saying. I wanted to go and listen, but it was like I was glued to the chair and unable to move.

As soon as I heard her hang up the phone, she came back to the kitchen and sat down across the table from me again.

"I just finished talking to Dinah and Vincent, and they are leaving first thing in the morning to come down here. Tomorrow morning I'm calling your father at work to break the news to him. I don't want Ellen to know anything about this. When Dinah and Vincent get here, the four of us will sit down and decide what to do."

End of discussion. They would decide what the fate of my baby and I would be. Then she tore the letter to smithereens and flushed it down the toilet. So much for that! Until Dinah and Vincent arrived two days later, she didn't let me out of her sight.

After Dinah and Vincent got there, Momma, Daddy, Dinah, and Vincent sat down and brain-stormed about what to do. The first thing they decided to do was for the four of them to gang up on Tom and try to force him to marry me. That didn't work. Short of forcing him down the aisle with a gun in his back, it was not going to happen. The only thing that tactic produced was to make Tom even more hostile toward me.

I tried with every ounce of energy I had to stand up for myself, but I was outnumbered. My life was out of my control. There was one thing that I was determined to fight to the finish for, and that was that I would not, under any circumstances have an abortion. I was not going to kill my baby. Aside from that, apparently everything else was going to be decided for me.

Meanwhile, I was still trying to come to grips with *this* Tom. What had happened to the Tom I thought I knew and loved? The one that had said he loved me too. The one that I had so many happy memories with. Had he just vanished into thin air, and been replaced with this alien creature that was causing me so much pain and despair? *This* Tom had turned my life into a living nightmare. A hell on earth. Who was this hateful and cruel person? Where had our love gone, and when had it been replaced with this loathing that he felt for me? That was what, no matter how hard I tried, I was never able to figure out.

Every time the *four planners of my future* would tell me that I had to give my baby up, I would plead with them to please let me keep my baby, but my pleas fell on deaf ears. In the end I was beaten, and I resigned myself to the painful truth. My baby would be given to strangers.

The only consolation I could find in all of this, was that at the time, I truly did believe without question, that the applicants for adopting a child were scrutinized very carefully, and that only the cream of the crop, the pillars of the community, were approved. One day, I would find out what a cruel lie that was.

It was decided that Momma and I would move into a duplex apartment that a friend of hers owned. It was located in a sparsely populated area of the county, out in the country where I wouldn't run into anyone I knew. They chose to hide me there so that I wouldn't bring shame to my family. I was to stay there until I was in my sixth month of pregnancy, and then I would be sent to a home for unwed mothers that was located in the central part of the state.

I felt like I had been banished into a lonely world of shame. I was cut off from the rest of the world with no one to talk to, and unable to let anyone, besides a few members of my family know where I was. My whereabouts were top secret.

By this time I was resigned to my fate, and I was very sad. I had been made to feel so ashamed of my unwed pregnancy that I wouldn't even venture outside for a walk in the yard. I was afraid that someone would see me, and then my secret would be revealed for all the world to see, leaving me open for further condemnation by a society too quick to judge.

By the end of my sixth month of pregnancy the time had come for me to be released from my current exile out in the country, into the next phase of my exile at the home for unwed mothers. I would stay there until after my baby was born.

I had no idea what the home for unwed mothers would be like. I was very apprehensive about it, and I know that Momma was feeling anxious about it too. We were both feeling sad that it had come to this, but we were resigned to the fact that this is the way it would be. I do believe that my family thought they had made the best decision for me. Society didn't judge unwed mothers or their children very kindly at that point in time.

I wondered, how does a person prepare for something like this? I don't think one can. It was too much for me to deal with. My mind was unable to deal with my life as being my reality. I felt detached from myself, like it was happening to someone else in a movie or a novel.

Even though I hadn't known what to expect, the home was not as I had imagined it would be at all. It looked like a beautiful southern plantation taken from the pages of a civil war novel. It was an imposing white, two and a half story structure with massive columns that supported a wide covered veranda that led up to a very impressive double door. After opening the door we found ourselves in a huge wide entryway.

The second floor was where the main dormitory was located. It was a huge room that accommodated about twenty-five to thirty girls. Everyone had their own twin bed and a small chest of drawers. Upstairs there was a smaller dormitory. That was where the older girls stayed. I was assigned a bed on the second floor.

Down the hall was the bathroom. There were four toilet stalls, four showers and four sinks. Further down the hall was the nurse's office and examination room. Just off the examination room there was a sun room. The sun room was where the nurse gave me the orientation speech and tried to indoctrinate me into the experience of my new living arrangements. She also told me what to expect during labor and answered any questions that I had. Next door to the nurse's office was the maternity ward where the girls stayed after giving birth and upon return from the hospital. There were three beds in there and the girls stayed there for about a week after coming back from the hospital.

There was a lake in back of the house where there was a small dock. At the end of the dock was a covered seating area with built-in benches on three sides. That's where the smokers hung out.

My first few days at the home were mostly spent trying to learn how to fit in. Everyone was sizing me up, and I was doing likewise to them. It didn't take long to figure out who the bullies were, and which ones were the nice ones that I might want to make friends with.

The bullies always tried to intimidate the newcomer. If you let them get away with it, you were doomed for a life of relentless taunts for the remainder of your stay. I knew that I had to stand up for myself from the get-go. My life was already a living hell. I wasn't about to let anyone make it anymore hellish.

After several days of observing how badly some girls were taunted, I considered myself fortunate to have only one girl come after me. She tried to lure me into a confrontation by entrapping me with her mean-spiritedness. She lost because I made her look foolish. After that neither her, nor anyone else tried to bully me.

It was kind of weird living with so many pregnant young girls. After being there for a few days, I started to feel pretty comfortable. We were all in the same boat so there was no reason to feel ashamed, and there wasn't any fear of being exposed. The youngest girl there was fourteen years old. The oldest was twenty-one.

Our schedule and routine was very regimented and very well organized. Our day started promptly at 7:00 AM. We were awakened by a bell that sounded just like the ones used in schools to signal the start or end of a class. Upon getting out of bed, the first thing we had to do was to make up our beds. They had to be made up to specific specifications. There was no just pulling up the covers. No wrinkles were allowed, and you had to make hospital corners. After our beds were made, we quickly got dressed and went down to breakfast, which was served promptly at 7:30.

As soon as breakfast was over, the girls who hadn't graduated from high school yet went upstairs where a classroom was provided for them. The rest of us would start doing our chores to which we were assigned. We were required to wash our own clothes, which we had to do in a special laundry pavilion using big washtub sinks.

My first work detail was to clean the bathroom, but that only lasted for a week, and then I was assigned to the kitchen to wash dishes. It was hard and heavy work lifting those big baskets of dishes from the wash water to the first of two rinse water sinks. Then drying them all and putting them away. Everyone worked as fast as they could so that we could get out of there fast. We did the dishes in this manner three times a day.

After our chores were done, we were free until twelve noon when lunch was served. From 2:00 PM until 3:00 PM, we were required to lay down and rest, and then we were free again until dinner was served at 5:00 PM.

The home was run by the Salvation Army, so we were required to attend a short service in the small church on the property every evening at 7:00. After that we went into the very large great room in the house and sang a few hymns. From then until ten o'clock when the lights went out, some read, some talked among themselves, and others played games such as Scrabble.

Most of the conversation between the girls was about stretch marks, how many more days until their babies were due, and that sort of thing.

After I had been at the home for about a month, a bed in the smaller dormitory upstairs became available, and I was given the opportunity to move up there if I wanted to, and I did. There were only about ten beds up there, and the girls up there treated each other with more respect than the younger girls in the second floor dormitory did.

My baby came right on schedule. I was lying down for an afternoon nap, when all of a sudden there was a strong movement in my abdomen. It didn't hurt. I think what happened was that the baby's head suddenly engaged in the birth canal. Next thing I knew water was pouring out of me. It was only a couple of minutes after that when the pain and contractions started. I was driven to the hospital sitting on top of a bunched up blanket because the water was still pouring out of me.

By the time I was admitted to the hospital the pains were becoming very severe. I had been told that I would be given "twilight sleep" for the pain, but they waited a very long time before giving it to me. I believe that the nurses knew that I was an unwed mother, and wanted to see me suffer because of it.

I had been told that labor would be very painful, but I was in no way prepared for the excruciating pain I was having to endure. I didn't know that pain of that severity even existed. I was crying and begging for them to please give me something for the pain, but they rarely came in to check on me, even when I would buzz the nurses' station.

At one point the doctor came in and examined me. He told me that I might have to have a cesarean section because there was a very narrow area that made a sharp turn in the birth canal. By then I was reaching the point of hysteria, and I probably would have consented to most anything that would make the pain stop.

The doctor decided to wait a little longer before proceeding with the cesarean section to see if the baby would be able to navigate through alright, and he did. Shortly before I delivered they finally gave me something for the pain that knocked me out completely, so I wasn't awake when my son was born.

The girls at the home were given the choice of seeing their babies one time, or not to see them at all. Some girls said no because they thought it would make it harder when the time came to relinquish the child. Some said no because they claimed to have no feelings for the baby they carried. I had made the choice to see my baby.

I will never forget the few brief minutes that I spent with my infant son that day. He looked like Tom. His hair framed his little forehead in little strawberry blonde ringlets. It was so amazing to me that my body had created this perfect little being whose eyes gazed into mine. I felt a love for him unlike anything I had ever felt before. It was heart-wrenching when the nurse came and took him from my arms.

The following day the nurse brought him back by mistake, but realized it right away and pretty much snatched him right out of my arms. It broke my heart as I watched her walk out the door with him, and my tears spilled down my cheeks in unrelenting sorrow.

I stayed in the hospital for about thirty-six hours, and then taken back to the Salvation Army home. I had only been back for a few hours when the social worker came in with the adoption papers for me to sign. It was the hardest thing I had ever had to do. It caused a pain in my heart that I know will be with me until the day I die.

When the day came for me to leave Aunt Esther came and picked me up. I had mixed feelings about leaving. I had come to feel safe there, and I was somewhat frightened about going back home to Ocean Shores. I didn't feel like I was the same person as the me who had been before. I knew that I would never feel like the carefree young girl I once had been . . . too much had happened. I didn't feel whole anymore because part of me had been left behind in Central Florida.

CHAPTER 17

▼

LIFE AFTER DAVEY

David was the name I had given my son. Not legally, but in my head where it would remain until the day I would be reunited with him again. Before he was born I made a promise to myself that one day I would find him, but that day was faraway. I would wait until he was grown so as not to disrupt his childhood.

I was feeling very low after leaving the home. Aunt Esther wanted to take me on a trip. She thought that a vacation getaway would help me to get over my sadness faster, but I didn't want to go anywhere and she didn't push me.

It was decided that I would live with Aunt Esther when we got back to Ocean Shores. She was living alone because Uncle Marty had died while I was in, what I referred to as my term in exile. It made me very sad when I was unable to go and see him before he died, or to attend his funeral. I wished that I had been able to tell him how much I loved him, and how much happiness he had brought to my life. The many summers I had spent at the farm would always be among my most cherished memories. I felt that my life had been very enriched because of him.

Living with Aunt Esther was working out well. Although I was living right next door to Daddy and Ellen, it made it much easier for me to avoid Ellen. She still had no clue of what I had been through. As far as she knew, I had been living in New York with Dinah and Vincent, and working in an upscale department store.

Another advantage to living with Aunt Esther was that I was close to Colleen and Nora. Colleen had no knowledge of my unwed pregnancy.

Although part of me needed someone to confide my painful ordeal to, I knew that my story would be painful to her, and I didn't want her to have that burden. Nora was now in kindergarten and was such a joy to be around. She always made me smile with the cute little things she would say and do.

After I had been home for about two weeks I started looking for a job. Aunt Esther was still trying to convince me to go to college, but I had no desire to do so, and eventually she quit trying. I got a job in a boutique in downtown Ocean Shores. I liked my job immensely, but working there posed a particular problem for me, I spent almost every penny I made on the neat clothes they sold. I didn't seem to be able to stop myself. It gave me a high to buy things.

A couple of weeks after starting my job, I got a call from Trevor. He had been discharged from the Air Force and wanted to see me. He asked me out on a date and after that our relationship quickly started to revert back to the way it was before he went in the Air Force. It was good for me. It gave me less time to sit at home and pine for Davey.

Nancy and Carolyn were no longer dating Chad and Bruce, so for the first time, it was just the two of us. My family was very happy that Trevor and I had started dating. They had always really liked him; whereas they had *never* liked Tom.

As for me, I still thought about Tom a lot. I really felt that even after all that had happened between us, I was still in love with him. I found myself fighting the urge to call him on a daily basis. One day, I just couldn't resist the temptation any longer, and I picked up the phone and dialed his number. My heart was pounding so hard that I was afraid it was going to jump right out of my chest. His sister answered the phone on the third ring. She told me that Tom had joined the army a couple of months ago, and that he was stationed in Germany. We talked for a few minutes and said goodbye.

After hanging up the phone, I felt very confused. I had such mixed emotions about Tom. On the one hand I felt relieved that he hadn't been there, due to my fear of him rejecting me again. I had felt afraid to call him not knowing what his reaction would be. I don't think I would have been able to handle it if he had hung up on me, or told me to get lost and never call him again.

On the other hand, I thought that seeing him or talking to him might provide me with some kind of closure. It would have given me the chance to see if what I thought I felt for him was real or not. I desperately needed some kind of closure in order to be able to move on with my life.

The fact that he was unavailable, in the Army and stationed in Germany, put him completely out of my reach, and in a way gave me the open portal I needed in order to be able to move on. It was out of my control and in the hands of fate, whether for right or wrong, or for good or for bad. It was too soon to say. Only time and the future would allow me the opportunity to get the closure that I needed. The only problem was, that I felt positively sure that I was still in love with him. I knew that from deep in my heart, and as the song says, how do you mend a broken heart?

Meanwhile, Trevor and I continued to date each other exclusively, and a couple of months later he asked me to marry him. I had my doubts about marrying him because of the feelings that I still had for Tom, but in reasoning with myself, I decided that maybe it was the best thing for me to do.

I told myself that after we were married I would fall deeply in love with him, and we would live happily ever after in our little house with the white picket fence. Before I said yes though, I felt that it was only right that he should know about Davey. I was nervous about telling him, but I felt that I could not go ahead with the marriage unless I did. He took it very well, and said that it didn't change anything. He still wanted to marry me. The next day we announced our engagement to our families. Everyone was very happy about it, and so we set the wedding day for May the twenty-third nineteen hundred and sixty-five.

Aunt Esther took on the task of planning the wedding. I guess she automatically assumed that I would be helping her, but I took no interest in it. I think that was because subconsciously my heart just wasn't in it. Aunt Esther was always trying to chase me down for my help and input, but I would just tell her that whatever she decided would be okay with me. I didn't even pick out my wedding dress. The only thing that I went shopping with her for was my wedding night negligee.

I must say that Aunt Esther did a fine job of putting things together. The wedding was very nice. We were married in the chapel of The First

Presbyterian Church of Ocean Shores. The chapel was just the right size to accommodate the guests, which was about fifty to seventy-five people. The chapel looked beautiful. It was all decorated with orchids that were all furnished by a close family friend that grew hundreds of them at his residence. He and his daughter owned a florists shop. Carolyn was my maid of honor, and Bruce was the best man. Trevor didn't ask Chad to be his best man because we knew that it would be awkward for Carolyn, seeing as how they had broken up under bad terms.

The reception was immediately following the ceremony. It was a catered reception held at Aunt Esther's house. Momma was at the wedding, but not at the reception because Ellen threw a tantrum about her being there. Ellen could still be so miserable sometimes.

Trevor and I couldn't afford to go on a honeymoon, but we did go to a very fancy restaurant for dinner that night. After dinner we went home to the little one bedroom furnished apartment that we had rented in Delray Beach. The apartment had originally been a single family home, but the elderly woman that owned it had converted the front into a separate apartment. Our apartment was separated from her living quarters by a door at the back of the hallway of our apartment. The woman was from Romania and spoke very little English. It was very hard to communicate with her.

When we got back to the apartment we opened a bottle of champagne that Trevor had bought for the occasion. While he was getting all of that setup I went and put on my beautiful negligee. It was a beautiful white lace that was lined with a very sheer material, and it had a long flowing lace robe to match. It was very sexy and I felt beautiful wearing it.

We were just getting ready to take our first sip of champagne when our landlady appeared at the door. There I was in my beautiful negligee trying to explain to her that there was no hanky-panky going on. "We got married this afternoon." I told her, while pointing to my wedding band. Finally she understood. Her unexpected visit had temporarily shattered our romantic evening, but we were able to pick up quickly where we left off without her visit spoiling anything.

The reason that we were living in Delray Beach rather than Ocean Shores, was because it was closer to Trevor's job. He had chosen photography as his vocation in the Air Force, and had been fortunate to get a job with a well established photographer in Palm Beach. I didn't mind that we weren't going to live in Ocean Shores because Delray Beach wasn't that far away.

The image of marriage that I had pictured in my mind required the *perfect* wife to prepare a nice breakfast, lunch and dinner. What I hadn't pictured was how unromantic and time consuming that *duty* was going to be.

The next morning I pictured myself dancing around the kitchen in my beautiful negligee with everything being like a romantic fairy tale. That image was quickly dashed as I began my role of trying to be the perfect wife I had always pictured myself as being.

When I got out of bed the next morning my plan was to fix a big breakfast of bacon and eggs, complemented with toast, orange juice and coffee. It was amazing how fast my plan fell apart. The first thing I did was to put some water on to boil to make some instant coffee. Since I had never made instant coffee before, I was assuming that you added the coffee granules to the water before it started to boil. As soon as I got that going I went back into the bedroom and climbed into bed with Trevor. My plan was to wake him up with a romantic kiss from his *perfect* wife. Well, one thing led to another, if you know what I mean, and I forgot all about the coffee. What jogged my memory was the smell of something burning. Whoops!

As I scrambled out of bed I was already sensing that my perfect breakfast wasn't going to be so perfect. So much for dancing around the kitchen in my sexy negligee as my adoring husband looked on. It was more like frantically running around the kitchen like a crazy person. Still, I was undeterred. I was determined that this little mishap wasn't going to affect my image of being the perfect wife. After all, we hadn't even been married a full twenty-four hours yet.

I took a deep breath, and silently said to myself, "you can do this." I was determined to be the perfect wife that I believed I was *expected* to be, and *should* be. I sure wasn't going to let a pot of burned instant coffee stop me. I quickly tried to regain my composure. That was when my acting ability came into play. That was when I decided that even if I didn't really feel like the perfect little wife, I would just pretend like I was, and nobody would know any different.

So, with jaws secretly clenched, I calmly washed the burned pot of instant coffee out and started over. I got the bacon out of the refrigerator and put it in the frying pan, and decided that I should multitask. While the bacon was cooking I started setting the table and poured the orange juice. Okay, I was thinking, this is going well . . . until there was a knock at the screen door.

I was so absorbed in my cooking that I forgot I was in my negligee, and went to answer the door. It was a male Jehovah's Witness. It wasn't until his mouth suddenly dropped open that I remembered I was still in my beautiful, sexy, white lacy negligee. Oh well, too late now. Just pretend like this is normal, and maybe he won't pay that much attention, I silently said to myself. Being that I was still trying to be the perfect wife, I couldn't be rude. Especially to a "man of the cloth." I couldn't very well slam the door in his face.

That being the case I tried to be respectful, and quickly told him that I respected his choice of religion, but that I was Presbyterian, and very much devoted to my own faith. Then without further ado he left. As I closed the door, once again I realized that being the perfect housewife wasn't going to be easy, or necessarily the fairy tale life that I had always dreamed it would be. Plus, oh no, my bacon was burning.

That was the moment that it hit me right in the gut. I was going to have to do a whole lot of acting in order to maintain my facade as the perfect housewife. I felt that I had to maintain that persona or else I would be considered a failure, not only by others, but to myself as well. I felt so disappointed and disillusioned because that was when I realized that life is not a fairy tale after all. What a letdown that was. I think it was even worse than when I found out that Santa Claus wasn't really alive and living in the North Pole with Mrs. Claus.

I couldn't let anyone know my feelings though, because then I wouldn't be the perfect housewife, and that had to be kept secret. At the time I felt I could never divulge my feelings to anyone, because I thought I was the only one that things like this ever happened to. I felt like I was a flat-out failure that didn't measure up to quality standards.

The second day of my marriage went a little better than the first day, but the fairy tale part was already gone, and my fairy tale husband had to go back to work.

Chapter 18

▼

Disillusioned Confusion

My marriage to Trevor wasn't at all what I had expected, or hoped that it would be, but I realize that my expectations were completely unrealistic, and totally impossible to attain. Part of the problem was that no one had prepared me for the nitty-gritty of life, or even given me a glimmer or inkling of what to expect once you are out there on your own.

No one sat down with me and told me what to expect, or how to be a responsible adult. I grew up watching television shows that depicted family life in a very idealistic way. There were misadventures and mischievous behavior along the way, but it was all portrayed in a playful way that made the characters even more endearing to the audience.

My favorites were, "The Donna Reed Show." I especially admired her because she was sophisticated, soft-spoken, patient, and loving. I think she was the most perfect T.V. mom of all. "Father Knows Best," had the best dad anyone could ever hope to have. "The Brady Bunch" was a bit too perfect. The show was about a second marriage where both spouses each had three children that they brought into the marriage, and they all got along just great. "Ozzie and Harriet", "My Three Sons" and "Leave It To Beaver" were all wonderful and delightful, and those programs were the inspiration for the life I expected to have.

The moms always wore really nice dresses and high heel shoes, even while vacuuming and cleaning the house. They were never late getting dinner on the table at the exact time that it was supposed to be ready. The parents never fought, and they always treated each other respectfully.

Having watched those shows when I was so young and impressionable had made me take it all to heart, and I absolutely expected for it to happen that way in my own life when I got grown and married. I never even considered the possibility that my life as an adult, would in any way resemble the dysfunctional family life I was growing up in.

That is the reason that I was feeling so disillusioned and inadequate. I felt that the reason my marriage wasn't as picture perfect as the ones portrayed on television was due to an inadequacy in me. I felt unable to live up to the standards that had taken shape in my mind during my formative years. The standards that I had set for myself were unattainable, but I didn't know that yet.

When I was growing up, the admission of any sort of dysfunction in my family was tucked away in a state of denial. Problems of that nature were never discussed, because that would mean that we would have had to acknowledge that there was something wrong. The acknowledgment that it existed was only spoken through body language, or through the eyes, and was never to be confirmed or conveyed verbally.

Money, or maybe I should say, the lack of money, was another huge problem for us during the early days of our marriage. We couldn't go anywhere, not even to visit our family or friends, because we didn't have the money to buy gas with. It was very depressing, and it was yet another example of how poorly I had been prepared for life.

I was miserable most of the time, but I tried to keep those feelings hidden. I put on a happy face, but inside I was crying. On top of trying to cope with the adjustment of marriage, I was thinking about Davey a lot, and that would break my heart anew.

I would try to imagine what he must look like. I wondered if he was a happy and well cared for baby. I wondered what his name was, what kind of food he liked, and what his adoptive parents were like, and where they lived. I would see babies everywhere I went, and sometimes wonder if one of them was him.

Deep down in my soul I knew that this was a sadness that would be with me for the rest of my life. I knew that no matter how many other babies I might have during my life, that one of them would be missing from the picture . . . but not forever. I had made up my mind that if it was the last thing I ever did, I would know the whereabouts of my son, and I would know if he was okay. I had made that vow to Davey, and to myself, and I intended to fully honor that vow. Someday. Somewhere. Someway. Somehow. Sometime.

CHAPTER 19

▼

THE SHOW MUST GO ON

I was unhappy, but I was too stubborn, and too determined to drop the ball now. I couldn't stop hoping. I still had too many unfulfilled dreams to see to fruition. To give up now would be a betrayal to my idealistically determined nature. It would have been an admission that life was not as I had dreamed of, and I had dreamed of it for too long to let go of it so quickly. So, with all of the energy I could muster up, I proceeded with my life in denial of the ugliness. I was determined to try and make it as wonderful as I had imagined it would be . . . in my sea of dreams.

I wanted to have a baby. I ached for one. I got so excited about the prospect of having a child that I decided to have a talk with Trevor about it. I wanted to feel him out on the subject, and see if he was receptive to it. I decided to talk to him about it that evening at dinner.

I decided that I would fix his favorite meal, which was lasagna, and I would set the table with candles to create a romantic atmosphere. I decided to open a bottle of wine and have a glass of it while I was preparing dinner, and in celebration of the possibilities that tonight's dinner might bring to life.

After I got everything going and the lasagna in the oven I went to find something casual, but sexy to put on, and went and jumped in the shower. I wanted to be at my best, so I washed my hair and shaved my legs, and I put some really good smelling lotion that Trevor had given me all over my body. Ooh la la!

I fixed my hair in a half up, half down style that looked sexy and provocative. I was feeling so happy and excited, and after I got it all together, I couldn't wait for him to get home. While I waited for him, I poured myself another glass of wine, and sat down to relax. I was feeling very full of myself.

As I sat there, I decided that some romantic music would be a nice touch, and went to put some records on the stereo. I went back and tried to relax on the sofa, but I was so eagerly anticipating the romantic evening that I envisioned, that I found it hard to sit still. I kept looking at the clock. I estimated that Trevor should be home any minute now. I had no sooner thought that when he pulled into the driveway.

As soon as I heard the car pull in, I rushed to the bedroom for one last check in the mirror. I was happy with the face I saw looking back at me, so I rushed back to the kitchen so that I would appear to be nonchalantly fixing dinner.

I heard the door open, and Trevor say, "Umm, something sure smells good."

In the next instant I felt his arms go around me, and he said, "You smell good too." as he nuzzled my neck with kisses.

"You've been working so hard, I wanted to fix you something special." I said, as I turned around to kiss him, quite passionately, I might add.

As he rubbed his hands up and down my arms, we kissed again, and again, and again. "As good as this smells, I'm feeling another kind of hunger that I need to take care of first." he said, as his hands moved all over my body, finally landing inside my panties and stroking ever so gently my most intimate parts.

"I'm feeling that same hunger." I said, as my hands found their way down to his swollen masculinity, and rubbed my hand against it. He started to murmur softly in my ear as he rubbed against me. With that I turned around and turned off the oven, and took his hand to lead him to the bedroom.

I said, "Lay down and let me undress you." As I removed each piece of his clothing, I stopped briefly to give each part of his body special attention. By the time I got him undressed, he was about to explode with passion and ecstasy.

I wanted to prolong our pleasure, so I stopped touching him and started to slowly undress myself in a provocative manner. By the time I was completely undressed, Trevor was beside himself with passion, and pure animal instinct took over. He pulled me down on the bed with him and plunged his manhood deep inside of me. The orgasms just kept on coming and coming, until we both were completely satiated and limp with pleasure, and could take no more.

"That was awesome." he said, and I said, "I know."

We laid there in each others arms for awhile, savoring our pleasure. Then Trevor got up and took a shower, and I got dressed and went back to the kitchen to finish cooking dinner.

Dinner turned out perfectly. By the time we started to eat it had gotten dark, and the flickering candlelight added the perfect ambiance for me to bring up the subject of having a baby.

We opened a new bottle of wine, and sat quietly for a few minutes enjoying our dinner. Trevor started telling me about his day. "We landed a really big account today." he said.

"Oh, what kind of account? I asked.

"It's with the elite crowd in Palm Beach." he said.

"What will you be doing with them?" I asked after taking a sip of wine.

"They want us to be their exclusive photography agent to photograph things like their charity events, weddings, bar mitzvah and bat mitzvah celebrations. Basically anything that would be mentioned in the society column pertaining to different aspects of their lives. Some of the photos are likely to be bought to be published in magazines as well as newspapers. We stand to make a lot of money out of it. I'll probably have to be working longer hours as a result though, but I will be making more money. I'm not sure how much more. We'll be discussing it all at work in the next few days."

"That's so exciting Trevor. Just think of all the celebrities and famous people you'll be meeting."

"Yea, I'm pretty excited about the whole scenario."

We ate in silence for a few minutes, and when I felt like he was through talking about work, I found my opportune moment to bring up starting a family.

"Trevor, there is something I want to talk to you about." I said.

"Okay shoot. What is it?" he asked in between bites of lasagna."I've been thinking that I would like for us to have a baby. What do you think?" I asked.

I think that after our afternoon delight this afternoon, we may have already started one. You didn't use your diaphragm did you?"

"No, everything happened so spontaneously. I didn't want to break the spontaneity of the moment. I was too heated to want to take the time to stop and put it in."

"Well, it's okay if you did get pregnant. I would like for us to start a family. It's good timing too, what with the new account we landed at work today." he said as he reached across the table to touch my hand.

I don't know for sure if it was that very afternoon that I got pregnant or not, but since Trevor and I both had a hearty appetite for sex, it wasn't long before I discovered that I was indeed pregnant. Trevor was very happy about the pregnancy, and that meant so much to me. It added such a positive touch to my happiness. My hopes and dreams were alive and well, and that's what kept me going.

As had been the case with Davey, I suffered terribly with morning sickness. The only good thing about it was that it made me feel very queasy to even think about having a cigarette. It even made me queasy to see an advertisement, or a picture of a pack of cigarettes. Another thing that would send me running to the bathroom gagging was to smell sausage or bacon cooking.

I was able to find a wonderful doctor that had been highly recommended to me by the wife of one of Trevor's childhood friends. We had become good friends since Trevor and I had gotten married and moved to Delray Beach. Dr. Graber suggested that I eat a few soda crackers first thing in the morning before having anything to drink, and that really helped alleviate the morning sickness.

Having gotten over the hurdle with the morning sickness, the rest of my pregnancy went fairly smoothly. I went into labor right on my due date, just like I had with Davey. This time I was given much better care from the nurses than I had been given with Davey. After about ten hours of grueling labor I was given what they called "twilight sleep" to help with the pain. It didn't take the pain away altogether, but it made it easier to endure.

After being in labor for almost twenty-four hours, on May twenty-sixth, nineteen hundred and sixty-six, I gave birth to a beautiful and healthy baby girl. She weighed six pounds and twelve ounces, and was nineteen inches long. We named her Abigail Marie O'Brien.

I had assumed that Trevor had been in the hospital while I was in labor, and when the nurse brought Abigail to me for the first time, I was wondering where he was. It was such a happy moment for me to be holding my baby daughter in my arms. She was so beautiful, and I was disappointed when he wasn't there to share this special occasion with me.

I asked the nurse, "Could you please tell my husband to come in here? Has he seen the baby yet?"

"He isn't here Mrs. O'Brien."

"Oh, I guess he must have gone to get something to eat, or he went home to take a shower. Did he mention anything to you?"

"No, I haven't seen your husband since I started my shift. Would you like for me to check at the nurses' station for you, and see if anyone there might have some information?"

"Yes please. I would really appreciate it if you would do that for me."

"I'll see what I can find out for you." she said as she turned to leave the room.

"Thank you."

Then she was gone, and it was just me and Abigail. In a few minutes the nurse came back and told me that no one had seen him. I tried not to let the disappointment show, but whether or not I was successful in doing so, I don't know. All I know is that it hurt me a lot for him not to be there. Just as had been the case with Davey, I was left to endure the birthing process alone.

It came to light later on that he had basically seen me through the admission process, and then gone out to celebrate his baby's forthcoming birth in a bar all night. That is not at all how I had envisioned it would be. It evoked a feeling of resentment in me, and created a deep sense of foreboding concerning unforeseen problems in our future.

I couldn't believe that he would just leave me at the hospital like that. It hurt in so many ways, and at so many levels of my very being, that at times it made it hard for me to accept it as fact.

Abigail and I stayed in the hospital for three days. Dinah and Vincent had driven down from New York a few days before so that Dinah could see the baby, and so that she could stay and help me for a few days once I got home.

I was so glad that she was here because I was feeling apprehensive about my abilities to handle it all. Together we obsessed endlessly over every aspect of Abigail's care, and by then I was suffering with postpartum depression. I don't know what I would have done if Dinah hadn't been there to console me. She confessed to me later, that although she had appeared to be calm, inside she was a nervous wreck.

The postpartum depression only lasted for a couple of days, and my happiness with being a mother overcame my insecurities of being one quickly. I adored my baby girl. She was the apple of my eye and my greatest source of strength. She kept me so busy trying to meet her needs that I didn't have that much time to dwell on the issues that I had with Trevor.

However, it did bring Davey's absence more to the forefront of my mind, and that made my heart hurt. It was such a deep sense of regret and loss that it almost made me unable to breathe sometimes. If I could only accept the finality of it I would have been better off, but I couldn't, and I knew that I would never be at peace with it.

In the meantime, I knew that somehow I was going to have to learn to live with that sorrow, regardless of the devastating impact it had made on my life. I knew that it was going to be an impossible task for me to achieve personally, but one that I would have to learn to present to the world outwardly. I didn't want anyone to perceive me as being the failure that I thought I was myself. It was an exercise in futility because you cannot fool yourself as easily as you can others.

I hadn't been prepared for the impact a baby has on ones' life. It didn't seem like there was ever enough hours in the day to keep up with the demands of being a wife and mother. It seemed like I would have no sooner gotten to sleep when Abigail would wake up and start crying. I was seriously suffering with sleep deprivation.

Being the neat and clean fanatic that I am, it was very stressful trying to achieve everything that I felt I needed to. It was an impossible challenge for me to achieve, but that didn't stop me from feeling like I still had to try.

If I wasn't busy with the baby, I was busy with the housework. If I wasn't busy with the housework, then I was busy with the cooking. All of these influences had an overwhelming and debilitating impact on my psyche. I felt so all alone in this circumstance because I thought that I was the only one who was affected in this way.

Once again the feelings of being inadequate were taking over again, and I felt extraordinary pressure trying to keep those feelings concealed from the outside world. I was ashamed of what I perceived to be my incapacity for being the perfect wife and mother that I desperately wanted to be. It was becoming harder and harder to put on that smiling face that I felt I must present to the world.

Before Abigail was born, Trevor and I had sat down and discussed these very issues I was confronting. We had mutually agreed that it would be my responsibility to get up and tend to the needs of the baby. I didn't feel that it would be fair for Trevor to have to get up and down all night because he had to be at his job at eight o'clock in the mornings. Especially since the job promotion he had received before Abigail was born. Not only that, but he was having to work longer hours, and his job was very demanding.

Trevor would help sometimes, but not too much, and not unless I asked him to. On occasion, if he was home in the evening he would be in charge of Abigail while I cooked dinner. He would sometimes rock her and sing to her, or feed her if she was hungry, but it came to an abrupt halt if I asked him to give her a bath, or change her diaper. If she became fussy or hard to please he couldn't handle it, and so the responsibility would be immediately returned to me. I need a break sometimes too, I would think as he would either hand her over to me, or put her down and just let her scream until I would go and pick her up.

I knew that it was going to take some time for him to get used to her. I just hoped that it would be sooner rather than later. I think he was frightened by her smallness, and by what he perceived to be her fragility.

Although Abigail was a good baby, she wore me out. I knew that if I didn't start getting more rest I would probably collapse at the rate I was going. I was going to have to make some concessions when it came to trying to keep up with everything so meticulously.

I decided that I would start taking a nap when Abigail took hers. If she wouldn't go to sleep in her crib, I would lay her on my stomach. You might say we laid tummy to tummy. She always went right to sleep when I did that, and I slept like a baby myself.

As the weeks and months went by Abigail and I created our own daily routine, and were on a schedule that was working well for both of us. I settled into motherhood quite naturally, but as time went by I started to feel isolated and lonely.

Trevor had gotten another promotion at work, and was working all kinds of crazy hours. He was promoted to Project Coordinator. It was great that he was making more money, but it came with a lot of responsibility and long and unpredictable hours.

Trevor was in charge of overseeing the photo shoots, but quite often he would have to work in the darkroom developing the film if they needed him to get the job done. He spent more hours at work than he did at home, and Abigail and I were on our own most of the time.

When he first started having to work the longer hours, I would sit up and wait for him to get home, but then he started coming home later and later because he started going out for drinks with his colleagues. He said that it was all very innocent, and that he just needed to unwind a little after work. That's when my feelings of isolation and loneliness started to make me feel resentful toward him.

The bad feelings weren't because I was mad that I couldn't go too. I was angry because he didn't take into consideration how insensitive his behavior was as far as I was concerned, or how it made me feel on so many different levels. I didn't have my own car, so I was stuck at home almost all of the time unless a friend or relative invited me to go somewhere with them. Plus I felt like I was raising Abigail all by myself. We rarely did anything together as a family.

After this had been going on for a couple of months, not only was he coming home later and later, but sometimes he would come home with his shirts torn because he started getting into fights at the bars. He seemed to relish the fighting.

The next thing I knew bill collectors started calling, and bounced check notices were coming in the mail several times a week. The situation just kept getting worse. It wasn't too long before I was searching the house looking for items to take to the pawn shop, or looking for soda bottles to return to the store so I could get the deposit on them back. You used to get two cents for each bottle you returned.

It wasn't long before my feelings of resentment turned to feelings of hostility. To make matters worse, somehow through all this mess, I had gotten pregnant again. At this point in time no one else knew that I was pregnant. It was my secret, but I needed someone to talk to. Keeping everything all locked up inside was beginning to seriously wear me down. Still, I told no one. After I missed my third period I knew that I was going to have to tell Trevor. That was going to be tough because he had become so aloof and distant. Most shocking of all was that he appeared to be so unaffected by the disarray that our marriage and finances were in. His solution was to keep writing and cashing checks, and try to get the cash deposited in the bank before the last check cleared. Sometimes it worked, but most of the time it didn't, and then we would be charged twenty dollars for every check that bounced.

I didn't see how I could continue living this way much longer. I had begun to regard Trevor contemptuously, and to feel sick at the sight of him. I didn't want to be in the same room as him. It got so bad that even the sound of his voice sickened me. I had never known such misery, and I had no intention of living under those conditions for very much longer. However, I had no idea of how I was going to get out of the situation. I felt trapped.

One day it all became too much for me to bear any longer, and the tears started to flow. I had no idea or warning that I was going to start crying. One minute I was cooking dinner, and the next thing I knew I was sobbing. Trevor happened to be home and came to see what was wrong with me.

"Grace, what's wrong? Why are you crying?" he asked with a bewildered look on his face.

Everything that was bothering me, all of my pent-up emotions came gushing out. "What's wrong? You want to know what's wrong? Are you really all that clueless Trevor, or is it that you just don't give a damn about me and Abigail?"

"Lets see, where should I start?" I said in between sobs. "There's so many things that are wrong, I don't know where to start. Okay, I'll start with your staying out until all hours of the night. Do you think that it's really okay for you to do that? Don't you think that maybe you should spend more time with your wife and child? Do you think that I like being here by myself day after day, with no money and no place to go; to never have any fun? I guess you must because you sure don't act like it concerns you one iota."

"Grace, I don't know what to say. I'm sorry."

"You got that right. You are sorry, and you're a poor excuse of a husband and father. You treat Abigail and me like we are nothing. It's a disgrace, and I'm sick of being given no consideration. You think it's all about you, don't you?"

He started to move toward me like he was going to give me a big hug, and then I guess he had the mistaken idea that would make everything alright. Is he really that stupid, I thought to myself.

"Get away from me! Get out of here. Go! Go be with your drinking buddies. They seem to be the only ones you care about, or want to be with!"

"Grace, calm down. Can't we talk about this? I'm sorry, I have been selfish. I know I've neglected you and Abigail, but can't we sit down and discuss it, and try to straighten things out?"

"I'm pregnant." There, it was out. I tried to gauge Trevor's response to this news by the look on his face. At first he looked stunned, but only for a second.

Then he started to move toward me and took me in his arms. It felt so good to be held close, and I let the tears flow until there were no more left to be shed.

We sat down at the table across from each other and began to talk. I felt like a heavy burden had been lifted from my shoulders, and we both laid all our cards on the table. All of the pressure that had been building up in both of us was finally out in the open.

Trevor said, "Grace, first of all I want to tell you that I love you and Abigail with all my heart. It's just that when I'm here, I feel uncomfortable in my role as a father. I feel left out. I feel like you and Abigail don't need me. It's like I don't know what to do, or what I should be doing."

We talked for a long time, and by the time we went to bed I felt a lot better. I felt like there was still some hope for Trevor and I to make our marriage work. Only time would tell if we could continue to keep the lines of communication open, and what our fate would be.

CHAPTER 20

▼

HOPE WHERE THERE WAS NONE

Both of us went to bed that night with a renewed sense of hope and commitment to each other. We continued to talk long after we had pulled the covers over us, and laid our heads on the pillow. Our talk had infused our relationship with the intimacy we had lost during our adjustment to parenthood. Instead of becoming closer during this phase, we had drifted apart. Now that we had reconnected, when we made love that night, we both felt that our marriage was fresh and untainted by the problems we had been experiencing during this period of adjustment. We felt like it was a new beginning, and it felt so good.

In the weeks and months that followed our reconciliation, it was plain to see that both of us were really trying hard to make things work out between us. Trevor stopped going out to the bars after work, and he wasn't writing anymore bouncy checks. I started trying to find new ways for Abigail and her Daddy to bond. Everything just got better and better.

As Trevor took on more parental responsibilities he started to feel more comfortable handling Abigail, and she in turn started to develop a closeness with him. It wasn't long before she had her Daddy wrapped around her little finger. When he came home from work in the evening, she would squeal with delight at the sight of him and go running to him. That pleased him to no end, and it just made him love her all the more.

Our little apartment was becoming too cramped for the three of us, and with the new baby coming we decided to start looking for a house to rent. We would really have loved to buy a house, but we didn't feel financially stable enough to just yet. We found a cute three bedroom, one bath house in a nice little development where there seemed to be a lot of young couples with small children. It wasn't all that convenient to Trevor's job, but not so far away that it caused a major problem.

We liked the house so much that we decided right off the bat to go ahead and give the landlady a deposit. "The rent on our current apartment is paid up for two more weeks. Would it be okay with you if we wait until then to move in?" Trevor asked.

"That's fine with me." she replied.

Our apartment had come fully furnished, which was a blessing for a couple of reasons as far as I was concerned. First of all, that meant that the only furniture we had to move was Abigail's crib and changing table. Secondly, and this was my favorite reason, it meant that we had to go furniture shopping. I was so excited to be able to go and pick out furnishings that reflected my taste, rather than my Romanian landlady's.

"Right now we're living in a furnished apartment so we're going to have to buy some furniture." I told her.

"If you would like to arrange to have it delivered here the day before you move in, that's okay with me." she replied.

"That's so kind of you. Thanks so much." I told her. "That will make it so much easier for us than having to contend with it being delivered when we're so busy moving in."

With that we exchanged phone numbers and left. "Trevor, I really like that house, don't you? The back yard is all fenced in for Abby, (we had started calling Abigail Abby) and we can get her a swing set. When do you want to start shopping for furniture? We could start right now." I said.

"Whoa Nellie! I know you're excited Grace, but take a breath girl. I need to go back to work for a little while. I just have a few loose ends to tie up for tomorrow's photo shoot. Besides, look at Abby. She's falling asleep in her car seat. After tomorrow's photo shoot I'll try to get home early. Maybe we can start then. If not, I do have the next day off, so for sure we can go then. Okay?"

"Yea, I guess it will have to be. Can we stop and get a paper? I'll look and see if there's any sales going on. Plus, it'll give me a chance to make a list of all that needs to be done; like switching the phone and electric, and stuff like that. I'll make a list of what furniture we'll need to buy, and curtains and stuff like that too. Ooh, I can't wait." I said, clapping my hands together like a little kid whose overcome with excitement.

Trevor was laughing at me, and I started laughing too. "I know I'm acting crazy, but I can't help it." I said.

"Don't apologize. It's nice to see you so happy." he said.

The next two weeks were really busy. Trevor wasn't able to help with the packing or the furniture shopping because he was so busy at his work. What I would do was drop him off at work and go shopping while he was working. If I found something that I liked we would go back on his day off to see if he liked it too. For the most part, he pretty much liked everything I picked out. I was glad about that because I'm pretty much spoiled when it comes to getting what I want.

What with having to pack everything plus shop for furnishings, and all of the million other things I had to take care of, I was constantly on the go. By the time moving day rolled around I was halfway through my sixth month of pregnancy, and beginning to feel tired and uncomfortable.

I couldn't believe how much stuff we had accumulated during our two years of marriage. At times I felt overwhelmed by it all. Sometimes if Trevor was at work and it was just me and Abby, I would get so stressed out that I would start carrying on like a lunatic.

To let off steam I would start belting out a song that I made up as I went along. It usually went something like this. "I'M SO SICK OF THIS! I CAN'T TAKE IT ANYMORE! I'LL BE SO GLAD WHEN THIS MOVE IS OVER THAT I'M GOING TO JUMP FOR JOY!" Then I would start dancing around the room saying things like, "AH HA! UH HUH! OH YEA! OH YEA! CAN'T WAIT! AH HA! UH HUH! OH YEA!"

Usually during these maniacal episodes Abby would be in her walker. She would start getting real excited, and she would start bouncing around in her seat, clapping her hands, and squealing with delight. It was amazing how these bursts of foolishness helped to alleviate the stress, and leave me feeling refreshed and ready to tackle the seemingly never-ending boxes once again.

A week before moving day we managed to finish picking out all of the furniture. We made arrangements to have everything delivered to our new house the day before we would be moving everything else, as well as ourselves in.

I loved everything we had chosen, and I couldn't wait to see how it all looked after we got it all arranged. Our landlady, Mrs. Brighton, said that we could paint inside as long as we didn't use any outrageous colors. That was fine with us because we didn't want to use any outrageous colors. It wasn't our style.

We got up real early on moving day and started loading the U-Haul trailer we had rented. We managed to fit everything in, so we only had to make one trip. That was a blessing because between all of the commotion with moving, and having to tend to Abby's needs, I was beginning to feel totally wiped out.

Trevor had managed to get a few days off for the move, and that was a tremendous help because that way he could entertain Abby while I put things away the way I wanted to.

During the move I had been on my feet a lot, and that had caused my feet to get swollen. The doctor told me that I needed to stay off of my feet as much as possible. That wasn't easy to do because Abby was running all over the house and getting into everything she could get her hands on.

We decided to buy Abby a youth bed so she would get used to sleeping in it before the new baby arrived. The new baby would be using her crib. At first it was a real struggle getting her to stay in her new bed when it was nap time or bedtime. Since I don't believe in spanking children, it was a real test of wills. Every time she would get up I would have to march her right back to bed. One day I counted thirteen times I had to do that before she finally quit getting up. There were times when I felt tempted to give up and just let her get away with it, but I never could bring myself to slip into that way of parenting. It paid off because after about a week she knew that she couldn't get away with it, and bedtime and nap time were no longer a struggle. Either Trevor or I would read her a story, and she was usually asleep by the time we finished reading it.

Life was going smoothly for us at this point in time. I had met some of the young mothers in the neighborhood and we had become friends. It was nice for me to have people to chat with as we sat in the back yard and watched our children play. About a month before the baby was due, the mothers gave me a surprise baby shower. They had even brought Trevor into the plan so that he could furnish them with names and addresses of friends and family living in Ocean Shores. I couldn't have been more surprised. It was lovely.

Three weeks later I woke up with a lot of energy and started going to town on cleaning the house. By mid-afternoon I started having cramps that quickly turned into pains with contractions. When the pains started coming about every fifteen minutes, with contractions lasting for about a minute, I decided that I had better call Trevor at work.

When I called they told me that he was on a photo shoot, but they said they would send someone to go and tell him that I was in labor. He called back about twenty-five minutes later. As soon as the phone rang I raced to answer it.

"Hello." I said, desperately hoping that it was him.

"Hey hon. I'm leaving work right now, and I should be home in about thirty minutes. In the meantime why don't you call Dr. Graber and let him know what's happening, and call Alicia and let her know that she needs to come and pick up Abby. If you don't feel up to doing that, don't worry. I'll take care of everything when I get home. I'll be there as soon as possible."

"Please hurry Trevor. Ouch! Ouch! Ouch! Trevor the pains are really getting bad."

"Lay down on the couch, and don't worry about a thing. I'll be there before you know it." he said, and then he was gone.

I was grateful that Abby was still napping. I took Trevor's advice and went and laid down on the couch. As soon as Trevor got home he came over to me and took my hand in his.

"Hey sweetheart. Are the pains coming any closer together?"

"No, but they are getting stronger."

"Did you call Dr. Graber or Alicia, or do I need to do that?"

"You need to." I said grimacing with pain.

"Are you having a pain right now?" he asked with a concerned look on his face.

"Yes. Oh, Trevor they are really getting bad. It hurts so much."

"I'm sorry you are hurting so badly. I'm going to call Alicia and see whether she can come over, or if we should bring Abby to her house. Then I'll call Dr. Graber's office and let them know that you're in labor and we're going to the hospital. Just hang in there for a few more minutes. I'll be right back."

He came back to the living room a few minutes later and said, "Okay, I got up with Alicia, and she is on her way over. She should be here in about ten to fifteen minutes. I called Dr. Graber's office and apprised them of the situation. I'm going to go and get your overnight bag that you packed and put it in the car. Do I need to get anything else?"

"Just my toothbrush and deodorant." I said, trying not to let the hysteria that was starting to build up in me show.

As soon as Alicia came Trevor started rushing me toward the door, but first I told him that there were a few things I needed to tell Alicia concerning Abby.

"Don't worry Grace, I'll take good care of her, and whatever she needs I'll figure it out. Don't worry, just get going. I don't want Trevor to have to deliver a baby while en route to the hospital. Now go on. Everything will be fine. Quit worrying." she said, as she helped Trevor herd me out the door.

With that we were out the door and at the hospital in about twenty-five minutes. Twelve hours later I was holding my newborn son in my arms. If he had been born two hours and thirty-five minutes later, he would have been born, not only on the same day as Davey, but also at exactly the same time. Trevor and I had decided that if the baby was a boy his name would be Joseph Daniel O'Brien.

I couldn't wait for Trevor to see his new son. I knew that he wanted a boy, even though he never really came out and said so. I expected him to come through the door any second now. I felt confident that he had waited at the hospital this time, but as I watched the hours on the clock tick by, I knew that this was just like all the other times. No one else was there with me to share the joyous occasion with.

I was shocked, and very hurt that he had done this to me again. I had thought for sure he would be here this time. Right then and there I knew that my feelings for him had forever been changed. I could feel whatever love I had ever felt for him waning its' way out of my body with every tick of the clock.

CHAPTER 21

▼

MY LIFE IS A TRAVESTY

Instead of going home from the hospital with a happy heart, I went home with a deep sense of dejection. The only thing I felt happy about was that I would get to see Abby. I had missed her so much. Other than that, the only other thing I felt was pure dread. My feelings for Trevor had no place for love anymore. His last betrayal while I was in the hospital had been the straw that broke the camel's back.

It was a real revelation to me to experience how fine a line there is between hope and hopelessness, and love and hate, and how quickly those lines can be crossed. As for myself, I felt that I must have been standing close to that line already, and it was a matter of just a quick step over.

It never entered my mind that Abby wouldn't be glad to see me, but as soon as she saw the baby in my arms she ran away and wouldn't have anything to do with me. She wouldn't even look at me. It broke my heart. I wanted so badly to hold her in my arms and tell her how much I had missed her.

Momma had come up for a few days to help me, and it was comforting to know that she would be with me. I wasn't ready to be alone with Trevor just yet. I needed some time to clear my head and to sort out my feelings for him first.

Joey was asleep so I went and laid him in his crib. I thought that if Abby didn't see me holding him she would come to me, but she didn't. When she continued to act like she was mad at me, I couldn't take her rejection, and I started sobbing.

At that point Momma picked her up and put Abby's head over her shoulder so that she would be forced to look at me.

In between sobs, I said, "Hey Abby, my sweet girl. I love you. Won't you come to Mommy so I can give you a kiss and tell you a story?"

With that Momma started to hand her over to me, but she started kicking and crying, all the while saying, "No! No! No!"

Her reaction caused me to start crying again. Then Momma looked at me and said, "Grace, you're the big girl here, and you're going to have to stop crying. Just give Abby some time. If you quit trying to make her come to you, pretty soon she will do it on her own. Now stop crying. Everything will be fine."

The next stunt Abby pulled was to not eat anything if I was looking at her. Like most mothers, I was concerned about my child getting the proper nutrition. I tried every trick in the book to try and get her to eat, including fixing all of her favorite foods. Tonight I had made fried pork chops, mashed potatoes and gravy and baby peas. Normally she would have gobbled them up, but tonight she wouldn't take one bite.

I tried to cajole her into eating by playing here comes the choo-choo train, or pretending that a little mouse was going to come and eat it if she didn't, but nothing worked. I decided to stop trying and just leave her there in her high chair to see what would happen.

I had come to the conclusion that she knew it made me unhappy when she didn't eat, and this was her way of getting back at me for bringing a new baby home. I went to the living room and sat down on the couch where I could still see her because the living room and dining area were combined. I pretended not to be looking at her, hoping that she would eat if she thought I wasn't looking.

It very soon became obvious that she wasn't ready to make up. The next thing I knew she was throwing her plate as hard as she could across the room. Food went flying everywhere. What didn't land on my new recliner landed somewhere in between. I sure hoped she wouldn't stay mad at me much longer.

Little Joseph Daniel on the other hand, was doing great, but I was getting worn out. Joey wanted to be fed every three hours whether it was day or night. During the day he would usually go right back to sleep after being fed, but at night he wouldn't go back to sleep unless I laid down with him and put him on my stomach. I guess you could say we laid tummy to tummy. The only thing I could figure out was that he was afraid of the dark, and he found it comforting to be laying against me where he felt the warmth of my body next to him, and he could hear my heartbeat.

I was becoming very deprived of sleep. It rarely worked out that Abby and Joey would be taking their nap at the same time so that I could grab a nap too. Not only that, there just didn't seem to ever be a peaceful moment when I could just sit down and relax for a few minutes. If it wasn't time for one to eat, it was time for the other one to. If one didn't need their diaper changed, the other one did, and if one didn't need to be held, the other one did. It seemed like I had a baby attached to my hip at all times.

One evening Trevor came home and found me sitting on the couch with a child on each knee, and we were all three sitting there crying our eyes out. He looked very surprised to have come upon such a scene, and he looked as if he was totally baffled as to what may have brought on such a display.

He asked, "What's wrong?" Duh! He just didn't have a clue. As the weeks and months went by things continued to go from bad to worse between us. If both of the kids were up during the night crying or whatever, it never appeared to occur to him that I could use some help.

Little by little he was reverting back to his old ways of staying out drinking and carousing with his buddies till all ours of the night. I knew that it was probably only a matter of time until the bounced checks started showing up in the mail. Sure enough the bill collectors started calling. It got so bad that I was afraid to answer the phone for fear that it was a bill collector. I expected them to come and repossess our furniture any day now. Once again, there were times when I had to take soda bottles back to the store to cash in so that I could buy such staples as bread and milk.

I was so miserable. Sometimes I would fantasize about Tom coming by and rescuing me from my private hell. It was quickly becoming harder and harder for me to live in the same house with Trevor. My resentment over his inexcusable behavior became so strong that I started to despise him.

Feeling the way I did, I couldn't stand for him to touch me. Consequently our sex life became another huge problem. I didn't know what to do, or where to turn. All I knew was that somehow I was going to have to find a way to leave him. There was no way I could continue to live under these conditions.

One weekend Colleen came up to visit me and I ended up telling her all of my problems. She was now twenty years old, and had been sharing a two bedroom apartment with her best friend Catherine ever since they graduated from high school. She had come up right after work on Friday afternoon.

As soon as I saw her car pull up in the driveway, I ran out to meet her and give her a big hug."Oh Colleen, I'm so glad you're here. You have no idea how happy I am to see you. Let me help you get your things out of the car, and we'll go in, open a bottle of wine, and get caught up with each other. You look great!"

"You do too." she said. "I've been looking forward to spending the weekend with you too, and I can't wait to see the kids. There isn't anything for you to carry in. I travel light. I figure if I forgot something, I'll borrow it from you." she said with a playful look on her face.

"Where's Trevor?" she asked. "Isn't he usually home from work by now?"

"I have no clue as to his whereabouts" I said, " and I couldn't care less. If he never comes back, it will be a joyous occasion, and one to which I will be celebrating big time."

That last remark had stopped Colleen dead in her tracks with a perplexed look on her face. I think at first she thought I was just joking, but on second thought, she wasn't sure if I was serious or not.

"What?" I said looking her straight in the eye. "Come on in and let's discuss it over a bottle of wine."

"Well, okay, but now I don't know what to make of the way you're talking and it's making me uneasy. Is everything alright with you and Trevor?"

Before I could answer her, Abby was at the door jumping up and down with excitement over seeing her Aunt Colleen.

"Come on, we'll talk when we get inside." I said.

As soon as we got in the door, Colleen had to put her bags down and pick up Abby, who was holding her arms outstretched for Colleen to pick her up. Then Joey started crying. He had been napping, but the commotion must have awakened him. That was okay. He needed to get up now anyway or else he would never go to sleep tonight.

After everything calmed down a little, I went in the kitchen and brought out a new bottle of wine. "Let's sit at the table." I suggested. "That way we'll have a place to put our glasses and cigarettes where the kids can't get to them."

You've got the house really looking good." she said. "I like how you've got everything arranged."

"Thanks. I like it too." I poured us each a glass of wine and we sat down.

"Okay now, out with it. What is going on around here." she said with a determined look on her face.

"Trevor and I aren't going to make it together. Our so called marriage is a joke, only it's anything but funny. Its been rocky for a long time now. I just haven't said anything."

"Why? What seems to be the problem?" Colleen asked, with concern written all over her face. "How long has this been going on?"

"Pretty much since day one." I said. "Marriage isn't at all like I expected it would be. My expectations were totally a fantasy. I know that now. I should have known it then, but I didn't. I was thinking that marriage would be like a romantic fairy tale; more like it is in the movies and on T.V. It isn't at all like that, believe me."

"Okay, so marriage isn't like a fairy tale, that still doesn't tell me what the problem is. With all we've been through with Momma and Daddy, and Ellen, I don't see how you could possibly think that way."

"I know, it doesn't make any sense, does it? I suppose I've seen too many movies where everything was portrayed that way. Somehow, I thought my marriage would be like Donna Reeds' on "The Donna Reed Show." In retrospect I feel foolish about it. That's why I haven't said anything about it to anyone. Well that's part of the reason anyway. The other part is that at first I thought the problems were because I didn't measure up to being the perfect wife standards I had always set for myself." I poured us some more wine and reached for a cigarette.

"The bottom line is that Trevor is hardly ever at home. After work he stays out until about two or three o'clock in the morning drinking with his buddies. Sometimes he comes home with his shirt ripped, because apparently he likes to fight. I never have the use of a car. I have no money, and I feel like I'm a single parent. And last, but not least, I can't stand him anymore."

"My God Grace. I had no idea." Colleen said, as she reached for a cigarette and lit it.

"He wasn't at the hospital when either one of our children were born. While I was writhing in the worst pain you can ever imagine, he was out partying. He never helps me with the kids. They can both be screaming their heads off for one reason or another, and he acts like he doesn't even hear them."

"Things were tolerable until after Abby was born. That's when he started staying out until all hours of the night. Then when I told him that I was pregnant with Joey he quit. We had a long talk about things that night, and I was hopeful that we would be okay."

"When he first started staying out, he told me the reason was because he felt left out after Abby was born. He said that he was uncomfortable in his role as a father, like we didn't need him, and he didn't know how to deal with it."

"He was good during my pregnancy with Joey, but once we came home from the hospital he started reverting back to his old ways again. He spends money that we don't have, and consequently, two or three times a week when I get the mail there are notices from the bank that another check has bounced. That's twenty dollars a pop, as you well know from working at a bank."

"Every time the phone rings I cringe, for fear that it will be another bill collector. There have been times that I've had to gather up every soda pop bottle I can find, just so I can get the deposit back, and hopefully have enough money to buy milk and bread."

"You poor thing. Why didn't you say something Grace? I would have been glad to send you some money."

"I know you would have, and I thank you for that, but I didn't want to burden you with my problems. It's just that now, I have to find a way to get out of here. I can't live this way very much longer, but I have no idea how I'm going to do it."

"I do." Colleen said, as she reached for the bottle of wine and poured us some more.

I was astonished when she said those two words. "How?" I asked, hoping that she wasn't joking.

"This is so ironic. You're not going to believe this Grace. Catherine is getting married in a couple of months, and I was going to find a new roommate, and guess what, I just did." she said, her face breaking out in a big grin.

"Oh my God Colleen. This is so great!"

"I know." she said, as we both got up and hugged each other. Then we started dancing around like two crazy people.

Abby, who had been playing quietly with her dolls, joined us in the dancing, even though she had no idea what had caused us to go from talking quietly one moment, to suddenly jump up and start dancing around the room the next. Joey, who was in his walker, joined in the fun by jumping up and down and clapping his hands. We were all laughing and feeling happy.

I felt like a big weight had been lifted off my shoulders. We finally got out of breath and sat back down.

"I can't believe this Colleen. It's a miracle. I need to pinch myself just to make sure it isn't a dream. Ouch! No, it isn't a dream." I said pinching myself.

"No, it isn't a dream Grace. This is going to work out so well. Abby can share my room, and you and Joey can have Catherine's room. Are you going to take all the furniture with you?"

"I plan to, unless Trevor gets ugly about it, but I'm not ready to tell him that I'm leaving just yet, so I can't say for sure."

"Well if you do, that will work out well too because everything in the apartment, except my bedroom set belongs to Catherine."

I'll probably be able to take it. Trevor will probably get a furnished apartment. I don't think he'll want to be bothered with moving a lot of furniture."

Then Trevor came home and we had to put a lid on it. I dreaded when the day would come for me to have to confront him with my plans, but I didn't plan on doing that until after Colleen went back home. So for tonight at least, I could breathe easy.

CHAPTER 22

▼

BROKEN DREAMS

After Colleen left the full impact of all we had discussed hit me like a ton of bricks. I started to have doubts about my decision, and to feel frightened. It was such a big step, and now in the clear light of day, I wasn't feeling so sure that it was the right one.

At least Trevor was at work so I had some time to think things over without any distractions from him. The kids were being good. Joey was laying on his blanket playing with one of his musical mobiles, and Abby was busy looking at my "S&H" green stamp catalog. She just loved looking through that catalog.

I was sitting on the couch watching them play, and all of a sudden I could feel the tears welling up in my eyes. I was thinking to myself, is leaving Trevor the right thing to do as far as my children are concerned? Is that what would be in their best interest, or am I selfishly considering only myself?

Then the self doubting kicked in and I started once again to think that there must be some shortcoming in me as a person, that makes me inadequate as a wife. Was Trevor staying out all night drinking because he wasn't getting his needs met at home? I was beating myself up but good, and then the tears started to flow. I cupped my hand over my mouth to keep from sobbing out loud. I didn't want Abby or Joey to see me crying.

As I sat there and thought about everything, I decided to give Trevor one more chance to do the right thing by me and the children. As I thought, I devised a plan. I would try to be as nice as I possibly could be to him when he came home. In my mind it was kind of a test I was giving myself to make double sure, one way or the other, that my misery was justified and that I wasn't making a rash decision. I figured that if I gave it my very best effort and he still remained distant from me and the children, then at least I would know that I had given it my very best shot.

I decided to fix Trevor his favorite meal of country fried steak for dinner. After I got the kids down for a nap I jumped in the shower, shaved my legs and washed my hair. I wanted to look pretty for him when he came home. I had given myself a big attitude adjustment, and I felt that maybe, just maybe, I hadn't given him the benefit of a doubt. Maybe if I tried my very best we may be able to work things out.

I wanted to keep the adrenaline pumping and my enthusiasm up for this, otherwise I wouldn't really be giving it my all. Only no matter how hard I tried, my heart wasn't really in it. I realized that in order for me to pull this off I was really going to have to put on a big act, and I didn't like to have to pretend, that would be self-defeating.

I needed some help here, so I decided to have a glass of wine. I hoped it would give me the boost I needed to get through this ordeal. Hey, this wine was good. By the time Trevor came home I was on my fourth glass and feeling pretty frisky. Maybe it wasn't going to be that tough to get through this after all.

I didn't want to fail again. I had already failed in my relationship with Tom, and even more importantly I had failed my first-born child, Davey. Feeling like such a failure was for the birds.

I tried to summon up good feelings for Trevor, but it was a chore to do so because it was all a lie. I knew that my love for him was dead and gone. In my heart I knew that none of the feelings I was trying to express through the guise of this lovely dinner and smiling facade I had planted on my face, wasn't going to change a thing. There was nothing to work with. Whatever love I had ever felt for Trevor just wasn't there anymore. It had evaporated into thin air. I felt so empty when it came to him, like I was in a void. The realization of it all hit me so hard that I felt like I had been punched in the stomach, and had the wind knocked out of me. Even so, I couldn't shake the feeling that it was somehow my fault. Trevor loved the dinner, but it had no meaning to me.

In the days and weeks that followed the situation was becoming harder and harder for me to deal with. Trevor still had no inkling of the plans that Colleen and I had talked about. Initially, I had thought that I wouldn't tell him anything until the move was imminent. I had thought that I could make it until then, but there was still a month to go before Colleen's friend Catherine would be moving out, and at the rate the tension in our house was building up, I was quickly starting to doubt that I could make it that long.

I played the charade for as long as I could, but if anything it only made matters worse. I was beginning to feel even more resentment toward Trevor, because here I had put forth all this effort, and nothing was changing.

He was still coming home late almost every night, and bounced check notices were still coming in the mail on a regular basis. I had finally reached rock bottom in the belief that there was even the slightest chance of things ever working out between us.

I felt so completely alone in my misery. My mind was spinning very fast, and every thought was a blur that I couldn't get a grasp on. The kids were asleep for the night, so even though it was only eight o'clock, I decided to go to bed. I managed to cry myself to sleep.

When I woke up my mind had stopped spinning, but I felt curious about the dream I had dreamt. In my dream I had been hit by a bolt of lightening, and the jolt had given my brain a powerful shock. In my mind's eye I could see myself falling in a downward spiral, plummeting toward an unknown abyss with great velocity. I knew that I had to find a way to stop the plunge because there was no one else there to do it for me. I managed to stop falling, but there was no place to run to, and there was no place to hide.

I had fallen to a place in the middle of nowhere. The landscape was devoid of anything. There wasn't even a single blade of grass, just me and empty space, but that no longer scared me because I knew at that moment that I had somehow found, through the grace of God, the strength that had stopped my downward spiral. I no longer felt panicky, because now I knew that I had found the strength to do whatever I needed to on my own.

I stood alone, but I didn't stand hopeless or helpless. I thought of the life that I had dreamed for myself just a few short years ago, and I knew that the life I was living was not meant to be my life. It didn't even bare a remote resemblance to that life. What had happened to the real Grace, I wondered. When had she disappeared, and where had she gone? Would I be able to find her, or was she gone forever? Was this new persona I saw reflected in the mirror all that was left of her? No, it couldn't be! That was a stranger staring back at me. How had I gotten so far off the path I had intended to travel, only to arrive at this desolate place. How would I find my way back to me? I didn't have all the answers just yet, but I thought everything would eventually sort itself out.

There was no doubt going to be some difficult decisions to be made, but I was starting to feel stronger,more like my true self. I prayed with all my heart that I would find a way to create a life that would be a good one for me and my children.

I went to their rooms where they were napping, and looked at my two beautiful children. I knew that for them I could move mountains if I had to. That's when I knew that everything was going to be alright.

CHAPTER 23

▼

LIFE ON THE MOVE

Now that my head was clear, I felt better about the decision I had made. Now all I had to do was find a way to implement it. I felt neither guilt, nor indecisive about what I was doing. I knew that I had given my marriage to Trevor my best shot, and I knew that it would never work out between us.

Remember the bolt of lightening that hit me in my dream? Well, that bolt of lightening had figuratively struck the right chord in my brain. Not only had it jolted me into seeing the true picture of my reality, it had cleared my mind of all the garbage and debris that didn't belong there. It had given me a blank canvas to work with. I was no longer plummeting into an infinite abyss. I was heading toward a straight target.

I wasn't happy about the situation. I felt saddened and hurt that my marriage had reached this destination. I felt sorrow, as if a loved one had died, and I grieved over the death of my marriage.

After my period of grieving was over, I felt a very calm peacefulness settle over me. If you have ever felt the presence of the Holy Spirit at work in your life, then you know exactly how I was feeling. That presence not only confirmed to me that I was doing the right thing, it also gave me the strength and courage I was going to need to get through this transition with myself and my children left in tact.

I decided to call Colleen. I was just about to hang up, when on the sixth ring she answered the phone. "Hello"

"Hey, it's me. You took so long to answer the phone that I was just about to hang up. What are you up to?"

"Oh, hi Grace. I was just helping Catherine pack up some things. She and Jack went house hunting over the weekend, and found a house that they fell in love with. They made an offer to purchase on it, and now they're just waiting to see if the owner accepts their offer. It's pretty much for sure that he will. They've already been to the bank and have been pre-approved for the loan. The only reason they might not get it is if there are multiple offers on it, which could potentially start a bidding war."

"Oh, I hope they get it Colleen. If they do, will Catherine be moving in before the wedding?"

"Yes, and you know what that means?"

"I could move in sooner. That would be so great. I don't know how much longer I can take living with Trevor. My nerves are shot."

"I'm sorry you're having such a hard time Grace. I hate it for you."

"Catherine should know if they're getting the house in a day or two. The owner was out of town, but he was suppose to be back yesterday. If they do get it, then Catherine wants to do some painting before she starts moving in, but that shouldn't take long. They're going to have a paint party, and there are five or six people that are going to help with that. Catherine will move in as soon as that's done. She wants to have it all set up nice so everything will be done when they get back from their honeymoon."

"Oh, I hope everything works out so I can get out of here. I'm trying not to get too excited though. I don't want to leave myself open for a big letdown." I said, even though I really couldn't help, but feel excited.

"Have you said anything to Momma about what's going on?" she asked.

"No, but I guess I better. You haven't mentioned anything to her or Daddy have you?"

"No, I'm leaving that up to you. I think it's your place to tell them, not mine. I do think that you should go ahead and at least let Momma know though."

"You're right. I dread it though. Do you think she'll be shocked?" I asked.

"No, she's pretty intuitive, and I think she already suspects that things aren't going well between you and Trevor."

"Okay, I'll call her today. Right now you're the only one that I've said anything to. I'm not going to say anything to Trevor until all my plans are in place. I have no idea what his reaction is going to be, but I want to have an escape plan just in case I need one."

"I think that's a good idea. I'll call you as soon as I know any more details about when Catherine will be moving. Hang in there Grace. It'll all work out. Try not to worry. I love you."

"I love you too Colleen. Bye."

By the time we hung up the kids were starting to wake up from their afternoon naps. I got them up, put Abby on the potty chair, she was almost completely potty trained thank goodness, and then I went and changed Joey's diaper..

Once I got the kids all settled, I started cooking dinner. Trevor would be getting off from work soon, and although I never knew if he would be home for dinner or not, I always tried to have it ready just in case.

Dinner was done, and no Trevor. That was not surprising. I decided to go ahead and get the kids fed. Maybe he would be home by then. Nope, still no Trevor. While the kids were playing I ate my dinner and put the leftovers in the refrigerator. If he wanted to eat when he came home he could warm it up himself. I was sick and tired of this kind of hogwash. I could feel the anger welling up inside of me. My whole body felt like it was going to explode from holding it all in.

Have you ever been so angry that you reach a point where your anger reaches its' maximum crescendo, and then a quiet, but eerie calm takes over? That's how I began to feel, and with that feeling came an ominous sense of foreboding.

I played with the kids for awhile, trying to ward off any of my negative thoughts that they might pick up on. As we played, their squeals of delight softened the ugly edges of my anger, and I began to relax a little. Soon it was time to get them in the bath and ready for bed.

After I got the kids in bed, I was feeling lonely and sad. I decided to call Momma. She was always a soft place to fall when I felt upset. Besides, like Colleen had said, I needed to tell her what was transpiring in my life.

I wasn't ready to tell Daddy and Ellen just yet. I didn't want to tell Aunt Esther either. I knew that she would probably just tell me that I needed to stick it out. I could hear her saying,"All marriages go through bad times.", and I knew that no matter what I said to her, or how I might try to explain or justify my actions, she would be listening with deaf ears through a brick wall. Although she would probably never admit it, her reasoning would be that it would cast a shameful shadow on the family. Maintaining proper social decorum was what seemed to matter the most to her.

Trevor still wasn't home, and he hadn't called, not a word from him yet. I decided to go in the kitchen and pour myself a glass of wine and lit a cigarette. A couple of glasses of wine and several cigarettes later, I picked up the phone and dialed Momma's number. She picked up on the fourth ring.

"Hello"

"Hi Momma."

"Hi sweetheart. How are you?"

I took a deep breath and proceeded to tell her my tale of woe. "I'm okay, but there are some things going on in my life that I felt I should let you know about."

"What's wrong Grace? Are the kids alright?" she asked with a trace of alarm in her voice.

"The kids are fine Momma. It's just that Trevor and I are going through some real rough times. It's nothing new. We've been having problems ever since we've been married. Only now they have become unbearable. We've tried to work things out several times before, but it just isn't ever going to work out. Believe me, this isn't a rash decision. It's something that I've given a lot of thought to. I want a divorce."

"Oh Grace I'm so sorry."

"Yea, me too." I said, "but I do have a plan. You know that Catherine is getting married."

"Yes"

"Well, when she moves out, me and the kids are going to move in with Colleen. It helps Colleen, because then she doesn't have to look for a new roommate, and it helps me because we can share expenses, plus she won't have to buy any furniture because we'll use mine."

"I've been thinking about moving myself." Momma said. "Maybe the three of us could look for a place. That way we could afford something bigger, maybe even a house with a back yard for the kids. That way you would have a place for Abby's swing set. Plus we could help you take care of the kids. If the hours work out, one of us could babysit while you're at work."

"That would be wonderful." I said.

"Maybe the three of us could get together and see what Colleen thinks about it." Momma said.

"That would be good." I said.

"Grace, what's the problems that you and Trevor are having about?"

"Oh my gosh, there are so many I don't know where to begin, but the root of the problem is that he stays out half the night drinking with his friends. He hardly ever spends any time at all with me and the children. He spends money that we don't have, and checks are bouncing all the time. I have bill collectors calling me day and night, and the list goes on and on. I really don't feel like talking about it any more right now. I just wanted to let you know what's going on. I haven't told Daddy or anyone else yet. You and Colleen are the only ones that know."

"Is there anything I can do to help?" Momma wanted to know. "Are you and the kids going to be okay until you can get out of there? Trevor wouldn't hurt you, would he?"

"He's already hurt me, not physically, but he has hurt me mentally and emotionally as much as he can. I'm filled with hurt. There isn't any space in me that he can squeeze anymore hurt into, but I don't believe that he would hurt me physically. The kids are fine. They just don't have a Daddy so to speak. Don't worry Momma, I can handle it. I promise. I'll call you back tomorrow okay?"

"Okay honey. Call me if you need to. I'll come and get you and the kids if you want me to."

"No, but I appreciate it Momma. I know I can always count on you, and I love you very much."

"I love you too sweetheart."

With that, we hung up. I was glad that I had called her though. That was one thing off of "my dread to do list" that I wouldn't have to worry about anymore.

I went in to check on the kids. They were both sleeping, so I decided to have a little celebration party all by myself. I went and poured myself another glass of wine, lit a cigarette and sat back and tried to relax. Things seemed to be working out so far and I felt a lot less stressed out. The only thing to do now was just to wait and see what happens as the situation unfolds.

CHAPTER 24

▼

BROKEN DREAMS/NEW DREAMS

I stayed up late that night waiting for Trevor to come home. As the hours got later and later, I got angrier and angrier, and tipsier and tipsier. I usually went to bed around eleven o'clock. If Trevor wasn't home by then, I had no idea what time he came home because I would be asleep. Tonight my routine would be different. Tonight I wanted to be awake and waiting for him. I decided that tonight was the night I was going to tell him exactly what my plans were.

Finally, around two-thirty I heard his car pull into the driveway. I had turned all of the lights in the house off because I didn't want him to know that I was still up. I wanted to watch him come staggering in, unaware that I was lying in wait. I wanted to see what he would do, and to observe his reaction when he realized I was still up.

I heard the car door slam and his footsteps approaching the front door. By this time I was eager to confront him. I heard him fumbling around for the right key. Then I heard him drop them on the front stoop and start muttering vulgar obscenities as he prowled around in the dark trying to find them. If I hadn't been so fed up, I probably would have found it amusing. Tonight however, I was not amused. I was sickened by the pathetic creature that was crawling around in the front yard at two-thirty in the morning because that creature happened to be my husband.

He finally managed to find the keys and unlock the front door. He still had no clue that I was sitting on the couch just a few feet away from him. I was tempted to blurt out something and scare the you know what out of him, but I decided to just let the situation take its' course and see what happened.

He stumbled into the kitchen and looked in the refrigerator for something to eat, grabbed a piece of bologna and some cheese, and threw a sandwich together. Then apparently decided that he was thirsty, he grabbed a beer and popped it open. He was still clueless that he was being observed.

It wasn't until he finally got himself situated and turned on the T.V. that he became aware of my presence. I wished that I had a camera ready to capture the moment. It was priceless. He had just taken a bite of his bologna sandwich, and was chasing it down with a slug of beer when he saw me. He nearly choked on the sandwich, and the beer came spewing out of his mouth like a geyser erupting.

For a second he looked mortified, but quickly gathered his wits about him. He then proceeded to ramble off some expletives about how I had scared the dickens out of him. "Damn it Grace. You could have caused me to choke. Why are you sitting in the dark lying in wait for me like this?"

"I waited up for you because I have something that I need to talk to you about, something that can't wait." I said.

"Is something wrong with the kids?" he asked.

"Yes" I said. "They need a father who plays a part in their lives, and I need a husband that behaves like a husband. I'm sick and tired of this so-called marriage we have, and I'm really sick to death of you. I want a divorce Trevor, and I want you out of this house tomorrow. It makes me sick to see what a debacle you have made of our marriage."

"You can sleep on the couch tonight because you're too drunk to drive, but tomorrow you need to make other living arrangements."

Right before my eyes I saw his face change. First to shock, and then to disbelief.

"I don't know why you look so surprised. Did you really think that I was going to put up with this nonsense forever? We have no marriage. We never do anything together as a family. I've stuck with it for as long as I can. I was hoping that things would get better between us, but I've gone as far as I'm willing to go."

By this time he was up and out of his chair. He stood before me, glaring down at me with a face so severely contorted with anger that I was alarmed. I had never seen anyone look that way before.

He got right in my face, and said, "Listen carefully to me Grace. I'm not going anywhere. Not tomorrow, not next week, not next month, or next year. Not ever. You got that Grace? I'll see you in hell before that ever happens."

I was scared to death that he was going to hit me. Then I heard Joey start to cry. I guess our yelling had awakened him. I was relieved to have a reason to get away from Trevor, so I jumped up to go check on Joey before he woke Abby up. I sure didn't want to have them both to contend with during this confrontational, and potentially volatile exchange that was going on between us.

Joey was easy to get back to sleep. All he needed was his pacifier and a few pats on the back. I lingered longer in his room than I needed to, simply because I was in no hurry to go back and face Trevor. I needed some time to reinforce my fortitude, so I sat down in the rocking chair in Joey's room and tried to calm myself.

After thirty minutes or so I didn't hear Trevor moving around, so I very tentatively tiptoed to the door and peeked around the corner to see if I could see any sign of him, and see where he was and what he was doing. I couldn't hear him or see him, so I ventured out into the hall and stole a quick glance out into the living room. Much to my relief he was sleeping on the couch. I let out a huge sigh of relief, then went and turned the light off and made sure the door was locked.

I then made a beeline for the bedroom and quickly got in bed. I figured if Trevor woke up and came and got in bed with me, I would pretend to be asleep. I closed my eyes and tried to relax my mind so I could go to sleep. The kids would be up in a few hours, and I needed to get at least a few hours of sleep before then. There was no telling what tomorrow would bring, but I needed to be ready for whatever it was.

The last thing I remember thinking before I dozed off, was that me and the kids were probably going to have to leave tomorrow while Trevor was at work. The only place I could think of for us to go was to Momma's. There was going to be a lot of things to take care of. I hadn't even gotten started and already I felt exhausted and overwhelmed.

Abby woke me up at seven-thirty. I coaxed her into bed with me and we cuddled and went back to sleep until Joey woke up a half hour later.

I had to drag myself out of bed. Boy, this was going to be a rough day. I was exhausted before my feet even hit the floor, and I was feeling hung over from all the wine I had drunk last night. My nerves were shot from the anticipation of knowing that I was going to have to deal with Trevor again. As I stepped into the living room, I was relieved to see that he was still asleep, but I knew it wouldn't be long before the kids woke him up.

I got the kids situated. Abby in her booster chair, and Joey in his high chair and gave them some dry Cheerios to snack on while I fixed their breakfast.

I could hear Trevor starting to move around behind me, but I didn't turn around and acknowledge his presence. I wanted to postpone having to look at him, or speak to him for as long as I possibly could. I pretended that I wasn't aware that he was standing behind me. I could feel his glare at my back so strongly that it felt as if the hatred he felt for me had actually penetrated my skin, and become a living thing that now resided within me. I could literally feel it, and it sent chills all over my body. I felt paralyzed with dread. Oh how I wished that either Momma or Colleen were here, but they weren't, so I quickly told myself to take a deep breath, turn around, and face the situation head-on. I hoped he wouldn't do anything to frighten the children, like yelling at me, or slamming cabinet doors and that sort of thing.

With that in mind, I turned around and tried to act like everything was normal for the kids' sake. I figured that if I didn't raise my voice or act mad, maybe he wouldn't either.

I said, "Good morning. Would you like some coffee? I'm fixing some scrambled eggs and toast. Would you like for me to fix some for you too?"

He responded very haughtily, saying, "Go to hell bitch."

At least he had said it without shouting, so the kids didn't seem to pick up on anything out of the ordinary. I was grateful for that.

He then turned around and left the room. I could hear him turn on the shower. After about thirty minutes he came out all dressed for work, and said, "I'll be home right after work. Be ready to talk because I have plenty to say. We're far from finished with our last conversation." Having said that he turned and was out the door.

I felt a moment of relief that he was gone, but that was quickly replaced with the frightening task of deciding what to do next. What I wanted to do was to flee from there as fast as I could, but that would have been a betrayal to my sense of what was the right thing to do. After all was said and done, I figured that I at least owed him the chance to say his side of the story, and for him to hear my side as well.

I desperately felt the need to talk to someone about what was going on, but not just anyone though. It had to be either Momma or Colleen. Since it would probably be Momma that would give me refuge, I decided to call her. I didn't like to call her at work, but my need to speak with her was so urgent that I decided to do it anyway.

Momma was currently taking a real estate course and working in a real estate office. Right now she was just working in the office doing clerical work, but her boss had told her that once she passed the real estate exam and got her realtor's license, he would hire her on as a full-time realtor.

As I dialed the number I prayed that she would be the one to answer the phone. She picked up on the third ring.

"Hopkins Realty, how may I help you?"

"Hi Momma. Can you talk for a minute?"

"Yes, but we're very busy right now, so I can only talk for a minute. Is something wrong?"

"Trevor and I really had it out last night. I told him that I want a divorce. He got very angry. He's at work now, but he told me before he left that we weren't through with the conversation we had last night. I really want to get out of here, but I feel that I at least owe him the chance to tell his side of the story, and for him to hear my side as well."

She listened to what I had to say, and said, "I'll call you back on my lunch hour and we'll sort it all out then. Try not to worry, everything will be alright. Okay hon?"

"Okay Momma. I'm sorry to have bothered you at work, but I really needed to talk to you."

"It's okay, I'll talk to you in a couple hours. By."

Her reassurance that we would sort it out later was very comforting to hear. I felt calmer now, but my head was still swimming from all the thoughts that were swirling around in my brain. I had so many things to think about that I didn't know where to begin to figure it all out. I decided to just go about doing my daily routine until after I talked to Momma, but I wasn't able to go about my daily routine as if everything was normal. It wasn't and there was no sense in trying to pretend that it was.

After getting the kids settled I decided to sit down with paper and pen and start writing my thoughts down. I was hoping that by putting it all on paper I would be able to think about things in a more rational manner.

Once I started writing, the words just came pouring out. My hand couldn't write fast enough to keep up with my thoughts. I made lists. I wrote down feelings, both happy and sad. When I finally put the pen down I had written eight pages. After I went back and read everything I felt more grounded. It was all there in black and white. Most of it was a sad commentary of my life as I saw it. Most of it was painful to read, and I couldn't hold back the tears. They streamed down my face and plopped on the paper, smudging my litany of heartbreak.

My reverie was broken by the sound of Joey screaming. Abby had taken a toy that he was playing with away from him. I made her give it back to him and then she started screaming. Oh boy, what I really wanted was to be left alone to wallow in my wretched unhappiness. I wanted to throw myself across my bed and cry until there were no more tears left to shed. I wanted to sob, to keen, to let my grief pour out with abandonment, but I couldn't. I had my children to attend to.

It was probably for the best that I wasn't able to wallow in unrestrained self-pity. What good would that have done? My experience had been that when things were the toughest, I had to be the strongest, and I wanted to be strong.

I was actually happy that the children had broken the spell. They had brought me back to reality and disrupted my melancholy. Left to my own thoughts, I probably would have been eaten alive by my burden of sorrow and broken dreams. I got down on the floor and the three of us played and laughed. It felt so good to laugh.

I had just gotten the kids down for their afternoon nap when the phone rang. It was Momma.

"Hi Hon."

"Hi Momma"

"Okay, now we can talk. Tell me what is going on and what I can do to help." she said.

"I hardly know where to start. From the very beginning of our marriage things haven't been good. It hasn't all been bad. We have had some good times when it seemed like we had worked everything out, and for a while everything would go fairly smoothly, but then he would revert back to his old ways of staying out really late at the bars with his friends after work."

"The kids and I rarely see him because we are asleep by the time he gets home, and we never do anything together as a family. He spends money like it grows on trees. Consequently the bill collectors are calling me on an almost daily basis, and checks are bouncing at least twice a week. I have no car, I have no money, and it's horrible."

"I've become resentful toward him for making us live this way. I don't love him anymore, and I'm not willing to keep on living like this."

"Last night I waited up for him to come home. He got home about two-thirty, and I told him that I want a divorce, and that I want him to move out of here today. We ended up having an ugly scene. I was afraid he was going to hit me. He got right up in my face, and his face was all contorted with anger. Then Joey woke up and started crying, so that gave me a chance to get away from him, and go and see about the baby. I stayed in Joey's room longer than I needed to because I didn't want to go back out there. I waited until I couldn't hear him moving around anymore, and then I took a sneak peek out to the living room, and he was asleep on the couch. After that I went to bed. I didn't get to bed until about four-thirty this morning."

"When I got up with the kids this morning he was still asleep on the couch. I started fixing the kids something to eat, and I could actually feel him glaring at me from behind, but I pretended like I didn't know he was there. I finally had to turn around and face him in order to give the kids their food."

"I decided to try and act as normal as I could because I didn't want to start arguing in front of the kids, for fear that it would scare them. So when I turned around, I asked him if he would like some coffee or something to eat, and he said,"Go to hell bitch." Then he said, "Be ready to continue our conversation when I get home today because this is far from over." I stopped to take a breath.

Momma said, "Are you afraid of him? I mean, do you think that he will become violent and hit you, or hurt the kids?"

"No."

"Well then this is what I think you should do. I think you should wait for him to come home, and listen to what he has to say. Then have your say. Then depending on how that conversation goes take it from there. After having your talk if you want me to come and get you and the kids, I will, but I want you to think long and hard about what you're doing, and make sure that whatever that may turn out to be, you won't have any regrets about it later on. This is a big step you're taking, and I want you to be sure it's what you want before doing anything drastic."

"I had sensed that there were problems between you two, but I didn't realize that it had gotten this bad. I thought that they were just bumps in the road that every marriage goes through." she said.

"These are not just bumps in the road Momma. This is a road to nowhere filled with endless potholes and boulders."

"Nevertheless, give it this one more shot and see how you feel about it then. I'll be at home tonight if you need me. I love you."

"I love you too Momma. Thanks for listening, and thanks for always being there for me."

It wasn't long after Momma and I hung up that Colleen called.

"Guess what, Catherine and Jack's offer on the house was accepted. The closing will be next week. That means that you can move in with me in about ten days. Isn't that great?"

"Yes it is. Just to catch you up to speed on things, Momma and I had a long talk just before you called, about my situation. I called her this morning because Trevor and I had a big fight last night. He says he's coming straight home from work this afternoon to continue the conversation. I figure I at least owe him the courtesy of listening to what he has to say, but I don't think there is anything he can say that will make me change my mind, so plan on me and the kids moving in with you just as we planned. Joey's crying, so I have to go, but I'll talk to you later, okay?"

"Okay, bye."

It was amazing to me how wonderfully things were falling into place. I saw it as a good omen, and I thanked God profusely.

True to his word, Trevor came straight home from work. I made myself listen to what he had to say, but none of it made any difference. It was too little too late.

CHAPTER 25

▼

THE TRANSITION

After our talk there was no doubt in either of our minds as to whether there was any hope for saving our marriage. We were both left feeling very bitter, each for our own perceived reasons . . . whether they were right or wrong. With each of us feeling that way we knew that we could not continue to live under the same roof. I was relieved that his angry outbursts from last night and this morning had seemingly passed. Consequently, it was mutually agreed upon that Trevor would go and stay with his parents. He grabbed some clothes and a few personal items and was gone.

Even though there was a part of me that felt bad because my marriage had ended, mostly I just felt a huge surge of relief that I would no longer have to live under such unhappy conditions. I felt as free as a bird. I felt excited about what the next phase of my life would bring. I felt hopeful and happy. There was no fear in me about it. I somehow just knew that everything would be okay, and that my children and I would be better off in the long run.

After I got the kids settled down and tucked in bed, I called Momma to let her know what was happening. We didn't talk for long.

"I'll come up to your house Saturday morning, and if Colleen wants to come with me, I'll bring her too. That way we can all sit down together and sort out a plan that will be workable for all of us." she said.

They came up Saturday morning, and we all sat down at the table and commenced making our plans. We each had paper and pen and started making a list of our wants and needs. After we got that done, we had to figure out how to achieve the desired results. My list was the longest and most complicated.

After all was said and done, it basically came down to this. We all wanted to live in Ocean Shores, and we all either wanted to either rent a house or buy one. No one wanted to live in an apartment. I would need a U-Haul truck to move mine and the children's things.

I was going to have to sit down with Trevor and talk about how our belongings were to be divided. He was going to have to give me some money, plus I was going to have to have a car. I dreaded the part about having to sit down with Trevor, but it had to be done.

Momma said, "You need to get a lawyer, and file for legal separation papers. You need to specifically ensure that you have legal custody of the children, and that Trevor will have to pay you child support."

I didn't know how I would be able to take care of all of this. I was beginning to feel that so much of what had to be done depended on Trevor's cooperation, and that was one of the great unknowns.

Another problem that had to be addressed quickly was the fact that my house rent was going to be due in ten days. I would need to be out by then.

Colleen told me, " Don't be concerned about that because Catherine will be moved out by then, and you and the children will be moved in with me."

That still left me with the problem of getting the money to rent a U-Haul truck, and coming up with my share of the rent on Colleen's apartment.

Momma said, "I don't think it will be too much of a problem with finding a house to rent. When I get back to work on Monday, I'll look through the listings on houses for rent. If I find something that I think would be suitable, I'll call Colleen and have her go and look at it. If we both like it, we'll call you, and see what you want to do."

I knew that the first thing I needed to do was to call Trevor and set up a time for him to come over so that we could hash things out. Oh how I dreaded the thought of that.

After we finished working out our plans as best we could, Momma and Colleen decided to leave.

"Since it's the weekend and Trevor's off from work, it might be a good time for you to get up with him and ask him to come over." Momma said.

As soon as they left I put the kids down for a nap. I grabbed a beer and a cigarette and sat down and put my feet up. I was trying to gather up my courage and get up with Trevor. Since I needed the car to go and buy some groceries, I figured that I could use that as a premise to get him to come over. That way he could stay with the kids while I went grocery shopping, and when I got back I would start a discussion about our separation and what needed to be done. It sounded like a good plan. Now, if I could only catch him at his parents' house.

With a great deal of trepidation I went and picked up the phone. I took a deep breath and made myself dial the number. I was just about to hang up, when on the sixth ring Trevor picked up. My stomach felt like it had butterflies flying around in it, and my heart was pounding because I was afraid he would say that he couldn't come over right now, but that didn't happen.

"Hi Trevor."

"Hey Grace. What's up?"

"I was wondering if you could come over. I need the car to go grocery shopping. I need some money too. Can you come over?"

"Yea, just let me finish eating lunch. I should be there in about thirty minutes. Okay?"

"That works for me." I said with relief. I had expected for him to make some excuse not to come over, and I was really surprised that he didn't hum and haw about giving me some money.

Twenty-five minutes later he walked in the door. I was all ready to go.

"The kids have had lunch, and they've been sleeping for about forty-five minutes. I should be back in about an hour." I told him.

With that, he handed me fifty dollars for groceries, and I was out the door. It felt good to get out of the house and have some time just for me, even if it was only to go grocery shopping. It gave me some time to think without any distractions.

Once I started thinking about all that lay before me my head started to swim, and for a minute I could feel a panic attack ready to make an advance on my sensibilities. I couldn't let that happen. I had to try to ward it off before it got a grip on me. I had too much to do, and only a short time to do it in.

In order to keep the panic attack at bay, I started saying to myself, as calmly as I could, "Everything is going to be just fine. Everything is going to be just fine."

I guess you could say that I had a mantra going. I was saying it very calmly, but inside I felt more like screaming the words out. Since the calm voice wasn't really the way I genuinely felt, it really wasn't helping.

I decided to just let it all out, be true to the way I was really feeling. Pretty soon I was shouting at the top of my lungs, oblivious to what the people in the cars around me thought. That is, until I stopped at a traffic light, and realized that everyone within shouting distance was staring at me.

Noticing the looks on their faces, I broke out laughing hysterically. I laughed and laughed and laughed until there were tears coming out of my eyes, and I felt like I was going to wet my pants. The thought of wetting myself sobered me up, but thankfully I had squelched the panic attack.

At first I took my time grocery shopping. I hadn't been in any hurry to go back and talk to Trevor, but then all of a sudden I felt the need to get it over with quickly. Prolonging it was only making it worse. Better to just do it and get it over with. Why prolong the agony. I needed to know what I was going to be dealing with, especially as far as money was concerned.

On the drive back home I decided to do my best to avoid getting into a screaming and shouting match with him. I desperately wanted for us to be able to work this out in a civilized manner. I decided that I would invite him to have dinner with us, so that we could have some time to talk. I had picked up some beer and wine at the store hoping that maybe a glass or two of wine, or a couple beers would help us both to relax.

As soon as I pulled in the driveway and got out of the car I could hear Joey crying. He probably needed to have his diaper changed. Trevor would change a wet diaper, but not a dirty one. Thinking this, I felt a flicker of anger flare up inside me, but remembering my mission I quickly dismissed it. I grabbed as many groceries as I could and went on in.

Sure enough Joey had on a dirty diaper. Toys were scattered all over the floor. Abby's nose needed wiping and her hair needed to be brushed. It was sticking up in all different directions, and wet with perspiration. I knew this was what I would come home to. This was what happened whenever Trevor took care of the kids for more than an hour. I could feel that twinge of anger trying to rear its' ugly head again. This time I had to clench my jaws together very tightly so that no words could come out. That little voice in my head was telling me to remember my mission, and this was one tough mission.

I picked Joey up and said to Trevor, "There's some beer and wine out in one of the bags out in the car."

I was pretty sure that would inspire him to go out, and at least bring in some of the groceries. If I was lucky, maybe he would even bring all of them in.

After I got the kids all set and happy I went and got me a beer.

I asked Trevor, "Can we sit and talk for a while?"

"Sure." he replied.

We sat down at the kitchen table. Joey was content in his swing, and Abby was sitting on the floor happily looking through her S&H Green stamp catalog. So far so good, I thought taking a deep breath.

"Trevor, just to catch you up on everything, Momma and Colleen came up this morning, and I told them what was going on between us. Colleen's friend Catherine is getting married and moving in about a week or so. Colleen said that the kids and I could move in with her when Catherine moves out, and that's what I plan on doing."

"That sounds reasonable." he said.

"Before I move, I think there are a few things that we need to come to an agreement on. For instance, I'm going to need some money to get moved with. I need to pay Colleen my half of the month's rent, and I need to rent a U-Haul truck to move my things. I'm hoping that you will agree to let me have the furniture, and I need to know how much money I can expect from you, not only for the move, but as child support on an ongoing basis."

So far the discussion was going very well. I had been concerned that it would turn into a shouting match that would leave us both feeling more resentment than ever toward each other.

So far, Trevor was listening very intently to what I had to say, and giving me the courtesy to say what I needed to without interruption. Then I in turn respectfully gave him the chance to respond.

Things were going so smoothly that I literally had to pinch myself to make sure this wasn't a dream. I thought it was amazing that there was no anger between us. The frankness and the ease with which we were able to talk to each other was a rare blessing.

I think it made us both realize that even though we didn't belong together as man and wife, we could still have a civilized relationship with each other. Our lifestyles were separated by a chasm too large to build a bridge across for any other kind of relationship to work. We had both been too immature in the beginning of our marriage to see how big the gap was, and how incompatible our views on life were.

The next phase of our discussion was going to have to address the division of our belongings, such as furniture, and the real whopper, the money factor. This is where things are liable to get ugly, I thought to myself, but once again I was pleased to be proven wrong.

Trevor said, "You can have all of the furniture. I plan on renting a furnished apartment, and I don't want to have to deal with moving a lot of stuff. Since we won't be paying next month's rent on this house, you can have that money too."

"I haven't told the landlady that we're going to be moving yet." I said.

"I'll go down and tell her that we'll be moving out at the end of the month." he said, "and since we paid first, last, and security when we moved in, maybe she'll give us the money that would be for the last month, and the security deposit back. You can have whatever money she gives us for that too."

Our rent was $90.00 a month, so if she did give us that money, and Trevor gave me the money we would ordinarily be paying for the upcoming month's rent, I would have $270.00 to make the move with.

We didn't discuss any legal issues. I felt that we had resolved enough for one day. The legalities would be taken care of in due time.

CHAPTER 26

▼

ON THE MOVE

The following week was extremely busy. The fact that I didn't have the use of a car at my disposal made it very difficult for me to get things done in a timely fashion. For instance, I was always running out of boxes to pack things in. If it hadn't been for a neighbor lady that I had become friends with, I don't know what I would have done. Every time she went to the grocery store she would get as many boxes as she could for me, and if I needed for her to pick up a few things for me while she was there, she did that too.

Trying to pack and take care of the kids was very trying on my nerves. I was worn out mentally and physically. Joey was crawling now, and grabbing everything he could get his hands on, and Abby was into everything. She would take things out of boxes I was packing and run off to another part of the house with them. She hid the items in closets and behind furniture because she couldn't understand why I was putting our things in boxes and sealing them up. I couldn't pack any of her or Joey's belongings while she was awake because she would scream and pitch a fit. It was horrible. I finally came up with the idea to get the biggest box I could find, and let her use it as her playhouse. That did the trick. She was happy as a lark, and so was I.

Momma and Colleen came up the weekend of the move to help me load things up, and to help me with the children. I rented a U-Haul truck to move everything in. Colleen and Momma had each driven their own cars up so that I could put items such as diapers, children's clothes, and baby food in the cars where they would be close at hand.

Momma said, "I'll drive the U-Haul truck, and you and the kids go in my car Grace." She hadn't been able to find a house for us to rent that would meet our needs yet, so I would be moving in with Colleen until we could find something suitable for all of us.

By mid Sunday morning we had everything loaded up, and we all went about the business of giving the house a final cleaning. I wanted to make sure that everything was left in shipshape so that I would be sure to get the security deposit back. By one o'clock we had everything done and were ready to leave. I called the landlady to ask her if she could come over and inspect the house. I wanted to make sure that she had no complaints. She only lived three doors down, so she was there in just a few minutes. She was pleased with the condition I was leaving the house in, and she even gave me the check for the security deposit and the last month's rent we hadn't used right on the spot.

There was just one more thing I had to do before leaving. I had to call Daddy and let him know what was going on. I dreaded doing this, but it had to be done. I couldn't put it off any longer. I went to the cooler and grabbed a beer, hoping that would calm my nerves. I lit a cigarette and picked up the phone, which wasn't going to be disconnected until the next day.

I dialed his number, hoping that he would be the one to answer, not Ellen, even though she and I had been getting along very well ever since I had gotten married and moved out of the house. Nora answered the phone. It was hard to believe that she was ten years old now.

"Hi Nora. How are you doing? It seems like I haven't seen you in so long." We talked for a few minutes, and I asked her, "Is Daddy home?"

"He's working out in the yard" she said, "but I'll go get him for you."

My heart was pounding harder with every second that passed.. I took a big gulp of beer and lit another cigarette. It seemed like it was taking an eternity, but Daddy finally picked up the phone.

After the usual pleasantries had been exchanged I took a deep breath, and commenced to tell him everything.

"Daddy, I'm sorry to spring this on you like this, but Trevor and I have split up. The kids and I are moving in with Colleen."

"Is this just a temporary separation?"

"No it isn't. We've been having problems for a long time now. We've sat down time and again and tried to work things out. Afterward everything seems to be okay for a while, but before long we're right back with the same problems. Its' finally gotten to the point where we both know our marriage just isn't going to work. We're able to part under fairly friendly terms, and I'm glad for that because I didn't think we were going to be able to because I had so much resentment building up inside of me. I had gotten to the point where I was beginning to feel a lot of bitterness toward him."

"Basically, these are the problems. He spends money we don't have by going out to the bars after work. Consequently, checks are bouncing left and right. I dread picking up the phone for fear it will be a bill collector, and it usually is. It's usually after midnight when he comes home, and the kids and I are already asleep. I'm stuck here without a car, and I have no money to go anywhere even if I did. I think the children and I deserve better than this, and I'm not changing my mind. I refuse to live this way anymore."

"When are you moving?"

"I've got everything packed up and loaded in a U-Haul truck. I'm moving today. I'm sorry that I didn't let you know before. I know I should have, but even though the problems have been going on for a long time, things reached the boiling point about two weeks ago. That's when I decided I had to get out of here. I just didn't know how I was going to do it. Ironically, that's when Colleen told me that Catherine was moving out, and I decided that the children and I would move in with her. I didn't want you to worry, and I didn't know how to tell you."

"Why not? I had no inkling all this was going on Why didn't you tell me? Does your mother know about this?"

"Yes, in fact she and Colleen came up this weekend to help me get everything packed up and loaded in the U-Haul. They're waiting on me. Momma's going to drive the U-Haul, and I'm driving with the kids in her car. Listen, I don't mean to cut you short Daddy, but we really need to get going. I want to get everything out of the U-Haul before it gets dark"

"Call me when you get here, and I'll come over and help you unload. It's a hell of a thing to hear about right out of the blue like this.

I wish you had said something before Grace. I don't know why I've been the last to know. All of this has been transpiring, and you couldn't even pick up the phone and call me?"

"I'm sorry Daddy, please don't be angry. There was really nothing you could have done about it. I kept hoping that things would get better between us, but we're just too different. Our objectives in life are not the same. He doesn't want to be an active part in me and the children's lives. If you like, we can talk more about this later, but I need to get going."

"Okay, I'll see you in a little bit."

"I love you Daddy."

"I love you too sweetheart."

With that we hung up. I just needed to stand there for a minute or two. I was shaking. I had known the conversation wasn't going to be an easy one, but that had been a lot harder than even I had anticipated. I took a few deep breaths, and was out the door and on the road.

I knew as well as I knew my own name that my marriage to Trevor could never have been a happy union for either one of us, and I felt certain that leaving was the right decision. Even so, I still felt incredibly sad that it had come to be so.

CHAPTER 27

▼

WHAT NEXT

The drive to Ocean Shores was a long one, not literally, it just seemed that way. The tears ran down my face all the way there, and the kids were both tired and fussy. Driving was difficult because of the tears. I might as well have been driving through a heavy rainstorm.

Although I did feel sad about the breakup of my marriage, I also felt relieved to be leaving the misery of it behind me. That wasn't the entire reason that I was crying. I was crying, in part because I was scared to death. The realization that I was actually going through with my plan hit me like a streak of lightening, and brought cold hard reality crashing down on me like a ton of bricks. Here I was embarking on a life as a single mother, I had no job, no car, and very little money. Those were the facts, and they jolted me very quickly into a full blown panic attack.

On top of all that, I was both mentally and physically exhausted. What I really wished was that I could crawl into bed and pull the covers over my head. I would have liked to be able to stay there indefinitely, without any interruptions or responsibilities.

I was snapped out of my muse when all of a sudden a big ruckus broke out in the back seat. Abby had dropped her "blankie" that still trailed along behind her most of the time, Joey had lost his pacifier, and at the moment we were all three driving down the highway crying in unison.

The first chance I got to pull over I was going to stop and try to get the kids re-situated and calmed down. I put my blinker on so Momma and Colleen would know that I was stopping. I took the opportunity to change Joey's diaper, and while Momma kept an eye on Joey I took Abby to the restroom. That started another round of crying because I wouldn't let Abby drag her blanket along with us, and she didn't want to go to the potty, but she was in her training pants and I didn't want her to have an accident in Momma's car.

After I made sure Joey had his pacifier and Abby had her blanket, I took a few deep breaths to calm myself and we were back on the road again. Once I was back in the car, I just kept telling myself, "okay Grace, you can do this. Everything is going to be fine." I kept repeating the words over and over to myself as fast as I could. I thought if I could keep saying the words fast enough, it wouldn't leave any time lapse for negative thoughts to permeate my brain.

By the time we got to Colleen's apartment, (and my new home) both kids were asleep. The first thing we did was to setup sleeping pallets for them on the floor in Colleen's bedroom. We put them in her room because that would be the quietest room in the apartment during our unloading of the U-Haul.

The next thing I did was to call Daddy and let him know that we were here, and ready to start unloading the U-Haul truck. I was really hoping that Ellen wouldn't be coming over with him. I just hoped that his common sense would prevail as far as that was concerned, and it did. He and Nora arrived about thirty minutes later.

I was feeling a little apprehensive as I watched Daddy approach the door. I felt like a little girl who thought she might be in trouble, and was afraid that she was going to get a lecture from her Daddy for some wrongful behavior. I tried to brace myself for whatever the situation called for. I hoped he wasn't going to start asking me a bunch of questions about everything. I just didn't feel like talking about it right then. He must have sensed that because after giving me a big hug, we just went about the business of getting everything unloaded.

I wasn't quite as lucky when it came to Nora's inquisitiveness though. "Why are you moving in with Colleen, Grace? Where is Trevor going to live?"

"Right now I'm really tired Nora, and busy with getting everything unloaded. I promise you that one day soon we'll sit down and talk about it. Okay?"

That seemed to satisfy her for now, and she started helping with the unloading by bringing in some of the smaller items. She was a tremendous help when the kids woke up. After I changed Joey's diaper and took Abby to the potty, she pretty much took over taking care of them and keeping them occupied.

Momma went to Burger King and got food for everyone, Nora fed Joey his baby food, and by the time Momma got back everything was unloaded. We ate, got Joey's crib and my bed setup, and decided to call it a day. Everyone was exhausted by then. At least the next day was Sunday and no one had to go to work.

"Thank you Daddy and Nora for coming over and helping so much. We'd probably still be unloading if it wasn't for you." I said as I walked with them to the car. They both gave me a big hug and then they were gone.

When I got back to the apartment, Momma was getting ready to leave. "I'll come back tomorrow and help you unpack some of these boxes and get things put away." she said.

"Thank you for everything you've done. I love you." I said as she went out the door.

"Love you too hon." she said looking back over her shoulder.

After everyone was gone and the kids were in bed asleep, Colleen and I grabbed a couple of beers out of the refrigerator, and plopped down on the couch. My furniture fit well in the apartment, and with the exception of a few boxes that still needed to be unpacked, everything was pretty much in order. Although I was worn out by the day's events, I felt more relaxed than I had in many a moon, and it felt great.

Colleen and I sat up and talked for several hours. We talked about a lot of different things, but mostly about ideas for getting my life as a single parent on track. We went over different scenarios.

"The first thing I need to do is find a job. Do you get the paper?" I asked Colleen.

"Yea, in fact I think I've still got today's, but it might be kind of icky because I knew I wasn't going to have time to read it, and I threw it in the trash. I'll go get it if it's not too messed up." she said as she headed for the kitchen garbage can. "It's in good shape Grace. Do you want another beer while I'm up?"

"Are you gonna have one? If you're having one, I'll have one too." I answered back. "I think I'll come in there and sit at the table. It'll be easier to spread everything out in there. Where can I find a pen to mark the ads I want to check into?"

"I'll sit in here with you, and while you check out the classifieds, I'll read the paper. I've got a pen in here you can use."

"Okay, I'm gonna check on the kids first. I'll be there in a minute." I told her as I headed down the hall. They're sleeping just like the babies they are." I said as I sat down at the table.

"Now, let me see here, are there any great jobs available for someone that has no particular training, except for changing baby diapers, wiping runny noses, cleaning spit-up from the drooling mouths of babies, has little to no experience, but needs to make a lot of money. Nope, I'm not coming across any jobs like that."

We both chuckled, but inside I could feel a butterfly or two in my stomach.

"Right now I'm just looking for just about any kind of job I can get." I said. "Any port in the storm so to speak. It would be good if I could get something close by, a job that I could walk to, or something that I could get to by taking the bus."

"If you can't, maybe we could work it out to where either you take me to work, or vice versa until you can get a car." Colleen said.

"Thank you little sister;for everything." I said reaching across the table to pat her hand.

"You're welcome." she replied with a smile on her face. I think she was trying to keep everything lighthearted. She didn't want me to get too serious or worried.

"No really Colleen, I mean that from the bottom of my heart."

"I know you do," she said, "but you would do the same for me if I needed help. That's what sisters do. Just don't get discouraged. You can't work everything out in one day, but you'll see, everything will fall into place."

"I know you're right. It's just that I've got three priorities that do need to be worked out, maybe not in one day, but quickly. I've got to find a babysitter, get a job, and work out the transportation issue. There's just so much to think about, and so much to do, but you're right, it will all work out.."

"And you know what else Colleen?"

"What?"

"I don't feel scared or worried anymore. I feel at peace, and even a little excited about the challenge. I'm ready to see what this new chapter in my life will be like, and you know what else Colleen?"

"What Grace?"

"I feel the presence of the Holy Spirit is with me, and I feel so comforted by it. I know that God will see me through this maze of confusion and uncertainty, and that means so much to me. I'm so grateful for that."

When I finally crawled into bed that night, I felt very positive about the future. As I laid there random thoughts would meander through my mind. Things like, I don't have to worry about where Trevor is tonight because I don't care, and tomorrow when the phone rings, I won't have to worry that it will probably be a bill collector. Then I would realize that I had a big smile on my face, and I felt so blessed by all the love that surrounded me. I slept so good that night.

The next morning it was such a pleasure to get up and not have to deal with the feelings of resentment that had been such a prevalent part of my mornings with Trevor. Instead I woke up to a household where everyone was feeling happy and energetic. Momma came over about eight-thirty. I fixed cheese omelets for everyone, except Joey, who was happy with his squashed bananas and baby food egg yolks. Yuk!

After we finished eating and cleaning up the kitchen, we sat around the table talking about future plans, and just enjoying each others' company. There was so little unpacking left to do that none of us felt under any pressure to get it done.

Colleen and I filled Momma in on the things we had talked about last night, and Momma said, "I think I'll go pick up a Sunday paper. We can look in the Help Wanted Ads. They'll be new ones in it since it's the beginning of the week, and we can also see if there are any houses for rent."

While Momma was gone, the phone rang. It was Ellen. "Hi Grace. I just wanted to let you know that if you need for me to babysit while you look for a job, I'll be happy to do so."

"Thank you Ellen. I was wondering how I was going to handle that. I don't think a prospective employer would look too favorably about hiring me if I showed up at the interview lugging an almost three year old and an infant along with me."

We both laughed, and Ellen said, "I think you've got that right."

"But it would be a good way to show how much experience I have." I said. "I could show what a whiz I am at changing dirty diapers and cleaning spit-up off the furniture. Maybe he would even hold Joey and play with Abby while I do it." Again we laughed.

"Well you could be right about that, but I would advise you not to chance it." Ellen said.

"Seriously though Ellen, I really do appreciate your offer. It's a big load off my mind not to have that concern, and to know that they will be in good hands."

We talked for a few more minutes, and I told her briefly why I had left Trevor.

She surprised me when she said, "It sounds like you made the right decision."

After we hung up I told Colleen about our conversation. I really thought that it was a very nice gesture on Ellen's part. I felt a sincere sense of gratitude, and a new sense of appreciation toward her. I had never expected that from her. If anything, I had expected her to gloat over the failure of my marriage. It taught me a lesson about automatically making assumptions about others. People could, and did change.

When Momma got back with the Sunday paper we started looking through the classified section. Colleen was playing with the kids. I don't think she realized how big of a help that was to me. I felt such a rush of love for my family wash over me. I felt so fortunate to have them.

The paper was full of Help Wanted ads. Looking at all the different categories of employment that were listed, made me realize how few I was qualified for. That set off an alarm system in my head. I could feel a panic attack trying to invade my psyche. I had never planned on being the breadwinner for my family.

There were, however a few that I planned on checking into. One was at a doctor's office for the position of receptionist, and the other one was for a position for a saleslady in an upscale women's clothing store in downtown Ocean Shores.

"You can use my car tomorrow if you want to go job hunting. You can drop me off at work and have the use of the car for the rest of the day." Colleen said.

"Thanks Colleen, but I think I'll finish the unpacking and just try to get my bearings before venturing out to look for a job right away."

Now that I was facing the fact that I was going to have to leave my children with a babysitter, I was feeling reluctant to do so, but I knew that I had no other choice. I only hoped that I could find someone that I would feel completely comfortable leaving them with. In the meantime I had Ellen as a backup until I could find someone on a more permanent basis.

My plan was to call the doctor's office and set up a time for an interview. I had decided not to pursue the saleslady position because I knew that I would be tempted to spend too much of my paycheck on clothes. Another reason that I liked the possibility of working at the doctor's office was because it wasn't too far from the apartment, and I could catch a city bus just down the street that would take me right to the front door..

The next morning, as soon as I got the children fed and settled, I called the doctor's office and set up an appointment to come in the next day for an interview, then I called Ellen to see if she would be available for me to bring the kids over while I went on the interview.

Ellen told me, "I am available, and if you get the job I'll babysit until you can find someone suitable on a more permanent basis."

Was this the same Ellen who had caused me so much grief just a few short years ago? She seemed to have metamorphosed into this really nice person who was a stranger to me, but the more I got to know her, the more I liked her.

The kids were happy for the moment. Abby was watching Captain Kangaroo, and Joey was in his swing looking like he was about to doze off. I was glad they weren't fussing. I don't think I could have handled it at the moment. My nerves felt very fragile. I could tell that if I didn't get a grip, I would probably have a full-blown panic attack.

My mind was in a whirl again, and sometimes I felt like I was losing it. These episodes would just come on me with no warning, and stop me in my tracks, like a deer caught in headlights. Sometimes I knew what brought them on, and sometimes they seemed to hit me for no apparent reason. This particular one, I believe, was brought on because I was feeling overwhelmed with uncertainty about the road that lay ahead of me, and I started to doubt myself, afraid that I might have made the wrong decision about leaving Trevor.

Even though it was only ten-thirty in the morning, I felt like I needed a beer to calm my nerves. I went to the refrigerator and was very happy to see that there were four beers left. I grabbed one and sat down at the kitchen table. I guzzled about half of it down in one gulp. Then, the fact that I was drinking a beer at ten-thirty in the morning made me start to fret because I was doing so at such an early hour of the day. I sat there and chastised myself for a good fifteen minutes, all the while still wolfing down the beer. After I finished drinking it I felt a little calmer. By this time I had finished chastising myself, so I went and grabbed another beer. I figured if one had helped, just think how much two would. Okay, this was much better.

The kids were still being good. Abby was now watching Mr. Rogers, and Joey had fallen asleep in his swing. I finished my second beer and was feeling much better. "Okay" I said to myself, "you can do this." I grabbed a tablet I had found in the "junk" drawer, and scrambled through the drawer looking for a pen. "Okay" I said to myself again, "let's get going on a plan of action."

Making lists had always worked well for me, so I started making a list of everything that I had to do for "Phase One" of my new life.

> List of Things To Do
> Phase One
> 1. Find a job
> 2. Find a permanent babysitter that will come here
> 3. Get a car

That was as far as I got, but that was okay. I wasn't ready for "Phase Two" yet. Why boggle my mind with clutter that I didn't need to deal with right now? All that would do would cloud my mind with unnecessary stress. Looking at my list made me feel much calmer because I could see that I had already made progress on the first two items. I was going for an interview the next day, and arrangements for the children had been taken care of—even if it was only temporary.

By the time Colleen got home from work I was feeling happy as a lark, and very much in control of things. That is until Colleen said,

"You really should think about getting a lawyer and filing for a legal separation. You need to see about that right away so that Trevor will be legally obligated to pay child support."

That's when "Phase Two" started working its' way into my brain, and I could see another panic attack looming just over the horizon.

CHAPTER 28

▼

REALITY CHECK

Okay everybody, rise and shine! This is how my day started. I got up with the kids at six-thirty. Then, hurry, hurry, hurry. I got them fed and dressed by seven-thirty so I could drive Colleen to work. She had to be there by eight o'clock. From there I dropped the kids off at Daddy and Ellen's house, and rushed back home to get dressed for my interview which was scheduled for ten o'clock. I was really glad that I'd had the foresight to pick out what I was going to wear the night before. Otherwise I never would have made it. This new routine was going to take some getting use to. I wasn't use to all this scrambling around first thing in the morning, and neither were the kids.

As I gave myself one last check in the mirror before leaving, I was glad that at least I wasn't having a bad hair day. In fact, I was quite pleased with the way I looked. I thought I looked very professional. I had borrowed a short-sleeved, pale aqua two-piece suit from Colleen. It was lucky that she and I wore the same size clothes because I didn't have many interview appropriate attire in my wardrobe at the present time.

The location of the doctor's office certainly would be convenient, I thought to myself as I pulled into the parking lot about five minutes later. I could even walk to work if need be. The office is in a nice building, I observed as I walked in the front door. I located the building directory and looked for Dr. Tranzen's office location. That's when I found out that he was a pediatrician. This is getting better by the minute, I thought. This could really be a lucky break for me if I got the job. Maybe I could even get free medical care for my children, or at the very least a discount. That would be a tremendous help. I was certainly going to do my best to get this job.

I got off the elevator and walked into a very nice waiting room. It was filled with mothers and their children waiting to see the doctor. I walked up to the check-in window to introduce myself. "Hi, I'm Grace O'Brien. I have a ten o'clock interview with Dr. Tranzen for the receptionist position."

The woman I spoke with looked to be in her late twenties. "Oh yes." she said very pleasantly, as she came around and opened the door for me. "Come on in." She took me down the hall to the doctor's office. "Dr. Tranzen will be with you shortly." she said as she turned around to leave.

After about ten minutes Dr. Tranzen walked in the door. He was young and very good looking. He shook my hand and said, "Good morning, I'm Dr. Tranzen."

"It's very nice to meet you, I'm Grace O'Brien."

He sat down and asked, "What kind of experience have you had Miss O'Brien?"

"The only work experience I have is working as a saleslady at an upscale women's clothing store. My husband and I have recently separated, and up until now I haven't worked. I have two small children who have, believe me, given me plenty of experience. I'm a fast learner and I'm very dependable.

"Unfortunately," he said, "I need someone with experience in taking medical dictation, and who can transcribe medical records and reports. I need someone who is familiar with medical terminology that already has experience. I'm sorry, but your experience just doesn't meet those qualifications. Thank you for coming in, and I wish you luck in finding a job."

With that said we both stood up and the interview was over. I felt disheartened as I left. I had really wanted that job, but I vowed not to let myself be so easily discouraged. Instead of going to pickup Abby and Joey right away, I decided to go back to the apartment and look through the Help Wanted ads again.

On my way back to the apartment I happened to pass a cute little restaurant with a Help Wanted sign in the window. I decided to stop and check it out. It turned out to be a good time to stop because it was between breakfast and lunch, and there weren't very many customers inside.

A waitress that looked like she was about my age picked up a menu and started to seat me. "No, I'm not here to eat." I said. "I saw your Help Wanted sign in the window, and I would like to apply for the job."

"Oh, okay. The boss isn't in right now, but I can give you an application to fill out. You can sit right here and fill it out if you want to, and I'll make sure he gets it when he comes in."

I quickly filled out the application and left it with the waitress. Oh well, back to the drawing board, I said to myself. Things just didn't seem to be going too well for me today.

As soon as I got back to the apartment the phone started ringing. It was the man from the restaurant. He wanted to know if I could come in for an interview later on that afternoon. "It's too close to lunchtime right now, and we'll be getting busy. Can you come in about two o'clock?"

"Yes, I sure can." I said. Alright! Maybe things were looking up. I wasn't really that gung ho about working in a restaurant, but considering what my qualifications were, I really couldn't expect to get the great job I had anticipated I would find. Reality was giving me a rude awakening. I was getting a big dose of it too.

Since I had about two hours to kill before my appointment, I decided to kick off my shoes and sit back and relax for awhile. I tried to sit back and do nothing, but it isn't in my nature. It makes me nervous. The harder I tried to just sit there, the more nervous I became. Maybe a beer would calm my nerves. I know! I shouldn't have a beer right now. After all I have a job interview to go to, but I didn't have to be there for another hour and a half. What could it hurt? Any effects it might have on me would be gone by then anyway. So what's the big deal, I asked myself.

Having justified that to myself, I felt more relaxed already. I got up and did a little dance over to the refrigerator, grabbed a nice cold beer, and lit a cigarette. Ah! This was much better than just sitting there and making myself be still.

I thought I better call Ellen and let her know what was happening. I didn't want her to get mad at me. The line was busy. I waited five minutes and called back. She picked up on the third ring. "Hello."

"Hi Ellen. I just wanted to call and let you know what's happening."

"Oh, how did your interview go? Did you get the job?"

"No, the doctor wanted someone who is familiar with medical terminology, someone who can take dictation and transcribe medical reports. I was disappointed that I didn't get it, especially after I learned that he is a pediatrician. It would have been great. I was thinking that maybe I would get free medical care for the kids, or at least a discount."

"Yes, that would have been good. I'm sorry, but don't get discouraged. After all, that was your very first interview."

"I know. How are the kids? I hope they're being good for you."

"Oh yes, they are being little angels. Right now we're eating lunch."

"I'm glad they're being good for you. I really appreciate you watching them for me. In fact I don't know what I would have done if you hadn't offered to keep them for me. That's mainly why I'm calling. After I left the doctor's office, I happened to see a Help Wanted sign in the window of this really cute restaurant, and so I decided to go in and apply for the job. It's for the position of a waitress, which I'm not exactly wild about, and I have no experience, but at least it's a job until I can find something better. At least I will have some money coming in, you know. Anyway, to make a long story short, when I went in to apply the boss wasn't there, but the waitress gave me an application to fill out."

"When I left, I was going to come and pick up the kids, but I decided to come home and change my clothes first. Well, I hadn't been home more than five minutes when the phone rang. It was the owner of the restaurant, and he wanted to know if I could come in for an interview at two o'clock. He said the lunch hour rush would be over by then. Anyway, I was wondering if you could watch the kids until after I go for this interview."

"Absolutely, like I said, they're being really good. I'm actually enjoying looking after them. I really get a kick out of Abby. She has so much to say, and Joey mostly just grins. Should I put them down for a nap since you'll be awhile?"

"Yes please do. They get cranky if they miss their naps."

"Okay, so don't worry, just go for the interview and don't worry about a thing."

"Thank you Ellen. Wish me luck ."

"Good luck Grace. I'll keep my fingers crossed for you. Bye."

After we hung up I decided to turn on the T.V. and watch my favorite soap opera, "As The World Turns." I still had forty-five minutes to spare before I had to leave for my interview. When the T.V. came on Lisa and Bob were having marital problems again. I wished that they would get their problems worked out. That may sound silly, but if you've ever been a soap opera fan, you are bound to understand how you really get to where you take the story to heart, like the characters are real people that you know. I had to laugh at myself because I realized that my own life was pretty much a soap opera, in and of its' self.

Finally it came time for me to go to my interview. I was glad because I was more than ready to get it over with. It had been a long day and I missed my children. It only took about four minutes to drive over to the restaurant. I could easily walk to and from work, I thought to myself. The name of the restaurant was "Gabby's." Under the sign was a smaller sign that said, "Where You Are Always Welcome To Come In And Gab With Us." I liked that. It sounded like a friendly place.

As I walked in I took more notice of the place. It was really cute. There were a lot of hanging baskets with beautiful plants hanging down, and the tables were set up in a way that gave it a casual, yet intimate atmosphere. There was a lot of folk art (which I'm a big fan of) on the walls. It was a cozy and welcoming atmosphere. Yea, I thought, I could be happy working here.

The same waitress that had given me the application was still there, and she greeted me with a warm and friendly smile. "The owner, whose name is Ted, is in his office." she said as she led me down the hall to it. The door was open, but she lightly knocked before we went in.

"Ted, this is Grace O'Brien. Grace this is Ted Gablonsky." We shook hands, and the waitress turned and left.

Ted appeared to be about thirty years old with sandy brown hair, and the greenest eyes I had ever seen. He motioned for me to sit down, and then he asked me to tell him a little bit about myself.

"I was born and raised in Ocean Shores. I just recently moved back here from Delray Beach because my husband and I are getting a divorce, and I wanted to be closer to my family. I have two small children, a little girl named Abby, who just turned three, and a baby boy whose name is Joey. Joey is almost eight months old."

I dreaded the part of the interview when I knew he would start asking me about my job experience, but to my surprise, he didn't seem to care that I didn't have any. He simply said, "I'm sure you'll catch on fast."

He went on to say, "We're only open for breakfast and lunch. Your hours would be from 7:00 A.M. until 3:00 P.M. five days a week. We're closed on Sunday, and your other day off would be on Wednesdays. If you would like the job, it's yours."

"We have a good breakfast and lunch crowd. The other waitresses average about twenty dollars a day in tips, and I pay seventy-five cents an hour.

Doing some quick math in my head, I figured I would make about twenty-six dollars a day, which would give me about one hundred and thirty dollars a week. I felt like I could make it on that.

"The waitresses wear beige bermuda shorts with a red T-shirt, and white shoes like nurses wear. You'll also need a red apron with pockets in it for your tips. If you want the job you can start tomorrow." he said.

"I definitely want the job." I said. "But, could I possibly start the day after tomorrow? I already have a pair of beige bermuda shorts, but I'll have to go shopping for the other items."

He said, "The day after tomorrow will be fine. Thanks for coming in, and I look forward to working with you. Do you have any further questions?"

"No, I can't think of anything." I said. With that, we shook hands again, and I left his office. I was so happy to have a job that I felt like I was floating on air.

I still had a couple of hours left before it was time to pick up Colleen, so I decided to go on over to Daddy and Ellen's house to pick up the kids. The children were still napping when I got there so I stayed and visited with Nora and Ellen for a while. Ellen was happy for me when I told her I had gotten the job, and she reassured me that she would continue to watch Abby and Joey until I could find someone else. I couldn't get over how much nicer our relationship had become. That made me happy. It just made it so much nicer all the way around, not just for me, but for all of us.

Abby woke up about forty-five minutes after I got there. She was so glad to see me. She ran to me as fast as she could shouting, "Mommy,

Mommy!" Her shouting woke Joey up, but that was okay. It was almost time for me to go pick up Colleen anyway. I went in to pick up Joey, and as soon as he saw me he started grinning and moving his little arms and legs, eager for me to pick him up. The love I felt for my children was so intense that it brought tears to my eyes.

CHAPTER 29

▼

LEARNING THE ROPES

The following day I took Colleen to work again so that I would have the use of the car to go shopping. By the time that I paid for the shoes, a couple of red T-shirts, a couple of aprons, and another pair of beige bermuda shorts, I was glad that I had a job to go to the next day. The aprons and the T-shirts were cheap, but the shoes were expensive.

I would be okay though. I had given Colleen my share of the rent for the month, filled her car up with gas, and bought enough groceries to last us for at least a week. After paying for the things I needed for work, I figured that I had about a hundred dollars left out of the two hundred and seventy I had started out with.

I decided to stop by the bank and open a checking account. I deposited eighty-five dollars, and decided that it would be used for my "get a car" fund." I wanted to get my own car as soon as possible. In the meantime, Colleen assured me that we would work it out using hers. She seemed to be thrilled that we had moved in with her, and she made the children and I feel very welcome and very loved.

It was so nice living with Colleen, so different than my life with Trevor. It was so pleasant to have a grown-up to have dinner with, and someone to laugh and talk with. With Trevor, I had been alone most nights. It was wonderful not to have to go to sleep at night wondering where my husband was, and when he would be home.

Since tomorrow was going to be my first day on the job, I wanted to go to bed early so I would be well rested. I had to be at work at seven.

Colleen said, "Until you can get your own car, or find someone to come to the apartment to babysit, I'll take the kids over to Daddy and Ellen's in the mornings and pick them up on my way home from work. Just feed them and get them dressed and ready to go before you leave."

"I don't know what I would do without you Colleen. Thank you so much for everything." I said as I gave her a big hug, and tears started to well up in my eyes.

She gave me a quick hug and said, "Go to bed before you start getting all teary on me. Everything is going to be just fine."

I set the alarm for five o'clock. I figured that would give me enough time to get dressed and put my make-up on before the kids woke up. Then I could fix breakfast for Abby and feed Joey, and still have time to get them dressed. I planned to leave the house at six-thirty. It would only take me about ten minutes to walk to the restaurant. I wanted to get there a little early so I would have a little time to get my bearings.

Nothing could have prepared me for the scurrying around it took for me to actually implement my plan the next morning. Sure enough, the alarm clock went off at precisely five o'clock, but I wasn't the only one that it woke up. It woke Joey up too. I picked him up as quickly as I could because I didn't want him to wake Abby up. No such luck, she woke up too.

None of us were use to getting up so early, and consequently that made the three of us very grumpy and ill-humored. Was that Colleen I heard grumbling in the background? Yes, that was her staggering down the hall rubbing her eyes, and looking very unhappy.

I took one look at her and figured it was best for me not to say anything. Instead I busied myself getting the kids fed. As soon as I got Joey fed, I put him in his walker and dashed down the hall to the bathroom to put on my make-up. I left Abby at the table where she was still eating her breakfast.

Colleen had laid down on the couch with her pillow over her head trying to block out our noise and catch a few more Z's. She wasn't having much luck though because Joey had rolled his walker over to the couch where he was currently trying to pull the pillow off of her head, all the while talking his baby talk to her. I pretended to be oblivious to it all. What else could I do, I had to get ready for work. That was working for me until I heard Colleen let out a big loud noise of exasperation. After hearing that I couldn't ignore it any longer. I went and got Joey and brought him in the bathroom with me.

Joey, however, didn't like being shut in that little room. He started screaming and banging on the door with his little hands. All I could do was, to the best of my ability, try to pretend that this wasn't happening, and finish putting on my makeup and fixing my hair. The hair part was easy because since my hair was long, I was required to wear it pulled up at work.

Meanwhile, Abby had finished her breakfast and was banging on the other side of the bathroom door, where she was screaming for me to let her in. At that point I was praying that this madness wasn't an example of what our mornings to come were going to be like, because if it was, I had serious doubts about maintaining my sanity in the days to come.

I took a deep breath, and said to myself, "okay, you can do this." With that, I opened the bathroom door, ran down the hall, and grabbed the clothes the kids were going to wear over to Daddy and Ellen's. That started a whole new temper tantrum with Abby. She was at the age where she had established her own opinion about what she wanted to wear, and the outfit she picked out was just too outrageous to even consider. She wanted to wear a white shirt with purple polka dots with plaid shorts that had an array of colors, none of which matched the white with purple polka dotted shirt. Furthermore, she wanted to wear about ten different colored barrettes in her hair, and her bunny rabbit house slippers as her shoes. Thank goodness Joey didn't care what I put on him.

By now Colleen had given up on trying to block out the commotion, and had come to my rescue. While I got the diaper bag packed she dealt with Abby's meltdown. By the time I closed the apartment door behind me, I felt like I had already done a hard day at work.

During my short walk to work I tried to release the stress that had welled-up in me, but as soon as I was able to let that go, I started stressing out about what possible horrors might be lying in wait for me at my new job. Needless to say, I was feeling quite apprehensive as I walked into Gabby's, and I was seriously fighting the impulse to just turn around and bolt.

I got to Gabby's about fifteen minutes before it was time to open, and the same girl that had been there the other day unlocked the door and let me in. She had a nice friendly smile and I liked her right away.

She said, "I don't believe I introduced myself the other day. My name is Elaine, and I know your name is Grace. I'll try to help you as much as I can today. Why don't you take this menu and go sit down and try to familiarize yourself with it. Starting out you will only have two tables to wait on, and depending on how fast you catch on, you'll get more tables. Here's a check book to write the orders on."

I barely had time to look at anything before it was time to open the doors for business. There was a steady stream of customers for breakfast. I was really glad that I was only responsible for two tables. That was a huge relief to me because I was finding the job to be very nerve-wracking. The majority of customers seemed to be regulars and they told me what they wanted very quickly.

One of the trickiest things I had to learn was how to balance the food on the serving trays. By the time breakfast was over I had let two cups of coffee slide off the tray and onto the floor. The cups and saucers had broken on impact with the floor, but the coffee managed to spill all over my clothes on its' way down. I had given several orders of scrambled eggs to people that had ordered their eggs over-easy, and pancakes to people that had ordered toast, etc., but somehow it all got straightened out in the end.

Most everyone knew that I was a new employee and was very forgiving of my ineptitude. For the most part everyone was really nice and friendly. There was only one real grouchy couple that had gotten mad at me for not refilling their coffee cups often enough. Consequently they left me no tip, which I was told that in restaurant lingo meant that they had "stiffed" me.

For some reason lunch went much better for me. I didn't spill anything and I didn't make any mistakes with my orders. When I counted my tips I had made thirteen dollars and forty-five cents. I was told that was pretty good considering I had only two tables to take care of. All in all I was feeling pretty darn good about it all. Now, if I could just make it through tomorrow.

CHAPTER 30

▼

GETTING SETTLED

As the weeks turned into months my life settled down. I liked my job. Although I didn't want to be a waitress for the rest of my life, for now it served my purpose well. The hours weren't too bad, it was close to home, and at the end of the day I always had a little money in my pocket.

Trevor and I had now been separated for three months. I had no regrets about my decision to leave him. I did feel lonely sometimes, but it wasn't that I felt lonely for him. I simply just felt like there was a void in my life. I think that was because I never went much of anywhere, other than work, or to the grocery store.

Daddy and Ellen picked me and the children up for church on Sundays. Colleen wasn't attending on a regular basis. Sometimes Momma would come and pick us up afterward, and we would go to the beach, or out to dinner, but for the most part my social life was pretty much non-existent.

Every once in a while my two best friends, Carolyn and Nancy, who were now both married with one child each, would come over and visit me and let the kids play together. Carolyn's little girl Marcy was two months younger than Abby, and they got along really good with each other.

Nancy's little girl Jennifer, was a month older than Joey, and they didn't get along nearly as well as Abby and Marcy did. They were both at the age where they were crawling and pulling themselves up to a standing position. Whatever toy one had, the other one wanted. A lot of screaming went on as a result. They were always messing up what the two bigger girls were playing with as well.

If Abby and Marcy were playing house, the two babies always crawled over their tea sets and dishes, happily turning their setup topsy-turvy, and instigating huge outcries from the girls. By the time they would leave to go home, the apartment looked like a tornado had run through it, but those sorts of things didn't bother me in the least. I was glad to have their company, and glad for the kids to have someone to play with, even if they didn't always get along.

Another reason for my loneliness was because Colleen had started dating a customer she had met at the bank where she worked. His name was Stewart. They had only been dating for a couple of months, but they seemed to be getting serious about each other. Lately she had begun sleeping over at his house quite often.

I don't mean to imply that my life was so lonely and miserable that I just moped around feeling sorry for myself. To the contrary, I was making considerable headway as far as getting my life together for me and the kids. I no longer had to cash in soda bottles in order to buy milk. I didn't have to worry that every time the phone rang it would be a bill collector, and I didn't dread going to the mailbox for fear of another bounced check notice. What bills I had were always paid when they were suppose to be.

Other good things were happening as well. I had met a stay-at-home mother that lived in our apartment complex whose name was Pauline, and she had started babysitting for Abby and Joey. That was a tremendous blessing to me, not only because it was so convenient, but she was such a nice person as well. Abby and Joey loved her and I never had to worry when they were in her care.

There were other good things that were happening too. Daddy had a friend at the Elk's Club (where he was the chaplain) that was a lawyer, and he had agreed to handle my divorce at a discount, pay as you can rate. That was a tremendous blessing and a big load off of my mind.

Now that I was legally separated from Trevor, he was obligated by law to send me child support. Good thing too, because he hadn't been very reliable about sending me money up until then. He was now required to send me one hundred dollars a month.

Not only that, by being very frugal with my money, I now had five hundred and eighty-five dollars in my "get a car" fund. I decided that when I had a thousand dollars saved I was going car shopping. I figured that if I was really careful with my money, I should have that amount in a few more months. I couldn't wait to get a car. I knew that it would make my life a lot happier because I would be able to go where I wanted, when I wanted, without having to depend on anyone else for my transportation. All in all I felt that I was making good progress.

According to our separation agreement, Trevor had visiting rights to have the children every other weekend. He usually chose to pick them up once a month. Although it was nice to have a weekend to myself, I wouldn't have cared if he didn't pick them up at all. The reason being that they always came home looking bedraggled and worn out, usually with runny noses as well.

Trevor's leaving after dropping them off didn't bother Joey, but Abby always cried when he would leave. I would hold her and try to comfort her to no avail. She didn't understand why he didn't stay with us. Finally, out of desperation to try and console her, I decided to try and explain the situation in terms that she, hopefully, would be able to understand.

I told her that Mommy and Daddy loved her and Joey very much. I said, "We will always love you and Joey because you are our sweet and precious little girl, and Joey is our sweet and precious little boy. The reason that we don't live in the same house with Daddy anymore is because Mommy and Daddy don't make each other feel happy, but our love for you and Joey will never change, no matter what."

That seemed to do the trick. She stopped crying immediately, and we never had that problem again. Along with helping Abby, the situation had taught me a good lesson as well. It proved to me that children understand much more than most people give them credit for, and that what upsets them the most, are the things they don't understand and feel helpless to control. It reinforced my feelings that no matter how small the child is, or how petty the situation may seem to an adult, a child's feelings should always be respected and addressed accordingly.

My feelings of loneliness gave me more time to think, and more and more I found myself thinking about Tom. I struggled with trying to erase those thoughts from my mind. I was surprised that I hadn't run into him, or any of his friends that might make mention of him, but I never did.

I thought about him everyday. Thoughts of him crept into my mind unexpectedly and randomly, but always with longing. I struggled with the urge to pick up the phone and call him on a daily basis. Finally, one day while the kids were taking their nap, I had reached my limit of self-control and rationale over the matter. My feelings for him were complicated. I had a hard time understanding why I still felt such strong feelings for the person who had caused such indelible pain in my life. I don't know, but the truth of the matter was that I still felt like I was in love with him.

Colleen was with Stewart. The kids were sleeping, and once again I found myself struggling with the overwhelming urge to pick up the phone and call Tom's Mother's house. To try and distract myself, I turned on the T.V. hoping there would be a good movie on. Finding nothing good on T.V. to watch, I got up and started pacing around the apartment, all the while glancing at the phone as I paced.

I knew there was a bottle of Vodka in the kitchen cabinet and decided to fix myself a drink. I hoped that would relax me and get my mind off of Tom. I fixed myself a screwdriver and went back into the living room where I picked up a magazine that Colleen had left on the coffee table. I thumbed through the pages that had pictures of all the latest women's fashions, but I still couldn't shake thoughts of Tom from my mind. This is ridiculous I thought to myself as I threw the magazine back on the coffee table and started pacing again, all the while sipping on my screwdriver.

I went and checked on the kids. They were still sound asleep. I decided to go back in the living room and curl up with a good novel I was reading, but the pages might just as well have been blank. Even though I was reading the words, I had no idea what I was reading about. That's how preoccupied my mind was with thoughts of Tom. Finally, in exasperation I said to myself, "That's it." Then I lunged for the phone and dialed Tom's number.

Chapter 31

▼

The Call

My hands were trembling as I picked up the phone and dialed Tom's number. I didn't know what to expect. For all I knew he could be married, or he could be living somewhere else. All I knew was at that moment, I couldn't stop myself from picking up the phone. I had tormented myself about this moment for as long as I could. I had no idea who might answer the phone, or what I would say when they did. For all I knew I might panic and hang up without saying anything. The only thing I did know was that I had to make this call come hell or high water.

I didn't know what my true feelings for Tom were at this exact moment. All I knew was that I needed to find out if I still had the feelings for him that I thought I did, or was I just daydreaming about finding romance with him because I was lonely.

His mother picked up the phone on the fourth ring. My heart was pounding in my chest, and for a second or two I couldn't decide whether to say something, or just hang up. I wrestled with that decision for what seemed like a long time, but it was actually only a few seconds. It wasn't until I heard his mother say, "Hello. Hello." for the second time that I managed to open my mouth and speak. I didn't say who I was, I simply asked, "Is Tom there?"

"Yes, just a moment." she said. Then I heard her calling his name and telling him that there was a telephone call for him. As I waited for him to get to the phone, I still didn't know what I was going to say, or if I would just hang up and say nothing. All of these thoughts were racing through my mind. Then suddenly I heard him pick up the phone, and as soon as I heard his voice I knew that I wasn't going to hang up.

"Hello." he said. I would have recognized that voice anywhere. It had an unmistakable sultry baritone pitch to it. I swallowed hard and took a deep breath.

"Hi Tom, it's Grace." For a few heart-stopping moments there was nothing but the sound of silence, and then, "Hi! This is certainly a surprise. How are you?"

Once we both got over the initial shock of actually speaking to each other the conversation went smoothly.

He asked, "Where are you?"

"I'm in Ocean Shores. My husband and I separated a few months ago, and I moved back here to be close to my family."

"Oh, I was away for a while myself. I was in the Army, stationed in Germany for almost two years." he said.

We had only been talking for about five minutes when Joey woke up and started to cry. "Tom I'm sorry, but I'm going to have to go. My little boy just woke up and I need to pick him up before he wakes up my little girl."

He quickly asked, "Can I have your phone number? Would it be okay if I call you?"

I said, "Yes." to both questions, and then he was gone.

After we hung up I sat there in stunned silence for a few moments, and actually pinched my leg real hard to make sure I had actually made the call, and not just dreamed it. Ouch! The pinch brought me back to reality and I quickly ran down the hall to pick up Joey. I needed a moment to compose myself, and not to sound corny, but I really did feel like I was floating on air, in a dreamlike state, fringing on the outskirts of reality.

As I brought Joey into the living room to change his diaper, I felt lighthearted and happy. I was glad that I had finally made the call that I had been wanting to make for so long. It was a relief not to have that inner struggle in me any longer. I had done it, and now just let the chips fall where they may, I thought to myself.

I wanted to shout from the rooftops, "I called him!", but since Joey was the only one around, I shared my happiness with him. He just grinned back at me. At least he didn't say, "No! You shouldn't have done that!", or, "What did you do that for?"

Just as I was wishing that Colleen was here to share this delectable tidbit with, she walked in the door. I shot a big grin at her.

She knew something special was up because she said, "What are you so happy about?"

I didn't answer her right away. I wanted to savor my juicy little tidbit a tad longer, dangle it in front of her like something extremely tempting, but just out of her reach to obtain. I just shrugged and kept on grinning until she started to get mad at my teasing.

When she started to walk away in a huff, I said, "Wait! I'll tell you, I'll tell you! I called Tom!"

Her mouth flew open and her eyes got as big as saucers. I couldn't tell what she was thinking, but I could tell that she was definitely surprised, if not downright shocked about it.

"No, you're kidding aren't you?" she said.

"Nope, I'm not kidding you. I've been wrestling with wanting to call him for some time now, and today was the day I decided to quit wrestling with it."

"I want to hear every single detail" she said, "but first I need a drink, a strong one! Do you want me to fix you one too?"

"Yes mam, I sure do. I think that would be positively apropos for the occasion." I replied, shooting another big grin at her.

When she finished fixing our drinks she came and sat down on the couch with me. "Okay, out with it, and don't leave anything out. Tell me everything you said and everything he said, what you felt and what his response was. Okay now go." she said as she curled up comfortably on the couch, looking like she couldn't wait for me to get on with the story.

"Well, it's like this. I have never felt like I was ever completely over Tom. I've always felt that I still loved him, even when I married Trevor. Maybe that's one reason why our marriage never really worked, and now that I am basically single again, its been even more in the forefront of my mind. I've tried to get him out of my mind, but I can't."

"I've always sensed that you still had feelings for him, and I'm glad that you finally made the call that was pulling at your heartstrings. Why should you torture yourself like that? The worst that could happen would be that he would just hang up on you, or tell you that he never wants to see you again. I'm guessing by the grin on your face that didn't happen." she said, giving me an affectionate pat on the arm.

"No, that didn't happen. He asked me if it would be alright if he called me, and naturally I said yes, so we'll see what happens."

We must have been talking for about an hour when Colleen got up and fixed us both another drink. When she sat back down, she said, "Stewart and I had our first fight this afternoon."

"Why? What happened?" I asked her.

"He's getting too serious, and I'm not ready to be as committed as he wants me to be. He's too controlling, or at least he tries to be. Sometimes it's so bad that I feel like I'm being smothered, and it makes me feel like I can hardly breathe. He wants to take our relationship to the next level, and he wants me to move in with him. I'm not ready for that. I want our relationship to be more open. If I meet someone else that I'm attracted to, I want to feel free to do that, and vice versa for him to feel free to do that as well." she said.

She didn't seem to be very upset about the breakup. I didn't know if that was because she didn't care for him as much as I thought she did, or if she was in denial of her true feelings for fear of getting hurt.

"I'm here for you if you need to talk." I said.

Just as Abby was waking up from her nap, the phone rang. It was Momma. "I was wondering if you all would like to go out to dinner with me, my treat." she said.

"I do. Let me check with Colleen." I said.

We ended up going to Hill's Bar-B-Q Barn for some ribs.

Colleen and I agreed that we wouldn't mention anything about Stewart or Tom to Momma. I don't know what she would have to say as far as Stewart was concerned, but I knew that she would have plenty to say about Tom, and it wouldn't be good.

I knew that I was feeling distracted at dinner because I kept thinking about Tom, but I didn't know that my distraction was so obvious until I felt Colleen kick me under the table. It was then that I heard Momma say, "Grace! What is the matter with you? I've asked you the same question three times."

"Oh, I'm sorry." I said.

After that, I tried my best to pay attention to what was being said, but it wasn't easy. I knew that it was outlandish for me to be acting like a dreamy-eyed teenager, but for the life of me I couldn't help it.

By the time we got back home and I got the kids bathed and in bed, I was feeling exhausted. It had been an emotional day for me and I decided to get ready for bed earlier than usual. Tomorrow was a work day and I had to get up early. I took a quick shower, brushed my teeth, and just as I was about to close my eyes the phone rang. It was Tom.

▼

ONCE AND AGAIN

"Hello."

"Hi Grace, this is Tom. I hope I didn't wake you up."

"No, I was just getting ready for bed." I said, trying to keep my mouth from going dry and my heart from beating out of my chest. Once again I had to pinch myself, but this time I wasn't doing it to make sure that I wasn't dreaming. This time I was trying to keep myself from fainting. In fact, I had to pinch myself really hard twice in order to regain my composure. What is it about this man that makes me so inexorably attracted to him, I wondered to myself, in the split second that it took for that thought to flash through my head.

"I was momentarily in shock when you called me today. You rendered me almost speechless. I didn't think I would ever hear from you, or ever see you again. I knew that you had gotten married because my sister Sharon sent me the wedding announcement from the newspaper. I was in the army at the time, stationed in Germany."

"How long have you been out of the army?" I asked.

"I was drafted in February of nineteen-sixty-five, and I was discharged in February of nineteen-sixty-seven. Listen, I would really like to see you."

"I would like to see you too Tom."

"When can we get together?" he asked.

"You can come over tomorrow night if you want to. I'm sharing an apartment with my sister Colleen. It's on Marlin Drive. Twenty-seven nineteen Marlin Drive, apartment nine."

"When would be a good time?" he asked.

"Well, why don't you come over about eight o'clock. That will give me time to have the kids bathed, fed, in bed, and hopefully asleep." I said.

"Eight it is then." he replied, adding, "I look forward to seeing you Grace."

"I look forward to seeing you too Tom."

With that we said goodnight and hung up the phone. Although I had been sleepy when the phone rang, I sure was wide-awake now. My heart was still pounding, and I was giddy with the excitement of seeing him the next night. There is no way I can lay down and go to sleep now, I thought to myself.

I decided to fix myself a nightcap before turning in. I needed something to calm me down, plus I just wanted to curl up on the couch with a drink and a cigarette, and savor the endless possibilities that tomorrow night might bring. I finished my drink and was still feeling too wound up to go to sleep, so I went back in the kitchen and fixed myself another drink. After this, I have got to go to sleep, I thought to myself. The second drink did the trick. I went to bed and was able to fall asleep quickly.

When I woke up the next morning I wasn't sure if Tom had really called, or if I had just dreamed it. I was still wondering as I stepped into the shower. It wasn't until I went in the kitchen and saw my empty glass from the night before in the sink, that I knew for sure I hadn't dreamed it. Knowing that I was going to see Tom tonight gave me a tremendous rush of energy. I felt like I could take on the world if necessary.

I had just finished getting ready for work when I heard the kids starting to stir. Since I had met Pauline, the stay-at-home mom that was babysitting for me, my mornings were no longer as frantic as they had been when I had first started working. Pauline was truly a blessing. She fed the kids breakfast and got them dressed. All I had to do was take them two doors down from my apartment to her apartment. I paid her forty dollars a week, and it was worth every penny.

After taking Abby and Joey down to Pauline, I decided that I should run in and tell Colleen that Tom was coming over tonight. She was just waking up to get ready for work when I went in. Actually she was just laying in bed enjoying a few more lazy moments before having to get up.

"Colleen, guess who is coming over tonight?" I said.

"Let me guess. Let's see. You're grinning from ear to ear, I heard the phone ring last night, and you are making me guess. It must be non-other than Tom." she said, acting like she had just solved a big mystery.

"You're right Sherlock." I said.

"Since I won't be seeing Stewart tonight, I was just planning on staying home. So if you want me to, I'll babysit Abby and Joey if you and Tom want to go out somewhere." she said.

"Oh, I love you, I love you, I love you Colleen. You're the best sister anyone could ever hope to have." I said, as I danced a lively two-step out of the room.

"Just be careful! Take it slow! Do you hear me Grace?" she hollered from her room.

"I hear you Colleen. I promise I will be careful, and I will take it slow." I said just so she wouldn't worry. Actually I didn't know if I would take it slow or not. "Don't say anything about Tom to Momma or Daddy, okay?" I hollered as I went out the door. I practically skipped to work. I felt so alive, so happy. It felt wonderful to have something to look forward to, and knowing that I would see Tom tonight was just what I felt I needed.

We were very busy all day at work. All of the snow birds and tourists had descended on south Florida for the winter months. I was glad that we were busy because the busier we were the more tips I got. Our regular year-round customers weren't too happy about it though. They didn't like having to wait for a table to become available.

The only thing I didn't like about being so busy was that all the employees were under so much pressure to accommodate everyone in a timely fashion. It made the cooks grumpier and harder to deal with, and our orders were more likely to get messed up. The orders would come up incomplete frequently. For instance, if someone ordered eggs and toast, their eggs would be ready, but their toast wouldn't be. By the time their toast was ready, their eggs would be cold, etc. Cold eggs with warm toast, or warm eggs with no toast did not make our customers happy campers. Consequently, they would not leave us a good tip. If the waitresses complained to the cooks, the cooks would get mad and mess up our orders on purpose. We hardly had time for a bathroom break. It was a nightmare at times.

During the tourist season there were four waitresses on the floor. When I had first started the job it had been the off-season and we had worked at a much slower pace. Then it had just been Elaine and me. I was thankful that I had not had to train for the job during the busy months because it would have been too frantic for me to cope with.

My co-worker Elaine, and I worked well together. If she was real busy and I had a minute to help her I would, and she did the same for me. Elaine and I had become fairly close friends, and I had confided the truth about my past relationship with Tom to her. That is why when I got a free moment at work that day I told her that I had talked to Tom over the weekend, and that he was coming over to see me tonight.

She said, "I noticed a special sparkle in your eyes this morning, and I knew their was something going on, but I couldn't put my finger on it. I'm happy for you because I can see that it makes you happy, but take it slow. I don't want you to get hurt again."

Being so busy that day had made the time go by faster, and before I knew it the clock said it was time for me to go home. As I was leaving Elaine said, "Have a good time tonight, but remember what I told you." I just smiled at her and went out the door.

Elaine was a couple of years older than me, and she and Dinah had been in the same grade. They had never been close friends because they didn't run around with the same crowd. Never-the-less, from time to time Elaine would ask how Dinah was doing. Since Dinah and Vincent were planning a trip to south Florida in a couple of weeks, I decided to invite her over for dinner while they were here.

When I got home I called Pauline and asked her, "Would it be possible for you to watch the kids for about another hour?"

"Sure." she said.

"Thank you Pauline. I'll see you in about an hour." I said.

I wanted to tidy up the apartment and take a shower before going to get them. I was apprehensive, yet excited about seeing Tom. I needed to see him in order to know what my true feelings were for him. I felt like I was still in love with him, but I wasn't sure if those feelings were real, or just some romantic notion that I had convinced myself of. At any rate, I felt the need to know in order to be able to move forward with my life. If there weren't any feelings of love between us then I felt like it would give me closure, rather than continuing to harbor the notion of a possible relationship with him in the future.

One underlying feeling that I don't think I was even consciously aware of at the time, was that I didn't want to feel that I had given up my virginity, and beared a child with a man that didn't love me. It hurt too much to think that after all that had happened, that the heartache, the excruciating and unbearable pain of having to leave my child behind, had all been for naught. That was extremely hard for me to come to terms with.

After tidying up the apartment and deciding what I was going to wear, I went down and got the kids. I wanted to get them fed and bathed early, but when I got back to the apartment Colleen was already home from work.

She said, "Why don't you let me give the kids a bath. I don't want you to have to feel rushed and nervous about getting ready."

I guess I must have seemed a little flustered and nervous because she was being very attentive to me.

"I stopped at the store and picked up a couple bottles of wine, some beer, and some cheese and crackers in case you might want to offer him something to drink and a little snack." she said.

"Do you think we could open one of those bottles of wine now?" I asked. "I feel like I could use a glass to calm my nerves. I feel so nervous Colleen."

She came and gave me a hug, and said, "I know. Just be yourself and everything will be fine. However it turns out, you will survive. So just try and relax, okay? Remember, I'm right down the hall if you need me."

A little before eight o'clock Colleen said, "I'm going to take the kids with me to my room. Don't worry about a thing. I'll see to their every need and keep them amused until they go to sleep."

But, all of a sudden I felt like I didn't want to be all alone out in the living room when Tom came over.

"I'd really rather that you stay out here, you and the kids. I don't know what to expect. It might end up feeling awkward for both of us. Will you stay with me? Please!"

"Of course I will if that's what you want. I just thought that you might like to be alone."

"Thanks Colleen, for everything you do for me. I really don't know what I would do without you, and I mean that from the bottom of my heart. You're a wonderful sister."

Knock! Knock! Oh my gosh that's him! I went to answer the door with a feeling of trepidation. I didn't know what my feelings would be once I opened the door, but I was fixing to find out.

CHAPTER 33

▼

WHAT'S NEXT

I didn't rush to answer the door. In fact, right then I wasn't sure that I wanted to answer it at all. In the first few seconds that followed the knock, the first thought to flash through my mind was this is the man that abandoned me and made me give up my baby. For a few seconds I felt nothing but disdain for him. I turned and looked at Colleen and noticed a bewildered look on her face. I wanted to give her an explanation for my behavior, but for the moment I was unable to move my body or my mouth. I felt like I was frozen in time.

Then the knock came again, and momentarily broke me free from my reverie. Colleen and I gave each other a little nod that said, "It's okay, go ahead." I went to the door and opened it with somewhat of a flourish, making sure to plaster a big smile on my face. It all felt like it was unreal, like I was moving in slow motion while in a trance, an out-of-body experience, having no sense of being propelled forward by my own will. Then there he was, standing there smiling at me, and something stirred in my heart, bringing me back to reality. The hate was gone for now anyway.

"Hi Tom."

"Hi Grace."

"Come in." I said. The surreal feelings had left as suddenly as they had come. I was glad to see him, glad that he was standing in my doorway. "You remember my sister Colleen, and these are my children, Abby and Joey." I said gesturing toward them.

"Of course. Hi Colleen. How are you?" Then looking at my children he said, "Hi, how are you? Your children are very cute." he said with a smile that I could tell was sincere.

We all had a brief moment of feeling awkward, but it disappeared instantaneously into thin air, leaving without a trace, as though it had never even happened. In those first brief moments I knew that I still loved this man.

"Have a seat and make yourself comfortable." I said. "Would you like something to drink? We have either beer or wine, or there might be some vodka in there. I'd have to check on that."

"A beer sounds good." he said.

"Colleen what would you like?" I asked her in a certain way that I knew she would get the signal that I wanted her to stay with us. I wasn't ready to be alone with Tom yet.

I went to the kitchen to get our drinks, feeling the need to get away by myself for a few minutes. My feelings were so intense that I needed to catch my breath. Abby followed me into the kitchen saying, "I thirsty too Mommy. Who that man is Mommy?" I told her that he was a friend. "I don't like him Mommy." she said.

"You don't even know him Abby. It isn't nice to say unkind things. He might hear you, and it would make him feel bad if he heard you say that you don't like him. What would you like to drink? You can have some apple juice or chocolate milk."

"I want chocolate milk."

"Okay, you go back in the living room and I'll bring you some, and Abby I want you to be a good girl and be nice to Mommy's friend, okay?"

"Okay Mommy, I be nice."

I finished getting the drinks and went back to the living room. I had no sooner sat down when Joey started going after Abby's glass of chocolate milk. Luckily Colleen moved fast enough to grab it before he knocked it over, but then he started to scream because she wouldn't let him have it. Oh boy, this is just great, I thought.

I was trying hard not to lose my composure, but it wasn't easy. I went over and picked up Joey, and told Tom, "I'll be right back." and headed for the kitchen to fix Joey a bottle. While I was in there, I said a little silent prayer asking God to help me get through this evening without anymore uncomfortable distractions. Thankfully, the bottle did the trick for Joey and he fell asleep in my arms while drinking it.

Meantime, Abby was sidling her way over to Tom. She crawled up in his lap and said, "You color." He couldn't very well say no, so he started coloring with her. "No, do blue." she said as he was picking up a red crayon. After about an hour of this disruptive activity I was able to get Abby in bed. Joey was still sleeping.

I had no sooner sat down when Abby came back out saying that she was thirsty. That's when Colleen came to my rescue and said, "Come on Abby, I'll get you a drink, and then we'll go in our room and I'll read you a bedtime story."

Now it was just me and Tom. I looked over at him, and was about to ask him if he would like another beer, but all I saw was this huge grin on his face. He was slowly nodding his head from side to side. I asked him, "What are you grinning about?"

"It's just so new and different to see you in this context; to see how you interact with your kids. They're beautiful children."

"Thank you." I said.

After that brief exchange there was a moment of silence between us. I don't know what Tom was thinking, but I know that I was thinking of our precious son. I was wondering where he was and what his circumstances were, and feeling sad, so very sad.

For a moment I felt such bitterness for Tom. I wondered how in the world had my life come to this. How could I have feelings of love for him one minute and feel such contempt for him the next. What kind of a person did that make me? I felt so confused within myself, and I wondered; who am I and what am I doing? Why had I allowed myself to invite him back into my life? Then with the sheer determination of will, for now anyway, I realized I had to shake myself free from this line of thought and just get through tonight. I would try to figure it all out at some later date when I had more time.

I think that Tom must have sensed some of what I was feeling. A few brief moments of reflection passed between us, and then the feeling passed as quickly as it had come. The next thing I knew, we had gravitated into each others' arms and were sharing a tender kiss. I knew our underlying issues were lying in the shadows somewhere, lurking, waiting to leap out and pounce on us, probably when we were least expecting it, but for the moment they were nowhere to be found.

After our kiss ended we talked for a little while, just speaking in generalities. Our kiss had stirred up powerful emotions in me that I had forgotten I had, and I wasn't sure if I was ready for them just yet. I needed some space, some time to digest the feelings that were brimming up inside of me. They were coming to a boil too fast, getting ready to carry me away to a place that I wasn't sure I wanted to go. I felt like I had lost my brakes and was barreling down some highway out of control, headed to some unknown destination that I wasn't sure I wanted to reach.

At that point I put up a wall between us. It felt like natural born instinct to do so because my feelings made me feel very vulnerable. I didn't want to leave myself open to be hurt again. I felt that if I allowed hurt to get in the door it would destroy me. I felt like what I imagine a trapped animal feels like when staring down the barrel of a gun, knowing that death could be imminent. At that moment I wished that Tom was a stranger, not someone I had given my whole heart to, only to be broken into a million pieces.

As I walked with Tom to the door to say goodnight, he asked me, "Will it be alright if I call you?", and like the fool that I am, I said "Yes."

In the weeks and months that followed our first meeting, Tom and I fell right back into a relationship that felt new and fresh and wonderful. We couldn't get enough of each other, and it was good, so good, but it probably wouldn't last this time anymore than it had before. We just weren't able to let each other go. We had an obsession for each other that surpassed all logic, and it sunk its' teeth into me with a vicious and tenacious grip. It had worked itself into the very core of our being, and become as much a part of us as our own flesh and blood. It could no more be shed than the shedding of our own skin.

CHAPTER 34

▼

AND SO IT GOES

There is nothing more wonderful than love when it is new and unspoiled, and nothing more heartbreaking than when it starts to sour. I should have known that it was too good to last. Things so seemingly perfect simply cannot last forever. We humans aren't meant to live a life without trials and tribulations. Who knows why, only God knows why. I guess that if our lives went unblemished we would never experience the full spectrum that is the phenomenon of life. If we can trust that our lives are controlled by God and His infinite wisdom, and happen as they are suppose to as part of His plan, that is truly a blessing, but when we are hurting it is so hard to come to terms with that logic, and to feel peace.

Not only was my relationship with Tom unraveling, but my life as I had known it was also falling apart in a way that had once seemed unfathomable. On an otherwise sunny afternoon in August of nineteen-sixty-seven, my heart was broken and shattered into a million pieces, leaving it forever damaged and unable to ever be put back together as a whole again. From that day on my heart would never be free from some degree of sadness. Not one day would go by that at some point utter desolation would creep in and make sorrow a permanent part of my life, scarring my heart forever.

I sensed that something was wrong the minute I answered the phone. I'm not sure why because it was something intangible in Daddy's voice. "Hello, oh hi Daddy."

"Hi, I was wondering if you and Colleen are both at home."

"Yes we are."

"I'm coming over. I need to talk to both of you."

"Is something wrong Daddy?" I asked, but he didn't reply.

"I'll be over in a few minutes." he said, and then just abruptly hung up the phone.

I relayed the conversation to Colleen and we both became alarmed, consequently starting to speculate on any number of possibilities as to what this sudden visit from Daddy could mean. Out of all the possibilities we conjured up between us, the real reason never even entered our minds.

After about twenty minutes of speculation, Daddy knocked on our door. By that time Colleen and I were both on the brink of panic, our minds having run the gamut of possible conclusions for Daddy's impromptu visit.

Daddy looked very grim. Pain was etched on his face. "You need to sit down." he said to both of us. Meanwhile the kids were scrambling to sit on his lap. He picked them both up and gave them a kiss. I noticed that his hands were shaking. After he had both kids situated on his lap, he dropped a bomb that sent us careening into a pit of sorrow of such magnitude that we went into a state of shock.

No! He couldn't have said what I thought he did. No! Take it back! The words he had spoken were so overwhelming that they couldn't possibly be true. We had to be imagining this. It was too horrific to be real. Soon we would wake up and find that it was a very, very bad dream.

What my father had come to tell us was this, "Girls, I don't know how to tell you this, but there has been a tragedy. Your sister Dinah committed suicide earlier today. I'm sorry, but she is gone. No one knows why she did it."

I covered my mouth with my hand to try and stifle the hysterical cry of denial that was welling up inside of me, and trying to escape from my mouth, but I couldn't. I'll never forget the sound of that wail, or the keening that followed from me and Colleen. I ran down the hall and threw myself on my bed. Colleen followed me and laid down beside me. We held each other, and cried, and cried, and cried. I don't know how long we stayed that way. I remember hearing both of the children crying, probably because they were frightened and had no idea why

Colleen and I were down the hall crying. I remember hearing Daddy say to them, "It's okay my precious babies. Mommy and Aunt Colleen will be alright. Come with Pop Pop. We'll go outside for a walk." Then I heard the door close, and the only sound that remained were the sobs coming from me and Colleen as we laid there in total sadness.

After the initial shock had worn off to a degree that we were able to function at the most infinitesimal level, Colleen and I got up and went to find Daddy and the kids, and went back to the apartment and made plans for going to New York for our sister Dinah's funeral.

We were all in a daze. It was as if we ourselves weren't real, but more like we had literally become a part of a surrealistic dream of nightmarish proportions. We moved by rote as if we were robots on automatic pilot, only the outer shells of our true selves.

Daddy, Momma, Colleen and I were going to drive to New York together for the funeral. Abby and Joey were going to stay with Ellen. I called Trevor to let him know what had happened, and where the kids would be. After that I called Tom and left a message with his sister.

I remember wishing that our relationship was such that he could take me in his arms and give me comfort, even though my mind hadn't accepted the reality that my sister was really dead. I still longed to wake up and find that it was all a hellish nightmare.

We left that night. The trip was long, but that didn't matter because it gave me longer to wake up from the dream that I had convinced myself this nightmare had to be. None of us slept, we just drove. There was no talking because our psyches were numbed into silence. Any verbalization, any utterance of words spoken would be more than our fragile minds could handle. We could not speak because that would give validity to something that none of us were willing to accept as the truth yet, and so we just drove and drove and drove.

Once we got there, nothing could have prepared me for the moment of truth. When I walked into the funeral parlor and saw the still body of my beautiful sister lying in her casket. I heard a wail of unbelievable sorrow fill the room, and as I fell toward the floor, I realized that the cry had come from me. All that was left of me at that moment was a profound sadness that had steeped itself way down deep into my soul.

In the days following the funeral we tried to find an explanation for this tragedy, but everywhere we turned to look we came up with nothing but a blank. No one could, or would, ever offer us any reason for what had happened.

We would never know why the life of my beautiful, vibrant and vivacious sister that I had adored, had come to such an inexplicably sad and violent end. There was no closure for any of us, and there never would be.

CHAPTER 35

▼

PICKING UP THE PIECES

We arrived back home as shattered people, forever fragmented, and missing valuable parts of ourselves. We had been to hell, and parts of us had been left there, unable to escape the hideous horror of hell on earth. We would suffer the consequences if its' wrath, to some degree for the rest of our lives.

The only thing that kept me going during those first weeks and months following Dinah's death, the only reason I had for getting out of bed each day, was my precious children. Holding them close to me was the only thing that brought me comfort. Even Colleen and I could not help each other very much because we could not speak of Dinah without breaking down into relentless crying. We tried to avoid that at all cost because of the children.

For several months we didn't go anywhere except to work and the grocery store. We were always glad to return to our home, our place of solitude. It was our sanctuary where we could retreat and try to deal with our sorrow privately, away from the prying eyes of others. Our pain could not be shared. It was too painful, too private.

During this time I didn't see Tom. I didn't want to. I would have had to be civil to him, and I wasn't capable of that yet. I would have had to make polite conversation and smile, and that would have taken more energy and more emotion than I had to give to anyone other than my own flesh and blood. I knew that Colleen was struggling with the same feelings that I was, and she in turn knew my pain as well. Words were not needed, only an occasional hug and close proximity to each other would suffice. Momma spent more time with us during this trying time in our lives. We three were each others' lifelines that kept us from drowning in a sea of tears.

One afternoon about three and a half months after Dinah's death, Momma came over and gave us a reason to have something to look forward to. She told us, "A house has been listed through my real estate office. It can be purchased through an F.H.A (Federal Housing Authority) loan. That means that only a small down payment is needed. It's a four bedroom, two bathroom house with a carport and a fenced-in backyard. Would you be interested in going to look at it?" she asked Colleen and I.

"If we all like it, we can look into the possibility of the three of us going in together and buying it. Do you want to go look at it?" she asked us.

Colleen and I looked at each other and simultaneously said, "Yes! Can we go look at it right now?" we both asked. It was the first time since Dinah's death that we had felt even a glimmer of excitement about anything. We all piled in the car to go and look at it.

All three of us loved the house, and we most definitely wanted it. The only setback was that for me, it was too far from my job to be able to walk to work. I would definitely have to buy a car, and probably have to make other arrangements for daycare for Abby and Joey. Although those were two major concerns for me, it didn't put a damper on my enthusiasm about buying the house.

I guess that Momma had been pretty sure that Colleen and I would go for the idea because she already had the necessary forms with her, ready to be filled out. We were all very excited about the prospect, not only of becoming homeowners, but also about the five of us living together as a family.

After we had looked at every nook and cranny of the house, we piled back in the car. "Let's go get some burgers and fries to go, and go back to the apartment and start the process of filling out the necessary applications." Momma suggested.

The fact that Momma worked in a real estate office was an extra bonus because she was familiar with all of the forms, and the steps that needed to be taken in order to secure a loan.

"We can get the ball rolling as early as tomorrow morning if we do all of the necessary paperwork tonight." she told us.

That was not a problem because we were all highly motivated to do so. In fact, we were all so excited that we wished we could start moving in that very night.

Buying a house was just what we needed in more ways than one. Not only was it a smart move financially, but it gave us a boost mentally as well. It gave us something positive to think about, something exciting to look forward to, and that helped us to get to a point where we could think about something other than the constant and unrelenting grief that we all felt over Dinah's death.

We got lucky. Momma stopped by one afternoon. When she first came in she was acting kind of gloomy, and then all of a sudden she got this really big grin on her face, and she said, "Guess what? The approval for our loan went through. We got the house!"

We were all so excited that we were literally jumping for joy. The loan had gone through quickly and smoothly. The timing had been perfect because my divorce from Trevor had been finalized just a few weeks before we applied for the loan. Had we still been married it would have made things significantly more complicated.

Rather than dreading the packing and moving process, we couldn't wait to get started. Our closing was scheduled to happen in a couple of weeks. Colleen and I would have to pay another month's rent because the day of the closing fell in the middle of the month. We would have liked to have been able to use the rent money for other things, but it ended up working out well because we used the two weeks after the closing to get the house move-in ready.

When we had first looked at the house all of the rooms were painted white. We wanted to have some color so we utilized the two weeks for painting, putting in shelf paper, hanging curtains and that sort of thing. We went through all of our belongings and decided what to keep and what to get rid of, and we went ahead and started moving some of our things in. What we didn't need or want, we either gave to the Salvation Army, or put an ad in the newspaper to sell. Between the three of us we had more than enough furnishings for the house. Consequently, when moving day arrived we were in good shape and were able to get settled in quickly.

The issues that I had been concerned about how I was going to get to and from work, and the babysitting issue were working out as well.

Momma said, "Until you can get a car, I'll make sure you have a way to and from work." Colleen had also said, "I can help you with that too. If Momma can't get you there, you'll have a backup with me."

My babysitting concerns were working out as well. When I told Pauline that we were moving, and that I didn't know what I was going to do about babysitting arrangements, she told me, "Since your job is close by, why can't you continue to bring them here?"

In retrospect, I thought gee, why didn't I think of that? I was glad the children would still be being babysat by Pauline. I didn't want too many changes in their lives to be happening all at once.

It worked out well with all of us living together because we worked as a team in all matters. We all liked for the house to be neat and clean so everybody pulled their own weight with doing chores. The house had come furnished with a stove and refrigerator, and Momma already had a washer and dryer, which was a special blessing for me because I hated having to go to the Laundromat.

Although we were all still grieving terribly over Dinah's death, the move had given our spirits a lift. We talked more, and even laughed some. Momma and Colleen helped me considerably with taking care of Abby and Joey, and Tom had started coming over. Momma still didn't like him, but she tried never to show it because she knew that his presence made me happy.

About a month after the move Daddy helped me buy a car. We bought a nineteen-sixty-six light blue Ford Fairlane. I was so happy that you would have thought I had won a million dollars.

CHAPTER 36

▼

UNEXPLORED TERRITORY

My life as I had once expected it would be was turning out to be something completely different. The hopes and dreams I had envisioned in my childhood in no way mirrored my life as it was in reality. That was a hard pill to swallow because my dreams had once been so real, I had believed they were reality. It had taken a long time for me to realize that what I had envisioned was no more than a fairy tale. Consequently, I had spent a lot of time thinking that I was a failure because I didn't measure up to the fairy tale standard that I had unwittingly imposed on myself.

Shortly after we moved into the house I quit my job at Gabby's and took a job working at night. I really would rather have worked days, but working nights meant that I didn't have to put Abby and Joey in daycare because Momma and Colleen had offered to babysit for them. It was better that way for several reasons. It meant that I didn't have to pay for daycare, and therefore I was able to save more money, and I felt that it was better for real little ones like Abby and Joey to be at home with family.

I took a job at a popular downtown eatery that was open until 2:00 A.M. It wasn't long after I started working there that I became friends with a crowd of other waiters, waitresses, and bartenders that worked the late-night hours. They would go out for drinks in order to unwind after work, and I started joining them. It was a fun group of people that were easy to be with. A lot of laughing and merriment went on, and it comprised most of what was my social life. The only problem was that I started drinking more than I should have.

My relationship with Tom was on and off, touch and go. He came around when he felt like it, without any commitment or consideration for my feelings. It wasn't unusual for weeks, or sometimes months to go by without a word from him, but never-the-less I was always willing to see him every chance I got. I was a complete and utter fool when it came to him. I couldn't help myself. He was an obsession that I couldn't shake. It wasn't uncommon for him to call me in the middle of the night wanting to come over. He would beg if I didn't respond according to his will, so for the most part I would acquiesce to his pleading.

Most of these visits were pretty much the standard for our relationship, such as it was. He would come over basically apologizing for his lack of attention to me, telling me how much he loved me, and then seduce me into making love with him. He would usually vow to change his wayward ways and do better by me. I was so blinded by love and hope that I would choose to think that maybe this time he really meant it, and so it would go, and go, and go.

I was stupid. There is simply no other word to describe what a complete and utter fool I was when it came to Tom. I loved him with an intensity that was larger than life.

To compound my stupidity, because our encounters were so sporadic, and because after each tryst I would vow to myself not to let him weasel his way into my life again. I wasn't on birth control pills, and even though Tom used a condom, I got pregnant again. I was mortified. I dreaded the shameful ordeal of having to break this very disconcerting news to my family. I was aghast to be in this position again. We had faithfully taken precautions to prevent my getting pregnant again, but somehow it hadn't worked.

There was a possibility that Tom would do the right thing this time, but knowing him like I did, I didn't really expect that he would. I was probably in this alone. I was resigned to the fact not to expect anything positive about my pregnancy to come from Tom. He wasn't inclined to do the right thing for anyone other than himself. It saddened me to think that I could feel so much love for someone whose character and integrity was so flawed. There must really be something very wrong with me, I thought. Was I a glutton for punishment, or simply a garbage disposal when it came to the men I chose to love.

I held off for as long as I could before telling anyone. I wasn't ready to confront the backlash that I knew was inevitable once this news got out. After I had missed two periods I called Tom and told him. His reaction was pretty much what I had expected. All he said was, "I'll come over and we can talk about it."

His aloofness was so blatantly cold that I wondered if I really knew him at all, and if I did, why would I want to. Why would I, such a touchy, feely person, have a relationship with a man that was apparently made of ice.

I think the reason was that I had known a caring Tom at one time, and that is who I had fallen in love with. The reason I held on to him so tenaciously was because I so fervently believed *that* Tom was the *real* Tom. I just couldn't accept that his dark side was the *true* Tom, the Tom that came out when push came to shove. I was unwilling to believe that I could love such a person, but I did and it hurt, and it kept on hurting until I was filled up with nothing but cold, hard, debilitating hurt.

I tried not to let my feelings show, but on the inside they were eating me alive. That's what caused me to spill my guts out to Colleen late one night when just the two of us were home. The kids were home, but they were sleeping. We were watching television when out of the blue, without any warning, I broke down in uncontrollable sobs. They wracked my body and left my feelings defenseless against anything but the truth.

I'll never forget the look on Colleen's face when the sobbing started. She was shocked, just as I was at this confounding state of mind that had erupted from me so unwittingly and unexpectedly. I was horrified. Colleen was initially astounded, and then alarmed because she had no idea what was going on with me. At first she jumped as if the boogeyman had suddenly burst through the door. Then she panicked because she thought that I was in pain, which I was. It just wasn't the physical pain that she had automatically perceived it to be.

It was emotional pain that my body and mind could no longer hide or disguise. There was no trying to pretend that I could conceal it indefinitely anymore. It wasn't going to go away like some bad dream I could forget about, and it wasn't a situation that I could bluff my way through. The dye was cast, and there was no turning back now.

CHAPTER 37

▼

THE SAGA CONTINUES

Life does go on, even when you wish you could stop the clock, and stop time. As soon as the sobs escaped my body the gig was up.

After Colleen's initial jump of alarm, with her eyes as big as saucers, she said, "Grace, what's wrong? Are you in pain? What should I do? What can I do to help you?"

"There's nothing you can do." I told her.

"But why are you crying? Please, tell me what is wrong so I can help you." she said with pleading eyes that were full of concern.

"I'm pregnant, and Tom doesn't care. He doesn't want to take any responsibility for it."

"Oh Grace, oh my God. Are you sure?"

"I'm sure, and I've told Tom. Basically, to be blunt about it, he doesn't give a rat's ass."

"Have you told anyone else?" Colleen wanted to know.

"No, and I wouldn't even have told you if it hadn't been for my emotions betraying me. I'm not ready to let it be known. I have to come to terms with it myself first, and I'm a long way from doing that right now."

"How far along are you?"

"I've missed three periods, so I guess I'm about two and a half months. I can hardly believe it. Tom and I were always careful. He always used a condom. I don't know what to do. I don't know how I'm going to break the news to Momma and Daddy, or to anyone else for that matter."

"Grace, I hope you know that I will be with you every step of the way. Look at me and know that I speak straight from my heart. You are not alone. I am here for you now, and I will be here for you always."

"Thank you Colleen." I said in between sobs.

"I think that you should go ahead and tell Momma and Daddy."

"No, I told you I'm not ready to cross that bridge right now."

"I know you did, and I understand why you are hesitant about it, but just think about it for a minute. Wouldn't it be a big relief not to have to carry this secret around any longer? You're going to have to tell them sometime, so why carry this burden around any longer. Get it over with. You'll feel better once you don't have to worry about breaking the news to them. I'll be there with you, right by your side every step of the way. You are not alone. Besides, what is the worst that can happen? They aren't going to stop loving you, and they're not going to kill you."

Colleen offered me nothing less than her complete love and support that night. There were no words of admonition, only words of encouragement and hope. Knowing that she didn't judge me as a complete fool meant the world to me. She assured me that I would live through this, that it wouldn't destroy me, or mean that I was a bad person, or a bad mother. She just kept saying everything will be okay over and over again, until I believed that it actually would be. She was a great comfort to me that night, and by the time we finished talking I was feeling a lot better.

We decided that I should go ahead and break the news to the rest of the family. The sooner the better, so I could quit worrying about it. We talked a little bit more, and then went to bed. After all of that we both needed rest.

The next day was Sunday and we both had the day off from work. We decided that we should go to church and pray for strength and guidance to get us through the emotional ordeal that I had ahead of me. We also decided that after church we would go over to Daddy and Ellen's and let the cat out of the bag so to speak.

I was very worried about what Daddy's reaction to this bombshell was going to be. I knew that he already despised Tom with a vengeance, and I knew there was going to be hell to pay for my latest transgression. All of that aside, the part that I hated the most was going to be the disappointment I would see in Daddy's eyes.

I soon found out that my premonition about an angry response from Daddy was an understated version of what his actual response was when I told him. It was a living nightmare. Aside from what I know his disappointment in me was, he was in a far greater rage over what I told him Tom's reaction to the pregnancy had been. I think if Tom had been within his reach at that moment, Daddy would have either killed him, or inflicted serious and permanent bodily harm on him.

Surprisingly enough, it appeared that Ellen was going to be one of my biggest supporters throughout my pregnancy. Maybe that was because she had been through a similar situation herself. Whatever the reason, I appreciated all of the hope and understanding anyone gave to me because I was my own biggest critic.

At the beginning of my pregnancy I spent a lot of time admonishing myself for my stupidity, and feeling very humiliated that Tom, once again had left me in a lurch. I soon realized that sort of thinking was counterproductive, and that the only choice I had was to pull myself up by the seat of my pants and take full responsibility for my own actions. It was one of the hardest situations to come to terms with, but like so many other predicaments in life that we find ourselves in, nobody else can take care of it for us.

There are so many times in life that no matter how much someone else would like to take away our pain and make it go away, the harsh reality is that most of the time we are the only one that can ultimately get ourselves through it. There is no magic trick that can make the consequences of our own bad choices, or unfavorable behavior disappear. Many times we are left with indelible emotional scars, both seen and unseen, even to ourselves. The bottom line is, are we strong enough to do it.

My pregnancy would probably be fraught with anxiety and stress, but with God's help I hoped to get through it. I worked through the sixth month of my pregnancy, but at that time my obstetrician told me that I needed to quit work and stay off my feet as much as possible.

Since Momma, Colleen and I had bought the house and started sharing household expenses, I had been able to save enough money, that along with child support and food stamps, I would be able to continue pulling my own weight.

I liked not working and being able to spend more time with the kids. Abby had started kindergarten in September so she was at school from 8:30 A.M. until 2:30 P.M. Being able to spend that extra time with them was very special, and the joy that they brought into my life helped tremendously in keeping my spirits up.

I rarely heard from Tom during this period, but that was no surprise, it was what I had expected. He had agreed to pay for the doctor, and for the hospital stay when I gave birth. That was a big relief to me. Other than those two means of support, Tom wasn't involved in anything else to do with me or the baby. It hurt a lot, but these days I tried to make myself numb when it came to Tom.

Momma was as solid as a rock for me during my pregnancy. She and Colleen were unwavering in their loyalty toward helping me to get through this as best as we could. That being said, it was still a stressful time for me, and I was depressed to a certain degree most of the time.

I was lonely to a great extent most of the time. Although I wasn't sent into exile by my family this time, I had inexorably imposed one on myself. The only people that I had contact with, besides my family, was my best friend Nancy and her husband Jake. Nancy was a good seamstress, and she told me that if I would pick out some material she would make me some maternity clothes. She would call and check on me on a regular basis, and she visited me as often as she could. Her children were about the same age as Abby and Joey, and they played together well. That gave us a chance to visit. She was my lifeline to the outside world.

Trevor's reaction to my pregnancy had surprised me. When I told him I was pregnant he asked me if Tom and I were getting married. When I said we weren't, he offered to give the baby his last name. I thanked him, but I had already decided to go to a lawyer and have my last name changed to Walker, which was Tom's last name. I did this because I wanted my last name to be the same as the baby's.

I was glad that Abby and Joey were still small. That way all they had to know was that Mommy was going to have a baby, and that they were going to get a new brother or sister. I didn't need to explain anything else. However, they were very curious about the baby, and everyday they would ask me if today was the day the baby was going to come out of my tummy.

The baby was due on November 14, 1971, but when I was a week into my eighth month I started having severe cramps with contractions.

I didn't tell anyone. I just continued with my daily routine, which was pretty much taking care of the kids and cleaning the house. That didn't continue for very long though because on the second day the cramping and contractions became so strong that I had no alternative but to tell Momma and Colleen.

They immediately called my obstetrician, who told them to bring me to the hospital right away. He met us at the hospital and did a sonogram. The sonogram showed that the problem was a condition called abruptio placentae. It means that there is a premature detachment of the placenta from the wall of the uterus. My doctor admitted me to the hospital because he said, "If I send you home and the condition worsens, the baby could suffocate and you could bleed to death before you're able to get to the hospital."

I stayed in the hospital for a week and was given several blood transfusions, which I hated. At the end of the week the doctor came in and said, "I will allow you to go home, but only if there is someone around that can take care of you. You have to have complete bed rest, and only get up to use the bathroom or take a shower. Will you be able to arrange that?"

"I'm pretty sure that I can. I just need to make a couple of phone calls to be sure."

"Good." he said. "I'll leave instructions at the nurses' station, and you can just let them know, okay? Just remember that you are not to get up for any reason other than what I just told you. We need to try and keep that baby in you for the rest of your pregnancy. The longer he, or she stays inutero, the better the chances are that your baby will be born healthy."

"I understand Dr. Wood, and believe me, I won't do anything that could possibly hurt my baby."

The first person I called was Momma. I just wanted to let her know. I knew that she, or Colleen wouldn't be able to take off from work for an indefinite period of time. Next I called Daddy to let him know what was going on. A few minutes after we hung up, he called back and said, "I just spoke with Ellen and she wants you and the kids to come to our house."

"Are you sure Daddy? You didn't put any pressure on her to do this, did you?"

"No, she volunteered as soon as I told her what the doctor had said."

"Okay then, I'll let the nurses know, and I'll call you back and let you know when they can discharge me. Thank you Daddy. I hate hospitals. I'll call Ellen as well, and tell her thank you. By."

I did good for the first twenty-four hours or so. After that I became extremely bored with just laying in bed. I couldn't see what harm could come from just walking out to the living room and sitting and watching T.V., but after a couple of hours I started getting very bad cramps again.

I guess Ellen must have seen me squirm, or simply sensed that something was wrong, because right away she asked me, "Are you alright Grace? Are you having pains?"

"Yes I am. They just started a few minutes ago, but they're really strong, and the contractions don't stop. It's just one continuous contraction."

"Walter! Grace needs to go to the hospital!" she hollered to Daddy, who was in another part of the house.

Daddy came running into the room, and Ellen said, "Here is her overnight case for the hospital. You need to go right now. I'll call her doctor and tell him that you are taking her to the hospital. Just hurry and go!"

Abby and Joey were already in bed for the night, so I didn't get to tell them I was leaving. Ellen said, "Don't worry about that Grace. I'll tell them when they wake up in the morning, and I'll tell them that you asked me to tell them that you love them. Don't worry about anything. For Pete's sake quit dallying and get going!"

Once the doctor examined me he told Daddy and I, "She's in labor and has started to dilate. I'm going to admit her and put her in a labor room." Eleven hours later, at 6:10 A.M on October 10, 1971,. Dinah Jean Walker was born.

I had decided that if I had a girl I would name her after my sister Dinah. That is how my Dinah got her name. I only got to see her through the window of the nursery on the first day because her chest was covered in a rash, and they had to run some tests to see if her rash was contagious. Her rash wasn't contagious so I got to hold her for the first time when she was twenty-four hours old. They determined that the rash had been caused by some medication that I had been given, and that it would disappear on its' own after a day or two.

Other than the rash, Dinah was a healthy baby. Having been born four and a half weeks early, she was very small. She weighed five pounds three ounces and was seventeen inches long. Since she weighed just a little less than five pounds when I was ready to be discharged, I was able to take her home with me three days later.

I had been planning on getting a youth bed for Joey and using his crib for Dinah, but I hadn't gotten that done because I had gone into premature labor. For now I was thinking that I would put Dinah in the bassinet until I could get Joey a youth bed, but when I got home, I was delightfully surprised to see that Momma and Colleen had bought Joey a youth bed, and had already setup the crib for Dinah in my room.

I was anxious to see how Abby and Joey were going to react to their new baby sister. I kept thinking about how Abby had shunned me when I brought Joey home. I really hoped that wasn't going to be the case this time. Much to my relief that didn't happen. In fact it was just the opposite. They were constantly hovering over her and wanting to hold and kiss her.

Tom stopped by quite frequently the first few weeks after I brought Dinah home, but then I guess the novelty of being a father wore off, and his visits became fewer and farther between. It did make me sad, but I didn't let it get me down too much. I was determined to give my children the best life I could, and that was what I focused on.

Shortly after Dinah was born, Momma was ready to take her real estate exam. I helped her with her studies by asking a set of questions after she read each chapter. Through helping Momma to prepare for her realtor's exam, I began to think that maybe real estate would be a good career for me to pursue sometime down the road. For now the only thing I could focus on was taking care of my children.

I planned on getting a job and going back to work when Dinah was six months old. Elaine, that I had worked with at Gabby's called me one night to see how I was doing.

"Hi Grace, it's Elaine. "I'm just calling you to let you know that I've been thinking about you, and I wondered how you and the baby are doing." She went on to say that, "I'm not working at Gabby's anymore. I recently started a new job at the International Pancake House. I've been doing very well there. I make a lot more in tips there, than I was making at Gabby's. If you would like, when you're ready to go back to work, I could put in a good word for you with my boss."

"Thank you Elaine, and thanks for thinking about me. You should come over for a visit sometime. I would really like that."

"I would like that too." she said. "I need to come and see that new baby of yours. Bye now, take care and stay in touch."

"I will." I promised as we hung up.

Dinah was a good baby, but nevertheless I was very tired during the months following her birth. She slept from about nine o'clock at night until about twelve-thirty A.M. By the time I would give her a bottle and rock her back to sleep it was usually one-thirty going on two. She was usually back up at five o'clock. I would give her another bottle, and by the time she finished that it was almost time for Abby and Joey to be getting up. I would fix breakfast for them and then start getting Abby ready for school.

Getting Abby ready for school was no small accomplishment. She always gave me a hard time about what she wanted to wear. We would generally go through just about everything in her wardrobe before finding something that she would agree on. She would pitch a fit if I tried to insist on her wearing something that she didn't want to, and it was exhausting trying to force her to do so. After finally getting through all of that, I would load the kids in the car and take Abby to school. Most of the time I had to wake the baby up, consequently she would cry most of the way there and back.

By the time I got back home I had usually had about six cups of coffee. I drank a lot of coffee during that time. It was the only thing that kept me awake. I was pretty much constantly on the move for the rest of the day. I couldn't take a nap when the baby napped because I had to be up with Joey. Sometimes I would get lucky and have them both asleep by one o'clock in the afternoon. On those occasions I would set my alarm to go off at two-thirty. That way I had time to wake them both up and have them in the car ready to pick up Abby at two-forty-five. In those days I went to bed early. As soon as I had all three of my children sleeping, I went to bed too.

By the time Dinah was six months old I was pretty much ready to go back to work. I knew that I didn't want to work nights anymore.

I wanted normal daytime hours. Aside from just plain not wanting to work nights anymore, I really didn't see how I could because the baby still wasn't sleeping all night. That meant that she would probably be waking up just as I was going to sleep. I certainly couldn't expect Momma or Colleen to get up with her and then have to go to work the next morning.

It wasn't going to be easy, but I started trying to work out the necessary arrangements for my children's care because I wanted, and needed to get a job. My savings were practically gone, and I felt that it would be good for me to be out among other adults who were not members of my own family. I felt like I was getting in a rut.

I decided to make a list of everything that would need to be taken care of in order for me to be able to go back to work. Abby would be finished with her school year in another month. I decided to wait until then to get a job. The First Presbyterian Church had a daycare, and I decided to start by inquiring there. Having been a member there my whole life, I knew almost everybody there, and I had heard other people whose children were enrolled there saying nothing but good things about it.

Next year Abby would be in first grade and attending the same school that she was currently attending. Joey was now four and would be attending prekindergarten. I was hoping to get him in at First Presbyterian for that. That left Dinah. I didn't want to put her in a regular daycare setting because I was afraid they would just leave her in a crib all day, and probably not change her diaper as often as it needed to be, plus I didn't want her to be exposed to all the germs. I figured germs would be all over the place from little ones coughing and sneezing all over everything. That was my dilemma, and offhand I couldn't find a solution for

I had been mulling this over for about a week when Tom happened to call. I was telling him that I needed to find someone to take care of Dinah so I could go back to work. Out of the blue he said, "I know just the right person. Remember Sam Grant that we went to high school with? Well, his mother runs a small daycare out of her house. She never takes in more than four kids at a time. Would you like her phone number?"

"Yes I would." I told him.

As soon as we hung up, I called her and made an appointment to go and meet her the following day. Mrs. Grant was just the type of person I was looking for. Her home was small, but neat and clean with a fenced in backyard.

"Presently I only have two children in my care, and I would be happy to watch Dinah for you. I charge by the day, and I would need to be assured that you would be bringing her at least three days a week in order for it to be feasible, money wise for me. That's because I don't take anymore than four children at a time."

"That won't be a problem because more than likely I'll be working five days a week." I told her. I planned on finding a job where I would have weekends off to be with the kids.

We said our goodbyes, and I told her that I would be in touch with her as soon as I found a job and knew my hours. She seemed to be the grandmotherly type, and that was just what I was looking for. It certainly wasn't the ideal way to raise children, but it was an acceptable one. Besides I had no choice.

CHAPTER 38

▼

STRIVING FOR NORMALCY

What are the basic components of normalcy? Does anyone really know? That's the question I have pondered more times than I can say. I don't think there is any pat answer. After all, aren't we all different? So, if we are all different how can the same things be considered normal for everyone, and why is the appearance of being normal so important to most of us?

At this time in my life I was trying very hard to at least appear to be what I considered normal, albeit inwardly I rarely felt that I was. Since I didn't feel that way naturally I tried to exude it in my outward demeanor, but since I didn't know what normal looked like I never really knew if I was coming across as appearing to be so.

My self-esteem was running very low. Having been rejected by Tom twice had really done a number on me. I wondered why he didn't love me as I loved him. I didn't think that I was *that* bad, but I thought that I must be, otherwise he would love me. Wouldn't he? Inside I felt like I was a real loser. I was twenty-five years old and already I had made a mess of my life. I can't begin to tell you how disillusioned I was with the direction my life had taken. Not only was I disillusioned, I was very disappointed in myself because I wasn't living up to the standards I had set for my life. I knew where I had started to go wrong, but I couldn't help it if I had fallen head over heels in love with someone I would come to find out didn't return that love, could I?

I wanted my children and I to be a normal family. I didn't want them to be considered by others as being from a dysfunctional, or broken home. To me that was a stigma I didn't want for them. It made me try even harder to create a stable and loving family life.

Outwardly life was seemingly going pretty well for us. We were all in good health, and we had a nice home that was filled with love. I was so thankful that Momma, Colleen and I had bought the house. We were a team. Everybody pitched in and did their share as far as paying the bills and taking care of the house. Not having to be responsible for everything took a lot of pressure off of me.

My biggest source of aggravation was that Trevor and Tom were always delinquent with the child support payments. It not only put me in a bind, it made me feel very resentful towards them. There was no valid reason for them not to send me the child support. They both had good jobs and had no one to take care of but themselves.

The kids were always needing new shoes or something else, and it was their responsibility, as much as mine to help provide for them. The children were healthy, but even so, they did need to go to the doctor from time to time, and that was always a big expense.

At first I tried to resolve the child support problem by talking to them in a diplomatic way, but that produced no results so I decided to get a lawyer to handle it. When the papers my lawyer had drawn up were served on them, they were both enraged. I was dumbstruck as to how they saw themselves to be the victims in this matter, but it really didn't matter to me that they were angry. It did give me some degree of satisfaction to see their reaction.

Each case had to be held separately. Trevor's was scheduled first. When I finally got my day in court the judge ordered him to pay me one hundred dollars a month, plus what he owed me in arrears. If looks could kill, I would have died on the spot. To this day I'm still amazed when I think about it. How could he possibly think that he had absolutely no responsibility towards taking care of his children, and the audacity to turn it around, and in his viewpoint think that he was the one being wronged. It was outrageous!

Tom was no better. He had paid the obstetrician and the hospital bill for me and Dinah, but the buck stopped there. I had heard stories about delinquent dads from time to time, and I never could understand the mind set of such thinking, or how they could sleep at night without wondering if their children were okay, or if they had some needs that needed to be provided for.

I wondered why I kept picking such losers, and I wondered what that said about me. After a while I started to think that maybe I didn't deserve anyone any better, but I knew that my children did. Tom didn't come by very often to see Dinah. He went through spells where he would be in our lives for a day or two, then we might not hear from him for a month or more. Even so, God help me, I was always happy when he was around.

I just didn't seem to be able to resist him. I don't know why I loved him so much. Loving him was hurtful and very detrimental to my well being, but yet I found it impossible to break it off with him completely. I clung to the hope that one day he would stop treating me this way, and love me the way that I wanted him to, and I clung to that hope with a fierce tenacity. I think I was obsessed with the determination to make that happen.

I did on occasion date other people, but it seemed that no matter who I was with, I was always wishing that I was with Tom instead. Thoughts of him ran through my mind daily. I just couldn't shake them loose, and once again I started feeling very depressed.

Being depressed was nothing new for me. I have a long history with depression. The first time I remember feeling that way was when I was about four years old. I remember sitting on my grandmother's front porch steps and feeling very sad because my mother didn't get after me like my neighbor Molly Boyle's mother got after her. I know that probably doesn't make any sense, but that's what I mean when I say, "How do you define normal?"

My first episode of depression didn't last very long because I remember Momma sitting down beside me and asking me what was wrong. As soon as she told me that she would start getting after me more I was happy again. I've read that children actually want to be disciplined by their parents, and I suppose I was feeling discipline deprived.

The first long-term bout with depression I experienced occurred when I was in the second grade. I felt depressed most of that school year because I didn't feel that my schoolwork was up to par. I got better than average grades, but I didn't feel like that was good enough.

I'm a person that needs more assurance than most people, and I didn't always get it. I don't think my need was recognized by my parents because if it had been, they would have given me all the reassurance that I needed. I must have appeared to be more well adjusted than I really was. That was because I kept my feelings all bottled up inside. I was ashamed for people to know that I felt that way, so I kept those feelings hidden.

The feelings of inadequacy were more or less a part of my psyche, and that is what I was struggling with at this point in time. I felt that I didn't measure up to whatever standard that I was supposed to in order to be a good mother to my children, or a woman that Tom would want for his wife.

Oddly enough I didn't blame him for his rejection of me. I blamed myself for not being *that woman,* the woman of his dreams. I got so down about it that I didn't want to go on living anymore. Eventually I worked myself into such a frenzy that I lost control of my ability to reason, and I decided to commit suicide.

On that day, "kill yourself" became the phrase that kept repeating itself in my mind over and over again until I couldn't focus on anything other than attaining that goal. I waited until Momma got home from work and asked her if she could watch the kids. Then I got in my car and proceeded to carry out my plan. I had decided that I would go to several drugstores and buy some sleeping pills. When I had purchased eight hundred of them, plus a tablet and pen to write suicide notes to my family, I drove to a motel and registered under a fictitious name.

After I checked into the room I just sat there for a little while. I was feeling sad, and a little bit scared about my plan to kill myself, but that didn't deter me from my plan to carry it out. I got some water and started swallowing the pills. It was hard to swallow so many, but when I got all eight hundred of them down, I laid down on the bed and waited for them to take effect. I don't know how long that took, but the last thing I remember thinking was that at least I would see my sister Dinah soon.

Sometime during the night I woke up and had to rush to the bathroom to throw up. I remember literally bouncing off the walls from the effect of taking all those pills. I remember hearing the sound of glass breaking, but I didn't know what it was that I broke. After I finished throwing up I stumbled back to bed.

The next thing I remember was going outside and getting in my car. The manager of the motel came over to my car and asked me, "What are you doing? Where are you going?"

"I'm going to the beach." I told him.

All I had on was my panties and bra. Somehow he got me back in the motel room and called for an ambulance. By this time I was hallucinating. At first I thought I heard my children talking, and I remember saying, "Please don't let my children see me this way."

The next minute I was back in the motel room laying on the bed and having a hallucination that a giant "Planters Peanut" man was towering over me. By then the ambulance had arrived to take me to the hospital.

On the way to the hospital I started to feel so thirsty that I started begging for some water, but they wouldn't give me anything to drink. Then I started hallucinating again. As I looked out the window of the ambulance, I thought I saw people walking on the side of the road. The really weird thing was that from the chest down their bodies were underground, leaving only their head and shoulders visible.

When we got to the hospital the doctor gave me something to make me throw up some more. I threw up until there was nothing left to throw up. Then an attendant came and took me to a big room that had jail cells all around its' perimeter. When I saw that we were headed for one of the cells, I broke down and started begging them not to put me in it. By this time they were dragging me because I refused to walk to that hell hole. I saw another woman in the cell they were going to put me in. She was very disheveled and wild and scary looking.

The inside of the cell was all concrete except for the door. It was solid steel except for a tiny peephole with bars. It was very dark and dank looking in there. I was doing everything within my power not to get locked in there with the crazed-looking woman. There was no telling what she might do to me. The doctor must have heard all the ruckus, and thanks be to God, he came in there and stopped them from locking me in that cell.

I ended up in a hospital bed close to the entrance to "the jail room." I don't really know how long I stayed there. What I do remember is that being there was like being in the middle of a horror show. I was surrounded by all these jail cells, and every one of them had a crazed person locked inside. They were all yelling obscenities and carrying on out of their minds. Had they not been locked in, it would have been terrifying for me to be in their midst.

At some point, I guess as soon as they thought I was out of danger from overdosing, the police came and took me to jail. I remember getting a mug shot and having my fingerprints taken, then pleading with them not to put me in a jail cell. They said it was for my own protection. Evidently they called my mother because she came and got me, in what appeared to be the middle of the night.

CHAPTER 39

▼

DO WHAT YOU HAVE TO DO

Okay, so life is tough and you didn't know that it was going to be this way. Oh well, like they say, "When things get tough the tough get going." Or, "When life gives you lemons, make lemonade." After my brush with death I realized that just because life hadn't turned out to be the fairy tale that I had so innocently imagined it would be, in the end you must deal with cold hard reality, and play with the hand you are dealt. First and foremost, I was so grateful that God had seen fit for me to live. I decided that I was going to try my very best to be worthy of that blessing. I had become a stronger person because of God's faith in me, and I was determined to live up to that faith to the best of my ability. I know an evil demon was in possession of my mind on the day I had felt driven to kill myself, and I vowed that it would never get its' grip on me again.

I made a pact between myself and God, that no matter how tough things may ever get, I would never give up no matter what. I kept telling myself that I was indestructible so often that I came to believe it with all my heart, and that made me one determined person. I told myself that nothing short of death would keep me from finding a way to take care of my children. I held so fast to that belief with such a ferocious tenacity that it empowered me to believe in myself enough to do it.

I no longer had the time or patience for self-pity, whether for myself, or from anyone else. There is no honor or integrity to be found in someone who sits around saying, "Oh, poor me."

Yes, I felt strong, but would I be able to maintain that strength indefinitely? That question was always lurking on the fringes of my mind, but for now at least, I could shoo it away. For now it seemed that the worst was over and I was able to accept the imperfect circumstances of my life.

Abby was now six years old and ready to start first grade. Joey was now four years old and would be attending prekindergarten at the First Presbyterian Church of Ocean Shores. Dinah Jean would be two years old in October, and she was going to continue to be in the care of Mrs. Grant four days a week while I was working.

I was now wishing that I had gone to college so that I would have a successful career and be able to provide for my children better. I was still doing waitress work because the hours that I worked suited my family life better, and I made good tips. I had briefly worked in a doctor's office, but I made more money working as a waitress.

Other than work, for the most part my life was spent seeing to the needs of my children. I did go out on dates occasionally, but for the most part I found dating to be more trouble than it was worth. It still seemed that no matter who I went out with, I was still wishing that I was with Tom instead. Plus, I found that it was almost always a hassle trying to avoid unwanted advances from the men I dated. I wanted nothing to do with casual sex, or having to deal with men that I did not love trying to grope my body.

Although my life was busy, and more or less going well, I found myself still having to fight off my ongoing bouts with depression, and I hated that. I was ashamed to feel that way, and I didn't share those feelings with anyone, or give any outward hint of what I was feeling inside. Almost everyday I was filled with self-loathing.

I tried to look at myself objectively, hoping to find a glimpse of how others might see me, thinking that maybe I could talk to myself the way a good friend might. Maybe I could give myself some good advice that way.

In the evenings after I got the kids to sleep I started doing a lot of introspection. I would get myself a beer or some wine, and if Momma or Colleen were at home I would go to my room and think. If they weren't at home I would go to the living room, turn off almost all of the lights and think. By looking at my life as if it were someone else's helped me to see things a lot clearer. It also helped me to feel more detached from my problems.

The downside to it was that as I thought, I drank. Usually I would drink until I felt quite drunk, and then stagger off to bed. I knew that I was drinking too much, but I didn't really care. All I really cared about was feeling some kind of peace. If that meant drinking until I could go to sleep, then so be it.

Through my soul-searching, I had been able to reach some conclusions and make some decisions. I reinforced those pearls of wisdom into my brain every night. I came to believe them so strongly that I felt I couldn't be swayed or convinced to change my mind by anyone; not even Tom.

It had been about a month since I had heard from him. I decided that I didn't want to see him anymore. I still loved him, but I knew that loving him would bring me nothing but more heartache and pain. I had gotten myself to the point that I wasn't willing to let him continue to hurt me. I nursed my resolve as I drank, and I willed myself to think of only the bad times I had been through with him. I knew that if I allowed myself to think of the good times, I would lose my new-found strength and determination to have him out of my life forever.

Every time I would find my mind wandering in his direction I would think of my Davey, and if that wasn't enough to make me despise him, I would think of my little Dinah Jean. I would think of what an irresponsible sorry excuse for a man he was for not being a part of her life.

I wanted Tom to call because I wanted to reinforce my resolve to have him out of my life permanently. There was no doubt in my mind that he would eventually call. I just wanted it to be sooner rather than later so I could have it over and done with and get on with my life.

Finally, after about six weeks had gone by without hearing from him, he called. He wanted me to meet him at a cocktail lounge for a drink.

I said, "No, I don't want to see you anymore."

"Oh, come on Grace, don't be like that." he said trying to sound as alluring as possible.

I knew that he probably had a smile on his face, thinking that he could always charm me into giving in to him. Thinking that made me only more determined to end this relationship.

"No, I'm not kidding Tom. I'm tired of playing this game with you. I don't see any future in this relationship, and I'm through wasting my time with you. It's over. Don't call me anymore. I'm looking for more in a relationship than this farce of one that we share. I'm tired of being used and dumped on by you and your buffoonery and horseplay. I deserve more, and my children deserve more. Everything is a joke with you, and I'm tired of being the brunt of your asinine antics."

"I don't believe you really mean what you are saying Grace"

"I really do Tom. Goodbye. I wish I could say that its' been nice knowing you."

"Wait a minute! Can't we at least talk this over? Come on. Just meet me for one drink. Please!"

"No, it would just be a waste of time Tom. I'm through. I have nothing more to say. Goodnight." With that said, I hung up the phone.

I was shaking all over after I hung up, and to my horror, I found myself sobbing uncontrollably. I was glad that the kids were asleep, and that no one else was at home to see me cry. It was like a dam had given way and I was crying a flood of tears. Damn him for causing me so much pain and heartache! Why did my life have to be so full of pain and disappointment, I wondered. I don't know how much time had gone by before I stopped crying. I just let myself cry, and cry, and cry, until there were no more tears left in me.

Logically I knew that I had made the right decision to end my relationship with Tom, but inside my heart was broken to think that I would never be able to feel his arms around me again. I felt like part of me had died, just like I had felt the last time I had held Davey in my arms, only to have him taken away from me forever. I fell into bed and cried myself to sleep.

CHAPTER 40

▼

GET UP AND TRY AGAIN

When I woke up the following morning, at first I wasn't sure if I had really talked to Tom the night before, or if I had just dreamed that I had. After a few seconds my head cleared and I knew that I really had talked to him. I felt sad about it, but I felt proud that I had followed through with my conviction to have him out of my life. I knew that any future with Tom would only be a repeat of our past, and I wanted more than that.

I went and woke up Abby and Joey and proceeded with the process of getting them ready for school. Thank goodness I was off from work today so I could let the baby sleep until we were almost ready to leave. While Abby and Joey were eating their breakfast I went and threw on a pair of shorts and a T-shirt, then went in and woke up Dinah Jean. I changed her diaper and fixed a bottle of juice for her to drink in the car. She and I would have our breakfast when I got back from dropping Abby off at her school, and then taking Joey to his preschool.

Since I didn't have to work today it would give me a chance to just play with the baby, and get use to not having Tom in my life anymore. In essence, I could just relax, or at least try to. I felt so sad that my relationship with Tom had to end this way, but I knew that it must.

The morning passed very quickly and before I knew it, it was time to go and pick Joey up from preschool. I decided to take Joey and Dinah Jean to McDonalds for lunch. It was such a nice day that I thought it would be nice to take the kids to the beach after I picked Abby up from school. That way they could run and play, and I could just sit and watch them have fun. At least that's what I thought. As it turned out, they wouldn't have any of that sitting and watching from me. They wanted me to play too. It was just as well because too much thinking isn't always the best way of dealing with things, and playing with them helped to take my mind off of thinking about Tom.

By the time we got home and everyone had taken a bath and eaten supper, the kids were so tired that none of them put up the usual fuss about going to bed. After I read them a bedtime story and got them tucked in bed, I went out in the living room to talk to Colleen. Neither her or Momma knew anything about the conversation that I'd had with Tom last night.

"I'm getting a glass of wine Colleen. Would you like one too?" I asked her as I went in the kitchen to get it.

"Sure." she said somewhat absentmindedly. She was reading the latest issue of Glamour magazine.

After I came back with the wine, I asked, "How was your day?"

"Pretty much the usual, except that Stewart came in the bank and came up to my window. He wants us to get back together, but I don't want to, and I told him so. He's too controlling. I don't like that. I'm my own person and I don't need to be told what to do and when and how to do it. At least we were in the bank and he wouldn't dare make a scene in there. I have no regrets about it whatsoever." she said while turning the page in the magazine.

We hadn't been talking for more than five minutes when the phone rang. Since Colleen was sitting right by it she answered it.

"Oh hi Tom. Here's Grace." she said, then started to hand me the phone.

"Tell him I don't want to talk to him."

She gave me a funny look, then said to Tom, "She says she doesn't want to talk to you Tom."

"Tell her to cut the crap and come to the phone." he said so loud that I could hear every word. I shook my head emphatically to indicate no.

"Look Tom, I don't know what's going on between you and Grace, but she refuses to talk to you, and I'm through relaying these messages between the two of you. I'm going to say goodbye and hang up. I'm sorry Tom, goodbye."

"What in the world is going on between the two of you?" she wanted to know.

"I've been doing a lot of soul-searching lately, and I decided that the best thing for me to do is to get Tom out of my life for good. If he ever wants to have a relationship with Dinah Jean, he can talk to a lawyer about it. I'm done with him." I said.

"I knew that something didn't seem quite right with you. You've been keeping to yourself so much lately, but I got the feeling that whatever it was, you didn't want to talk about it, and that you just wanted to be left alone. What's going on Grace?"

Before I could answer her the phone rang again. "Just let it ring." I told her, but after about the tenth ring she picked it up.

"Hello."

"Hi Colleen, it's Tom again. I'm going to keep calling until Grace agrees to talk to me. If you take the phone off the hook, or just let it ring, I'll come over there. Now tell her to come to the phone. Please!"

"Okay, just a minute, and I'll see what I can do. Grace, he's not going to give up until you at least talk to him. If you don't talk to him he says he'll come over here. Now, what do you want to do?"

"Oh! Alright then!" I said as I snatched the phone angrily from her hand. "Tom, what do you want? I told you last night that I don't want to see you anymore. I haven't changed my mind, nor will I, so just leave me alone. If you decide that you want to have a relationship with Dinah Jean, perhaps we can talk about that another time. Right now I don't want to talk to you or see you, so please stop calling." With that I slammed the phone back down on the receiver.

"What in the hell is going on with you two?" Colleen demanded to know.

"I'll tell you, but first I want to get another glass of wine. Do you want some?"

"Yes! I have the feeling I'm going to need it. Bring the whole bottle!"

I had barely gotten started telling her what was going on when there was a loud knock on the door. We both knew who that was. The curtains were closed, so he couldn't see us. The television wasn't on, so we decided to pretend like we had gone to bed, but he kept knocking so hard that I was afraid he was going to wake up the children.

"I whispered to Colleen, "Will you please open the door and tell him that I am in bed asleep?"

She didn't want any part of that scenario. She picked up her glass of wine and scurried down the hall to her bedroom and shut the door.

CHAPTER 41

▼

WHAT TOMORROW BRINGS

One never knows what tomorrow may bring. Sometimes when we least expect it, what we thought was lost to us forever turns up right outside our front door.

After I heard Colleen close her bedroom door I was in a quandary as to what my next move would be. I was fervently wishing that the persistent knocking would stop, and that Tom would turn around and leave. I didn't trust myself to see him without letting my guard down, and I had come so far this time. I had psyched myself up to where I was ready to end my relationship with him once and for all. It hadn't been easy to get to this point, and now it looked like it might all have been for naught. Damn it! Why wouldn't he just go away.

With each moment that passed the incessant knocking got louder and louder as he went from knocking to pounding. By this time Momma had come out to see what was going on.

"Grace, what in the world is going on? Who's pounding on the door? Should I call the police?"

"Momma it's Tom. I told him last night that I didn't want to see him anymore. He called earlier, and I told him the same thing again. Now he won't go away, and I don't want to see him. I don't know what to do." By this time it had become clear that he wasn't going to leave until I opened the door.

Momma said, "Grace, I don't know what this is all about, but you're going to have to open the door before he wakes up the kids and the whole neighborhood. Now do what you have to do and get rid of him before the neighbors call the police."

With that she gave me a look that said she meant what she said, and that I had better do it right now. Then she turned around and went back to her bedroom. Now I was really angry. I did not need this aggravation. I took a deep breath and opened the door with a flourish.

"What part of I don't want to see you anymore don't you understand? I want you to leave Tom. Don't make this difficult. Please just go!"

"I just want to talk to you for a minute Grace. Let me come in so we can discuss things. Please Grace. I don't want to end things like this. At least let me come in and say what I need to. After that, if you still want me to leave I will. Just hear me out."

"I've said everything that I need to Tom. There is nothing more to be said. I want you to go. Please leave Tom." With that he pushed past me and into the house.

"I'm not going anywhere until we sit down and talk about this. If you want to call the police then go ahead and do it, but I'm not leaving."

"Okay Tom, you win for now, but whatever you say it isn't going to change my mind."

With that said, I went in the kitchen and sat down at the table. Tom followed and sat down across from me. I waited for him to start talking, but he just kept looking at me. It seemed that he wanted me to be the one to initiate the conversation. I wanted to get this over with as quickly as possible, before I had a chance to change my mind. Still, he said nothing. The silence between us was becoming awkward.

Then finally he asked, "Do you have anything to drink?" I got up and fixed us both a screwdriver. I needed something stronger than a beer.

I sat back down and asked, "What do you want to say to me Tom?"

"Why all of a sudden did you decide that you don't want to see me anymore?"

"Because there is no future for me in this relationship, and I want more than you are willing to give. I never know when I'm going to see you. It seems that the only time you call is when you have nothing better to do, or else you're horny and don't have anyone else to have sex with.

I feel like I'm nothing more than an afterthought with you, and that's no longer good enough. I want there to be more than that Tom. I need for it to be more in order to be happy."

I went on to say, "I don't hold it against you. You can't help it if you don't love me as much as I love you, and I think that we should both move on with our lives."

The truth is that I did hold it against him, but I wasn't saying so. I felt like he had not only wasted years of my life, but that he had also caused me immeasurable pain and heartache in the process. I had had enough. That was the bottom line. He waited until I had said all that I wanted to say, and then he started to talk.

"I do love you Grace, more than I've ever loved anyone, but I'm scared to death of commitment."

"Tom, I think everybody is a little skeptical of commitment, but there is very little in life that is guaranteed. That's where a leap of faith comes into account. If you have enough trust in what you are doing, then you have to give it a chance."

"Okay, I tell you what, we'll ask your mother what she thinks we should do, and if she thinks that we should get married we'll drive to Georgia tonight and do it. Okay?"

I was so surprised by this that I wasn't sure that I had heard him correctly, and I wasn't really sure if he really meant what he said, or was just trying to pacify me. I thought, okay, I'll play your game, and went down the hall to get Momma.

She wasn't too happy about being pulled into the situation, but she got up and came and sat down at the kitchen table with us. I had decided that I was going to let Tom do all the talking. After we were all seated, I said to him, "Okay go ahead and tell her what's going on."

"Grace and I have been talking about getting married, and we want to know whether you think we should or not. If you think we should get married that's what we'll do. If you don't think we should then we won't. Your answer is the deciding factor. If you say yes, then we're going to drive to Georgia tonight. We'll leave right now. It's up to you. We respect your judgment."

Momma squirmed in her seat, and looked at me long and hard. I don't think that she liked being put in this position. It seemed to me that she really wanted to say no, that she didn't think that we should get married, but she was hesitant to say so because she knew how much I probably wanted her to say yes.

After what seemed like an eternity, but was actually just a few brief moments, she said, "It's pouring down rain out there. I'm not so sure ya'll should be driving in this weather."

Neither Tom nor I said anything at first. We waited for her to give us a definitive answer one way or the other. Still, she kept quiet.

"So you don't think that we should?" Tom finally asked her.

Momma's eyes darted back to me. I guess she saw the pleading look in them, because she said, "No, I think that you should."

"Okay then, that's what we'll do." Tom said with conviction.

"Just please be careful driving in this weather." Momma said.

"I'll go and pack a few things." I said.

Soon Tom and I were headed for Valdosta, Georgia.

This was insane, and downright unbelievable, just plain crazy. I couldn't believe that we were actually in the car, in the pouring down rain at eleven o'clock at night on our way to Valdosta, Georgia to get married.

It was raining so hard that we could hardly see where we were going, but going we were. I had dreamed of marrying Tom for so long, but I had never envisioned it happening this way. If I hadn't been so afraid that given any time to reconsider, Tom might be likely to change his mind, I wouldn't be driving to Georgia to get married tonight. We could have planned a small ceremony with our family and closest friends to share in the celebration with us, but I was so determined to see this through that I couldn't take that chance.

I felt sure that once we were married everything would be fine. I felt that everything that had gone wrong between us in the past would be rectified once we were married. I had absolutely no reservations about that. I believed with all my heart that this was what was meant to be, and that once we were married, Tom would be a good husband to me and a good father to my children.

The trip was going to be a long one. The rain made it seem even more so because it was so hard to see. The glare from the headlights of the oncoming traffic were magnified by the reflection of the standing water on the road. We kept thinking that we would be out of it soon, but after driving for four hours we were still driving in torrential rain.

We decided to stop and get a motel room and continue on our way the next morning. It was just too crazy to keep driving in this weather. Tomorrow we could start fresh. Hopefully, he wouldn't change his mind in the morning, but that was a chance I would have to take.

We slept in the next morning until about nine o'clock and went down to the restaurant in the hotel to have some breakfast. The fact that the sun was shining did a lot to perk up our mood. We were eager to get back on the road, so we ate our breakfast quickly and got on our way. Looking at the map, we figured that we had about another four or five hours to Valdosta.

The weather was good for the remainder of the trip and we were able to make good time. Nevertheless we arrived too late in the day to think about getting married. We decided to check into a motel room first and then go shopping.

I had packed a few things, but Tom had only the clothes he had on his back, and they were getting rather messy looking. We found a shopping mall and decided that we each should get a new outfit to get married in, along with some toiletries so that we could freshen up. By the time we finished shopping we were both starving, but we decided to go back to the hotel and freshen up before going out to eat.

On the way to our room we stopped at the hotel desk and asked the desk clerk if he could recommend a good restaurant. We had decided that we wanted surf and turf for dinner. Our mood was festive and happy, and it looked like Tom wasn't going to change his mind about getting married. For the first time since we had started this journey I felt like I could relax. Life was good.

Chapter 42

▼

Our First Day Of Marriage

When I awoke the next morning at first I didn't know where I was. Then I looked over and saw Tom, and remembered that this was my wedding day. I still couldn't believe that this was actually going to happen. It sure wasn't the way that I had envisioned it would be. Tom was awake too, and he looked over and smiled at me. That made my heart melt because he looked so happy.

We had found out the day before that we would have to go to the Health Department and get blood test before we could get married. It was required in order to rule out the presence of venereal disease. If one had it, you weren't allowed to get married until you received treatment for it and found to be free of it. Neither one of us had anything, so after getting proof of the results we headed for the courthouse where we were directed to the judge's office where the marriage would take place.

This was all starting to feel surreal to me. I think the reason for that was because I had dreamed of this moment for so long, I had begun to think that it was never going to happen. I was afraid that it was all a dream that I would awaken from at any second, and then cold hard reality would set in. That would be so disappointing that I didn't know if I would be able to handle it.

The judge was in his office and he was available. He came out to perform the ceremony right away. It was all over in about five minutes. It amazed us to think that the circumstances of our lives could be so dramatically changed in those few brief minutes. I remember walking down the steps of the courthouse and wanting to shout, "We finally did it! We got married!"

We had decided the night before that immediately following the ceremony, we would head for home. By the time we got close to home, Tom said, "I'm starving. Why don't we stop and eat dinner before we stop at my Mom's. How about you, are you hungry?"

"Yes, that sounds like a good idea. I'm so hungry I could eat a cow."

"There's a good bar-b-que restaurant just a little way down the road. Does that sound good?" Tom said looking over at me to see my response.

"It sounds perfectly marvelous my darling husband." I said, returning his gaze with a smile.

As soon as we finished eating we headed to Tom's mother and sister's house, which was about fifteen miles away. When we went in they both came out to the Florida Room to great us, having no hint of the news that we were about to tell them.

Then Tom said, "I'd like for you to meet my wife."

They looked at us with confusion on their faces. I think they thought they had misunderstood what he had said. After several seconds of them being rendered speechless, he said it again.

"I said, I would like for you to meet my wife."

Then they finally got it. After they recovered from the initial shock they were happy for us, but stunned by the news. That was the last thing they had expected to hear just out of the blue. I thought their surprised reaction was very amusing.

We didn't stay at their house for very long because it was getting late, and after all the traveling and excitement of the trip, we were beginning to feel worn out. When we arrived at my house everyone was asleep. We showered and got in bed. We were feeling excited about the fact that this was our first night together as husband and wife.

Tom spoke with relish when he said, "Now we have to consummate our marriage."

Afterward Tom said, "Marriage isn't hard at all, in fact I like it."

I found that to be very amusing, seeing as how we hadn't even been married for twenty-four hours yet. I didn't laugh or say anything though, I just wanted to savor every bit of happiness that I could.

We were filled with desire for each other so we fell back into each others' arms and consummated our marriage, over and over again.

CHAPTER 43

▼

HAPPY EVER AFTER?

For the first week or so after our marriage, we stayed at the house that Momma, Colleen and I had bought. Tom had bought a large three bedroom, two bath house with a family room about six months earlier, and we planned to eventually move there. Since Tom wasn't a very good housekeeper, or decorator, we decided to get it all cleaned up before we moved in.

His house was in a different school district, so that meant that Abby would have to change schools. I was a little concerned about how she was going to adjust to the change, but being an engaging and precocious little trouper, she adjusted very well with no problems.

Tom and I were relatively happy in our marriage for about six months, then the honeymoon was over. In retrospect I realized how stupid I was for thinking that our marriage would make all the difference, and that he would once again be the Tom I had first fallen in love with, a good man, loving, responsible and considerate, but it was not to be. I knew the true Tom, the man I knew he wished he could be, but for whatever reason he was afraid to let that Tom show himself.

Tom didn't give a rat's ass about the house, the yard, or family life. I did what I could to try and make the house look pretty, but Tom wasn't willing to spend a penny toward any cosmetic improvements whatsoever, and there was a lot that needed to be done. The whole inside of the house needed to be painted. There were no drapes or window treatments, no landscaping, quite a few windows that wouldn't open, and the list went on and on.

It was a good thing that I was working because any repairs or improvements that were needed on anything, either I paid for, or it just stayed broken or undone. He never paid for any groceries, doctor bills for Dinah Jean, or anything I bought or needed for the house, like paint drapes, etc. It didn't take very long before I started to feel resentful, frustrated, and very angry about it. Plus, he was so messy and he never picked up or cleaned up after himself.

On top of all that, it didn't take him long before he reverted back to his old habits of hanging out at the bars after work with his buddies. It wasn't unusual for him to stay out all night whenever he took a notion to. It was all starting to feel like déjà vu, just like it had been with Trevor, only worse. Tom thought it was funny to be just coming home as I was getting the children and myself ready to leave in the mornings. He would make jokes about having been kidnapped, or something else equally ridiculous.

It was practically unheard of for him to eat dinner with us, and forget about being any kind of father figure to the children. On the rare occasions that he was at home at night there was no sense of us as being a family. He never played with the kids, read stories to them, or tucked them in at night.

We never had discussions about making any plans for our lives, present or future, what our dreams were, how our day had been, issues concerning the kids, nothing. If I tried to communicate with him, or just have a discussion, it was like talking to a brick wall. Most of the time he would just stare at anything but me, and say nothing. He didn't answer me, laugh, grunt, or acknowledge that I even existed, except to tell me what a bad mother and wife I was. Our so called home became a house that was filled with tension so thick that it permeated the very air that we breathed. You could feel it on your skin and in your bones. It prickled and it was chilling.

Most afternoons after getting off at work and picking up the kids, weather permitting, I would pack up some food to cook at John Lloyd Park, and the kids and I would go to the beach for a couple of hours. It got us out of the house and into the fresh air. The kids could run and play and I could have fun watching them. We usually stayed until about six o'clock. After we got home I would get the kids cleaned up and into their pajamas, and then I would help Abby with her homework.

After the kids were asleep, I would usually get myself a glass of wine and sit down and relax, or at least try to. Then the loneliness would set in. Usually by the time I went to bed, Tom would still be out. On the rare occasions that he came home before I went to bed, he was usually drunk and mentally abusive to me. He always said what a bad mother and wife I was. I knew that wasn't true, but if a person keeps telling you that day after day, a person more than likely will start to doubt themselves, and that is what started happening to me. I started to wonder if he might be right.

The tension and animosity just kept on building up until the whole house became almost impossible for me to inhabit any longer. At that point it started to affect the kids because they could feel the tension, and it was causing them to have mental anguish. That was the final straw because I wasn't going to tolerate that. I moved up to the front part of the house where the children's bedrooms were. By that time Tom and I were virtually living apart, and our relationship as man and wife was non-existent. We were legally still man and wife, but in reality we were strangers.

After several months of living this way, I told myself that I had to get out of this relationship before it destroyed me. I had to, not only for my own sake, but for the sake of my children as well. I knew that if I continued to live this way I would become so depressed that I would be no good to myself, and if I was no good to myself, how could I be a good mother to my children? That was the clincher. I had to get out of there, and quickly.

I considered going back to the house and living with Momma and Colleen, but in the long run, I didn't think that would work. I felt that there needed to be distance between me and Tom. I knew that if I continued to live in close proximity to him, we would never get the closure we needed to overcome our obsession with each other. Only time and distance could do that.

The next day I told Abby and Joey that we were going to go on a vacation in a few days. I had decided that I wanted to move to North Carolina. I had always loved Western North Carolina. The beautiful mountains full of trees had always made me feel at peace when I was among them, and that is what I needed, peace and tranquility. I also thought that it would be a good place to raise my children. The only thing I needed to decide now, was where in North Carolina did I want to move to.

After I got off from work the next day, I picked up the kids and decided to go visit Momma and Colleen. I needed to tell them what was going on with me, and what my plans were. They knew that things were not going well between Tom and I, but they had no idea of just how bad it actually was. I hoped that they would both be at home so I could tell them both at the same time. I was in luck, both of their cars were in the driveway.

"Hey! What a nice surprise." Momma said as we walked in the door.

Abby and Joey ran to her and gave her a big hug. Then, having heard all our voices, Colleen came and joined us in the living room. After a few minutes went by, Abby and Joey asked if they could go out in the back yard and play on the swing set. I was glad they would be out of earshot. It made telling Momma and Colleen what was going on easier, without having to worry about them overhearing what was being said.

After the kids went outside, Momma, Colleen and I sat down at the kitchen table. For some reason, the kitchen table was where we always ended up when we wanted to talk.

"So, how are things going?" Momma asked.

"Not good." I said. "Not good at all. My marriage is virtually over. The kids and I have been staying in the front part of the house for the last couple of months. The tension in the house is so thick you can cut it with a knife. I'm moving out. I can't, and won't live that way anymore. The kids are feeling the tension too. I can just tell that they are."

"Oh hon, I'm so sorry. I know you had such high hopes, and it was something that you had wanted so badly for so long. When do you plan to move back here, or are you moving back right now?" Momma asked.

"We can go start getting your stuff right now." Colleen said, giving me a smile of encouragement.

"Well, that's what I wanted to talk to both of you about." I said. "I feel like I would like a glass of wine, or a beer if you have any."

"It just so happens that we do." Momma said as she went to the refrigerator. "Which would you rather have? We have both, or there is some vodka in the cabinet."

"I'll take a glass of wine, no, on second thought, I'd like some vodka and lemonade, if you've got lemonade."

"We do, and I'll join you. What about you Colleen, what do you want?"

"Might as well make it unanimous. I'll have the same as you're having."

When the drinks were made we sat down at the kitchen table. "Let me just check on Abby and Joey real quick, and then I'll tell you what my plans are." I took a peek out the back door and saw that the kids were fine. They were playing on the swing set. Dinah Jean was happily playing with some toys on the kitchen floor. Okay, now I can relax I was thinking.

"I guess you're wondering why I called this meeting together." I said jokingly.

"Yes we are. Will you get on with it for Pete's sake." Colleen said impatiently.

"Okay, I hope you're not going to be upset with me, but I don't plan on moving back here. It's not that I don't like you." I said, trying to lighten up the mood, because I could see some alarm on their faces.

"I've been doing a lot of thinking about what I should do after Tom and I split up. I've known for some time now that it was inevitable. I just didn't know exactly when it would happen, or what would be the final straw that would make it happen. I feel that I need to put some distance between us. If we continue to live in close proximity to each other, I don't think that either one of us will ever get the closure we need to once and for all, end our inexplicable obsession we have for each other. We need to get on with our lives and let the past go."

"Like how much distance are you talking about here?" Momma wanted to know.

"Yea, I hope you're not moving to Timbucktoo Grace." Colleen said. I could tell that she was trying to throw a little humor into the conversation, but at the same time, I could also see and feel the apprehension she was feeling.

"I've decided that I want to move to North Carolina." I said. Dead silence filled the room. They didn't like the sound of that idea one iota. That much was clear without even another word being said.

"Before you go getting all upset, let me explain my reasoning. The first thing, like I said is the need for distance. That aside, you know how much I have always loved North Carolina. The mountains with their beauty are so serene. I need tranquility in my life, and I think I can find it there. Plus, I think it would be a good place to raise my children."

"But Grace, where would you go? You don't know anyone there, you have no job. Where would you live? There's too much uncertainty to just go riding off with three small children under those circumstances. I don't think it's a good idea."

Colleen just kept quiet. I don't think she wanted to get in the middle of Momma and me, and I didn't blame her. I'm sure if she had the choice of making the decision for me, she would rather that I stay in Ocean Shores.

"Momma it may sound to you like I have lost my mind, or that I'm not thinking clearly, or maybe you just think that I don't have good sense, but I have thought this out, and I just know that it will work out, and that it's what I should do. Don't ask me how or why I know this, but I can tell you that I am not scared at all about making this move. It just feels right, and in my heart I know it will all be okay. Please, you have just got to trust me on this."

"Grace, you're going to be the death of me. Honestly, I never know what to expect next when it comes to you. So where do you plan to go, and when do you intend to do it?" she asked with worry and exasperation in her voice.

"I plan to move to a town called Greenwood. It's in the southwestern part of North Carolina"

"And may I ask how you decided on this place called Greenwood." she asked.

"You can, but you're not going to like my answer."

"Try me." she said, sitting back and crossing her arms across her chest.

"Well, first I got a map of North Carolina, and then I took a protractor and drew a circle around the area that I wanted to live in, which was definitely the mountains, and then I closed my eyes and put my finger on the map. The first few times it didn't work because my finger fell in an area that I didn't want to live in, but on the fifth try it landed on Greenwood."

Both her and Colleen's mouths dropped open with disbelief and utter amazement. I know they thought I was either just plain crazy, or just plain stupid.

"Anyway, the bottom line is that me and the kids are going on a vacation to Greenwood, North Carolina next week. My plan is to find us a place to live. That's the only thing that would keep me from going, not having a place to live. I feel confident that everything else will work itself out."

"There's something else that I need to talk to you about, but first let me check on Abby and Joey again." They were still playing well together and having fun so I went back to the table and sat down.

"Once I move, I won't be able to contribute my share of the house payment anymore, so I want to be removed from being part owner. I hope this won't leave you in a lurch, but I just won't be able to afford it anymore."

"Well, although I hate to do that, it is the most logical thing you've said so far today." Momma said. I could tell that she was upset with me, and that she was concerned about the well being of the children and I going off into unknown and untested territory.

"I plan on taking a week off from work, and leaving the beginning of next week. I've already cleared it with my boss. Of course, he doesn't know that I plan on moving, he just thinks I'm going on vacation. I don't want to tell him about the move just yet because he would probably just let me go and I need to continue working until the day before I leave for good."

I stayed and talked to Momma and Colleen for a little longer, trying to reassure them about my decision to move, but I don't think it really did any good. They still thought I was making an irresponsible decision.

With that part taken care of, now came the really hard part, telling Tom. I was filled with both dread and sorrow at the prospect of what that conversation would be like. I didn't have any idea of how he was going to react to the decision I had made. For all I knew, he might jump for joy at the opportunity to get rid of me. He had to know that the life we were living together wasn't good for any of us, but on the other hand who knew. He might be very angry. I never knew what to expect from him.

On the best days of our marriage, he would have come home at a reasonable hour, we would have gone to bed together, gotten up the next morning, kissed each other goodbye, and wished each other a good day. Then, many times when he came home that afternoon, he wouldn't be on speaking terms with me. Of course he never clued me in on what the reason he wasn't speaking to me was.

But then, none of that really mattered anymore because for all intents and purposes it was all over between us, so what was there to be worried about. My mind was definitely made up, and nothing was going to change that, so why was I feeling so anxious about it?

In my heart I knew why, but I couldn't let my heart rule in this case. I had to be strong and carry through with my plans. I had to admit to myself once and for all that I had to let Tom go. There was no longer any room for doubt or denial. This roller coaster ride I had been on with him had gone on far too long as it was, and it was making me physically and mentally sick.

I made a vow to myself that I would get it over and done with at the first opportunity, but I had to wait until I thought the time was right. I didn't want to have this conversation, for example on a morning when he had been out all night, and was still drunk when he came home. I didn't want to attempt to broach the subject when he wasn't on speaking terms with me either. I wanted for there to be a time when just the two of us could sit down and try to end the relationship amiably.

I knew it would be difficult under the best of circumstances, but I wanted it to be under the best conditions as possible. My chance came a few days after I had told Momma and Colleen what my plans were. The kids were spending the night with them as they occasionally did on the weekends.

It happened one Saturday morning when neither Tom or I were working. We happened to meet in the kitchen just as I was making some coffee. We didn't speak to each other for a minute or two, and then I asked him, "Would you like some coffee?"

"Yes I would." he said.

"Do you think we could sit down and talk for a few minutes? I need to discuss something important with you." I said.

He was agreeable with that, so I thought, okay, so far so good. I suppose that I appeared calm outwardly, but inside I had so many different emotions and feelings brewing that I began to wonder if I could get through this without having a complete breakdown. This was one of the hardest things I had ever had to do. My heart was broken that this was what our marriage had come to. I had never loved a man as I loved Tom. He had been the love of my life, and in just the few minutes that it would take for me to say what I had to, it would all be over between us.

As soon as the coffee was ready we sat down at the kitchen table that was in a little alcove by a bay window. It was one of my favorite places in the house because it was always filled with sunshine, and I had a lot of really nice houseplants growing there. It was like an indoor garden.

We both took a couple of sips of our coffee before either one of us said anything. Then I took a deep breath and said, "Tom, the children and I will be moving in a few weeks. I've decided to move to Greenwood, North Carolina. We should file for a divorce before I leave."

Just for a split second, I had seen a flash of emotion in his eyes, but then it was gone as quickly as it had come. I wished that I knew what that flash meant, but I never would because he said nothing. There was no need for me to say why I was moving, we both already knew the reasons.

CHAPTER 44

▼

THE END OF AN ERA

As with so many situations I have dealt with in my life, many times I've found that most of the ones I have expected will be the hardest, have turned out to be the ones that are the least difficult. That was the case with the conversation Tom and I had on that Saturday morning. There was no bitter animosity or playing of the blame game. It was just what it was, plain and simple, no explanations necessary, only the need to get on with it.

We simply picked an attorney out of the yellow pages, and made an appointment to file for a divorce. It was a simple divorce because Florida has a no-fault divorce law. We didn't have to have legal grounds, or put the blame on either one of us.

The only details that had to be worked out was the custody issue for Dinah Jean and the child support issue. There was no problem with the custody issue because Tom didn't want custody, and the child support we agreed on was one hundred dollars a month.

If I had been feeling vindictiveness toward Tom, I probably could have gotten his house, but I didn't want to cross that line. Basically I just wanted it over and done with so I could move away. Since I wouldn't be living in Florida when the divorce became final, we made Tom the petitioner for the divorce.

With that taken care of we got in the car and went back home. On the way home, Tom said, "I feel so relieved to have that ordeal over and done with." I did too really, but for different reasons than Tom, so I concealed my anger because I didn't have the energy to do otherwise.

I knew that we were both very unhappy in our marriage, and I had reached the point that the only thing that mattered was to have it over and done with so I could put it behind me. I had reached my saturation point for misery and could hold no more of it without self-destructing.

I felt like I had been double crossed and deluded by Tom, and what he had led me to believe his feelings for me were. I had a heap of wrongs that would never be righted. In particular the loss of my son Davey. I had a slew of regrets that could never be readdressed, and a lot of broken dreams that were comprised of, and defined by, the travesty of what Tom had expressed as his love for me.

I had no fear of what lay ahead, only excitement for a new start in life for me and my children. I felt like we were starting a great adventure, and who knew what that adventure might be. I didn't even want to know. I wanted to be surprised every time I turned the page in this new chapter of my life. Everyone who knew my plans couldn't understand how I had the nerve to make a move like this with three small children, to a place I had never been to before, didn't know a soul who lived there, and without a job lined up. The truth was, I wasn't scared at all. I just knew that it was going to work out.

As soon as Tom and I had scheduled our appointment with the lawyer, I had arranged to take two weeks off from work. So the day following the appointment, the kids and I left on the vacation I had told them we were going to take.

I had bought some items that I hoped would keep the kids entertained, but I knew the trip was going to be hard on them. Abby was now eight, Joey was six, and Dinah Jean was four. I had calculated that it was about seven hundred and eighty-nine miles to Greenwood. I had made up my mind in advance that I wasn't going to push the limit on trying to get there as soon as possible, but rather to gauge when to stop based on how the kids were doing. As it turned out we made pretty good time the first day because all three of them slept a good deal of the time. That was a blessing. The first day we made it to just over the Georgia state line.

Since there was a couple hours of sunshine left in the day I decided to try and find a motel that had a swimming pool. I knew the kids would like that, and it would not only give them a chance to play after being cooped up in the car all day, it would also wear them out so they would be able to go to sleep early. I wanted to go to bed early myself because the long drive had worn me out. As soon as we got checked in and brought in what we needed for the night, we all four got into our bathing suits and headed for the swimming pool.

After an hour or so of playing in the pool we were all getting hungry. We went back to our room, got showered and bathed, and went to dinner at a diner across the street from the motel. By the time we got back to the motel we were all ready to put on our pajamas and lay down and watch T.V. The kids were asleep within an hour and I fell asleep right after they did. Abby and Joey were in one bed and Dinah Jean was in bed with me.

We got an early start the next morning. I really wanted to get to Greenwood before dark if possible. I wanted our first impression of the place to be in the daylight. Again we made good time and arrived there about four o'clock in the afternoon. We were not disappointed at what we saw.

The sign that greeted us as we entered the city limits said:
WELCOME TO GREENWOOD, NORTH CAROLINA
Population 4,569

Greenwood certainly lived up to its' name. It truly was a charming little town, set in the middle of a valley surrounded by mountains that were covered with beautiful trees. Every building in town was old, but they were all well maintained and added to the ambiance of the place. It made you feel good just to be there.

We checked into a motel that was right in town, and decided to do some exploring; check the place out and see what it had to offer. We didn't explore for too long because there wasn't too much time left before it would be getting dark, plus the kids were tired and so was I.

We spotted a café right on Main Street and went in to eat dinner. The waitress was real friendly and greeted us with a welcoming smile. After she put our order in and brought us our drinks, we struck up a conversation.

She said, "I don't believe I've seen you folks before. Are you from around here, or are you on vacation and just passing through?"

"Actually, we're planning on moving here from south Florida." I said. "We're on a vacation/find a place to live combination. My name is Grace, and these are my children, Abby, Joey and Dinah Jean."

"Well it's sure nice to meet you. My name is Jenny, and I hope you'll be able to enjoy your vacation, and find a place to live. What made you decide to move to Greenwood? Do you have family here? I might know them if you do. I've lived here all my life."

I was about to answer her, when Abby spoke up. "You know how my mommy decided to move to Greenwood?"

I thought, oh no, this girl is going to think I am absolutely crazy out of my mind.

"No I don't know. What made her decide to come and live here Abby?"

"Well, she got a map and drew a circle on it, and then she closed her eyes and put her finger on it, and her finger landed on Greenwood. That's how she decided."

I took a quick look at Jenny to see what her reaction was. She did look surprised, but she didn't look at me like she thought I was nuts.

"Well, that's certainly an interesting way to decide where you want to live." she said, and we looked at each other and laughed.

"I know it sounds crazy." I said.

Then the cook called her to let her know our order was ready. After she brought our food to the table and asked if there was anything else that we needed, she said, "I don't mean to get in your business, but if you have any questions, or need any information, I'll be glad to answer anything you would like to know, if I can."

"Thank you Jenny. That's very kind of you and I appreciate it. First and foremost, I need to find a place for us to live. I'd like to find a three bedroom, two bath house to rent if possible. That's my primary concern right now. After we find a place to live, we'll take a little time for a mini vacation, and go back to Florida and pack our belongings. Then once we get moved in, I'll need to find a job."

"That's probably more questions and information than you volunteered for." I said, apologetically.

"No, no, no, not at all." she said. "As a matter of fact I have a friend that's a realtor. I can call her if you like and tell her what you're looking for, and if she knows of anything to show you, I'll give you her name and phone number. Her office is just down the street actually, so it will be easy for you to find. She's probably closed for today, but I'll give her a call at home. You go ahead and eat your dinner before it gets cold, and I'll come back and let you know what she said."

"Thank you so much Jenny. I really appreciate it." I said gratefully.

When we were finished eating Jenny came back to the table and told me, "I talked to my friend and she said she would check her listings and try to find something suitable for you. Here's her phone number and the name of the real estate office. Her name is Brenda, and she said to wait until around ten o'clock tomorrow morning and meet her at her office."

"Great! Again thank you so much Jenny."

She asked us if we wanted any dessert, but we were all too full. They gave very generous proportions around here.

Before she left the table, Jenny gave me some more useful information. She told me where the Chamber of Commerce was, and sort of a verbal tour of the town. She also mentioned some local attractions that she thought the children and I might be interested in checking out. By the time we had finished dinner, I felt like I had made a new friend.

After dinner we went back to the motel. We were all tired, but Joey and Dinah Jean were downright cranky and whiny. I got them in the bathtub and suddenly remembered that I had forgotten to call Momma and Colleen to let them know that we had arrived safely. While I took a minute to call them, Abby helped Dinah Jean get bathed and into her pajamas.

Abby had become such a help to me. She was so mature for her eight years of life. I didn't know if that was good or bad because I wanted her to be able to be the child that she was, and unencumbered by responsibility that was before her time to be so.

Once settled in bed with a T.V. program to watch the kids fell asleep quickly. That's when I could finally relax. I went out to the car and brought in a bottle of wine that I had bought just for this occasion. The celebration of our arrival in Greenwood, and the beginning of a new chapter in our lives. Ah! It felt so good to sit down, put my feet up, and speculate as to what our lives might be like here. It was all good, and I slept like a baby that night.

CHAPTER 45

▼

A NEW CHAPTER BEGINS

The next morning my first thought upon awakening was, this is the first day of the rest of my life. That thought caused me to smile to myself, and I felt very happy and very excited. The kids and I got up early and had breakfast at the same café we had eaten dinner at the night before. From there we went to the real estate office that Jenny the waitress had referred me to. My first priority was to find a house to rent, and once I had that taken care of I could relax and do some fun things with the kids.

As it turned out, there weren't very many choices in the rental department. There very few houses, and even fewer apartments for rent. I wasn't interested in an apartment. If I didn't have any choice, due to availability then so be it, but I really wanted a three bedroom, two bath house, close to town if possible. I felt that a house would feel more like a real home and be a more private setting. Having lived in an apartment before, I knew how nosy and complaining neighbors could be, and how everybody seemed to know and talk about everybody else's business.

Just when I was beginning to lose hope of finding a place that would suit our needs, the realtor took us to see a house that was farther out of town than I had hoped for, but as far as the house itself, it was just what we needed. It was out in the country about five miles outside of town, but it wasn't in an isolated area. There were other houses scattered around. That made it okay, because the thought of being out in the middle of nowhere all by myself, with three small children gave me the willies.

I decided to go ahead and rent it even though it didn't come supplied with a stove or a refrigerator. I didn't want to have that expense, but I figured I would pick up some used ones. The only drawback to going ahead and renting the house now was that I would have to start paying my house rent beginning today. I hated that because by the time I got back to Ocean Shores and got everything packed up then drove back to Greenwood, it would almost be time to pay another month's rent. However, I felt that I had no choice but to do so.

Having our living accommodations taken care of was a big relief, but it just made me all the more anxious to get back to Ocean Shores so I could start packing up. I was eager to have us moved and settled before school started so that Abby and Joey would be settled in their new school, and not have to be disrupted once school had already started.

However, I had promised the kids that we would do some fun things while we were on vacation, and I couldn't break that promise. One day we went to the Cherokee Indian Village. Abby and Joey liked the Indians, but Dinah Jean was afraid of them, so I had to carry her almost the whole time we were there.

One day we went to Gatlinburg, Tennessee where we rode on the Gatlinburg Sky Lift. The view was amazing. It was a clear day and you could see everything so clearly. It was so beautiful it took my breath away. It was a little hair-raising however, because once again Dinah Jean was frightened. She cried most of the way, and she kept saying, "Me fall down Mommy." All I could do was hold her tight and tell her, "Mommy won't let you fall Dinah Jean. Mommy is holding you tight so there is no need for you to be scared. Look, see all the pretty mountains?"

On the last day of our vacation we visited the historic Biltmore House in Asheville, North Carolina. It was extremely beautiful and I really enjoyed seeing all the rooms decorated with very ornate antique furnishings. The kids on the other hand didn't see what all the fuss was about. All they wanted to know was when are we leaving, or can we go now.

Their becoming bored worked out well though, because after that they were ready to go back home too. I was more than ready to leave and get started on the packing, so the next morning we left Greenwood and headed for Ocean Shores. Now all Abby and Joey wanted to know is when are we coming back. Dinah Jean didn't give a hoot. Abby and Joey were enthralled with the mountains. They loved the woods and all the little creeks that rambled through them. I felt like I had made the right decision about moving there. It all just seemed to fit right.

I dreaded the drive back to Ocean Shores. I glanced back at the kids who were all sleeping, and I wished that I could just lay down and go to sleep too. My goal was to at least make it to the Florida state line before stopping for the night. That meant that I had about three to four more hours before reaching my goal.

To pass the time and break up the monotony, I decided to play a little game as I drove. It was one that I had played with the kids, but since they were sleeping I would have to play it by myself. Ho! Hum! The game was to pick a color and see who could spot the most cars that were that color. That's how bored I was. What I really felt like doing was to let out a big loud yell just to blow off some steam, but I didn't want to wake up the kids. I picked the color red, and after counting three or four red cars I had had enough of the game.

For my next attempt at trying to amuse myself I started singing whatever I was thinking. The first chorus went something like this. "I'm so sick of driving I don't know what to do, but I have to, oh yes I have to, boo hoo hoo, hoo hoo." I know that sounds silly, but I was desperate, and so I just sang whatever thoughts or words came into my mind.

I still had about two hours worth of driving before reaching the Florida state line, when all of a sudden I heard Joey say, "Who are you talking to Mommy?"

"No one honey. I was just feeling bored and lonely so I made up some games that I could play by myself."

He asked, "Can I play the game with you?"

"Sure." I said. I was glad to have his company. There are no rules to this game. You just start singing about whatever comes into your mind. It can be about anything, maybe something that you see, or something that you are thinking about; anything."

He said, "Okay Mommy, but I want you to go first."

"Okay, here goes. Oh how I love my children. They are the most wonderful, fantastic, and terrific kids in the world. There are no others as wonderful as my Joey, my Abby and my Dinah Jean. Oh yea! Oh yea! Oh yea! Dee dee, dee dee, dee, dee dee!"

Joey seemed to like the song. He was smiling, but I think he thought that I was a little crazy. "Okay, now it's your turn." I told him, and away he went. I was interested to see what he would come up with.

"I have a silly Mommy, but I love her, yes I love her, and I'm getting hungry! I have to go to the bathroom! How much further is it until we get to the motel? I really have to go to the bathroom bad Mommy! Oh yea, oh yea, oh yea."

His last stanza was sung so fervently that it made us break out in laughter and woke up the girls. It was good timing though because we were just coming up on a gas station to take care of Joey's needs, and I needed some gas anyway. I figured I'd get the kids a light snack to tide them over until we stopped for the day while I was at it. According to my calculations I figured it would take about another hour to make it to the Florida state line.

The next morning we got an early start and made it back to Ocean Shores before it got dark. I decided to go straight to Momma and Colleen's and spend the night. I wanted to tell them all about our trip and the house that we had rented; plus I really didn't feel like seeing Tom just yet.

▼

CHAPTER 46

NORTH CAROLINA HERE WE COME

It was wonderful to pull into Momma and Colleen's driveway and get out of the car. The kids were glad to be able to get out and run around too. Joey wanted to tell them all about the Cherokee Indian Reservation. That was his favorite place we had gone to on our trip, but when he started talking about the Indians, Dinah Jean started crying.

She started stomping her feet and saying, "No Mommy. I don't like Inyans."

"It's okay Dinah. There aren't any Indians here. Brother is just telling Grandmother and Aunt Colleen a story about them. Come here and sit on Mommy's lap. There's nothing to be afraid of. Then Abby started to tell them about the Sky Lift we rode up the mountain in Gatlinburg. I guess Dinah Jean felt safe in my arms because she started laughing.

"I think I fall down." she told Momma and Colleen.

Momma, Colleen and I sat up quite late that night talking about my trip. They wanted to know what Greenwood was like, and what the house I had rented was like; in short they wanted to know everything.

I could tell that they were still somewhat dubious about the move, but I was so certain that it was the right move for me that I think my enthusiasm lessened their anxieties a little bit anyway. I truly did feel that God had led me to make this decision, and therefore I had not a single shred of doubt about doing so. I simply felt that it was meant to be.

On the way back to Tom's house the next morning I stopped at the grocery store and picked up some groceries, and I asked them if they had any empty boxes that I could have for packing up our belongings. They gave me all they had and said they would save some more for me when their next delivery came in on Tuesday.

I knew that I was going to have to leave a lot of things behind because I could only take what I could fit into a small U-Haul trailer that I intended to hitch to the back of my car. There was no other way to do it. I couldn't afford to hire a moving company, and I couldn't rent a big U-Haul truck because it would be impossible to fit the four of us into the cab of one. Besides, I didn't feel comfortable hauling my car behind a big U-Haul truck. Consequently, deciding what I was going to take was going to require a lot of thought.

I was relieved to see that Tom's car wasn't in the driveway when I pulled in. Whenever he was there the tension in the air made everyone feel on edge. Besides, I just wasn't ready to have to deal with him on any level right then.

I unloaded the car and got the kids some lunch. Then I started trying to figure out where to begin as far as what to pack up, and what to leave behind. I felt so overwhelmed by it all that I couldn't bring myself to make a move. After a few minutes of complete inertia I decided to try and figure things out in a more orderly way, rather than just plowing in haphazardly.

By this time the kids had finished their lunch, and Joey and Dinah Jean were starting to become fidgety as to what to do with themselves. Abby just wanted to be helpful and help me get things packed up, which was certainly within her capabilities.

Abby is a very loving child who has been blessed with the gift of discernment, and consequently she has an inner sense as to how to proceed when an occasion calls for it. Especially when it comes to me because we are so close. That being her nature, she immediately offered to help me get started with the packing. The only trouble was that Joey and Dinah Jean wanted to help too, and that was not helpful!

I told Abby, "The best way that you can help me right now is by playing with Joey and Dinah Jean. Maybe you could read them a story or color with them. "Mr. Rogers" will be coming on in a few minutes, maybe all of you would like to watch him."

I liked for the kids to watch "Mr. Rogers" because he always emphasized to the children how special each of them were. He was also very kind, with a very positive theme to his show. He always emphasized the importance of good ideals and values as well.

I got the kids all setup to watch him in the family room with their pillows on the floor in front of the T.V. I hoped that they were all so tired from our travels that they would fall asleep while watching his show. Once they had all the stuff they needed, like Dinah Jean's "blankie", Joey's teddy bear, and Abby's book that she was reading, I snuck off.

I decided to sit down and make a list of what to pack up and what to leave, along with any other business that I needed to take care of before moving day. Before commencing this task I needed to find a tablet and a pen, and sit down at the table with a cigarette and a beer while I tried to gather my thoughts. I was still overwhelmed, but I knew that I needed to get as much of this done while I still had a few more days off from work.

I sat down at the table and started the easy part of my list while I smoked my cigarette and drank my beer. There were certain things that were no-brainers, such as some sheets and towels, blankets, our clothes, some dishes and pots and pans, silverware, etc.

Other things required more thought, so I decided to go on a room by room tour, taking inventory and adding to my list of what I wanted to take with me as I went. I didn't want to take anything that had been in the house before Tom and I got married. I felt I had no right to those things. By the time my tour had reached the family room, I noticed that all three of the children were sleeping. I was glad for that time of respite.

I found myself thinking of all the times I had wished that Tom would come home at a reasonable hour, but ironically I found myself thinking the exact opposite now. Now, I was wishing that I would never have to see him again before I left. I began to realize how much bitterness I felt toward him. At that moment I felt no love whatsoever for him.

All I could think about was how much trouble and heartache he had caused me. That gave me a surge of energy because then I could only think about how quickly I wanted to be away from all this pain and heartache. It was then that I started to pack with such ferocity that before I knew it, I had filled every box that I had on hand. If I would've had more, they would have been filled too.

It was then that I heard the door open and saw Tom come walking in. He must have been drinking because he started talking very loudly. In this instance, once again trying to make a joke out of everything.

Looking at all the boxes I had already packed, he said, "Boy, you must really be in a hurry to get out of here."

I forced a fake chuckle, and then I said, "You got that right. I can't get out of here fast enough. The kids are all taking a nap in the family room, and I would appreciate it if you would stop talking so loud. Are you going to be around for a while? I need to go get some more boxes."

He sarcastically replied, "Maybe I will and maybe I won't." Then he shot a lascivious grin at me. I knew that he wouldn't go off and leave the kids alone, and since I didn't intend to be gone longer than twenty or thirty minutes, I grabbed my purse and away I went.

Someone had once told me that boxes from liquor stores were good to use for packing because they are very strong. There were two liquor stores right in our neighborhood, so I stopped at them to see if they had any. I got lucky. They both had some, and between the two of them I was able to get twelve boxes. I was very happy to get them because I thought they would be excellent for packing books and other weighty items in. I didn't want to make the boxes so heavy that I wouldn't be able to lift them. Besides, I had a lot of books. I had a set of encyclopedias, children's books, and a large variety of others that I had accumulated over the years, none of which I wanted to leave behind.

By the end of the day, I was quite proud of myself for getting so much done. At the rate I was going, I would be able to leave much sooner than I had anticipated, but I planned on working another week before leaving just to give myself some extra money.

Tom was giving me a thousand dollars, so I felt that I had some breathing room as far as not having to feel too pressured about being able to get to Greenwood and getting us setup with whatever we were going to need. I knew that I would need security deposits for the utilities, and I knew that the kids and I would needing to get some winter clothes. Even though I planned on buying a used stove and refrigerator, I had no idea how much all of that was going to cost.

By the time I had to go back to work I had finished packing everything except what we needed on a daily basis. During those last days in Ocean Shores Tom wasn't around very much, but when he was he either acted very aloof, or like he thought what was happening was somehow a big joke on me. It hurt me to think that he was able to look at all that had happened, and all that was continuing to happen as being very trivial. It appeared that he placed no value whatsoever on what we had once been to each other.

My last week at work was filled with mixed emotions. I had become close with some of my co-workers and regular customers, and it was sad to think that I might not ever see some of them again. After we closed on my last day they had a surprise "Farewell Party" for me, and took me out to dinner. My fellow workers, along with most of my regular customers had all contributed to what they referred to as, "a little traveling money" gift. I was overcome with their generosity and love when they handed me a goodbye and good luck, we'll miss you type of card that contained two hundred and seventy-five dollars.

My plan was to leave for North Carolina two days after my last day at work. Everything that I was taking was all ready to be loaded into the U-Haul, which I was going to pick up the evening before we left. Tom had recruited a friend of his to help load everything up. I was really counting on him, and I was praying that he wouldn't let me down like he had so many times before.

In those last few days before leaving, I tried to spend as much time as I could with Momma, Daddy, Colleen, Ellen and Nora. My moving was emotional for all of us, but it didn't take away from my excitement about starting this new chapter in my life. My feeling that it was the right thing to do did not waiver one iota. I felt at peace.

Tom was true to his word, and he and his friend Bob loaded up the U-Haul just as he had promised they would. I guess that he wanted to make sure that I left.

The trip was pretty much uneventful. We didn't have any car trouble or anything like that. I had been a wee bit nervous about pulling the U-Haul behind me, but after having gone fifty miles or so, I started to feel very comfortable about it. I had one bad experience of having to back up with it, but after that I made sure I parked in a location where backing up was unnecessary.

The only other problem I had was when I tried to go up the dirt road to our new home. My car just didn't have the power needed to get up the hill with the U-Haul. The more I persisted in trying, the worse it got. I finally had to give up and try to seek help, but from whom? I didn't know a soul except the realtor who had shown us the house, and the man from whom we had rented it.

I had to have help, and it was getting dark very quickly. I decided to take the kids and walk over to the nearest house I saw. I sure hoped they were the friendly type. Thanks be to God, they were. They were a young couple with two young children. The man happened to be my landlord's son, and he had a four wheel drive truck. They were very nice, and he was happy to help us. I was so relieved. I don't know what I would have done without his help. He and his wife turned out to be very good neighbors during the brief time that we lived in that house.

The important thing was that we had made it, and thus begun the new chapter in our lives. I couldn't wait for it to unfold.

Chapter 47

▼

Getting Settled

It was almost completely dark by the time our neighbor got the U-Haul backed up to where it needed to be, and boy oh boy is it ever dark way out in the country where there are no street lights. This was going to take some getting use to. It was spooky, but I couldn't let on to the kids or else they would have gotten spooked too.

We were all really happy to be out of the car and at our new home. That first night all I really concentrated on unloading from the U-Haul was some blankets, sheets, pillows, our toothbrushes, and something for us to sleep in. We had stopped at a restaurant and eaten dinner before coming to the house, and I had picked up some snacks as well.

Fortunately the electricity was working. I planned to go into town the next day to take care of setting up the account in my name, and also to make arrangements for getting a phone installed. For tonight however, we were all so tired that as soon as I got our sleeping arrangements setup (we were all sleeping on the floor huddled up in the living room) we were all asleep in no time.

Early the next morning we got up and got dressed to go into town. The first thing on our agenda was to get some breakfast. This eating out was getting expensive, so I added getting a stove and refrigerator to my "To Do List." I found a store that sold new and used appliances and was able to buy both the stove and refrigerator and get them delivered the same day. Once I had made those purchases and put down all the utility deposits, I was alarmed at how fast my money was being spent.

My neighbor whose husband had helped us with the U-Haul came over to see how we were doing, and she gave me a lot of helpful information.

She said, "I wasn't sure if you knew when school will be starting, or if you even knew what school district we're in, so I thought it might be helpful for me to fill you in on a few things."

"That's so kind of you. Please come in. Would you like a cup of coffee? You'll have to excuse our lack of furnishings. I couldn't bring very many things with me."

"I would love a cup of coffee." she said, as she came in and sat on our only chair. As I started making our coffee she continued talking. She said, "If you need information about anything else, I'll try to answer your questions about anything I can."

"Coffee will be ready in a minute." I said coming back to the living room. "I sure do appreciate your thoughtfulness in coming over to fill me in. Actually I need answers to everything you mentioned, and then some."

"I'm at your service, ask away." she said, and we both smiled. Her name was Caroline, and I really liked her. She was comfortable to be with because she made you feel that you had known each other for a long time.

"Okay, I think the coffee is ready so why don't I move your chair into the kitchen. That way you can set your coffee on the counter, and I'll sit on the counter while we talk.What do you take in your coffee?"

"Just sugar."

Once we got situated in the kitchen, I started with the questions. "I guess the first thing I need to know is when school starts."

"School starts the day after Labor Day, and Abby and Joey will be going to Cullasaja Elementary. The bus picks them up at the end of the dirt road. If you want me to, I can go with you when you register them. I'll be going there anyway to find out which teachers my children got, and also to get a list of all the school supplies they will need."

"It would be wonderful if I could go with you to see where the school is at. When are you planning on going? I'll be glad to drive. In fact I would prefer to because that way I'll pay more attention as to how to get there." I said.

"Sure. I was planning on going this coming Friday. That way I have all weekend to shop for their school supplies, plus that's the only day that you can register. You'll need to have proof of what vaccinations they have had, and if they need any, you can get them at the Health Department."

"They're all up to date on that, but I'll need to dig through some of these boxes to find the papers. My other concern is to find a daycare for my little on, Dinah Jean. She's four."

"Why don't you checkout the Head Start Program for her? As far as I know they base what you pay on your income."

"That's a great idea. Right now I have no income to base it on, but that will be changing soon. At least I hope it will. As soon as I get the kids in school, I'm going job hunting."

"What kind of work are you looking for?" Caroline asked.

"At this point, just about anything. I'll take whatever I can get, and look for something better when I'm able to. Right now I'm just concerned with having a paycheck every week."

I asked Caroline if there was a local Unemployment Agency in town, and she said yes. Then she told me exactly where it was. It was right in town, so at least I didn't have to worry about getting lost trying to find the place.

On Friday Caroline and I went and got the kids registered for school, and then she offered to go with me to the Head Start office. I couldn't believe my luck when they told me they had an opening for Dinah Jean. That was such a relief.

As soon as I got the kids settled in on their first day of school, I went about the business of trying to find a job. It didn't take long before I became very discouraged because the job opportunities, I quickly learned, are few and far between in such a small town.

Another problem was with the hours I would be able to work, being as I had to be home by the time the school bus dropped Abby and Joey off from school, and pick Dinah Jean up from Head Start. By the end of the day I was starting to feel a panic attack coming on. On my way home from a day of job hunting the reality of the risks I had put myself and my children in was beginning to dawn on me. All of a sudden I started to question my sanity about moving to a place where I knew no one, and had no job to go to. If I only had myself to worry about there wouldn't be any problem, but that wasn't the case. What had I been thinking when I made this decision? I knew that I had better stop this line of thinking before I reached the point of no return and let myself nose dive into a full blown panic attack.

I took a deep breath, and thought, hmm that seemed to help, so I took several more. Okay girl, you can do this. Then I started singing. At first I was making up the words as I went along, just like Joey and I had done on the trip back to Florida. Then all of a sudden the song, "I Am Woman" sung by Helen Reddy came on the radio, and I said to myself, "Yes! That's me! I am strong, I am invincible, I am woman, hear me roar, and I let out a great big lion roar."

Those up and down roller coaster rides with my emotions have been an ongoing problem for me for as long as I can remember. Sometimes they culminate in a panic attack, and at other times they may end up in a long bout with depression. I can't hide the panic attacks, but to a certain degree I can hide the bouts with depression.

The kids were all in good spirits when I picked them up, and that in turn picked my spirits up. They were all bubbling over about the new friends they had made and all that they had learned that day. Abby and Joey had met some kids that lived within shouting distance from our house. When we got home Abby and Joey insisted that we walk over to their house so that I could introduce myself to their parents, and check them out to make sure they would be good playmates for my children. By then it was time to go home and cook dinner, and by the time I was back home with the kids I had calmed myself down.

Since our dining room table hadn't been an item that I was able to fit in the U-Haul, we had been putting a tablecloth down on the living room carpet at mealtime and pretending that we were having a picnic. We made a game of it and the kids thought it was fun. I, on the other hand would have preferred to be eating my meals at a dining room table, but the important thing was that we were all together, in a safe place with plenty of food to eat, and clothes on our backs.

Tomorrow I would go right back out with new resolve, determination, and purpose. If I didn't find a job tomorrow, then I would get up again and go right back again and again until I found something. Yes! "I am strong. I am invincible. I am woman, hear me roar!"

CHAPTER 48

▼

THIS FEELS SO RIGHT

Now that we were settled in as much as we could be, considering that we didn't have hardly any furniture, and I still didn't have a job, we were feeling that this was exactly where we were suppose to be. The kids absolutely loved living out in the country and so did I. Small town life was what I loved, and since my great great great grandfather had settled in North Carolina in 1754, I felt like this was where my true roots were.

The only thing that was discouraging was the choices for, and the availability for employment. Initially I had gone to the unemployment office and searched for employment through them. I wanted to get away from doing waitress work if possible. I had taken business classes in high school, but I wasn't very skilled at them because I hadn't applied myself to the curriculum like I should have. Now I regretted it, but it was too late to be moping around about it now. Now it was just get a job, whatever was available until I could find something better. A port in the storm so to speak because my money was dwindling away at an alarming rate.

A good portion of it had gone toward getting winter clothes for all of us. Having come from south Florida, sweaters were about the extent of our winter clothes. Winter weather would be here soon, and the holidays would be upon us before I knew it. I decided to take whatever job I could get.

After dropping the kids off at school I went into town and started going to every business establishment in Greenwood. First I started looking for a job as a sales clerk. There were none to be found. Next I started going into every restaurant in town looking for a job as a waitress. The third restaurant I went in there was an opening. The name of the restaurant was called "Granny's Home Cooking." It was in need of some remodeling and updates, but at least it was a job.

There were two men that owned the restaurant, but the one that interviewed me was a stern looking man of few words. I found him to be very intimidating. He came across as being a very hardened and unhappy person. My hours would be from 7:45 A.M. until 2:30 P.M. He had wanted me to start at 6:A.M. and work until 3:00 P.M., but I couldn't because I had to be able to coordinate my hours with the children's schedule, and I needed weekends off. After informing him of those stipulations he glowered at me, and for a moment I held my breath because I thought he was going to tell me that those stipulations wouldn't work for him, but then he said, "Can you start tomorrow?" Even though it was a far cry from a job I thought I would like, I felt like jumping for joy. At least I had a job and would have some money coming in.

Not long after starting my new job I met a lady that worked in a real estate office right next door. It was owned by the same men that owned Granny's Home Cooking. The lady's name was Cora, and we would strike up a conversation whenever she would come in for coffee or something to eat. I told her that my mother was a real estate agent in Florida, and she was interested in learning about the real estate market in Florida.

One day, a couple of months after I had started working at "Granny's Home Cooking" she called me at home one afternoon and asked, "I was wondering if you could meet me in town on your next day off. There's something that I would like to show you."

Although my curiosity was piqued, I sensed that she didn't want to discuss the reason for her call over the phone so I didn't ask any questions. I simply said, "Sure, I'll be happy to meet you. My next day off is Saturday. I'll have to bring my children with me. Is that okay?"

We agreed to meet at the real estate office at 10:00 A.M. She had called on a Thursday, so at least I wouldn't have to wait very long to find out what this was all about. We met on Saturday as planned.

She said, "It would probably be better if you follow me in your car."

I still had no clue as to what the mystery was all about, but I was very excited to know that I would have the answer very soon. After about a three minute drive I found out. What she wanted to show me was a new house that was still under construction, but was almost completely finished. It was being built as a "spec" house, and it was being sold through The Farmers Home Administration. That meant that just a small down payment was required and that the buyer's mortgage payment would be based on their income. It was a three bedroom, one and a half bath, with a full size unfinished basement. The basement was already plumbed to put in a bathroom, and it had a washer and dryer hook-up. It would be perfect for me and the kids. It still had to be painted and sodded, steps needed to be built, but it would be move-in ready in a month or so.

I, of course was very excited about the prospect of being able to buy a house, but I was concerned about being able to come up with the cash for the down payment, even though it was only $600.00. I was also concerned about being able to qualify for a mortgage on my own.

Cora didn't seem to think that it would be a problem for me to qualify, and I felt encouraged to at least give it a try. After all the worst thing that could happen would be for them to say no. After leaving the house we went back to her office and started doing the necessary paperwork. Lady luck was with me on this for several reasons. Since I worked for the owners of the real estate office they were more than willing to help me fill out all of the necessary information, and they knew exactly what to put down to make the application go through.

Another reason that I felt lady luck was on my side was because they had a vested interest in getting the loan approved, namely the commission they would receive from the sale, but that's not all. One of the partners' wife was just getting ready to open a physical fitness center and they asked me if I would be interested in taking a job there as a physical fitness instructor. I jumped at the chance.

Although I was overjoyed about having the opportunity for this new job, there were some important details I was going to have to work out to make it feasibly possible. My hours would be from 10:00 A.M. to 5:00 P.M. Monday through Friday. My employers had worked with me as far as giving me weekends off, but they said they couldn't make any other concessions when it came to the hours they needed me to work. The ten o'clock part was great. It was the staying until five o'clock that posed the problem. Dinah Jean could stay at Head Start until five-thirty, so that part was fine. The problem was going to be finding someone to meet Abby and Joey at the bus stop at three-fifteen.

I went home and put my thinking cap on and came up with the idea to ask my neighbor Caroline, if it would be okay for Abby and Joey to get off the bus at her children's bus stop and stay with her until I could get home at about five-thirty. I told her I would pay her $25.00 a week if she could do that for me. She said it wouldn't be a problem for her. Okay, another problem solved. I felt like I was on a roll.

The next problem I needed to tackle was getting the down payment and homeowner's insurance money lined up so I could buy the house. I hated to have to ask to borrow money from anyone, but after sitting down and figuring everything out, I saw no other alternative. After figuring out exactly how much cash I was going to need, I decided to ask Momma for part of it, and my lifelong friend Nancy and her husband for the remainder.

I didn't want to have to do it, so I put off making the phone calls for the time being, grabbed a beer and a cigarette and sat down to calm my nerves. Finally, after a couple of beers and several cigarettes later, I made myself go to the phone and make the calls. It took all of about twenty minutes and I had all the money I needed all lined up.

Thank God for good friends and family, and thank God for providing the means for everything I had needed to get me where I was thus far.

CHAPTER 49

▼

LET'S GET FIT

Okay ladies, let's get to shedding those pounds and looking like a million bucks! I was so excited and thankful for the way my life was going, that I really did feel like I had a brand new life, one that was filled with happiness and fulfillment.

I was to start my new job the very next day, but I had no idea as to what exercises I was going to do. The only training I had been given was on how to use the various pieces of exercise equipment, but I did happen to have a magazine at home that I had bought a while back, and that particular issue of the magazine was focusing on exercising and physical fitness. It had page after page of exercises with pictures of how to do them, and under each picture was a description of what area of the body that particular exercise firmed up, and what muscles it toned up.

I went home and studied all the exercises. I wanted to make sure that I had an exercise program that was well balanced, and well rounded that worked on each counterpart of the body in unison. I started practicing on doing them correctly and I found out very quickly just how out of shape I was. Whew, was I ever winded. Pretty soon the kids started doing them with me. We were all laughing and having great fun.

Doing all those exercises had worn us out. I fixed a quick dinner, got Dinah Jean bathed and in bed. Joey was now old enough to bathe himself, so while he was taking a bath I helped Abby with her homework. By the time Joey had finished bathing and put his pajamas on, Abby and I were finished with her homework. Now it was time for her to get in the bath and for me to help Joey with his homework. By the time we were finished with all of that, it was bedtime for them, and I was so tired I couldn't wait to take a shower and get in bed myself.

The next morning went real smoothly. Not having to be at work until ten o'clock was going to work out really well for me. It gave me plenty of time to fix the kids some breakfast and get them ready for school without having to rush. I reminded Abby and Joey that they were to get off the bus at the same bus stop as my neighbor's children, and I told them that I would be there to pick them up at about five-thirty.

They seemed to be looking forward to getting off at my neighbor's house because they would have their children to play with. Their little girl was a year older than Abby, and their son was a year older than Joey. However, there were a couple of concerns that I had about it. My biggest concern was that they had two pit bulls that ran loose. I told them to be leery around the dogs, and not to go near them or try to pet them. The second concern was that their son, who was seven, had a little motor scooter that he rode around their yard. I told both Abby and Joey, that under no circumstances were either one of them to get on that scooter. I also told my neighbor Caroline, that Abby and Joey were not allowed to ride on the scooter.

My first day at work went really well, and I felt like I was really going to like the job. They told me that for the first few days I would be in training, and that I wouldn't be leading any exercise sessions during that time. I must admit that I was glad to hear that because I didn't feel like I was ready to take that leap yet. Those first few days I learned more about the exercise equipment. I was instructed on the correct way to use it and which part of the body that particular piece of equipment worked on. They taught me the procedure for signing up new members and the correct way to take their measurements.

The other part of my training was to participate in every exercise session. They had a session every hour and a half. Whoa! I became aware of muscles I didn't even know that I had.

The first week that I started leading the exercise sessions were hard because I was so out of shape. During that time however, there was another girl that had been hired at the same time as I was and we led the sessions together. That worked out well because she was out of shape too, and we worked it out that when one of us got winded, the other one would take over. Within two weeks time I had gotten in such good shape that I could have exercised until the cows came home and not get winded at all. I loved it! After about a month I looked and felt great.

The arrangement that I had with my neighbor Caroline was working out real well too. Her children and mine got along good and seemed to have a lot of fun playing together. I was still uncomfortable about the pit bulls running loose, but so far they hadn't been a problem. Nevertheless I was scared to death of them. Whenever I went to pick up the kids they would both come rushing toward the car barking, and I really had to build up my courage to get out of the car. What made it even worse for me was that I had always heard that animals can somehow detect when a person is afraid of them, and then they really go after the person. That meant that I always had to psyche myself up to a place in my mind where I felt that I could fool the dogs into thinking that I wasn't afraid of them. That was an extremely difficult challenge for me.

Money was tight. I wasn't getting any child support on a regular basis, so it became necessary for me to apply for food stamps and energy assistance in order to provide for my children. Being put in the position to have to apply for these programs was humiliating for me, and I dreaded the process of applying, but I was approved to receive both. Afterward I realized that I had to put those shameful feelings aside, and instead just be grateful to have the assistance.

Everything was coming together for me. The loan for the house had been approved and the house would be finished and ready to move into in April. I still had to buy homeowners insurance before the closing, but because I had been being very frugal, not only out of necessity, but with the foreknowledge that I would be needing money for that, I had made sure that I had money put aside for it.

Our new house was right in town. I liked that because it made everything so much more convenient. It took me about four minutes to drive to work, and being closer to everything meant a big savings on gas for going to and from work, for grocery shopping, running errands, etc.

The only negative was that Abby and Joey had to change schools, but actually it was a positive in the long run because there was an elementary school just three blocks from the house. Another positive element was that the school had an after school program, so that eliminated the necessity of having to find a new babysitter. All in all life was very good, and I felt very blessed and grateful for that.

Because the house was brand new there wasn't too much cleaning to be done. It was a nice home for me and the kids. Now all I needed was some furniture. I was looking forward to the task of furnishing and decorating the house because I could pick out exactly what I wanted without having to have anyone else's approval. It was fun because it gave me the chance to use my own creativity in putting the finishing touches on it, and when I got finished, I was happy with the results.

CHAPTER 50

▼

LIFE IS GOOD

Our life in Greenwood was turning out to be among the best years of my life. The kids were thriving in school as well as out of school. Most of the time I liked being a single parent. That way I could raise my children as I saw fit without the interference of a spouse that was, in my experience, good for nothing except causing problems. That being said, there were plenty of times that I felt very lonely. It would have been nice to have a partner to share the good times as well as the bad times with, but that wasn't in the cards for me just yet.

I had formed good friendships and the children had as well. Life wasn't perfect, life never is. There are always bumps in the road, and the road ahead is never certain, but through the grace of God we got over those bumps, even if sometimes it was by the skin of our teeth.

There were two reasons for this. The first one was that the Holy Spirit guided us through the hard times and blessed us with His protection and undying love. The second reason was that my children and I were a team. Even though the children were so young, they were such a tremendous source of strength and love for me. They gave me the strength and courage to keep plowing ahead, and to never consider failure as an option. Like the saying goes, where there is a will there is a way. I believe that with every fiber of my being. It doesn't mean that the way ahead of us will be easy, or the way that we might choose for it to be, but it is a way that if we have the strength and courage we will get through it, even if at first it may seem impossible.

The road map of our lives isn't necessarily that big, but it does cover a large territory. At times the roads can be quite curvy, or appear to go in circles without end, but many times if we study our route more closely we will discover a straighter course to take.

Our lives can take us to many interesting places. Some may be very beautiful. Some may be very empty and desolate. Along our route we will pass many smiling faces, but many will be places where rivers have overflowed from many tears.

The road map that the Lord has given us provides a very beautiful landscape, especially when the sunlight reflects off of its' surface and everything is in harmony. At times the road is dark and may be barely discernible. Then it can be a very empty and desolate place, very isolated and off the beaten path. That is when we can often get lost and things can get scary.

Often our road map approaches busy intersections and we are not sure which way we should go, or which road we should take. At other times we are able to decide which way to go very quickly, yet more often than not we are unsure.

At those uncertain times we may start to panic, then our hearts may start to pound and the road map gets blurred with the perspiration dripping from our brow, or the tears that are flowing from our eyes. That is when we have to be brave and strong like a lion, knowing that we are never alone because the Holy Spirit is always traveling with us.